# The Other Mother

## MICHEL BUSSI

Translated from the French by Sam Taylor

WEIDENFELD & NICOLSON

First published in Great Britain in 2021
by Weidenfeld & Nicolson
an imprint of The Orion Publishing Group Ltd
Carmelite House, 50 Victoria Embankment
London EC4Y 0DZ

An Hachette UK Company

First published in French as *Maman a Tort* by Presses de la Cité
a department of Place des Editeurs, Paris.

1 3 5 7 9 10 8 6 4 2

A CIP catalogue record for this book is
available from the British Library.

ISBN (Hardback) 978 1 4746 0671 4
ISBN (Export Trade Paperback) 978 1 4746 0672 1
ISBN (eBook) 978 1 4746 0674 5
ISBN (Audio) 978 1 4091 7312 0

Typeset by Input Data Services Ltd, Somerset

Printed and bound in Great Britain by Clays Ltd, Elcograf S.p.A.

MIX
Paper from
responsible sources
FSC® C104740

www.orionbooks.co.uk
www.weidenfeldandnicolson.co.uk

To my mother, of course.

*I have several mothers.*
*It's a bit complicated.*
*Especially as they don't like each other.*
*There's even one who's going to die.*
*Maybe some of it's my fault?*
*Maybe everything happened because of me?*
*Because I can't remember which one is the real one.*

# I
# Marianne

# 1

Malone felt his feet leave the ground, and then he could see the lady behind the window. She was wearing a blue suit, a bit like a police uniform, and she had a round face and funny glasses. In her booth, she reminded him of those ladies who sold tickets for the merry-go-round.

He felt Maman's hands trembling slightly as she held him up.

The lady looked him straight in the eye, turned to Maman, then looked down at the little brown book that lay open in her hands.

Maman had explained that the lady was checking their photographs. To be sure it was really them. That they really were allowed to catch this plane.

But the lady didn't know where they were going – that is, where they were *really* going.

Only he knew that.

They were flying to the forest of ogres.

Malone placed his hands on the ledge so it would be easier for Maman to hold him up. He was looking at the letters on the lady's jacket. He didn't know how to read yet, of course, but he could recognise a few letters.

J . . . E . . . A . . . N . . .

The woman signalled to the child's mother that she could put him down now. Normally, Jeanne wasn't quite so scrupulous. Especially here, in Le Havre's little Octeville airport, which had only three counters, two baggage carousels and one vending machine. But the security staff – from the car park attendants to those guarding the runway – had been on high alert since the early afternoon. All of them recruited in a game of hide-and-seek with an invisible

5

fugitive, although it seemed highly improbable that the fugitive would choose to go through this backwater.

Anyway, it didn't matter. Captain Augresse had been explicit on that point. They had to post photos of the men and the woman on the walls of the lobby and warn every customs official, every member of the security staff.

These people were dangerous.

One of the two men in particular.

An armed robber, to start with. Then a murderer. A repeat offender, according to the police report.

Jeanne leant forward slightly.

'Have you ever been on a plane before, dear? Have you ever travelled this far away?'

The child stepped sideways and hid behind his mother. Jeanne didn't have any children. She had to work ridiculous hours at the airport, and that was enough of an excuse for her two-faced boyfriend to dodge the issue whenever she brought it up. She had a way with little ones, though. More than with men, in fact. That was her gift, knowing how to deal with kids. Kids and cats.

She smiled again.

'You're not afraid, are you? Because you know, where you're going, there's . . .'

She deliberately paused until the end of the boy's nose came out from behind the mother's legs, squeezed into a pair of skin-tight jeans.

'There's a jungle . . . Isn't that right?'

The child recoiled slightly, as if surprised that the woman had been able to guess his secret. Jeanne examined the passports one last time before vigorously stamping each of them.

'But there's no reason to be scared, sweetie. You'll be with your mother!'

The child hid behind his mother again. Jeanne felt disappointed. If she was losing her knack with kids too . . . But it was an intimidating place, she reassured herself, especially now with all those idiot soldiers walking back and forth with their pistols holstered on their belts and assault rifles hanging from their shoulders, as if

Captain Augresse might watch the tapes afterwards and give them bonus points for their zeal.

Jeanne tried again. It was her job, security. And that also meant her customers' emotional security.

'Ask your mum. She'll tell you all about the jungle.'

The mother thanked Jeanne with a smile. She didn't expect the child to do the same, but he did react – and his reaction was very strange.

For a moment, Jeanne wondered how to interpret that brief movement of the boy's eyes. It was only a fraction of a second, but when she had said the word 'mum', the boy had not looked at his mother. He had turned his head the other way, towards the wall. Towards the poster of the woman she had pinned there a few minutes before. The poster of the woman the entire regional police force was looking for, and that man standing next to her. Alexis Zerda. The killer.

She was probably mistaken.

The child was probably looking at the large bay window just to the left of the wall. Or the planes behind it. Or at the sea in the distance. Or maybe his head was in the clouds already. Maybe he was just miles away.

Jeanne thought about questioning the mother and her son again, she had an inexplicable foreboding, an impression that something about the relationship between this child and his mother seemed a little bit off. Something unusual, something she couldn't put her finger on.

But all their papers were in order. What excuse did she have to hold them any longer? Two soldiers with shaven heads stomped past in their boots and camouflage fatigues. Providing security by scaring ordinary families half to death.

It was just the pressure, Jeanne reasoned with herself. The unbearable way airports felt like a warzone every time some dangerous madman was on the loose with the police on his heels. She was too emotional, she knew; she had the same problem with men.

Jeanne slid the passports through the opening in the toughened glass window.

'Everything seems to be in order, madame. Have a good trip.'

'Thank you.'

This was the first word the woman had said to her.

At the end of the runway, a sky-blue KLM A318 Airbus was taking off.

\*

\*   \*

Captain Marianne Augresse looked up at the blue Airbus as it crossed the sky. She followed its progress for a moment as it flew out over the oil-black ocean, then continued her own weary climb.

Four hundred and fifty steps.

From fifty steps further up, JB came running down towards her.

'I've got a witness!' the lieutenant shouted. 'And not just any witness . . .'

Marianne Augresse gripped the guard rail and caught her breath. She felt drops of perspiration trickling down her back. She hated the way the slightest bit of exertion made her break out into a sweat – and it got worse with every gram she put on. She hated being in her forties: lunch on the go, evenings on the sofa, nights spent alone, her morning jog always postponed to another day.

Her lieutenant hurtled down the rest of the stairs, then stood in front of Marianne and handed her some kind of grey and grubby cream rat. Limp. Dead.

'Where did you find that?'

'In the brambles, a few steps higher up. Alexis Zerda must have thrown it there before he disappeared.'

The captain did not reply. She just squeezed the cuddly toy between her thumb and index finger, its fur worn, almost white from being constantly hugged and sucked and pressed against the trembling body of a three-year-old. Its two black marble eyes stared at her as if frozen in some final terror.

JB was right: this thing was a witness. A mucky, broken witness, its heart torn out. Silenced forever.

Marianne hugged it, imagining the worst.

*The child would never have abandoned his favourite toy.*

Distractedly, she ran her fingers through the rat's fur. There were brownish stains on the acrylic fibres. Blood, no doubt. The same as the blood they'd found in the shelter a few hundred steps below?

The child's blood?

Amanda Moulin's blood?

'Let's go, JB!' the captain ordered, her tone deliberately harsh. 'Get a move on!'

Lieutenant Jean-Baptiste Lechevalier did not argue. In a flash, he was already five steps ahead of his superior officer. Marianne Augresse forced herself to think as she climbed, partly so that her fatigue wouldn't slow her down, and partly so that she could begin to string together the theories that were accumulating in her mind.

Although, when it came down to it, there was only one question that needed an urgent response.

*Where?*

Train, car, tram, bus, plane . . . There were a thousand ways Alexis Zerda could escape, a thousand ways he could disappear, despite the warning that had been sent out two hours previously, despite the posters, despite the dozens of police who were out searching for him.

*Where and how?*

One step, then another, one thought leading to the next.

*Or how and why?*

She avoided asking herself the other question. The main one.

*Why throw away the toy?*

Why tear this beloved creature from the child's hands? A child who would surely have screamed, refused to climb one more step, who would have preferred to die on the spot rather than be separated from the toy rat that bore his smell, his mother's smell.

The breeze blowing in from the sea brought with it the unbearable odour of crude oil. Out in Le Havre's navigation channel, container ships were queuing up like gridlocked cars at a red light.

The veins in the captain's temples throbbed. The stairs seemed to stretch away towards infinity, as if each time she climbed one step, another magically appeared at the edge of her vision.

The same question ricocheted around the walls of her skull.

*Why?*

Because Zerda had no intention of being burdened with a child? Because the kid was of no more use to him than the cuddly toy? Because he would also get rid of the child, in a ditch somewhere? Because he was just waiting for a more discreet place to commit the act?

Another Airbus streaked across the sky. The airport was only a couple of kilometres away, as the crow flies. Well, at least Zerda wouldn't be able to escape through there, Marianne thought to herself, remembering the huge security presence she had installed at the tiny local airport.

Another twenty or thirty steps. Lieutenant Lechevalier had already reached the car park. Captain Augresse's fingers tightened around the ball of grey and cream fur, kneading it, as if checking that its heart and tongue had been torn out, that this cloth rat could never tell anyone its secrets; that it was definitely dead, after all those endless private conversations with Malone, those conversations that they had listened to repeatedly, she and her men.

The captain's fingers played through the stiffened fur for a second or two, then suddenly stopped. She slid her index finger another couple of millimetres along the fabric, then looked down, not expecting to find anything new. After all, what could this gutted bit of cloth possibly reveal?

Marianne Augresse's eyes narrowed, focusing on the faded letters. And suddenly, the truth exploded.

In a single moment, all the pieces of the puzzle fell into place. Even the most unlikely ones.

The rocket, the forest of ogres, the pirates and their wrecked ship, the amnesia of a tropical rodent, the treasure, the four towers of the castle, all those nonsensical phrases that she and her men had fruitlessly mused over for five days.

The tales of a child with an over-active imagination. Or so they had thought . . .

Yet it was all written there. Malone hadn't invented a thing.

It was all there in four words, attached to the fur of this mute witness. They'd all held it, this cuddly toy, but none of them had noticed anything. They had been wholly concentrated on what it had to say. It was very talkative – they had listened to it, but they hadn't looked at it. This cloth rat, murdered so that it would never talk again, then abandoned by its murderer on the slope.

The captain closed her eyes for a second. She suddenly thought that, if anyone had been able to read her thoughts, to intercept them the way you sometimes overhear a fragment of conversation, they would think she was crazy. A cuddly toy can't speak, it can't cry, it doesn't die. No one over the age of four believes that stuff – six at a push, eight max.

Yes, if someone began the story at this point, they would think she was out of her mind. She certainly would have, when she was rational. Five days earlier.

Marianne continued to clutch the toy to her chest as she peered down the hundreds of steps she had just climbed and felt a sudden rush of vertigo. In the distance, all she could see was an infinite stretch of empty sky, a sky that was almost as dark as the ocean, the grey of the waves mingling with the grey of the clouds.

JB had already started the car; she could hear the engine purring. Summoning all her strength, she accelerated up the final few steps.

There was only one question worth asking, now that the truth had been revealed.

*Was there enough time to stop them?*

*Four days earlier*

# MONDAY

The day of the moon

# 2

*Little hand on the 8, big hand on the 7*

'Maman was walking fast. I was holding her hand and it hurt my arm. She was looking for somewhere to hide. She was shouting but I couldn't hear her, there were too many people.'

'Too many people? Who else was there?'

'Just people, doing their shopping.'

'So there were shops around you?'

'Yes. Lots. But we didn't have a trolley, just a bag. My big Jake and the Netherland Pirates bag.'

'Were you and your mother shopping too?'

'No. I was supposed to be going on holiday. That was what Maman said. A long holiday. But I didn't want to go. That was why Maman was looking for somewhere we could hide. So that no one would see me have a tantrum.'

'A tantrum like the one you had in school? Like the one Clotilde told me about? Crying. Getting angry. Wanting to break everything in the classroom. Is that what you mean, Malone?'

'Yes.'

'Why?'

'Because I didn't want to go with the other Maman.'

'That's all?'

'. . .'

'OK, let's talk about that some more later, about your other mother. But first, let's see if you can remember anything more. Can you tell me what you could see? When you were walking fast with your mother?'

'There were shops. Lots of shops. There was a McDonalds too,

15

but we didn't eat there. Maman didn't want me playing with other children.'

'Can you remember the street? The names of other shops?'

'It wasn't in a street.'

'What do you mean?'

'Well, it was a kind of street, but we couldn't see the sky.'

'Are you sure about that, Malone? You couldn't see the sky? Was there a big car park outside?'

'I don't know. I was asleep in the car and I only remember what came after, in the street without a sky with all the shops, when Maman was pulling my hand.'

'OK. It doesn't matter, Malone. In a moment, I'm going to show you some photos. Tell me if you recognise anything.'

Malone waited on his bed, motionless.

Gouti didn't say anything, as if he were dead. Then he started talking again. He often did that. It was normal.

'Look, Malone. Look at the pictures on the computer. Do they seem familiar?'

'Yes.'

'Were these the shops you saw with your mother?'

'Yes.'

'You're sure?'

'I think so. There was that red and green bird. And the parrot too, the parrot dressed up as a pirate.'

'OK. That's very important, Malone. I'll show you some other photos in a bit. But now let's go back to your story. You went and hid somewhere with your mother. Where?'

'In the toilets. I was sitting on the floor. Maman closed the door, so she could talk to me without anyone else hearing.'

'What was she saying, your Maman?'

'She told me that everything in my head was going to go away, like the dreams I have at night. But that I had to force myself to think about her, every night before I go to sleep. That I had to think hard about her, and our house, and the beach. The pirate ship. The castle. That was all she said to me, that the pictures in my head would go away. I didn't really believe her but she kept saying the same thing, that the pictures in my head would fly away if I didn't think about them each night in my bed. Like leaves falling off the branches of a tree.'

'This was before she left you with your other mother . . . is that right?'

'The other one isn't my mother!'

'Yes, yes, Malone, I understand, that's why I said your other mother. And what else did she tell you? Your first mother, I mean.'

'To listen to Gouti.'

'And this is Gouti? Your cuddly toy? So you had to listen to Gouti, is that what your mother told you?'

'Yes! I must listen to Gouti, but in secret.'

'He must be very powerful then. How does Gouti help you remember?'

'He talks to me.'

'When does he talk to you?'

'I can't tell anyone, it's my secret. Maman made me swear. She told me another secret too, in the toilets. The secret that protects you from ogres when they want to take you into the forest.'

'OK, it's your secret. I understand. But she didn't say anything else, Malone?'

'Yes! She said that.'

'What do you mean?'

'Malone! She told me it was a nice name and that I had to answer when someone called me that.'

'But you weren't called Malone before that? Do you still remember your other name?'

Malone remained silent. An eternity passed.

'Don't worry, it doesn't matter. And what happened after that?'

'She cried.'

'OK. So what about your house, from before? Not the one you live in now. The other one. Can you remember that?'

'A little bit. But almost all the pictures have gone away, because Gouti never talks to me about that.'

'I understand. But can you describe the pictures you have left

17

of the house? You were talking about the sea earlier? About a pirate ship and the towers of a castle?'

'Yes. There was no garden, just a beach. If you leant out of my bedroom window, the sea was right there. I could see the pirate ship from my room – it was broken in two. I remember the rocket too. And that I couldn't go far from the house because of the forest.'

'The forest of ogres, you mean?'

'That's right.'

'Can you describe the forest for me?'

'That's easy. The trees were as high as the sky. And there weren't just ogres in the jungle, there were big monkeys too, and snakes, and giant spiders . . . I saw them once, the spiders. That was why I had to stay in my room.'

'Do you remember anything else, Malone?'

'No.'

'OK. So tell me, Malone . . . I'm going to call you Malone, if that's OK, until we remember your name from before. Your cuddly toy. What kind of animal is it?'

'Well . . . it's a Gouti.'

'A Gouti. I see. And you say it really talks to you. Not just in your head? I know it's a secret, but can you tell me just a little bit about how it talks to you?'

Malone suddenly held his breath.

'Quiet, Gouti,' he whispered.

Malone heard footsteps on the stairs. He always listened very carefully to the noises in the house, especially when he was in his bedroom, under the sheets, listening in secret to Gouti.

*Maman-da was coming.*

'Quick, Gouti,' whispered Malone, 'you have to pretend to be asleep.'

His toy stopped talking just in time, before Maman-da came into the room. Malone held his furry rat close. Gouti was very good at pretending to be asleep.

Maman-da's voice was always a bit slow, especially in the evenings, as if she was so tired she could never finish her sentences.

'Everything OK, sweetie?'

'Yes.'

Malone wanted her to leave, but just as she did every evening, Maman-da sat down on the edge of his bed and stroked his hair. Tonight, the stroking went on even longer than usual. She put her arms around his back and pressed her heart against his chest.

'Tomorrow, I'm going to see your teacher at the school, remember?'

Malone did not reply.

'They say you've been telling stories. I know you love stories, sweetie, and that's normal for a little boy. In fact, I'm proud that you can invent things in your head. But sometimes grown-ups take those stories seriously; they think they're true. That's why your teacher wants to see us, do you understand?'

Malone closed his eyes. It was a long time before Maman-da made a move.

'You're sleepy, my darling. I'll let you get some rest. Sweet dreams.'

She kissed him, turned off the light and finally left the room. Malone waited, cautiously. He glanced at the cosmonaut alarm clock.

*Little hand on the 8, big hand on the 9.*

Malone knew he shouldn't wake up his toy until the little hand was on the 9. Maman had taught him that too.

He looked at the calendar of the sky pinned to the wall, just above the alarm clock. The planets shone in the darkness. When the lights were turned off in his room, all you could see were those planets glowing in the night. Today was the day of the moon.

Malone couldn't wait for Gouti to tell him his story. His own. The story about the treasure on the beach. Lost treasure.

# 3

*Today, Mimizan beach. I took off my bikini top just for Marco, my boyfriend. He likes my breasts. So did the fat pig lying next to us, visibly.*
Want to kill
*I stabbed his fat gut with the end of the parasol, right through his belly button.*

*Convicted: 28*
*Acquitted: 3,289*

www.want-to-kill.com

The telephone rang, waking Captain Marianne Augresse with a start. For a brief instant, her eyes remained fixed on her cold, naked skin, then she removed her arm from the bath where she had been dozing for the past hour and picked up the phone. Her forearm knocked the little tray of toys balanced on the laundry basket and plastic boats, wind-up dolphins and small fluorescent fish scattered over the surface of the water.

'Shit!'

*Number unknown.*

'Shit!' the captain repeated.

She had been hoping it was one of her lieutenants: JB, Papy, or one of the other duty cops at Le Havre police station. She had been waiting for a call since the previous day, when Timo Soler was spotted in the Saint-François quarter, near the pharmacy. She had stationed four men between the Bassin du Commerce and the

Bassin du Roi. They had been searching for Timo Soler for nearly a year: nine months and twenty-seven days, to be exact. The hunt had begun on Tuesday 6 January 2015, during the armed robbery in Deauville. The surveillance camera had immortalised the face of Timo Soler just before he vanished on a Münch Mammut 2000, taking with him the 9 mm Luger bullet, lodged, according to the ballistics experts, somewhere between his lung and his shoulder. Marianne had known she wouldn't get a wink of sleep until the following morning and so had planned only to doze – in the bath, then on the sofa, then in bed – hoping to jump up in the middle of the night, grabbing her leather jacket and abandoning her crumpled sheets, her Tupperware box of food and her glass of Quézac mineral water in front of the dormant television, pausing only to throw a handful of biscuits to Mogwai, her cat.

'Yes?'

Her index finger slid across the wet glass. She gently patted the iPhone with a towel that was hanging close by, desperately hoping that this would not end the call.

'Captain Augresse? Vasily Dragonman. You don't know me. I'm a school psychologist. A mutual friend, Angélique Fontaine, gave me your mobile number.'

*Angie* . . . For fuck's sake, thought Marianne. She was going to tear a strip off that little slut, with her lacy bras and loose tongue.

'Is this a professional matter, Mr Dragonman? I'm expecting an important call on this number at any moment.'

'Don't worry, it won't take long.'

He had a soft voice. The voice of a young priest, a hypnotist, or a telepathic magician from the East. A smooth and confident talker, with just a hint of a Slavic accent.

'Go on,' sighed Marianne.

'You're going to find what I have to say slightly disconcerting. I'm a school psychologist. I cover the whole region north of the Havre estuary. For a few weeks now, I've been looking after a strange child.'

'Strange how?'

Marianne's free hand played with the water between her

half-submerged legs. There were worse things than being woken in your bath by a man, even if he wasn't calling to invite you to dinner.

'He claims that his mother isn't his mother.'

The captain's fingers slid over her damp thigh.

'Sorry?'

'He claims that his mother isn't his mother, and that his father isn't his father either.'

'How old is this kid?'

'Three and a half.'

Marianne bit her lip.

An over-zealous shrink! Angie must have been completely taken in by his smooth psychobabble.

'He expresses himself as if he were a year older than that,' the psychologist continued. 'He's not particularly gifted, but he is precocious. According to the tests that . . .'

'And his parents really *are* his parents?' Marianne cut in. 'Have you checked with his teachers? He's not adopted, or in foster care, or anything like that?'

'There's no doubt whatsoever. He really is their child. The parents say the kid has an over-active imagination. The headmistress is meeting them tomorrow.'

'So, the situation is being dealt with then . . .'

Marianne suddenly felt guilty about the curt way she had replied to the soft-voiced shrink. Just below the surface of the water, the fin of a mechanical dolphin tickled her legs. It had been at least six months since Grégoire, her nephew, had last stayed over; and, given that he would turn eleven next month, it was far from certain that he would ever return to binge on pizza and DVDs at his aunt's house. She ought to throw these toys away, along with the Pixar films and the Playmobil boxes, throw them all in a bin bag like so many regrets, instead of allowing them to taunt her.

'No,' the psychologist insisted. 'It's not being dealt with. Because, as odd as this may sound, I have a feeling the child might be telling the truth.'

'What about the mother?' the captain asked.

'She's furious.'

'You don't say! Please get to the point, Mr Dragonman. What do you expect me to do about it?'

Marianne used her knee to push away the dolphin. She felt flustered by the voice of this stranger, particularly as he almost certainly had no idea that she was naked as she spoke to him, her thighs in the air and her feet resting on the edge of the bathtub.

The psychologist left a long silence, allowing the captain to sink a little deeper into her hot, damp thoughts. Although realistically, the idea of sharing a bath with a man didn't get her that excited. She had too many hang-ups, perhaps. And there wouldn't be enough space to cram her body between the cold wall of the bathtub and the muscles of an ephemeral but well-built lover. Her real dream, though she could never admit it to anyone, was to share her bath with a baby. To spend hours splashing around with a little mite who was as chubby as she was, the water gone cold, surrounded by plastic toys.

'What do I expect you to do? I don't know. Help me?'

'You want me to open an investigation, is that it?'

'Not necessarily. But you could at least do some digging. Angie told me that's what you do. Just check out what the boy is saying. I have hours of recorded interviews, notes, drawings . . .'

The dolphin was back. It was obsessed.

The longer the conversation went on, the more convinced the captain became that the simplest thing to do would be to meet this Vasily Dragonman. Especially as it was Angie who had sent him. Angie knew what she was looking for. Not a man; Marianne couldn't care less about men. At thirty-nine, she had at least another twenty years in which she could sleep with all the men in the world. No, Marianne had hammered the message home to Angie during their girls' nights out: in the coming months, the captain would be going in search of a single, mythical creature: a FATHER. So, in sending this guy her way, Angie was perhaps thinking . . . After all, a school psychologist would make the perfect father. A man with a professional understanding of early childhood, quoting Freinet, Piaget and Montessori while other blokes were content to read magazines such as *L'Equipe*, *Interview* or *Detective*.

'Mr Dragonman, the usual procedure for a child in danger is to call one of the child protection organisations. But I must admit that this case you have described seems . . . well, unusual. Do you really want to notify the authorities on the basis of the child's declarations? Does he strike you as mistreated? Do the parents appear dangerous? Is there anything that might give us a reason to separate them?'

'No. On the face of it, the parents seem completely normal.'

'OK. So there's no emergency. We'll make some enquiries. We wouldn't want to put the parents in prison just because their son has an over-active imagination . . .'

A shiver ran through the captain's body. The bathwater was now cold and faintly pink, as if the mixture of lavender, eucalyptus and violet essential oils she had poured in had gone stagnant. Marianne's breasts emerged from the pale surface, large in comparison to the little yellow plastic boat that floated over her belly. A vision of the end of the world, thought Marianne. Two virgin islands polluted by a liner dumping its toxic waste.

The psychologist's voice snapped the policewoman out of her reverie.

'I'm sorry, Captain, please don't take this personally, but you're wrong. That is why I was so insistent with Angie, and why I felt compelled to call you this evening. This *is* an emergency. It's urgent for this child. Absolutely urgent. Irreversible, even.'

Marianne's voice rose. 'Irreversible? For God's sake, you told me the kid wasn't in any danger!'

'Please understand, Captain. This child isn't even four years old yet. All those things he remembers today, he could easily forget tomorrow. Or the day after tomorrow. Or in a month or two.'

Marianne stood up.

'What are you trying to say, exactly?'

'That this child is clinging to fragments of memory in order to convince me that his mother is not his real mother. He talks about a castle, a pirate ship, a forest of ogres . . . other things. But in a few days, or maybe a few weeks, as surely as this child will get older, he will learn new things – the names of animals and flowers and letters and the rest of this infinite world that surrounds him – and then his older memories will be erased. And that other mother, whom he remembers today, that previous life that he tells me about each time I see him, will simply cease to exist!'

# 4

*Little hand on the 9, big hand on the 12*

Malone listened to the silence for a long time, making sure that Maman-da was not on her way back up the stairs.

His small fingers reached beneath the sheets until they felt Gouti's heartbeat. His toy was slightly warm. When he had completely woken up, Malone hid under the sheets and got ready to listen. It was the day of the moon. It was the day of the story about Gouti and the hazelnuts. Malone couldn't remember how many times he'd heard it.

There had been many days of the moon, so many that he couldn't count them. But he didn't remember any days of the moon from the time before.

Malone put his ear against Gouti, as if the toy were a very soft pillow.

*

*   *

*Gouti was just three years old, which was already pretty big in his family, because his mother was only eight and his grandfather, who was very old, was fifteen.*

*They lived in the biggest tree on the beach, which had roots shaped like an immense spider. Their place was on the third floor, first branch on the left, between a tern that was almost always away on trips and a lame owl who had now retired, but who used to work on the pirate ships.*

*Maman said that Gouti was very similar to his grandfather – a daydreamer, just like he was. It's true that his grandfather spent a lot* of time dreaming, but that's because he was losing his memory. They would often find him asleep on another branch, his white moustache all dishevelled, or burying a grey stone instead of an acorn. Gouti liked to sit in front of the sea and imagine that he was climbing on a boat, hiding in its hold, secretly eating wheat or oats from a bag until they discovered a new island. He imagined himself staying on that new island and making a new family. He often thought about that and forgot the rest.

And yet he did have work to do. His work was always the same, but it was very important: gathering the hazelnuts from the forest and burying them close to the house. Because the reason the whole family was living in this place was the forest. Hazelnuts, walnuts, acorns, pine cones . . . this was the treasure that fell from the sky in the autumn and that had to be carefully hidden before winter so they could eat for the rest of the year. Maman didn't have the time to do this because she was busy with his little brother Mulo and his little sister Musa.

So, every day, Gouti would gather and bury the nuts, then he would look out to sea and daydream. And every evening, on the way back to their big tree, he would realise that he had forgotten where he had buried the nuts.

Under a large stone? Between the roots of a tree? Near a seashell?

It was impossible to remember.

But poor Gouti never dared tell his mother.

Days passed, all of them the same, and with each passing day Gouti felt more ashamed and less able to admit to his mother that he was too absent-minded for such a precise and meticulous job.

Then one morning, winter came.

Gouti's whole family left its branch and went to hide under the spider of roots. Theirs was a deep, clean burrow that Gouti's grandfather had dug a long time ago, but with the family growing so large there was no longer enough space to keep their food close by.

They slept for six months, but it felt like only a second.

When they awoke and went up to the surface, they thought they must have emerged on the wrong side of the earth.

Their big tree was no longer there.

No tern, no owl. Even worse, there were no longer any hazel or *walnut trees, any oaks or pines. There was no more forest.*

*A winter storm had blown down all the trees while they slept.*

*Their mother always knew how to organise things, even in a crisis such as this. The most important thing is food, she said in a calm voice, and she asked Gouti to go and dig up the food he'd buried in the sand.*

*Gouti started to cry.*

*The beach was vast. It would be easier to find a pine needle in a forest; they would all die of hunger before he found a single hazelnut . . . and the trees that lined this beach would never produce any more nuts because they were all lying on the sand, their branches broken, their roots in the air.*

*Maman did not scold Gouti. She simply said: 'We have to leave, children. We must find another place where we can feed ourselves.' And she asked Gouti to carry Musa on his back since she was still very little, while she would carry Gouti's grandfather, who seemed to have aged another two years during the second that their winter nap had lasted.*

*They went all around the world.*

*They crossed plains and rivers, mountains and deserts. They ate wherever they could, in cellars and attics, at the top of strange trees they had never seen before and at the bottom of endless holes that seemed to burrow beneath the ocean. They were chased away by brooms, they made children scream in schools and old ladies in churches, they travelled in trucks and on boats, and even once in an aeroplane.*

*And then one day, months or maybe even years later, one day when they were even more starving than usual, the grandfather with the white moustache, who had hardly uttered a word since the start of their voyage, told them: 'It is time to go home.'*

*Maman must have thought it was a ridiculous idea. But as grandfather never said anything, when he did speak, she felt she had to obey him.*

*So home they went. They were sad because they remembered the trees of their forest lying on the sand, the vast beach without a single leaf under which they could hide, the empty seashells and the dead branches.*

*At first they thought they must have come to the wrong beach.*

*Only grandfather was smiling, making his white moustache dance.*

*He asked the whole family to sit on a little pile of sand and began to talk: 'A long time ago, when I was young – around Gouti's age – I was very absent-minded and I used to daydream about going around the world. We were poor and thin, there were barely any trees on the beach, there was no forest, we had almost nothing to eat and, on top of that, every time I buried one of the few hazelnuts I had managed to find, I would forget where I'd left it. And then one day, from one of those forgotten hazelnuts – just one – a tree grew, and on its branches were a hundred hazelnuts. Then another tree. And another. A forest. The forest where you were all born.*

*'Home.*

*'No life passes without a storm, without having to start over again.'*

*And so they walked on over the sand.*

*And on the beach, where Gouti had buried and forgotten hundreds of hazelnuts, walnuts and acorns, there was the biggest, greenest, densest forest they had ever seen. Gouti's mother hugged him tight to her chest while Mulo and Musa ran between the trees and applauded with their little paws, watched calmly by the tern and the owl, who had come back long ago.*

*Then Gouti's grandfather said that he was very tired, that he would soon fall asleep, just for a second, but a second that would last longer than the winter. But first, he had one last thing to tell Gouti.*

*He took his grandson aside, and they walked until their feet almost touched the waves and his moustache was flecked with foam. Then grandfather spoke softly: 'You see, Gouti, the real treasure is not what we spend our life searching for; the real treasure was buried close by all the time. If we plant that treasure one day, if we cultivate it and water it every evening, even if we forget why, then one fine morning, when we have lost all hope, that treasure will bloom and grow.'*

\*

\*  \*

Gently, Malone let Gouti fall asleep once more. His toy would need to be wide awake tomorrow. Maman-da and Pa-di were coming to school to see his teacher. He was a little scared about what they would say.

He had to sleep too, but he didn't really want to. He knew the nightmares would return. He could already hear that icy rain falling, cold, shining, cutting. He didn't even want to close his eyes.

Not because he was afraid of the dark. When Malone closed his eyes, behind his eyelids, in his head, he saw only one colour, as if everything had been painted.

Just one colour.

Red.

Everywhere.

# TUESDAY

The day of the war

# 5

Vasily Dragonman waited patiently in the lobby, his bag resting on his knees. Policemen hurried past him. If it weren't for their uniforms and the psychologist's worn leather jacket, he could easily have passed for a pharmaceutical sales rep waiting in a hospital corridor, with overworked nurses rushing back and forth in front of him.

Captain Augresse appeared. She was walking more slowly, down the middle of the corridor, forcing her colleagues to flow around her, brushing the walls on either side as they passed. She called out to one of the policemen who was walking towards her.

'Papy, did you call the doctor back?'

Lieutenant Pierrick Pasdeloup slowed down. All of his colleagues called him Papy, not only because he was the oldest person in this particular station, only a few months from retirement, but above all because – at just over 50 – he already had six grandchildren scattered across France. Shaven-headed, with a thin salt-and-pepper beard, he had the gentle eyes of a faithful dog and the lean physique of a runner. The very oldest guys in the brigade thought he was still young, the younger ones that he was already old.

'He's busy with patients all morning,' the lieutenant replied. 'He'll call us back when he gets a moment.'

'But did he confirm that the man he stitched back together yesterday really was Timo Soler?'

'He's one hundred per cent sure. Timo Soler came to him a few minutes after we spotted him near the pharmacy in Saint-François. Professor Larochelle patched up our armed robber at the port – the Quai d'Osaka – hidden away between some shipping containers.'

'And the good doctor contacted the police immediately afterwards? Not too troubled by professional secrecy, this one . . .'

'No,' Papy confirmed with a smile. 'And you ain't seen nothing yet.'

Marianne Augresse blinked away the image of the wounded robber and turned to Vasily.

'Shall we go, Mr Dragonman? I've had to fit you in between two meetings, and I can't promise we won't be interrupted by an emergency.'

The psychologist's calm demeanour stood in sharp contrast to the general frenzy around him. He sat down without creasing his leather jacket, opened his bag, took out a notebook and spread the child's drawings in front of him. His light brown eyes – almost the colour of varnished wood, terracotta or golden pastry – scanned the documents like a laser. His Slavic accent seemed even more pronounced than it had been on the phone.

'These are Malone's drawings. I have an entire notebook filled with notes and comments. I started typing them up, but . . .'

Marianne Augresse lifted one hand, as if to make Vasily freeze so that she could observe him. This psychologist was incredibly charming. A bit younger than her, maybe, but she adored shy, reserved men, the type who seemed to burn with some secret, inner passion. Like a tragic character straight out of a novel by Tolstoy or a play by Chekhov.

'Excuse me, Mr Dragonman, but could you start at the beginning? Who? Where?'

'Yes, yes, I'm sorry. The child's name is Malone. Malone Moulin. He's in his first year of preschool. In Manéglise. I don't know if you know where . . .'

The captain signalled for him to continue, with a simple glance at the map of the estuary pinned to the opposite wall. Manéglise was a small village of around 1,000 people, surrounded by fields, about ten kilometres from Le Havre.

'It was the school nurse who brought him to my attention. According to her, Malone kept talking nonsense. I met him for the first time three weeks ago.'

'And that's when he told you that his parents weren't his real parents!'

'Exactly. He claims to remember another life, before . . .'

'And the parents deny this.'

'Yes.' He checked his watch. 'In fact, they should be meeting the headmistress of the school in Manéglise at this very moment.'

'Without you?'

'They didn't want me there.'

'The parents or the headmistress?'

'Well, both, really.'

The psychologist gave a sorrowful smile, his eyes imploring. A lost dog in the street, begging for a sandwich.

'It's hard to argue with their view, really, isn't it? Frankly, Mr Dragonman, if Angélique hadn't sent you . . .'

There was a sparkle in his golden eyes as he pushed the child's drawings in front of the captain.

'At least let me explain. These drawings, a few words. It won't take long.'

Marianne Augresse hesitated. This man really was irresistible, the way he kept apologising, stammering, hesitating, yet never letting go of his objective. She would have to ask sly little Angie where she had found him.

'OK, Mr Dragonman, you have fifteen minutes.'

At that moment, the door opened, and Papy broke the spell.

'We've got the doctor on the phone!'

'Jesus! Put him through to my personal line.'

'I can do better than that,' said Lieutenant Pasdeloup. 'I can project his face on to your wall, larger than life. This is Professor Larochelle, Marianne, he's a bigwig at the Monod hospital and his office is equipped with the latest videoconferencing technology.'

The captain asked Vasily Dragonman to leave the office for a few minutes.

'It's to do with the armed robbery in Deauville, in January, do you remember that?'

The psychologist nodded, more amused than annoyed, and went out to wait patiently in the corridor while a second lieutenant entered, pushing a trolley with a camera and a microphone on it.

'We need to update our equipment!' said the cop, pointing the camera at the white wall.

He crouched down next to the trolley. He was wearing a skin-tight white T-shirt and jeans. About thirty. Face of an angel, muscles of a bodybuilder, trainers on his feet and a general laid-back appearance.

Lieutenant Jean-Baptiste Lechevalier. Married. Two children. A devoted husband and contented father. And a walking, talking female fantasy.

'Hurry up, JB!'

Marianne was only grouching at him for form's sake. Her gaze lingered for a moment on the lieutenant's curved back, before descending to those square centimetres of exposed flesh between the bottom of his T-shirt and the top of his jeans.

Already taken. Hands off . . .

'All right, we're ready,' said JB, getting to his feet with a cat-like undulation of his pelvis.

Lieutenants Pasdeloup and Lechevalier both sat down. Marianne took a seat behind her desk. JB touched the remote control and the white wall of the police station was transformed into a sumptuous, high-tech vision. Everything in the image appeared to be square or rectangular, from the varnished wooden desk to the grey leather chairs, from the exotic wood furniture to the plasma screen hung on the wall, even the large bay window that bathed this entire room in light.

The surgeon appeared in a moment, the ice cubes clinking in the glass he held. His white coat, worn casually over a three-piece suit, seemed specially designed to match his carnivorous smile.

'Captain Augresse? Sorry, I only have a few minutes. There's a woman I have to meet. She's lying down, eagerly awaiting my organ!'

He paused for two or three seconds before continuing, as if the video system was equipped with canned laughter to punctuate every joke he made. His immaculate teeth looked like an advert for the work of his colleagues in orthodontics.

'I'm performing a liver transplant, so let's make this quick. You wanted to talk to me?'

'You treated Timo Soler yesterday?'

The surgeon lifted the glass to his lips. The liquid was copper-coloured. Whisky? Red Bull? In the corner of his office, some golf clubs protruded from a Hugo Boss bag. Every detail seemed like part of an expensive Hollywood set.

'The armed robber, you mean? I already told your detectives everything. Your fugitive called me yesterday, late afternoon. An emergency. We met at the Quai d'Osaka, out of sight of any witnesses. He was waiting for me in a white Yaris. I noted the registration number, of course. He had a nasty wound between the subclavian artery and the upper lobe of the left lung, caused by a nine-millimetre bullet that had lodged there and been extracted somewhat summarily a few months earlier. The wound hadn't been treated since then. According to what the man told me, the wound had reopened recently, following a nasty fall. He was in agony. I did what I could.'

'You managed to operate on him like that? In his car, at the port?' The captain didn't hide her surprise.

'Of course not! When I said that I did what I could, I meant: I did what I could to help you.'

'Help us?'

JB appeared to be spellbound by the surgeon's room. He could see what looked like a swimming pool behind the office window, or perhaps it was the sea? The office was located on a hill in Sainte-Adresse, the chic part of Le Havre.

The surgeon seemed annoyed. 'Yes. I wanted to help the authorities. Informing you about the presence of the man you've spent months searching for is the least any honest citizen would do, don't you think?'

'Of course, Professor. And what else did you do to help us?'

'I injected him with a double dose of nalbuphine, an analgesic that's twice as strong as morphine. That calmed him down instantly and will ease the pain for a good twelve hours. After that, I examined his wound, fiddled about with it and then sewed it up. From the outside, it looks like a piece of haute couture.'

The professor flashed another brilliant smile, then moved closer to the camera, as if he were about to impart a secret.

'But *inside*, Captain, I must admit that I made a holy mess of it. A scalpel cut here, another there. The pain will be unbearable for Timo Soler when the effects of the drug begin to wear off. He will have no choice but to call me again . . . and this time, you'll be waiting for him with the cavalry.'

Marianne swallowed before replying.

'Yes indeed. We'll be there.'

Larochelle emptied his glass.

'Perfect. I have to go now. The young lady is waiting for me to give her a new liver. And hopefully, *she*'ll be a liver. Not a dyer, if you see what I mean . . .'

After one last burst of laughter the line went silent, and the luxurious decor vanished instantaneously, as if it had never existed. The three cops continued staring at the white wall a moment longer.

'The man's a saint,' said Papy at last.

'Where would the forces of law and order be without committed citizens such as him?' JB added.

'OK,' grumbled Marianne. 'But all the same, if Timo Soler does resurface to get himself sewn up again, we're not going to stand by and watch. We're going to nab him.'

The captain turned to JB. 'Spielberg, tidy up your things.'

Then to Papy. 'You stay on Dr House's tail, on a minute-by-minute basis.'

And then, finally, she picked up the child's drawings that had been left on her desk. Four wavy, black vertical lines, and a fifth line, in blue, that went diagonally across them.

A child's scribble, nothing more.

'Give me fifteen minutes with that shrink. He's going to explain to me how a three-year-old's memory works.'

## 6

*Little hand on the 12, big hand on the 1*

The class dispersed and Malone found himself alone. Half of the children were already lined up in pairs, forming a noisy caterpillar, waiting to go through a little iron gate behind the playground that led to the canteen. The other half were running towards their parents. Mothers mostly. The fathers tended to come in the mornings or evenings. Each child grabbed a hand or two arms, hugged a neck or clung to a leg.

But not Malone. Not today.

'Be a good boy and wait here. They won't be long.'

Clotilde, his teacher, smiled at him.

It was true: Malone did not have long to wait. Maman-da and Pa-di arrived just after the other parents had left. Maman-da was rarely late, but she usually came on her own to fetch him for lunch, not with Pa-di.

Malone ran over to Maman-da and grabbed her hand. He understood – they'd reminded him again that morning – that they had to talk to the teacher today at lunch about the stories he'd been telling. It was strange to go back into the classroom when it was empty, to have all the toys to himself.

'Mr and Mrs Moulin? Please, sit down.'

Clotilde Bruyère looked slightly embarrassed as she gestured to the only available chairs in the classroom, which were all of thirty centimetres high. Meetings with parents were often held here, and normally it did not pose much of a problem for the adults.

Normally.

On his Lilliputian chair, Dimitri Moulin – one metre eighty tall and weighing in at one hundred and ten kilograms – looked like a circus elephant perched on a stool. With his legs folded up, his knees were almost touching his chin.

Clotilde turned to Malone.

'Will you leave us for a moment, my dear? You can go and play outside for a bit. We won't be long.'

Malone waited in the playground. He didn't care. He'd deliberately left Gouti behind – in the dolls' corner, next to the blue bed. No one would notice his toy there, and Gouti would tell him everything afterwards. He looked longingly at the slide and the tunnel, where the big kids usually played and he was never able to. He thought about seizing this opportunity, running over there.

The sky was very dark, as if it were about to rain.

The toilets were a long way from the slide and the tunnel, a very long way, almost at the other end of the playground. If the rain suddenly started to fall, he wouldn't be quick enough to escape the glass drops.

Then he heard Pa-di shout something, even though the classroom door was shut. Poor Gouti, thought Malone.

His toy was always a bit scared when Pa-di got angry.

Seated on the mat for car toys, Dimitri Moulin had unfolded his legs and was grinding his heel into the realistically printed houses, gardens and roads.

'Mrs Bruyère, I'll be blunt. I have better things to do than go back to nursery school! I've just got a new job. I had to negotiate with my boss to be allowed to start work at one today. I'm sure you don't care – you'll be paid every month until you retire, but that's not true for me.'

The usual rant against employees of the state. Clotilde responded with silence. She wasn't used to it yet – she'd only been a teacher for six years, and a headmistress for two – but she'd been warned about this when she started: it was a classic complaint, almost as common as moaning about the number of weeks' holiday teachers were given. She had chosen to teach pre-school because she was gentle and patient. These qualities were also supposed to be useful for calming down angry fathers.

'That's not what we're here to talk about, Mr Moulin.'

'So let's get to the point then. Look, I've brought everything with me. This should save us a long chat.'

From the bag he wore over his shoulder he took out a series of cardboard folders.

'His birth certificate! Our family record book, stamped by the mayor's office and the maternity ward. Photograph albums showing pictures of the kid since he was born. Go on, take a look. You really think he's not ours?'

Amanda, sitting next to him, remained silent. Her eyes drifted over to the dolls' corner. Malone had left his cuddly toy sitting on a high chair. Gouti stared at them as if he was absorbing every word of the conversation. As if he were spying on them, Amanda thought stupidly.

'Mr Moulin,' the teacher said calmly, 'we have never questioned the fact that Malone is your child. It's just that . . .'

'Don't treat us like idiots!' Dimitri Moulin interrupted. 'We understand perfectly well what that shrink was implying, that Romanian, Vasily whatshisname. And your insinuations too, those little notes left in my kid's exercise book.'

Gentle and patient. Clotilde stuck to her strategy. After all, Mr Moulin could scarcely be any harder to tame than Kylian or Noah, the two troublemakers in her class.

'Mr Moulin, the reason I wrote those notes and suggested this meeting was simply that your son is saying things that might be described as surprising for his age, particularly when he talks to the school psychologist. I simply wanted to meet with you so that you could give me a little more information.'

'You're talking like a cop!'

Clotilde moved forward a few centimetres and squatted down so that her eyes were level with Dimitri Moulin's. She was used to living eighty centimetres above the ground. The bulk and height of this rhinoceros would not give him any advantage in *her* classroom. Quite the opposite.

41

The headmistress glared at Moulin.

'Will you please calm down. No one has mentioned the police. This is a school. My school. So, in the interest of your child, we are simply going to have a quiet discussion.'

Dimitri Moulin looked as if he wanted to get up from his midget chair and storm out, but his wife put a hand on his thigh to restrain him. He stared at the teacher defiantly.

'All right. You seem like a good teacher, after all. But as for that shrink, I just . . .' He was silent for a moment. 'Can't parents refuse that kind of thing, their kid being seen by a shrink?'

'It's complicated. It all depends on why . . .'

'Well, doesn't matter to me anyway,' Moulin cut in again.

He seemed to have mellowed. Maybe because he was actually quite attracted to this little woman who was standing up to him.

'After all,' he went on, 'I know there's something not quite right about the kid. He doesn't talk much, he uses words that are complicated, there's a bit too much going on in his head. If it'll do him good to speak to someone, well . . . I'm glad. That he can speak to an adult, I mean. But this Vasily Dragonski . . . Don't you have anyone else? Someone more . . .'

'More what?'

'You know what I mean.' He laughed. 'More French. I'm not allowed to say that, right?'

He leant over and, pushing away the little cars, spread the photograph albums across the town printed beneath his feet.

'Anyway, you might as well have a look at them. So we haven't come here for no reason.'

Clotilde turned her eyes to the documents.

'Vasily Dragonman is not under my authority. He reports directly to the regional education authority. I am here today as a mediator. We will discuss the matter and afterwards, I will provide him with my conclusions. It will probably be necessary for you to meet him again. Briefly.'

Dimitri Moulin seemed to be thinking. His wife spoke for the first time.

'You mean that the school psychologist can alert the authorities without even going through you?'

'Yes,' replied Clotilde. 'If there's any doubt about the child's safety, he can speak first of all to the child welfare services, who will appoint a social worker . . .'

'First of all?' yelled Dimitri. 'What comes after that?'

Clotilde delicately removed a little fire engine that Moulin's heavy shoes were threatening to crush. Then she said in her thin voice:

'Informing the police.'

'The police? You're not bloody serious? For a kid who's not even four years old and can barely string together three sentences?'

Clotilde rescued a second vehicle. She felt she had control of this conversation once more.

'I didn't say we would do that,' she reassured him with a smile. 'I can see that Malone is an adorable little boy who is growing up in the normal way and who is being perfectly well looked after. Besides – just between us – the last thing I want is the police opening an investigation, interrogating the children in my class and all their parents.' She leant even further forward, her eyes fixed on his, her preferred position for addressing three-year-old big shots. 'In a little village like Manéglise, no one wants that, do they, Mr Moulin? So we are going to discuss this quietly and calmly, and you are going to try to explain why on earth Malone keeps telling us that you are not his parents.'

Dimitri Moulin opened his mouth to speak, but Amanda cut him off.

'Please shut up now, Dimitri,' she said, almost imploringly. 'Shut up and let me speak.'

\*

\*    \*

Outside, a first drop fell on the iron slide and trickled down to the sand.

A second. A third.

Each of them more dangerous than the last.

Malone had been lucky. None of the drops had touched him. Not yet.

He took one last look at the classroom window. All their drawings were stuck to it, and their handprints. They had put their hands in a tray filled with paint and then pressed them against a sheet of paper.

His was bright red.

Behind the windowpane, they must be talking about him. And about his Maman, perhaps. Not Maman-da, but his Maman from before. Maybe about pirates too, and rockets and ogres. The adults knew about all that. He could only remember because of Gouti.

Another drop, landing on his trainer.

He'd only just escaped. Malone started to run.

Another twenty metres until he reached the door of the toilets.

Open the door and shut himself inside, as Maman had taught him.

# 7

*Today, my little sister Agathe finished all the sweets in the house before I got home from school and Maman got home from work.*
Want to kill
*One of them had cyanide in it!*

*Convicted: 253*
*Acquitted: 27*

www.want-to-kill.com

Vasily Dragonman spread out the drawings in front of Captain Marianne Augresse. He pointed to the first, an almost blank sheet with four black vertical lines and one red zigzag scrawled on it.

'Look carefully at these lines.'

Mariane Augresse put a hand over the drawing to conceal it.

'No, Mr Dragonman! We're going to start at the beginning. Who is this child? Tell me about his parents. The short version.'

Vasily bit his lip like a child who'd been told off.

'The parents. Normal, ordinary people. There's nothing much to say about them really. The mother, Amanda Moulin, is probably just over thirty, but she looks more like forty. The father is older: he probably *is* in his forties. They've been married for years. They live in a little house in Manéglise, on a housing estate called Les Hauts de Manéglise, on the outskirts of the village. Place Maurice-Ravel, to be exact. That's about all there is to Manéglise: a tiny village centre and a huge housing estate. She works as a cashier at Vivéco, the village minimarket. He's an electrician, or something like that. I think he's been struggling to find a steady job. People also know him in the village because he coaches the children's football team.'

'Have you met them?'

'Once, yes, when it all started. I was less curious about the matter back then.'

Vasily almost seemed to be apologising, as if he felt guilty about casting suspicion on a seemingly innocent family. Marianne found it incredibly endearing, the way he was behaving like a little boy, embarrassed to be telling on someone. She promised herself that she would talk to Angie about him that night. She wondered if the little flirt had a thing for this handsome man too? It seemed unlikely: the guy seemed a bit too intellectual for a tart like Angie. Her friend preferred bad boys.

Papy walked past the office window just then, a cup of coffee in hand. She raised her eyebrows at him and he responded by shaking his head. No word yet from Professor Larochelle about Timo Soler.

'Very good, Mr Dragonman. So, let's get back to the kid. Tell me about these drawings.'

'Well, as I said on the phone, he claims to have had a different life before the one he's living now, before his bedroom in the little house in Manéglise, before his parents, Amanda and Dimitri Moulin. He had described that previous life in great detail to me, even though his teacher, Clotilde Bruyère, says that Malone Moulin is normally a very quiet, reserved child.'

'So why would he confide in you?'

'It's my job.'

Good point, Marianne admitted to herself. Vasily was gentle and polite, but he had an ego too. And what if he was the one who was making all of this up, the captain wondered? What if he had invented this whole affair to make himself look good?

'Look at these drawings,' the psychologist went on. 'On this one, the four vertical lines, according to Malone, represent the castle near where he used to live. Those are the four towers. The zigzag that slants up to the top of the page is a rocket. He says he remembers having seen it fly up into the sky. Several times.'

Marianne sighed. None of this was convincing. She was only listening to what the shrink had to say because it killed some time while she waited for the surgeon's call, after which she would send five police cars to trap Timo Soler at the port. Her eyes drifted over to her computer screen for a moment. The website *want-to-kill.com* was flashing at the bottom of the screen. Naturally, she thought of Angie.

Was that little tramp playing a joke on her? What if this man, this supposed psychologist, was just a friend of hers, playing a role?

'You forgot the pirates,' she said distractedly. 'You mentioned a pirate ship too, yesterday.'

Vasily did not notice the irony in her voice.

'Yes! Exactly.' He grabbed another drawing. 'The blue shading represents the sea. Malone claims that he could see it from his bedroom. And the two little black dots . . . that's a ship.'

'One pirate ship or two?'

'Just one, but it's been cut in half. He said he could see that from his bedroom too. It's that kind of detail that I find troubling. Everything he says, from one meeting to the next, is very consistent. He never contradicts himself.'

Marianne's finger traced the blue sea.

'And the forest of ogres? There were ogres in the kid's story too, weren't there?'

She leant forward over the desk. Whether this was one of Angie's jokes or not, it was time to put an end to this farce.

'Frankly, Mr Dragoman, what do you expect us to do, realistically? Did you really think I would just accept all this? You're not telling me you believe this kid is telling the truth based simply on his ramblings and some scribbles?'

Vasily Dragonman's eyes flashed with panic, their terracotta sheen shattered. As if this was the first time he had ever come up against the walls of a cold, cruel, pragmatic world.

'Yes, Captain, in spite of everything, I *do* believe him! Eight years of study and as many working in the field should have taught me that this child has created an interior world with its own symbolism, a psychological labyrinth in which we should advance with caution.

But call it what you want – instinct or intuition – I am convinced that the majority of this child's memories are real. Even if it doesn't fit with what I know about psychoanalysis. I am certain that he really experienced all these things that he has drawn pictures about.'

'In that little house in Manéglise?'

'No. That's the point.'

For God's sake! thought Marianne. Her hands tensed under the desk. She felt she was setting off on an impossible journey, her sole motivation being that it was more pleasant to spend the time waiting for her cavalry charge staring into those gingerbread eyes than staring at the vending machine.

'Do you have anything else, Mr Dragonman? Anything . . . more concrete?'

'Yes.'

Vasily bent down over his patched leather satchel, then took out a series of photographs of a shopping centre.

'You recognise this?'

'Should I? There are a thousand just like it in France, aren't there?'

'It's the Mont-Gaillard shopping centre. The biggest in the region. Malone claims that it was in this shopping centre that his mother – the real one – handed him over to his second mother, Amanda Moulin. I showed him several pictures of it. Malone recognised the McDonald's, the Auchan logo, the drawing of the Pirate Island, a red and green parrot. The only place where those three shops can be found together is in this shopping centre. The child couldn't have invented it . . .'

The captain took the time to look at the photographs in detail.

'That doesn't prove anything,' she concluded, after a moment. 'He could be confused. Or he could simply be citing a place he's familiar with. He's probably spent every Saturday since he was born in that place. It's a shopper's paradise! Everyone north of the estuary goes there at the weekends.'

'He's not confused, Captain. It's difficult to explain to you in such a short time the subtle differences between implicit and episodic memory, but this is not confusion, believe me!'

Handsome, proud and stubborn as a mule, this shrink.

Marianne sighed. 'According to you, how long ago did this exchange of mothers take place?'

'Several months ago, at least. Maybe a year. It's not a direct memory. It's a memory of a memory, if you like.'

'I'm sorry, I don't understand.'

'A memory that he forces himself to think about every night so that he won't forget it. A memory that he is hammering into his brain like a nail. A nail to which he's attached a kind of sheet in his brain, so he won't have to see what's beneath it.'

'What's beneath it?'

'Whatever he experienced *before* the exchange in Mont-Gaillard. What he is able to express only in the form of drawings. The ogres, the pirates, and the rest. A reality that is too difficult to look at directly.'

'So you're saying that he is concealing a trauma?'

Suddenly, Vasily seemed more sure of himself. He smiled like a happy child.

'Yes, that much seems obvious to me. The rest is open to question, I guess – whether his mother is real or false, the honesty of Amanda and Dimitri Moulin. As far as I'm concerned, one thing is certain: this boy endured a traumatic experience and has built some incredibly high walls in his memory to keep it out of sight.'

The psychologist realised that he had the captain's attention, so went on, taking care not to speak too quickly.

'Except that . . . how can I explain this? It doesn't appear to be a classic case of trauma. He doesn't seem to be scared of his new parents, for example. He likes them, in fact. It's just that he thinks they're not his parents.'

'Paedophilia, or violence from a close relative – not necessarily his father or his mother – could that have provoked this behaviour?'

'Not as far as I know. I haven't detected anything of that nature.'

Marianne looked down at her watch.

12.20 p.m.

For several minutes now, a rainstorm had been hammering against the window of the captain's office. This was a common occurrence in Le Havre. It never lasted long – the rain, at least. The humidity lasted, though, that grey dampness, as if the water had soaked up the concrete from the city centre, the gravel from the port and the pebbles from the beach.

Behind the other window – the one that looked out on to the corridor – officers continued to walk past unhurriedly, their body language a sure sign that Timo Soler had still not shown any signs of life. Or of death, if the justice rendered by Larochelle's scalpel had been a little too heavy-handed.

Marianne decided to continue the interview for a while longer, and not just because of the shrink's beautiful eyes. He was talking to her about early childhood, about Malone Moulin, about children aged between zero and four. About those sweet little kids, similar to the one she hoped to carry in her womb one day.

'Mr Dragonman, I'm going to be honest: I'm finding it very hard to follow you. Everything you've told me seems like a bad joke, but last night you said it was urgent, an emergency. That was what worried me. You claimed that this child's memory could vanish if we didn't act quickly. Explain that to me. What will happen if no one except you believes this boy's story?'

# 8

*Little hand on the 12, big hand on the 4*

There was an opening about ten centimetres high between the white tiles and the bottom of the door, presumably to make it easier to clean the floor. Malone peered through the gap. Water was accumulating in front of the toilet block, forming a little puddle: the same, only smaller, as the one in the sand at the bottom of the slide. All he'd have to do is jump over it. It'd be easy, even if he wasn't good at jumping or running fast, all those things that the big boys did.

It wouldn't be a big deal if his trainer got wet. Once the water had fallen from the sky, it wasn't dangerous any more, because it died when it crashed onto the ground. Like bees: once they'd stung someone, they died. Maman-da told him that; she often talks to him about bees, mosquitoes, ants and other little creatures.

Yes, he'd just have to jump over the water.

When the rain was over.

Not straight away.

Malone could still hear the rain falling on the roof of the toilets and he didn't know if it was the drops that were already dead falling from the branches of the trees or the roof, or if it was the others, the ones that sting like a thousand snakes, like a thousand arrows from a knight's bows, if you didn't have time to hide.

He crouched down to look through the gap again. On the other side of the playground, through the classroom window, behind the raindrops that splashed against the pane and the handprints stuck to the glass, he could make out the face of Maman-da.

'I don't feel comfortable here, Miss.'

Amanda Moulin had removed a few bits of plasticine from the nearest shelf and her fingers were kneading them into tiny balls. Dimitri Moulin, still contorted on his miniature chair, now seemed to have little interest in the conversation.

'School was never my thing, you see,' Amanda went on. 'This is the school I went to. I started here nearly thirty years ago, in 1987. Mrs Couturier was the headmistress. Back then, there weren't all these toys outside and in the classroom. There was just one class-room, and there were only about a dozen of us. So, you see, I ought to feel at home, but, even if I force myself, this place doesn't bring back any good memories. I'm telling you this to try to explain why the village fairs, the elections for the parent–teacher association, selling cakes after class, all that stuff . . . it's just not my thing. It's not that I wouldn't like to take part, or that I don't think it's impor-tant. It's just . . .'

Amanda hesitated. Her fingers moulded two balls, one red and one white, into a single pale pink ball streaked with scarlet veins. Clotilde stared at her, listening attentively.

'It's just that, to be perfectly honest, school was always a bit of a burden for me, like a ball and chain that I dragged around with me from the age of three. And I'm probably not the only one who feels like that, am I – there are always more dunces than geniuses! When I'm working the till at Vivéco, I chat to everyone, I've been there six years. Anyone will tell you. I'm not really shy. But here, it's like I become shy again. I tell myself there must be loads of other people who are more intelligent than me, who can speak, or know something, or have an opinion, all of those people who actually liked school.'

The soft pink ball moved from one hand to the other. I was warned about this, thought Clotilde. Some parents are suspicious, hostile, aggressive even, as soon as they are back in a school play-ground; but it's only fear. A fear that goes back to childhood.

'Tell me about Malone, Mrs Moulin.'

'I'm getting to that, honestly I am. But I needed to tell you about me first, because it's important that you understand. So the reason we're here is that Malone is saying we're not his real parents and the school psychologist is taking him seriously. But how *can* you take his story seriously, Miss? Malone has lived with us since he was born. We brought you all the photos showing his first steps, his birthdays, parties with the neighbours, holidays, walks in the forest, going to the seaside, to the shopping centre. The longest we've been away from him since he was born is two days – when we stayed at my sister's in Le Mans, a year ago, for a wedding. They didn't swap him for another child then, you know. I think we'd have noticed!'

Clotilde forced herself to smile. With the tip of his shoe, Dimitri Moulin traced the road that wound its way around the printed carpet.

'I mean, you can ask anyone we know,' Amanda Moulin insisted. 'Our neighbours in Place Maurice-Ravel, my family, Dimitri's family, Malone's childminder, the other mothers who take their babies to the Parc des Hellandes. He's my kid! You know he is – I brought him here last May, to enrol him. And the mayor's office know it too! We registered his birth and we've got all the certificates.'

'Of course, Mrs Moulin, no one doubts that.'

Long seconds of silence filled the classroom, a silence that Clotilde never quite managed to obtain with her children. Amanda suddenly crushed the pink plasticine ball against her velvet skirt.

'They're not going to take him away from us, are they?'

Dimitri jumped. His foot banged into a little white ambulance. The headmistress didn't even have time to look surprised; Amanda was already talking again.

'We look after him as best as we can. We bought the house in Manéglise when I was pregnant. It was a mad thing to do, Dimitri will tell you. We didn't have the money, so we ended up with a thirty-year mortgage, even with a zero interest rate, but, well, we didn't want to bring him up in a council house in Mont-Gaillard. Besides, I knew there was a good school here. I thought so, anyway.'

Dimitri frowned at his wife. She didn't seem to notice.

'We're doing our best. Doing what everyone tells us we should do. A garden so he can play outside, meals with vegetables that we force him to eat, not too much telly, lots of books. We're really trying, so that he can have the opportunities we didn't really have.' She took a handkerchief from her pocket. 'If you only knew how much that kid means to me. We're doing everything we can, I swear to you.'

Clotilde moved closer to Amanda Moulin and stood right by her, the way she would if she were helping a child to blow their nose or brush their hair.

'No one doubts that, Mrs Moulin,' the teacher repeated. 'But then why is Malone telling all those stories?'

'Stories about rockets, and a castle, and pirates? Stories about another life he had before he lived with us?'

'Yes.'

'All children tell stories, don't they?'

'Yes . . . But there aren't many who say that their parents aren't their parents.'

Amanda seemed to be thinking about this. Dimitri stretched out his legs. He seemed to be in a hurry to leave now, and made a show of zipping up his jacket. Amanda took no notice.

'You think he's doing that because we aren't good at looking after him?'

'No,' Clotilde replied, too quickly. 'Not at all.'

'Because when I think about it, maybe that's it. Malone is better than us. More intelligent. He's advanced for his age, the shrink told us that at our first meeting. In fact, that's why we agreed to let Mr Dragonman see him. There are loads of things in Malone's head, stories, adventures, his own world, all these things we don't understand, Dimitri and me.'

'What do you mean?'

'Maybe we're not the parents that Malone would have wanted, that's what I'm saying. I'm sure he'd have preferred other parents, richer, younger, better educated, parents who could take him on an aeroplane, go skiing, visit museums. Maybe that's why he's inventing other parents.'

'Mrs Moulin, a child doesn't think like that.'

'I did! That's why I left my parents. Because I wanted to live a different life. Something more than just the countryside, the daily grind, bosses . . . I believed I could do it back then. I even thought I'd succeeded, before you summoned me here.'

'I didn't "summon" you, Mrs Moulin. And it's adolescents who dream about having another life, and parents, not three-year-old children.'

'But that's what I was telling you: Malone is advanced for his age.'

At that moment, Dimitri Moulin stood up. His six-foot frame unfolded and his silhouette suddenly overshadowed the room with its miniature furniture and its minuscule toys.

'I think we've been over this enough now. I'm already late for my shift. And my kid has been standing on his own in the playground for a bloody long time.'

His wife had no choice but to stand up too. Dimitri took a moment to look the teacher up and down. At the other end of the playground, Malone came out of the toilets.

It wasn't raining any more.

'Look at my kid,' said Moulin. 'Everything's fine. So you can give that shrink a message: if he's looking for trouble, he and I can settle this man to man. My kid hasn't been beaten or raped or anything like that. He's fine, you understand? As for the rest, I'll bring him up however I want!'

'I understand.'

Clotilde Bruyère opened the door, hesitated as she watched Malone come towards them, then decided to speak:

'But if you'll allow me to give you some advice, because I've been watching Malone in my class for several months now, and don't take this the wrong way, Mr and Mrs Moulin, but I think you need to dress your son in warmer clothes.'

'Why, is it going to get very cold?' worried Amanda.

'No. Because your son feels cold. Very cold. Almost all the time. Even on sunny days.'

The Skoda Fabia sped through the empty streets of Manéglise. Route de Branmaze. Pa-di drummed his fingers on the steering wheel. Behind him, on his booster seat, Malone hugged Gouti tightly in his arms.

*Little hand on the 1, big hand on the 4.*

He couldn't wait to get home, to go up to his bedroom and hide in bed with Gouti. So the toy could tell him everything.

# 9

'So you want to understand how a child's memory works, Captain, is that right?'

Marianne Augresse nodded. Vasily Dragonman took a deep breath and then launched into his explanation.

'OK. This might take a while. First, you have to bear one very simple principle in mind. In a child, the length of time that a memory is preserved increases with age. If you take a three-month-old baby, for example, its memories will last about a week. A game, a song, a taste. The memories of a baby six months last about three weeks. A baby of eighteen months has a memory of about three months, and at three years old memories are retained for about six months.'

Marianne did not appear convinced. She waved her hand irritably.

'Well, that's the theory. But a child's memory must depend on other criteria, no? A baby is more likely to remember something or someone that it sees every day, I imagine. Or an extraordinary event, whether it's something wonderful or frightening.'

'No,' the psychologist replied. 'It doesn't work like that. Your reasoning would apply to an adult memory, a memory capable of sorting the important from the incidental, the useful from the useless, the true from the false. But the memory of a child under three works in a different way. All the memories that are not reactivated inevitably vanish. Let me give you an example. Let's say you show a child the same cartoon every day, from the day he's born until his third birthday. He watches it over and over again, knows it by heart; the characters in the film are his closest friends. Then, for a year, you stop showing it to him and you don't speak about it for twelve months. On his fourth birthday, you take out the DVD and you let your child watch the show. He will have absolutely no memory of it!'

'Really?'

'Really! And what happens with a cartoon or a story can also happen with a close relative who's never mentioned again, a grandfather who dies, a childminder who gets a job elsewhere, the child next door whose family move house. But what confuses the matter is that it is very rare for us *not* to talk about an important event for several months, so it is reinforced. On the other hand, a young child will have an extraordinarily vivid memory of the immediate past: he'll know where he hid his dummy in the morning; he'll remember the colour of the slide in the park where he goes to play every week; he'll recall the dog behind the fence on the way to the bakery. Especially if these actions are repeated or brought up regularly in conversation.'

'So it's the parents who shape the child's memory?'

'Yes, almost one hundred per cent. That's true for us too, in fact. This is what we call episodic memory, or autobiographical memory. Our adult memory is almost entirely composed of indirect memories: photographs, spoken accounts, films. It's a bit like Chinese whispers – memories of memories of memories. We think we can recall precise details of holidays that took place thirty years ago – each day, every landscape, our emotions – but those memories are only images, always the same ones, that we have selected and reconstructed according to our personal criteria, like a camera that films only from one angle, shows only one part of the backdrop. The same is true of other memories, like the first time you fell off your bike, your first kiss, your cry of joy the day you got your exam results. Your brain sorts through everything and keeps only what interests it on a subjective basis. If you could go back in time or watch a film of the past, you would see that the actual events hardly ever correspond exactly with your memories. What was the weather like? What did you do afterwards? Who was there, apart from you? Nothing. No idea. All you have are flashes!'

As the psychologist was speaking, Marianne continued to watch her colleagues pass by outside the window to the corridor, holding cups of coffee or sandwiches. No one seemed particularly agitated. Timo Soler still hadn't called Professor Larochelle.

'I can well believe that, Mr Dragonman,' continued Marianne, 'even if it's a little disturbing. But let's get back to the memory of a child. At what age do we start to form memories that will last a lifetime?'

'It's difficult to say, precisely because of the phenomenon I just explained to you. Some people claim to remember things that happened when they were two or three years old, but those are always reconstructed memories or memories of things they were told. That's what happens in the case of adopted children, for example, especially those from other countries; how can they distinguish between real memories, the ones that have been repeated to them, and the ones they've imagined? Canadian studies have shown that adopted children who were told the truth about their past at a very young age, sincerely believed that they possessed actual memories of that first life, whereas that absolutely wasn't the case for children who didn't know they were adopted.' The psychologist looked down at Malone's drawings for a moment. 'So, in an attempt to answer your question Captain, I would say that most of us have no direct memory of anything we experienced before the age of four or five. Everything you do with your children during the first sixty months of their life – taking them to the zoo, to the seaside, telling them stories, celebrating Christmas or their birthday – you will remember all your life as if it were yesterday, but for them . . . nothing. A complete void!'

Marianne gave him a strange look, as if he'd said something heretical.

'A complete void? But those are the years that help build their identity, aren't they? Paediatricians always say that the first four years are the most important.'

Vasily Dragonman flashed a wide smile. He had taken the captain to the exact place he wanted to bring her.

'Of course! The first years are fundamental. And even the time before birth, if you look at theories around psychogenealogy and transgenerational trauma. A person's values, tastes, their personality . . . all of those things are shaped by the first years of existence. But looking at it purely from the point of view of our capacity to retain direct memories of events . . . there's nothing. It's a stunning paradox, isn't it? Our life is guided by events – acts of violence or of love – of which we have no real proof. Like a black box that we will never be able to access.'

'But the memories are still stored in that inaccessible black box?'

'Well, yes. It's quite a simple mechanism, really. Until the acquisition of language, thought depends on images, and therefore so does memory. From a psychoanalytical viewpoint, that means that memories cannot be stored in the unconscious, nor in the conscious, nor even in the preconscious.'

The captain widened her eyes to signify that she had no idea what he was talking about. The psychologist leant forward and continued to speak patiently:

'In other words, in a young child who seems to have forgotten everything, traces do still remain. We call this the sensory memory, or the sensorimotor stage of development. It occurs through the diffuse memory of emotions, impressions, and sensations. The most classic example is of the child who was circumcised when he was three months old and who, at the age of ten, remains terribly afraid of hospitals – their corridors, the colours, the odours, the noises – without having any real idea why, or any memory of having been in one before. Like the ghost of a memory.'

Captain Augresse was taking an increasing amount of pleasure in this conversation, and not only because of the glint that sparkled in the psychologist's hazel eyes each time he mentioned a new theory. She felt like an overenthusiastic student, as if she were travelling towards an unknown continent, a virgin territory filled with natives aged zero to four, so many destinies to be modelled by their parents – in their image, but without their flaws. The dream of every mother.

'I have a question, Mr Dragonman,' she said. 'It's probably stupid, but . . . What is the best thing for a teacher to do in the event of trauma? Should they help the child to forget or to verbalise the situation, talk about the trauma, so that the memory doesn't remain trapped somewhere in the child's brain?'

Vasily's reply was unequivocal:

'Any psychologist would tell you the same thing, Captain: denying trauma, as a form of protection, does not solve anything. To live with trauma, you have to confront it, verbalise it, accept it. That's the concept of psychological resilience which Boris Cyrulnik made famous.'

The captain liked to provoke. 'Well it's a bit stupid, isn't it?'

'Why?'

'I keep thinking about that film, *Eternal Sunshine of the Spotless Mind*. The story about the company that offers to erase painful memories. It's a seductive idea, don't you think? Rather than brooding over lost love, just wipe it from your brain.'

'That's science fiction, Captain.'

'For adults, I agree, it is science fiction . . . But according to what you've just told me, with a young child it is perfectly possible. For a grown-up whose memory is already fixed, I understand that it's impossible to suppress a trauma completely. We have no choice but to extract it, like a tumour. But for a child under four, it's different, because all of his conscious memories are going to vanish anyway. Maybe in that case it's better not to talk about the trauma, to let the memories evaporate, or blur, until they don't seem real. Even if the child retains a vague memory of trauma, he won't be able to tell it apart from a violent image from a book or on TV. A sort of containment theory, if you like. A bit like burying radioactive waste.'

The psychologist looked amused. 'Go on.'

'All right, imagine a child of one or two who's survived a genocide, like those Cambodians or Rwandans who come over to France as refugees. A child who's seen his whole family slaughtered before his very eyes. Which is better, Mr Dragonman? To allow everything from that child's brain to be erased so that they can forget the horror and grow up like any other kid? Or to make them carry that burden all their life?'

'To be frank, Captain, from a strictly psychoanalytical point of view, your theory is heresy! The child's sensory memory would contradict what the adults around him were telling him. You can't erase the ghosts of the past.' He paused. 'But the image you used to illustrate the idea of containment is correct, Captain. It would be just like burying radioactive waste. It can be effective for years, but then it can leak out at any moment.'

He smiled at the policewoman.

'In reality, there is no absolute rule. Suppressing a violent trauma can provoke amnesia, even in adults. There are also cases of re-covered memories: of sexual abuse in early childhood, for instance, denied, buried, but which come flooding back in adulthood. And then, how can you tell whether it's a real or a false memory? The ghosts of the unconscious are there, Captain, they stay with us all our lives, loyal and invisible. In the end, there is only one method for learning to live in harmony with them.'

'And what is that?'

'Love, Captain! What a young child needs more than anything is physical and emotional security. Stability. Confidence in the adults who are protecting him. Verbalising the trauma or not verbalising it ultimately makes no difference if that ingredient isn't there: the love of a mother, a father, or any other primary caregiver. That's all the child needs!'

Marianne let herself be gently lulled by Dragonman's words. On top of his accent and his clear oak eyes, he had an innate gift for teaching. A sense of rhythm, ellipsis, suspense. No wonder the Psychology lectures at the university were filled with female students.

She looked down at the child's drawings again and frowned.

'OK, Mr Dragonman. A mother's love . . . But let's get back to Malone Moulin. There's something I don't understand. You tell me that his story about exchanging mothers at the Mont-Gaillard shopping centre took place several months – or nearly a year – ago. So how can Malone remember it, if the memory of a child his age is so volatile? And then there's the stuff that goes further back, his supposed previous life, with pirate ships, rockets, ogres . . .'

'Because he's been reminded of those memories, every day, every evening, every week, month after month.'

The captain almost fell off her chair.

'*What?* Who's been reminding him? Who could possibly be talking to him about his previous life?'

Just as the psychologist was about to reply, Lieutenant Pierrick Pasdeloup burst into the room. He smiled broadly at Marianne while handing her a bulletproof vest emblazoned with the logo of the national police.

'It's showtime! The doc just called us. Timo Soler wants to see him, as soon as possible. They're meeting in less than an hour at a discreet spot at the port: the Quai d'Osaka, where Dr Larochelle sewed him up yesterday.'

Captain Augresse jumped to her feet.

'Ten men, five cars. We're not going to let him get away!'

Vasily Dragonman watched the whirlwind that had just hit the police station. Marianne was about to leave, slamming the door shut behind her, having completely forgotten about him, when he shyly raised a hand.

'Don't you want to hear the answer to your question?'

'What question?'

'Who's talking to Malone Moulin about his previous life.'

Marianne hopped about impatiently in the doorway, putting on her bulletproof vest.

'OK, go on then!'

'His cuddly toy.'

'Sorry?'

'His toy. Malone calls it Gouti. He swears to me that it's Gouti who tells him about his previous life, every evening when he's in bed. And, to be completely honest with you . . .'

This psychologist had starry eyes that could persuade you that there was life on Mars, that could convince you to get in a rocket with him and fly there to populate it.

'. . . to be completely honest with you, Captain, as strange as this might seem . . . I think he's telling the truth!'

# 10

Hidden behind the wall of containers that were piled up like multi-coloured steel bricks, Lieutenant Pasdeloup observed the white Yaris on the other side of the port. It was the only car parked on the peninsula that was separated from the rest of the docks by the Francis I lock.

All exits barred.

To the west, the ocean.

To the south, the Quai de l'Asie, and Papy, escorted by two cars.

To the north, the Quai des Amériques, where two other police cars waited, also invisible, hidden by giant cranes whose metal necks leant out over a Venezuelan liner.

To the east, the fifth police car – the one containing Captain Augresse and Sergeant Cabral – was positioned a little closer, on the same peninsula as the Yaris, behind the artificial dunes made of sand and gravel dragged from the bottom of the estuary to allow ever bigger ships to dock at the concrete quays.

It was a Sisyphean task. Digging out a few cubic metres of sand when the ocean brought in twice as much with each tide.

It had been quite a while since Lieutenant Pasdeloup had last walked around the port. Particularly on this side, facing the Francis I lock and its vertical lift bridge. The biggest in the world, they said when it was built, before the Belgians, then the Dutch, then the Chinese went one better. Inevitably, this thought sent Papy forty years back in time, to the days when he would ride his bike behind his father's, slaloming between the crates being unloaded by the dockers. Even then, Le Havre was practically still smoking from the bombardment of 1945 that had destroyed four-fifths of the city.

He wasn't old enough to remember what the city had been like before that, a town of villas and ship-owners, the casino and sea bathing. The remembrance of which made old people cry. His father. His mother. Le Havre before the Café and Océane docks were transformed into cinemas, concert halls, shops such as Fnac and Pimkie, fast-food restaurants like Flunch. Docks where young people came, just as he did forty years earlier, but to relax and have fun, not to work.

'Papy! Can you hear me?'

Jean-Baptiste Lechevalier was standing directly opposite him, to the north, on the Quai des Amériques, separated by five hundred metres of ocean and four kilometres of sea wall. Lieutenant Pasdeloup snapped out of his reverie and pressed the button on the walkie-talkie.

'Yeah, I can hear you. Can you see the Yaris too?'

'Yep. Got a perfect view of it, with Timo Soler inside. Officer Bourdaine's already got a few nice shots of him. He doesn't look too good. I reckon he's praying that Larochelle hasn't forgotten about him.'

Lieutenant Pasdeloup checked his watch. 1.12 p.m.

'What the hell is he doing, that bloody doctor?'

'He says he's on his way.'

Lieutenant Pasdeloup cut the walkie-talkie connection for a moment and looked through his binoculars again. Timo Soler was leaning back against the headrest of his seat. He kept closing his eyes, but never for more than a few seconds. The rest of the time, he scanned the space around him, alert. Papy could not see any weapons. Soler's hands continued to grip the steering wheel.

Because he wanted to be able to leave as quickly as possible?

Because he was in pain?

The lieutenant lifted the walkie-talkie to his lips again.

'Marianne? What should we do? We can't wait here all afternoon for the doctor. JB wants to go get him now.'

'And what do you think?'

'I think Timo would find it very difficult to get away from us. There's only one road to the south of the port where he's parked,

**65**

and two bridges to the north. We should be able to cut off all escape routes.'

'Yes. But Soler didn't choose that spot by chance. He has a 360-degree view of his surroundings. He'd see us coming from nearly a kilometre away, and we have no way of knowing if he's armed or not. Have you heard from the doctor?'

'According to JB, he's on his way.'

'Let's stick to the original plan then. Larochelle goes to meet him and gets him to swallow some sodium thiopental. That should send him to sleep in less than five minutes, and if that's not enough, Larochelle will make him lie down and start slicing him up while we approach the car. What kind of car does the doctor drive?'

'A Saab 9-3.'

Marianne whistled.

'It'd be a shame to start without him, don't you think? I can't believe he's agreed to dirty his tyres again on the gravel pits of the port.'

'Oh, it's a question of honour, old chap!' said Papy mockingly. 'Class solidarity. Don't forget that Timo Soler robbed the four biggest luxury boutiques in Deauville. Put yourself in Dr Larochelle's position: if we let the peasants do what they want, whatever will become of us?'

Captain Augresse interrupted her lieutenant's flight of fancy.

'I get your point, Papy. Let's wait another ten minutes for our superhero to turn up, and then we attack.'

The port looked deserted, giving the impression that the liners in the docks had been abandoned there, and that the gantry cranes had stacked the containers all by themselves, out of habit, rather than under the guidance of any driver. As if the machines and robots had taken over, the only things capable of surviving this steel and concrete wasteland. The containers seemed to be accumulating randomly, in accordance with some absurd logic that had been lost along with the last man.

To Papy, it seemed impossible that there was any rational order to the way in which these haphazard piles of boxes had been arranged.

Impossible, too, that any of the bookkeepers from the harbour master's office could have any idea of what was stocked along these kilometres of docks.

Lieutenant Pasdeloup, never taking his eyes off the white Yaris, remembered his father's words.

A port that is working is a port without boats.

A boat that is not at sea is a boat that loses money. And his father had been one of those swarms of dockers who had rushed towards each new liner to empty it as quickly as possible, the different teams trying to outdo each other, trying to break records.

Nowadays, thought Papy, a port that is working is a port without men.


'The doctor's still in Harfleur,' JB's voice crackled through the walkie-talkie. 'He says he's stuck in traffic, but my guess is he was probably flat out at work. He promises he'll be here in ten minutes.'

Papy looked at his watch again. The doctor was already seven minutes late for his meeting with Soler.

'What do we do, Marianne?'

'Nothing. We keep watching the Yaris and we wait.'


*We wait.*

A grey tanker moved slowly through the port. Russian flag. Gas or oil, probably. At the rate it was going, it would pass the Quai des Amériques in a few minutes and obscure JB's view of the peninsula.

Doesn't matter, thought Papy, at the other end of the port; he and Marianne still had an unimpeded view. The fine rain that had fallen on the concrete sea wall had given way to a patch of brightness in the faded sky, like a badly rubbed-out pencil drawing.


'Soler's on the move!' Marianne yelled into the walkie-talkie. Papy pressed the binoculars to his eyes just in time to see Timo Soler grimace, straighten up, and set off at speed.

The Yaris leapt towards the port, performed a U-turn in a cloud of dust, then headed north, straight towards a red metal bridge a few hundred metres away that stood at the entrance to the lock.

'Go, JB!' yelled Papy in turn. 'Soler's on his way towards you. Marianne's on his tail.'

Lieutenant Pasdeloup, positioned to bar any retreat towards the south by Timo Soler, between the oil tanks and the estuary road, was now forced into the role of spectator. Even though he was situated less than five hundred metres from the scene as the crow flies, more than two kilometres of docks separated him from Soler's Yaris.

He saw Marianne's car set off from the sand dunes, siren screaming, no more than a few seconds behind Soler.

The wounded robber didn't stand a chance.

He moved the binoculars a bit higher up, as if to anticipate the Yaris's route.

Jesus wept!

Lieutenant Pasdeloup bit his lip as he stifled another blasphemy. Soler had chosen just the right moment.

As the Yaris reached the lock, the bow of the Russian tanker was almost touching the edge of the vertical lift bridge. Soler's car accelerated again as the bridge slowly began to rise.

Echoing the police siren, the lock alarm went off. Three red lights flashed in front of the lock, the blue flashing light on the police car mingling with them to create a purple halo.

The Yaris drove onto the bridge. Through the twin lenses of the binoculars, it looked minuscule next to the tanker; a fly skimming the horn of a rhinoceros.

'We have to stop him before he gets away!' shouted Papy, powerless.

'I can't see a thing,' replied JB into the walkie-talkie. 'We're driving past that fucking Russian ship. If Soler gets across the lock, we should end up nose-to-nose with him.'

Or just after him, calculated Lieutenant Pasdeloup, watching anxiously.

Marianne's car had almost reached the red bridge. Cabral was driving. A solid cop. Reliable. Experienced.

'Hurry up, for God's sake!' the captain ordered him. 'If Soler can get over that bridge, then so must we!'

Marianne Augresse had undone her seat belt and had opened the window of her door to give her the best possible view.

And to shoot, if she had to.

Cabral didn't blink.

Papy saw Timo Soler's vehicle speed up and then launch itself through the air between the vertical lift bridge and the dock – a jump of one metre, maybe less. It was difficult to tell the distance from where he sat.

He had the impression that the Yaris bounced several times as it veered right, almost tipping over, but then it stabilised.

That bastard Soler must be screaming with pain, thought Papy. After being sliced up by Dr Larochelle, his wound open, the sudden movements of the car must be torture.

Not torture enough, though, apparently. One second later, the white Yaris sped off between the containers, along Avenue de l'Amiral-Chillou.

'Straight ahead!' yelled Papy to JB. 'He'll be right in front of you.'

The bridge was still rising, more than a metre off the ground now. Marianne's car was still accelerating. The sirens were deafening, the lights blinding.

'We're not going to make it!'

Cabral suddenly hit the brake.

The wheels of the police car locked a few metres from the bridge that was raised up into the sky. Captain Augresse did not have time to protest: her face smashed against the windscreen which was covered in wet sand.

Timo Soler's Yaris, followed by the two Renaults of JB and Deputy Sergeant Lenormand, disappeared from Pasdeloup's field of vision. His voice shook as he spoke into the walkie-talkie.

'Shit, are you OK?'

'We're OK.'

It was Cabral who answered.

'We'll be fine. The captain's a bit bashed up, and I reckon she'll give me hell once she's feeling better, but I'll take that any day over a dive into the lock.'

The bridge slowly descended. At last, the port came alive. Men ran out from behind containers like Playmobil figures coming out of their boxes. Amazed Russian sailors rushed to the railings of the tanker. JB's voice made Lieutenant Pasdeloup jump.

'Papy?'

'Yeah?'

'We've found the Yaris.'

'Really?'

'It's empty,' JB replied. 'Avenue du 16eme-Port. Let's seal the area. He must be continuing on foot, wounded. He won't get far.'

'If you say so.' Papy did not sound convinced.

He knew that area. Avenue du 16eme-Port went right around the Neiges quarter, a strange little village of about a thousand inhabitants, half industrial zone, half deprived urban area completely encircled by the port roads. An enclave. Isolated.

Timo Soler had not chosen his meeting place by chance, and even less so the place where he had abandoned his car. He had probably been hiding out in the Neiges quarter for months, and finding him there, if he had friends to help him, could take weeks.

Plenty of time for him to die first.

# 11

*Little hand on the 1, big hand on the 7*

Malone was playing with his little white and blue rocket on the living room carpet. Gouti watched him, leaning against the leg of a chair. Malone would have preferred to go up to his bedroom so he could listen to what his toy had to tell him, but he wasn't allowed.

We don't have time today, said Maman-da.

There was only time to warm up the pasta, set the table and quickly eat before returning to school.

Malone made the rocket blast off, in search of a planet where it could land. Poof-Poof seemed a good destination to him: a soft, purple, pear-shaped planet. In the kitchen, he heard Pa-di speaking loudly. He was drinking coffee and kept saying the same thing.

The teacher and Vasily. Vasily and the teacher.

He was angry. And even if Pa-di hadn't looked at him during lunch, Malone knew why.

It was because of him.

Because of everything he'd told Vasily.

He didn't care. Pa-di could shout at him or not talk to him at all. He could even punish him, if he wanted to. Malone didn't care! He would never tell him anything and he would keep talking to Vasily. He'd promised Maman.

Maman-da quickly drank her coffee, did the washing-up, kissed him on the forehead, swept up, and gave him another hug. Now she was tidying away all the things they'd taken to school: the papers, the notebooks, the photograph albums. She opened the big cupboard under the stairs, and then Pa-di called to her. He was already wearing his coat, but he couldn't find his scarf. Maman-da always said that she had two children to look after!

She went up to the bedroom to fetch the scarf while Pa-di waited in the kitchen in front of the telly, with his coffee, shouting up at her that he was going to be late.

Malone gently landed the rocket on Planet Poof-Poof. He walked over to the hallway, to that large black door which was never usually open.

He approached the cupboard and went inside. The only light came from outside, and the space grew even darker with his body blocking most of the light. He moved to the side, near the photo albums on the shelves. There was no point opening them: he'd seen them before – Maman-da showed them to him sometimes – but he didn't recognise himself when he was little. He remembered lots of things, thanks to Gouti, but not that. Not his face, not what he looked like when he was a baby.

Malone looked at the other boxes and objects crammed under the steps of the staircase. He spotted a large board. It was strange because it had big letters written on it. Malone didn't know all his alphabet, but he knew how to read his own name:

M A L O N E

In school, he had to be able to find the right label so he could hang up his coat.

M A L O N E

His name was written on that board hidden under the stairs, in large lettering, on white paper under glass, but it had not been written in felt-tip pen. Nor in paint. Nor with a biro.

Malone had to lean even closer to be sure.

He climbed over a few boxes and picked up the board with both hands so that he could bring it towards the light.

The letters of his name were spelt out using animals!

Tiny little creatures.

Ants.

Dozens of ants lined up, stuck to the paper, then crushed against the glass. Whoever had done this had taken great care. There was hardly a single ant out of place. It was pretty, and very neat, even if Malone was a bit sad for all those ants that had been killed in order to spell out his name. Unless the letters had been formed using ants that were already dead?

Who could have done this?

Not Pa-di, that was for sure. He hated colouring in, cutting up things, building things with Lego. Maman-da then, but why? To surprise him?

It would be a strange kind of surprise. He didn't really like ants. Especially not dead ones. He would rather have seen his name written in colourful felt-tip or finger-painted, like they did at school.

The front door banged shut, without Pa-di saying goodbye to them.

'Time to go, sweetie!' Maman-da shouted from upstairs in his bedroom. 'Can you get your coat?'

Malone came out of the cupboard under the stairs. He'd seen something else, too: other strange creatures, also dead.

And these creatures were bigger than ants.

# 12

The ugly bandage was stuck to both of Marianne Augresse's cheeks, squashing down her nose. She looked like a boxer, she thought, or a cougar who'd just had plastic surgery. She hated the thirty male eyes that were turned on her, particularly – for different reasons – those of JB and Cabral. But there was no way she could get out of this debriefing session. With Timo Soler on the run, she had to put as many men as she possibly could on the case, including those who'd been here less than a year, and it was essential that they all possessed the same amount of information about the Deauville armed robbery.

She moved to the centre of the room, resigned. When Marianne had first seen herself in the rear-view mirror of the police car on the bridge by the lock, blood pouring from her nose, it had made her cry. Weirdly, it was the first thing that had struck her, even before Timo Soler's escape: how long would it take for her face to get back to normal? A week? A month? Maybe several months, if her nose was broken. All that lost time in her personal countdown, because how could she find a man capable of giving her a kid if she had a nose like this?

*Ugh, this is becoming an obsession!*

The captain slid her USB key into the computer while folders were being circulated among the police officers. Anyway, she reminded herself, her nose wasn't broken. Larochelle had been quite reassuring when he examined it at the port, surrounded by dockers and sailors who had nothing better to do than watch her as if she were a stowaway who'd just emerged from a container. There wasn't even any need for stitches, the doctor had added. All she had was a big bruise that would disappear in a few days. At least Larochelle had been useful in that regard.

The surgeon had parked his Saab 9-3 next to the lock less than three minutes after Soler had escaped, and Marianne, as soon as she was bandaged up, had given him both barrels, even threatening to investigate him for obstruction of justice.

What if he'd held back deliberately? What if he had *wanted* Timo Soler to escape?

It was Papy – not exactly Larochelle's biggest fan – who had taken her aside and calmed her down. 'You're not thinking straight, Marianne,' he'd whispered to her. 'The doctor gave us the exact time and place of the meeting, and Timo Soler turned up as arranged. All we had to do was catch him. We're the ones who screwed up!'

He was right. It wasn't Larochelle's fault; it was purely down to their own incompetence. The surgeon was still smiling, apparently more amused than frightened by the swarm of cops around him.

'OK, Papy,' Marianne had muttered through gritted teeth. 'We'll deal with this later.' Her deputy had a point, anyway; they needed to take it easy on the surgeon, because they might need him again. Timo's ugly open wound was his handiwork, after all.

But still Marianne had brooded all the way back to the police station:

*Today, because of an asshole doctor, I let a criminal escape, and now I'm disfigured.*

Want to kill

*I grabbed the gun from my belt and I . . .*

She didn't have the imagination to invent an amusing or surprising punchline, not like the other users of *want-to-kill.com*, who were constantly outdoing each other with new and interesting ways to get rid of the people who'd annoyed them. The website's instructions were simple: write about someone who'd pissed you off so badly you wanted to kill them, and then describe how you might do it, if possible in a way that was joyful, moving or pathetic, then wait for the jury of online readers to give their verdict. Just another way for frustrated wishful thinkers to get their feelings off their chest without actually killing anyone. And in a way, the captain thought, that stupid website had changed her life.

She forced herself to stop thinking about it all and start the presentation. With relief, she felt the men's eyes move from her face to the map of Deauville. Marianne had asked Lucas Marouette – an intern who was spending a few bored weeks at the station before starting active service – to create a 3D animation on Google Street View. This was easy, apparently, if you knew how to download the basic apps. These virtual reconstructions were now the examining magistrates' favourite tool.

'It's the morning of Tuesday 6 January 2015,' began Marianne. 'Twelve minutes past eleven. The weather is cold and windy. The streets of Deauville are practically deserted. Two motorbikes stop at the city's central roundabout, between Rue Eugène-Colas and Rue Lucien-Barrière, very close to the casino. At the same moment, a couple walks along the pavement, arms around each other. An elegantly dressed couple. He is wearing a grey felt hat, she has on a silk headscarf. It is impossible to see their faces on any of the city's surveillance cameras.'

On the animation, two stylised figures in blue and red – no clothes or faces – walk along the shopping street in Deauville, each luxury store's sign clearly visible; a perfect reproduction of the captain's description.

'While the two motorbikes park, the couple separates. He goes into the Hermès boutique and she goes into Louis Vuitton. After that, everything happens very quickly. At the same moment as the two motorcyclists, armed with Maverick 88s, enter the two main jewellery shops on Rue Eugène-Colas – Godechot-Pauliet and Blot – the man in the hat takes out a Beretta 92 and aims it at the two saleswomen in Hermès while the woman does the same thing in Louis Vuitton. It takes them only two minutes to fill four bags, one for each robber. They know exactly what they're after, opting mostly for easily transportable objects. Watches, jewels, scarves, belts, wallets, bags, glasses . . . plus a few more rarefied pieces. Their gestures are precise and perfectly timed. All four of them emerge into Rue Eugène-Colas at exactly the same moment. The two bikers hand their bags to the woman. An alarm goes off at that point. The police station is only seven hundred metres away, at the end of the same street. A cop going outside to smoke a fag would have been able to see the two motorbikes.'

On Street View, the half-timbered Norman houses flash past on fast forward, as if filmed by a hand-held camera, before the image stops on the four robbers. Marianne goes on:

'I'll spare you the press articles about the robbers, their audacity, their recklessness even. Let's stick to the facts. The whole thing was expertly staged. The two bikes quickly drove back up Rue Eugène-Colas, almost to the police station, but turning about two hundred metres before it, on to Place de Morny. The objective was clear: to create a diversion. Force the police to chase them while their two accomplices made off with the loot. In theory, their bikes – two Munch Mammut 2000s – would be powerful enough to outpace the police cars.'

'Not just in theory,' sniggered one of the cops.

'True,' admitted Marianne. 'Which confirms that the robbers' actions were perfectly planned. They must have spent a hell of a long time preparing this: scouting the location, timing all their actions. But then the robbers got unlucky.'

Google Street span around again. An empty racecourse surrounded by opulent villas filled the screen.

'A police patrol was heading across town at that particular moment. It went past the racecourse on Boulevard Mauger and was in position to be able to intercept the two bikers. You know the rest, I assume.'

On the screen, the line of 3D houses vanished and was replaced by photographs. Extreme close-ups. Blood on the pavement. A helmet in the gutter.

'One of the bikers shoots first. Our men respond. The second biker, the one who hadn't fired, is hit. His bike ends up on top of him, his helmet hits the ground and the visor smashes. He is still partly protected from our men's gunfire by objects on the street – a lamp post and a skip. While the first biker continues to fire back, positioned behind the cars parked on the roadside, the second one takes off his helmet and drops it on the ground. Two surveillance cameras – the ones outside the racecourse and the Côte Fleurie hotel – catch his face on film.

The blurred face of Timo Soler appeared on the wall. A good-looking young man. Gentle eyes, with a hint of defiance.

'More shots. No one else is wounded. The gunfire lasts only eighteen seconds in total. Timo Soler gets back on his bike, the two bikers do a U-turn and turn off onto the road that leads to the stadium. They follow the train tracks for a short while, then leave the road to join the path that runs alongside the Touques river and disappear into the woods, probably heading towards Pont-l'Eveque. There's no way of following them. Despite the roadblocks, we don't see them again.' The captain pauses here and lowers her eyes slightly. 'With the exception of Timo Soler, who we saw again for the first time this afternoon.'

Marianne clicked on the mouse. Deauville city centre again, with the two red and blue figures.

'However, the diversion was only partly successful. This was the one glitch in the robbers' plan. As soon as the man in the hat comes out of the Hermès boutique, Florence Lagarde, the manageress, not only sets off the alarm, but is reckless enough to walk along the pavement of Rue Eugène-Colas with her mobile to her ear. Less than five seconds later, she is talking to Lieutenant Gallois at the Deauville police station and has the presence of mind to tell him that there are two groups of robbers: the motorcyclists heading towards the station, but also the two others, who are going the opposite way, on foot. Here too, everything happened very quickly, in less than two minutes.

'Still armed with a revolver, the man in the hat enters Rue Lucien-Barrière, turning around frequently, while the woman in the scarf, carrying the four bags, runs towards the beach. Their strategy seems clear: the woman is supposed to stash their haul while the man covers their tracks, making sure there are no acts of heroism from any of the local shopkeepers. By the time he reaches the convention centre, the woman is already on Rue de la Mer and has turned left, near the boardwalk. She passes the casino surveillance camera at 11.17 a.m. One minute later, the same camera films her again, running in the opposite direction – without the bags.'

The captain paused again, as if to emphasise the importance of this detail.

'At the same moment, the man in the hat who is protecting the woman's retreat is trapped by two policemen at the end of Rue Lucien-Barrière, in the pedestrian zone. We know every detail of the gun battle that ensued. The woman yells at the man to join her. He sprints. He is hit by a bullet in the leg, but he fires back, wounding Deputy Sergeant Delattre in the kneecap. He'll survive, but he'll have a limp for the rest of his life. They reach Rue de la Mer, but there they are caught in the crossfire from two patrols coming the other way. The man and the woman keep going along the street, slaloming between cars. Another one of our men, Savignat, is hit – in the shoulder this time, but it's not serious. The man and the woman try to cross the street, to get to the spa opposite, on the beach side of the road, shooting randomly. A few tourists are walking along by the seaside, mostly grandparents with little grandchildren. The cops aren't taking any risks. The two fugitives are shot dead as soon as they are out in the open, at the end of the street. The end.'

Another click. Two photographs appeared. A man and a woman.

'Cyril and Ilona Lukowik,' announced Marianne. 'Our very own Bonnie and Clyde. Cyril is from the area. He has a pretty long criminal record, mostly for drug-dealing, from the age of fifteen, after which he specialised in robbing holiday homes in the Pays d'Auge. He got a total of twenty-six months in prison, spread over four years and three sentences. He met his wife, Ilona Adamiack, when they were very young, in Potigny, the village where they both grew up, about twenty kilometres south of Caen. They were dealing together when they were in secondary school, and Ilona helped him with the robberies. Being a young woman who didn't look suspicious, she was generally the one who did the scouting.'

Marianne zoomed in close on the two faces of the robbers.

'Ideal suspects, it would appear. Except that they'd been pretty quiet for the last few years. They got married in 1997. Cyril got a job as a docker, first in Le Havre, then in other ports in France and abroad. She went with him. He came back to Le Havre in 2013. Apart from a few short-term temporary jobs, he'd not been able to find work. Seems enough of a motive for him to return to crime . . .'

The captain was silent for a moment as she let the cops stare for a while longer at the photographs of Cyril and Ilona Lukowik. Side by side, young, smiling . . . the first image might have made you think you were about to watch slides from a wedding or an anniversary, with some Elton John or Adele as background music. You could imagine the images that would follow: Cyril and Ilona as babies in their parents' arms, in prams, on bikes, disguised as Luke Skywalker and Princess Leia, newlyweds under a shower of confetti, tanned on Deauville beach.

Marianne clicked.

Another photograph. Two corpses lying on the ground, with a crowd of onlookers gathered around them.

'You'll find their detailed biographies in the folder. There is plenty more to say about this case, but essentially, since that armed robbery, the investigation can be summed up in three questions.'

A click.

Another slide.

Letters flashed, forming words, then a sentence.

That intern, Lucas Marouette, really knew his stuff. She'd like to see if he was just as talented away from the office.

Marianne coughed and read out the question projected onto the screen.

WHERE IS THE LOOT HIDDEN?

'According to the Deauville shopkeepers, the hoard is worth about two million euros: one and a half million in jewellery and watches, a quarter of a million in leather goods, and another quarter of a million in luxury clothes, glasses and perfume. Even if the shop-keepers were exaggerating for insurance purposes, it's a pretty good haul, and not too difficult to sell abroad. But what interests us more than the contents of those bags is how they were able to make them vanish. Ilona Lukowik had less than a minute to hide them, without being spotted by any witnesses – a sunbather on the beach, say, a doorman or a valet from the casino. Dozens of our men searched every house, checked every room in every hotel on the seafront. And nothing! Not a trace. There remained one obvious possibility: the ideal hiding place for four bags. The beach huts on the seafront. I know you don't need a description of them, they're the iconic image of Deauville. There are four hundred of them, facing the sea, each one bearing the name of a Hollywood star and belonging to a discreet but wealthy member of the Paris bourgeoisie. At that stage of the investigation, we had no choice: we had to open every single one of them until we got lucky.' Marianne rolled her eyes. 'Our colleagues in Deauville took five weeks to get this done. The mayor's office demanded a letter rogatory for each hut, signed by a judge, even though they were mostly just padlocked. It was a diplomatic minefield.' The captain suddenly raised her voice. 'And all for nothing! There wasn't a single trace of the hoard in any of the huts.'

She took a few steps across the room. The thirty or so cops listened to her intently, like fearful pupils faced with a strict teacher.

'So let's try to think about this in another way. Let's examine the strange behaviour of Cyril and Ilona Lukowik. How could they have hoped to get away, even if the diversion caused by the two motorcyclists worked? Even if they hadn't been intercepted by any police near the boardwalk? Even if, thanks to the hat and the headscarf, they hadn't been identified by the surveillance cameras? Deauville isn't Paris, Anvers or Milan. As soon as the first alarm went off, the police would have blocked every road out of the city, would have searched each car as it left, checking IDs. Cyril and Ilona could have waited a few days in Deauville for everything to settle down, of course, but we have not found any location – no apartment, no hotel room – with any trace of them. So, to sum up, as far as that first question is concerned, we have no answer at all. The location of the loot is a complete mystery.'

Click.

'Second question.'

The letters spun around before falling into the correct order.

## WHERE IS TIMO SOLER HIDING?

The captain's index finger, without her even realising it, was playing with the bandage on her nose.

'The only certainty is that, on 6 January, Soler was wounded. Quite seriously wounded, according to our ballistics experts. And that's not even counting the strain of having to lift up his motorbike in the middle of gunfire. All the hospitals in the area have, of course, been under strict surveillance since the robbery. Because one thing was beyond any doubt: if Timo Soler hadn't died somewhere, been abandoned or finished off by his accomplice, he would eventually have to resurface. Every police station on the estuary, from Caen to Rouen, has been on the alert.'

Marianne smiled, and felt it tug on her nasal septum.

'And we are the ones who've won the lottery! Soler has been hiding in Le Havre. Obviously, after this afternoon's fiasco, we will be the laughing stock of all our colleagues. So we need to catch this man, and fast. I want ten men patrolling permanently in the Neiges quarter, day and night.'

The captain exhaled.

Penultimate slide, announced the bottom of the screen. And not a moment too soon.

Marianne had only been speaking for twenty minutes, but already she felt spent. And to think that teachers had to do this eight hours a day.

## WHO IS THE FOURTH ROBBER?

She coughed again to clear her throat.

'We can't be certain about this, because the biker who accompanied Timo Soler kept his helmet on throughout the chase. However, we do have strong suspicions.'

Last click.

A photograph of a man in his early forties with an angular face. Thick, slanted eyebrows and stubble on his upper lip forming a sort of brown X, with a thin, straight nose in the middle; pale green, almost translucent eyes, closer to those of a snake than an Abyssinian cat. Two other details jumped out: an impressive silver earring in the lobe of his left ear, and a small skull-and-crossbones tattooed at the base of his neck.

'Alexis Zerda,' said the captain. 'A childhood friend of Cyril, Ilona and Timo. All four of them grew up in Potigny. They were in the same class, more or less, from nursery school onwards. They played in the same parks, messed around in the same holiday camps, hung out at the same bus stops. But of the four of them, Zerda is clearly the most dangerous. Although he has only been sentenced for four minor offences, he is the main suspect in several homicides. In 2001, during the robbery at the Banque Nationale de Paris in La Ferté-Bernard, he was suspected of opening fire on a police patrol. A young, married cop and another cop with children were killed instantly. Two widows, three orphans. Two years later, he was the main suspect in the attack on the Carrefour van in Hérouville. Five-thirty in the morning. A nightwatchman and a cleaning lady killed with bullets to the head. No evidence, no fingerprints, no witnesses, but all the same, the investigators had no doubt that it was Zerda. He would fit very neatly into what happened with the Deauville robbery, even if we don't have any proof so far. We are keeping a discreet watch over him. He travels a great deal between Le Havre and Paris. For the moment, we can't do anything, except watch him so closely that he can't risk walking around with a Hermès scarf round his neck, a Breitling in one hand and a Louis Vuitton suitcase in the other.'

The captain exhaled again, visibly relieved. Her nose was itching, but she resisted the urge to scratch under the bandage.

'And that's it, lads! An equation with three unknown factors. And the entire Normandy police force is counting on us to solve at least the second one.'

Stupidly, JB started to applaud. And, just as idiotically, all the other officers followed suit. It was probably a show of sympathy and respect; a show of support for their boss after the botched attempt to arrest Timo Soler at the port. Marianne should have taken it as that. Except that she thought she must look like a big fat turkey with a red face and a flat nose, who was – the cherry on the cake – thinking less, at that moment, about Timo Soler than about the drawings of a three-year-old boy, the strange speech of a mesmerising psychologist and, most of all, about the report that Lucas Marouette – the intern she had sent off to make discreet enquiries near Manéglise – was supposed to give her before the end of the day.

# 13

Vasily parked his motorbike in the car park of the mayor's office in Manéglise, close to the fence surrounding the school playground, but he didn't get off it straight away. He wanted to wait until the last parent had gone before entering the playground and knocking on the classroom door.

At the zebra crossing, the woman in the fluorescent yellow vest eyed him suspiciously, letting the giant lollipop dangle from her hand before concentrating once again on the school fence, on the lookout for any latecomers who might be tempted to rush across the road without looking both ways.

Vasily jumped.

A shadow, a presence behind him.

Clotilde.

Unsmiling.

The headmistress had spotted his bike and clearly didn't intend to give any ground. She opened her mouth, determined, but her words remained stuck in her throat: the mother of two pupils was walking slowly past them, at the pace of the two children clinging to the pram she pushed. The school psychologist took advantage of this diversion to calmly remove his helmet and his gloves. Clotilde waited until the mother was about ten metres away before launching her attack.

'You've got to stop this now, Vasily! I met the Moulin boy's parents today. I have no doubt about it – Malone is their son. They love him, it's blindingly obvious. I think that settles the question.'

Precisely, meticulously, Vasily folded his gloves inside his helmet. Behind the fence, they could hear the shouting of children who had stayed behind for the after-school club. In contrast to his calm demeanour, the psychologist's voice betrayed a mixture of anxiety and anger.

'So you're giving up on me? What are you afraid of, Clotilde? A red card from the mayor? The parent–teacher association? A coalition rallying against the school? All the inhabitants of Manéglise uniting to see off outsiders – you mustn't touch one of our own? Is that it?'

From the corner of his eye, he watched the lollipop lady, who stood like a statue on the pavement, holding out the green side of her lollipop sign. He lowered his voice.

'Come on, Clotilde! You know as well as I do that rejecting your responsibilities instead of assuming them, can end up hiding the worst . . .'

Vasily hesitated. Two of the bigger kids were watching him through fence. He knew one of them – Marin, a dyslexic boy. His despairing parents always left him in the after-school club for as long as possible because they couldn't stand the hours they had to spend helping him do his homework every evening. Clotilde turned her back on the children and exploded with rage.

'You end up hiding the worst monstrosities committed against children – is that what you're insinuating, Vasily? Physical abuse, incest, that kind of thing? See no evil, hear no evil, speak no evil. Is that what you're accusing me of?'

'Go and play over there, kids,' said Vasily.

Clotilde did not hear this. Or she pretended not to.

'Don't pull that kind of emotional blackmail on me, Vasily! Don't confuse the matter. You told me right from the beginning that this child wasn't in any danger from his parents. Isn't that right? But if you're suddenly now telling me the opposite, if you're implying that there's the slightest suspicion of Malone being mistreated, then I'll trust you: I won't take any risks, I'll go with you straight to the police station and report the matter. But all that crap you keep spouting about a previous life, and ogres and rockets, frankly . . .'

Vasily pointed vehemently, and this time the children obeyed him, running off, laughing, to the other end of the playground.

'There's no need to go to the station, Clotilde.'

The headmistress put her head in her hands.

'What do you mean?'

'There's no longer any need, is what I meant to say.'

'You're kidding! You haven't?'

Clotilde had raised her voice. This time, the lollipop lady heard and almost jumped out of her skin, briefly flashing a red stop sign at the cars to her right. She was employed by the mayor's office to work four thirty-minute shifts per day – morning, noon and evening – but she had no objections to working extra hours for free, chatting with the village's less busy mothers. A woman who believed in the importance of social ties. Even to the point of suffocation.

Vasily put his hand on Clotilde's back and gently steered her a few metres away from the unwanted eavesdropper.

'Don't worry, I haven't done anything official. I just wanted to check two or three things that bothered me. This is an unusual case, Clotilde. I can't just follow normal procedure, pass the dossier on to someone else, send the kid for tests. There's something else going on here, I can sense it.'

The headmistress glared at him.

'If Mr Moulin finds out about this, he'll kill you. For God's sake, I can't believe you went straight to the police without going through the proper channels. If Mr Moulin doesn't kill you, the school inspectors will!'

The children in the playground had now gone back into the classroom. The 4.30 p.m. rush hour was over, and silence reigned once again over the little square in Manéglise. Despite the added distance, the lollipop lady no longer had to make do with scraps of conversation overheard above the children's yelling and the roar of car engines; now she could hear everything they said.

Clotilde carefully articulated each word, just in case the lollipop lady was deaf and could lip-read.

'Well, while we wait for the shit to hit the fan, I'm banning you from going anywhere near Malone Moulin.'

'You're joking?'

'No.'

'What are you afraid of?'

'Of all the shit you're stirring. Especially what you're doing to this kid's life.'

Vasily grabbed the headmistress by the shoulders. She was small and slender, with slim fingers and legs, and a neck almost as delicate as the fine gold frame of her round spectacles.

'You have no right to stop me seeing Malone. This is my territory, and I am the only one fit to judge this matter. I'm the one who decides what is in the child's interests. The Moulins signed the authorisation before our first meeting. If you want to stop me entering your school, you'll have to inform the local authority and explain the reasons for your decision.'

A youngish father in a grey suit and tie came out of the school, holding the hand of a girl of about eight, who was breathlessly recounting her day. The father looked at her tenderly. The lollipop lady walked to the middle of the road, ensuring that they could cross without the girl's feet – or her tongue - slowing down in the slightest.

'But maybe,' Vasily went on, 'you don't want a story like this spreading beyond your little school? Maybe you're scared that the mayor will get angry with you and reduce your pencil and eraser budget by fifteen per cent? Or the parent–teacher association will refuse to man the coconut shy at the next school fete.'

'You're a bastard, Vasily.'

'I just want to protect this child.'

'I want to protect his family. Including him.'

Vasily took a step towards his motorbike. He gave a small wave to the lollipop lady, who nodded at him, embarrassed.

'I'll be here to see Malone on Thursday morning. As usual.'

'And what if the parents withdraw their consent? If they refuse to let you see Malone?'

'Just don't tell them they have the right to do so. We do that all the time, Clotilde – you know that as well as I do – with parents who are in denial about their child's problem.' His voice sounded a little worried. 'You haven't . . . you haven't told them they could put an end to the meetings? Did you advise them to withdraw their consent?'

Clotilde looked at him contemptuously.

'No, Vasily. I didn't tell them anything. But let me give some advice, if you're willing to listen: arrange a meeting with the mother. You don't have a monopoly on that kid's secrets. See the mother, Vasily, it's important.'

She smiled.

'And one other piece of advice: stay away from the father.'

# 14

*Today, after taking a bath with my lover, he told me
I had a fat arse.*
Want to kill
*I have news, girls! It really works, the old chest-
nut about throwing a plugged-in hairdryer into the
bathtub.*

*Convicted: 231*
*Acquitted: 336*

www.want-to-kill.com

Marianne hated the Amazonia fitness centre. Everything about it.
Seriously, everything.

The garish colour of the mats and the walls, the smell of sweat,
the type of men you saw there, the type of women you saw there,
the skin-tight shorts and leggings, the money she spent on it, the
smiles of the bimbos behind the reception desk, the smiles of the
little idiots in the changing rooms, the instruments of torture lined
up like it was a museum belonging to the Holy Inquisition.

Yes, that was it. This place was torture.

Marianne hated running on the spot. And pedalling a bike
without getting anywhere was even worse. Almost as ludicrous as
rowing without water.

The captain forced herself to keep going at the same speed. *7.6
km/h*, read the fluorescent numbers on the screen. Her trainer had
told her not to go below 7.

Eighteen months! She gave herself another eighteen months to play along, counting the kilograms, firming up her flesh, tightening her bum and strengthening the supposedly crucial 'core'. Come on, my poor muscles, keep going a bit longer, until a man falls under the spell of my bouncing breasts and gives you a helping hand by massaging you every night.

And, a year and a half from now, she'd give it all up. Sport. The diet. The whole healthy lifestyle thing. She'd even start smoking again. After all this effort, if fate – or God, or a flock of storks – couldn't even be bothered to send her a man who would give her a child, then the world had no right to judge her!

Another ten minutes on this treadmill and Marianne would stop. After that, she'd give herself a reward. The only comfort this hellish place could offer: a cooking pot into which sinners such as she could dive. A hot tub, then a sauna. The only reason she was willing to pay this club's subscription was because of its spa facilities. Seventy-three euros per month. At that price, the bubbles in the jacuzzi should be flavoured like champagne.

Lying in the sauna, naked on her towel, Marianne sweated buckets. She loved that, even more than the hot bubbling water. Especially when she had the sauna all to herself, as she did this afternoon.

She wiped the screen of her iPhone with the corner of her towel and checked her messages.

No news of Timo Soler. Not that she was expecting any. Not this soon. Soler had managed to remain hidden for ten months, apparently in the Neiges quarter. An area that they had searched from top to bottom. Something was now obvious: Soler had an accomplice. Maybe more than one.

He had gone back into hiding and would not come out again unless he thought he was going to die.

Marianne slid her finger over the damp screen: she'd received an email, which she opened, her heart aflutter.

lucas.marouette@yahoo.fr

An emoticon in uniform running after another emoticon in a

ski-mask. Nothing else, not even a word of explanation. But there was a document attached.

The captain sighed then clicked on the document that her intern had sent her. She had dispatched him to the little village of Manéglise that afternoon to tactfully dig up anything he could on Amanda and Dimitri Moulin. For her, it was a way of testing out this rookie – although a genius with computers – on a mission that was, theoretically, less dangerous than the car chase around the port.

Marianne was impressed. Lucas Marouette had written her a novel. Apparently, he was just as gifted with words as he was with technology.

She used one hand to wipe her chest, which was beading with sweat. Her thoughts drifted towards Vasily Dragonman. Alone in this pine box, she felt a bit like an odalisque, one of those voluptuous, seductive women who spent their lives in Turkish palaces, in tiled hammams, those sultans' favourites, free to parade their flabby bellies and their large breasts under their hijab, to gorge themselves on Turkish delight and give birth, year after year, to princes worthy of leading the Ottoman Empire's great army.

She slowly stroked her steam-softened skin, almost reconciled to her curves, then touched the mobile's screen, moving her thumb and index finger apart to zoom in on the text.

*Report, 3 November 2015*
*(Trainee Officer Lucas Marouette)*

*Neighbourhood survey*
*On Amanda, Dimitri and Malone Moulin*
*5 Place Maurice-Ravel, Manéglise*

Let's start with one thing we know for sure, boss. Malone Moulin was born on 29 April 2012, at the Estuary Clinic, weighing 3.45 kg. You'll be proud of me: I even got a photograph on my Samsung of the card announcing his birth - two little baby-blue slippers with laces in the shape of a heart. I took it at the house of Dévote Dumontel, 9 Place Ravel, the building directly opposite the Moulins' home. That may not sound like much, boss, but it wasn't easy. To obtain that picture, I had to swallow the godawful coffee that Dévote heated up in a rusty saucepan and poured into a Pyrex glass for me, her hands trembling but smiling proudly as if she believed that her saucepan had turned into copper and her mug into crystalware. I'll spare you the details, but that coffee forced me to visit the toilet soon afterwards! That was how I discovered that this kind old lady had all the birth cards she'd ever received on display in the loo. Malone Moulin's was pinned to the wall, along with those of her own children and grandchildren, who presumably don't come to visit her very often. If they did, surely they'd have bought her a proper coffee-maker?

Anyway, boss, other than the teary-eyed memories of Dévote Dumontel, I also got confirmation from the Estuary Clinic: there is no possible doubt about the birth of Malone Moulin and the identity of his parents. I also met the paediatrician who looked after the kid for the first two years of his life: Dr Pilot-Canon, a woman as skinny as a beanpole who, strangely enough, only has photos of vegetables, fruit and plants on the walls of her office. According to her, the Moulins are a perfectly normal family. The mother is very loving, maybe a bit too attached to her son according to Dr P-C, but no more so than most mothers. The father is more distant and crabby, but he still turned up to all the medical checks. The kind of bloke who'd rather build the bookshelf in the kid's room than read any of the books on it to his son, if you see what I mean. The kind who'd rather sow, plant and water the vegetables recommended by Dr P-C than get lumbered with the mush, the baby spoon and the sticky bib. Anyway, the doctor had everything written down in the kid's medical record

93

book: his weight, height, vaccinations, all that. After Malone turned two, a doctor from Montivilliers, Serge Lacorne, took over. I talked to him on the phone: nothing to report. He saw little Malone four or five times in his office, for a cold or a stomach ache. According to him, he's a fairly healthy kid.

As for the neighbours . . . The Moulins have lived in the Hauts de Manéglise housing estate for three years now. They bought their house exactly four months after Amanda Moulin found out she was pregnant. Before that, they lived in an apartment in Caucriauville. I spent an hour hanging around the housing estate in the middle of the afternoon, and honestly, boss, I didn't see a soul. There were plenty of dogs though – mostly Alsatians barking from behind six-foot-high hedges. All right, I'm exaggerating: I did see Dévote, standing at her window. And then, just before I left, I also met a guy who did the nightshift and was going home to sleep. A bloke who worked in a warehouse in the Fécamp industrial zone and who seemed happy just to talk to someone. They both know the Moulins personally; they do each other favours. Amanda Moulin feeds Dévote's parrots once a year, for example, when the old lady goes to see her children in Vendée, and the warehouse guy and Dimitri collect wood together. But that's all. They used to see the mother pushing the kid around in his pram from time to time, and now that he's bigger, they've seen him riding his bike around the estate, with his mother watching over him.

I hope you'll forgive me, boss, for not interrogating the Moulins' inner circle – friends, cousins, colleagues – but you asked me to be discreet, so I tried to make my questions sound casual and offhand. I did ask around in the village a bit, though, just to be able to cross-check anything you might have at the station. Amanda Moulin is quite well-known in the village because she lived there with her parents when she was young. She left home when she was a teenager, then came back years later. The prodigal daughter! She wasn't exactly a child prodigy, though. I found a retired schoolteacher who remembered her well. Said she was a good girl – not too bright, but she tried hard. A fighter. Not the kind to let someone walk all over her. Amanda Moulin is also fairly well-liked by the customers at the minimarket where she works. They say she's punctual, friendly, talkative. The last of those doesn't have to be a compliment, of course, but I think it was meant that way by the people I talked to.

I know, boss, I know – you're thinking that the Moulins of Manéglise sound a bit *Little House on the Prairie*, with Caroline Ingalls at least having turfed Harriet Oleson out of the grocery store. But don't worry, I did dig up some dirt on Dimitri Moulin! He's a qualified electrician, but for the past few years he's gone from one crappy job to the next, with long periods of un-employment in between. So he's been having a tough time. But there's more. This is my special surprise for you, boss: Dimitri has a criminal record. He was convicted of selling stolen cars in the Paris region, more than eleven years ago. He didn't know Amanda back then. He was locked up in Bois-d'Arcy for three months. Apparently, that calmed him down, because he's not been in trouble with the law since then. Do you want me to dig a bit deeper on that?

Lastly, while I was at it, I also checked out those key words you gave me: *Rocket. Castle. Pirate ship. Forest. Ogre.*

You won't believe this, boss, but strangely enough no rocket has blasted off from the estuary since little Malone was born. Even worse, no pirate ship has attacked the port of Le Havre in the last four years. And as far as the ogres are concerned, it's strictly omertà: maybe people are afraid to talk?

**95**

Sorry boss, don't mean to piss you off, but what exactly was the deal with those key words? Were they part of an initiation ritual or something?

To conclude, according to Dévote Dumontel, the Moulins have not left the housing estate for more than a week during the last three years. The last time they went away was when they went to Carolles, near Granville, the summer that Malone was two. There are postcards in her toilet too, near the birth announcements; they probably help her remember things. Dévote also remembers a wedding in Le Mans, and a trip to Brittany with the kid during last year's Christmas holidays.

And that's it, boss! I did what I could. I sought information with all the diplomacy I could muster, but I can't make any promises. You know what it's like in those little villages: no need for surveillance cameras to spot a nosy outsider. Anyway, I'm at your command if you want me to do anything else. Maybe some research into flying saucers, Martians and armies of trolls?

Seriously, though, should I keep digging or should I fill in the holes?

Marianne couldn't help smiling. The young cop hadn't done badly at all. She quickly typed a text to him:

*Keep digging!*

At that moment, the door of the sauna opened. Two slender blondes walked in, wrapped in pink towels, which they took off without embarrassment and carefully folded. Tanned skin, without even a white G-string mark. Painted fingernails and toes. Small bums and flat chests. It wasn't their contemptuous looks that finished off Marianne – the kind of look you give to an ugly house disfiguring a pretty landscape: she was used to that from other women – but the start of their conversation.

Only one topic on their minds: men.

Just so many dogs – mad, lazy, obsessed – to be kept on a leash. Husband. Lovers. Boss. The same struggle, repeated over and over.

Marianne left the sauna and went to take a cold shower. The first thing she did after that was check her phone. A professional habit.

Still no news from JB or Papy. Timo Soler was going to spend a night in hell.

7.23 p.m.

She had an hour before she was due to meet Angie at Uno. Well, at least she'd have plenty to talk about . . . and a few questions to ask her friend about a certain Romanian psychologist with eyes the colour of burnt sienna.

# 15

*Little hand on the 8, big hand on the 7*

Malone's eyes slowly closed, even as he tried to keep them open. Maman-da caressed him, rocking him gently to sleep. He liked her hugs – the tickles on his back, the kisses on his neck, the smell of her perfume.

But he also wanted her to go away.

While she was there, he couldn't listen to Gouti. And today, it was the day of the war! Malone had tried to speak with his toy before Maman-da came up to his room, so that Gouti could tell him what he had overheard at school, when Clotilde, Maman-da and Pa-di had shut themselves in the classroom. But he hadn't understood anything. It was all too complicated, and they were speaking too loud, or too quietly, or for too long.

Besides, he preferred his own story.

'Time to go to sleep now, darling.'

Amanda tucked Malone in tight, planted one last kiss on his forehead, and turned off the main light, leaving only the little nightlight that projected stars and clouds over the room's four walls and ceiling.

'Good night, sweetie.'

Then she added: 'Listen, I know Papa shouts sometimes, but it's only because he loves you so much. He wants you to love him too, to love him as much as you love me.'

Malone did not reply; the door gently closed.

Malone waited for a long time, his eyes wide open now. Staring at the green hands on the cosmonaut clock.

To make sure he didn't fall asleep, he would occasionally turn his eyes to the little calendar pinned to the wall next to his wardrobe. Every day of the week was represented by a planet, and to mark what day it was, a little magnetic rocket could be placed on any of them. Today, the red and white spacecraft had stopped on Mars. Malone made it take off every day, when he woke, and flew it to the next planet. From the moon to the red planet, this morning.

MARS.

*The day of the war.*

He knew the planets and the days by heart.

He knew Gouti's stories by heart too. One for each day.

Everything was calm.

Gouti's heart started beating again. Malone crawled under the duvet – in total silence; in total darkness – and listened to his toy's story.

He had to listen to these stories every night, just before the prayer to keep him safe from ogres. He must never forget. He'd promised Maman. His mother from before.

*

\*   \*

*Once upon a time there was a big wooden castle that had been built with the trees from the large forest that grew all around.*

*In this big castle, which could be seen from far away because of its four high towers, lived the knights.*

*In those days, the knights each bore the name of the day when they were born, and each day bore the name of a quality – a quality that everyone had to have on that day.*

*Do you find this a bit complicated?*

*Perhaps it is, so I'm going to give you an example. The knights from the castle born on the day of St Juste were called* Just; *those born on the day of St Courtois were called* Courteous, *and others were* Faithful *or* Friendly *or* Constant, Modest, Clement, Prosperous, *or* Prudent. *And on the birthday of the Friendly knights, everyone had to be friendly, you see? It's very simple, in fact.*

*Except that some of the days of the year corresponded to faults – bad*

99

qualities – because that's just how it is. And on those days – but only on those days – everyone was allowed to have that fault (but only that fault). For example, some knights were called Greedy, or Curious, or Joker.

The knight that we're interested in was called Naive. Where other knights wore a sword on their belts, he had a flute. Where the other knights wore metal armour, his was made from flower petals. And that wasn't all: his helmet was made from feathers, and the only shield he carried was a large book, which he was constantly reading. The bravest knights – Bold, Gallant, Valiant – were not allowed to make fun of him, except on one day: the birthday of the Mocking knight.

I have to tell you something else as well. There were strict rules in the castle. No one knew why – or, rather, no one dared suggest why, except on the birthday of the Frank knight, but that was not that day.

Two simple and very strict rules.

It was forbidden to go very far from the castle.

It was forbidden to leave the castle at night.

But one day – on the birthday of the Generous knight – Naive wanted to go and find a present for the other knights. It was a warm and sunny day. He had the idea of going out to gather a bouquet of flowers, the prettiest and biggest he could find.

I can see what you're thinking. You can guess what's coming next. The Naive knight is going to gather one flower, then another, then another, and suddenly he'll find himself too far away from the castle and he'll get into trouble. Not at all! I'm telling you the story of the Naive knight, not the Imprudent knight.

So Naive went to gather flowers in the forest, taking good care that he could always see the towers of the castle. As he was putting together his bouquet, he met a cicada, and he decided to play his flute for the creature. Then he met a bird and gave it a feather from his helmet for its nest. Then he met a rabbit and told it one of the stories from his big book. Then he met a butterfly and offered it his petals so that it would have somewhere to rest.

He had already gathered a huge bouquet and was about to go back to the castle when he saw the princess. She looked a bit like Snow White. In fact, you would have thought it really was her!

*She smiled at* Naive, *and gave him a little wave, then she walked away, laughing.* Naive, *still carrying his bouquet, followed her.*

*Now you can guess what happened next. Snow White disappeared behind the ferns, then reappeared in a clearing.* Naive *searched for her with his eyes and ears, then spotted a slender shadow amid the trees, and heard a laugh that melted into birdsong.*

*And, through this game of hide-and-seek,* Naive *ended up in an even bigger clearing. In the middle, he saw a large cottage. Smoke rose from its chimney. Snow White was waiting for him by the door, and she was even prettier close up. She took his hand and said:*

*'Come in!'*

*When he went inside, everyone was sitting at the table in front of the fireplace.*

*Everyone turned around, and* Naive *couldn't believe his eyes! Can you imagine? At the table there were other princesses who looked like Cinderella, Aurora, Beauty, Rapunzel, and lots of others, wearing elegant dresses and tiaras. There were little boys, too, who resembled Pinocchio, Hop o' My Thumb, and Hansel, and there was also Gretel and another little girl wearing a red hood.*

*They all smiled at him.*

*'Come in,* Naive. *Come and eat with us.'*

*There was an empty place next to Snow White.*

Naive *sat down and offered her his bouquet. She blushed.* Naive *had never felt so good, so happy. He had never eaten such delicious food.*

*He didn't notice the time passing. He didn't see night begin to fall outside. It was only when he heard the first cry that he realised; a cry that came from outside, but he couldn't see anything through the windows except darkness.*

*'What was that?'* Naive *said, worried.*

*'Nothing,' replied Snow White. 'It was nothing,* Naive.*'*

*Snow White was even more beautiful when she looked a bit scared.*

Malone poked his head out from under his duvet. He put his finger to his lips and made a shushing sound, asking Gouti to be quiet.

He had heard a noise too! A cry, just like the Naive knight had heard. It had come from downstairs. Maybe it was Maman-da and Pa-di arguing. Like they did almost every night.

Or maybe he had dreamt it.

This part of the story always frightened him a little.

Malone stayed there for a moment, listening. Then, when he was certain that no one was coming up the stairs, or scratching at his door, or moving through the dark towards his bed, he went back under the covers.

Gouti was waiting for him. And, as on all the other days of the war, as if he didn't care about monsters or ferocious beasts or the dark, he continued with the knight's story.

*The feast carried on.* Naive *heard other cries, all of them coming from outside. Growls too, and other strange noises, as if something were scratching at the door or banging against the walls.*

*Snow White was still smiling. The other princesses too.*

*'It's late,* Naive, *you should go home now.'*

*The little knight shivered.*

*Go home now? At night? Through this forest? So far from the castle?*

*'But I . . .'*

*And then suddenly, another idea entered his head. You might find this strange, but it hadn't occurred to him until that moment.*

*Where were all the baddies? He was sitting at a table with all the good people from the fairy tales, so where had the baddies gone? The wolves, the ogres, the witches?*

*As if reading his thoughts, Snow White leant towards him. She was even more beautiful when she was a bit scary.*

*'We've lived together for so long, we've ended up coming to an arrangement.'*

*'An arrangement?'* Naive *repeated blankly.*

*'Yes. We share the forest with them, but we never see each other. They let us have it during the daytime, and we let them have it each night. As long as it's like that, everything's fine.'*

*Naive agreed that it was a good idea, until another question occurred to him:*

*'But then what do the wolves eat? And the ogres? And the monsters?'*

*Snow White had gone bright red, and she looked more beautiful than ever as she lowered her eyes apologetically. It was the boy who looked like Pinocchio who responded, and his nose didn't grow a single inch.*

*'We feed them on* Naive *little knights who we lure deep into the forest. It was the only solution we could find so that we live in peace.'*

*And so finally the* Naive *knight understood. He took one last look at Snow White, and then he fainted.*

*When he came to, he was outside. In the forest. In the dark.*

*The cottage was still there, but the door was locked. He could see light coming from the windows and smoke rising from the chimney. Then he heard a wolf howl, so he started to run, very fast. He ran for a long time. Probably in circles, as he couldn't find his way out.*

*He sensed twisted shadows all around him, as if each tree branch concealed the claw-like hands of a witch. When he eventually came to a halt, too tired to go on, the monsters gathered around him. There were wolves, foxes, crows, snakes, giant spiders and other ferocious animals, though all he could see of them were their yellow eyes or their fangs. Suddenly, the circle opened to let through the chief of the monsters.*

*The great ogre of the forest.*

Naive *shrank back. The great ogre of the forest had a skull-and-crossbones tattooed on his neck and a silver earring that shone in the night. He burst out laughing.*

*'It's the birthday of the* Generous *knight,' said the ogre, leaning towards him. 'I see our friends from the cottage didn't forget that.'*

*He took out his big knife. The blade gleamed in the night, as if the moon in the sky above them were merely a piece of cheese that this immense weapon could slice into pieces.*

*Maybe you're a bit too frightened at this point in the story and you'd like me to stop for a minute, even if you've heard it before and you know how it ends. But you must also know that* Naive *was even more scared than you, especially as it was only much later that he found out what I'm going to tell you next.*

*While the monsters and the ferocious creatures closed in around* Naive*, licking their lips in anticipation, the cicada for whom he'd played the flute that morning had woken up and had jumped all the way to the castle to sound the alarm. The bird to whom* Naive *had* given a feather from his helmet had flown to the highest battlement of the towers to warn the guard, who was dozing against his lance. The rabbit to whom Naive had told a story had bounded over the drawbridge, and the butterfly to whom Naive had offered his petals had landed on a bouquet of flowers on the large table where the knights were eating their dinner.

'Naive is in danger!'

And so the drawbridge opened, and the knights galloped through the night, armed with real swords, real helmets, real armour and real shields.

There was Bold, Gallant and Valiant, but also Ardent, Robust, Battler, and even Cowardly, Fearful and Puny. All the knights of the castle.

They arrived just in time. The wild beasts of the forest and the wolves, and even the ogre, all fled.

Naive was saved.

He was still trembling when the oldest of the castle's knights, Placid, sat down on a tree trunk next to him.

Placid told him two very important truths. Would you like to hear them?

The first is that people who appear to be kind aren't always really kind.

But the second is even more important, and without it, the cicada, the rabbit and the butterfly that you helped wouldn't have come to warn us, and we wouldn't have got here in time to save you.

You see, even if it's true that people are not always as kind as they appear, if in doubt, always choose kindness! That's your best bet. I'm sure you won't understand all the things I'm saying to you. Some of it is a bit complicated, but by repeating them, you will end up remembering them.

In spite of the baddies, kindness is always your best bet. It is always kindness that wins out in the end.

# 16

*Is that all there is to eat tonight?*
*Want to kill*
*I dither between poisonous mushroom omelette and*
*tartar sauce curare.*

*Convicted:  49*
*Acquitted:  547*

www.want-to-kill.com

Angélique had had too much to drink.

The bottle of Rioja on the table was three-quarters empty, but Marianne had barely touched a drop. Through the window of the restaurant, the two women could see a tram passing without stopping at the deserted station before it disappeared between the buildings, heading towards St François Church, which looked like a giant altar candle.

'Careful, Angie,' Marianne warned her.

The waiter in Uno, a dark-haired man with a Catalan accent that went perfectly with the tapas he was serving them, placed a plate of tortilla in front of her. His gaze lingered a little too long on Angélique's profile, until she finally turned to look at him. Her long dark hair, held loosely in place by two hairclips, framed the perfect oval of her face. With a gesture that was almost unconscious – and no doubt terribly sexy in the eyes of the Catalan – she brushed her hair behind her ears, briefly revealing her forehead, her eyelashes, her cheekbones, her almond eyes, before the delicate curtain fell back in place.

An innocent game.

Angie didn't really seem to be fully aware of the power she wielded over men. She lifted the glass of Rioja to her lips and smiled at the police captain.

'Vasily Dragonman? Did you really fall for him, Marianne? I've only met him twice in my life. Both times at dinner parties given by my friends Camille and Bruno, where there were at least ten of us. The second time was last Saturday. He started telling us this strange story, about the kid who remembered a previous life, other than the one he has with his current parents. Vasily didn't give any names, of course. He said he'd come to a sort of impasse, and he didn't know what to do. It was clearly upsetting him. I got the feeling that he felt very alone – alone against everyone else: the parents, the school, the local authorities. But he didn't have enough evidence for his doubts to be taken seriously, or to make an official report. He needed help, it was obvious. Someone who could investigate, on the quiet . . .'

'So you gave him my number?'

'Yes. The story about the kid just seemed odd.'

'And that was the only reason?'

Angélique winked at Marianne.

'Well, he was cute, too. No wedding ring – and it wasn't in his pocket either; I checked with Camille. Knows lots about children, obviously. So because I'm a good friend, I thought about you!'

Marianne grimaced as the waiter arrived to clear away the empty tapas plates and replace them with an *arroz con costra*. She waited for him to move out of earshot.

'Thank you, Angie. You're too kind to your poor old grandmother!'

'Oh, give it a rest! You look after yourself like an Olympic athlete. You're extremely well preserved.'

'Yeah, well preserved . . .' She gazed out at the grey lines of the rectangular buildings in the Perret quarter. 'Preserved like a historical district. Soon to be classified by Unesco!'

She put a finger to her nose and the bandage that still covered it.

'But you'll have to wait for the renovations to be completed.'

Angélique smiled.

'The perils of your job, my dear. Anyway, why are you complaining? You're surrounded by virile men who all obey your every order. We can swap if you like: you take my place at the hairdresser's and spend your days turning kids with dark hair blonde and women with grey hair dark.'

Marianne burst out laughing.

She was aware that Angélique lived vicariously through her investigations. The captain was always careful not to tell her friend too much, not to break the rules of professional secrecy, but she would sometimes confide a few details to this budding detective. And Angie sometimes had surprising insights.

Although, right now, her friend seemed more interested in affairs of the heart. If anyone had been able to overhear their conversation – a waiter, a man at a nearby table, a spy who could read Marianne's mind – he might perhaps have taken her for a predator, obsessive, someone mostly concerned with evaluating whether she could seduce the men she met in everyday life: colleagues, witnesses . . . An impression all the more mistaken, as Marianne had climbed the ladder of the national police almost totally surrounded by men, yet having slept with hardly any of them. She was ambitious, not flirty, and actually quite sensitive when it came to any questioning of the equality between sexes in this profession where women, very much in the minority, had to stick together – and stick up for themselves.

As far as equality was concerned, though, Marianne was just beginning to realise the terrible injustice that fate had dealt her: a man had no biological clock to worry about. A bloke could go out on the pull at the age of fifty and become a father at sixty. But a woman, if she left it too late . . . Game over! Even if Prince Charming finally turned up, with apologies for his tardiness.

Yes, it *was* completely unfair, Marianne thought. Doubly unfair, in fact. Because it was the most liberated, most demanding women, those least inclined to throw away their youth on the first idiot they encountered, who – as their forties approached – would find themselves having to go out hunting for a man. A bit like a girl who doesn't really like shopping and who finds herself, the day before a big party, with nothing to wear, having to battle through the crowds she hates so much on the last day of the sales.

She'd talked about all of this thousands of times with Angélique. Beautiful, young Angie who had her whole life ahead of her, who adored window-shopping, crowds, sales and the first idiots she encountered.

'But Vasily isn't the only man in your sights, is he? What about JB?'

'JB?'

'Yeah, your gorgeous deputy. We spent our last night out together talking about him. I've been thinking about it. Verdict – he's too good-looking! Too kind, to be honest. He must be cheating on his wife, or thinking about it. Guaranteed. You should lead him on a bit, just to find out.'

'Are you kidding?'

Angie clinked her glass against Marianne's.

'There's no such thing as the perfect guy, you know that. Go for it!'

'For God's sake, Angie, he's married! He's the only guy in the force who'd give up on a stake-out so he could collect his kids from school. Anyway, he's my deputy. And anyway . . .'

'Exactly! Keep him close, it'll be your shoulder he cries on when the right moment comes along. Come on, Marianne, don't you realise how lucky you are? You're spoilt for choice! You're not washing women's hair or selling bread or looking after toddlers in a crèche – you're the captain of the local police force. To those guys you're iconic!'

'I was . . . I'm screwed now. We were tracking this guy today. I had ten men and five cars, and we still didn't catch him. Total incompetence!'

She touched her throbbing nose again. Angie dutifully rose to the bait.

'Shit . . . That guy you've been searching for since January? He's the one who got away? How did you find him?'

Marianne thought for a moment about mentioning the surgeon

and blaming him. After all, Larochelle was just as responsible for the afternoon's fiasco as she was. But she didn't want to fall into the same trap as he had and break the rules of confidentiality.

'We had a stroke of luck. A patrol at the port. They spotted him waiting close to the lock.'

The captain could, however, talk about the rest. The criminal's escape would be all over the front page of the *Havre Presse* within a few hours.

'And then he slipped through our fingers. Into the Neiges quarter.'

Angélique's eyes sparkled. The excitement of the hunt.

'I know lots of people in Neiges. Some of my customers live there. I could ask around.'

This was true. Marianne was aware that a hairdresser with an ability to extract confidences from her customers could be more effective than a whole army of informers. When the captain touched her nose again, Angie gave a professional assessment of her facial damage.

'It doesn't look too bad. Don't worry, when you wake up tomorrow just put on a bit of foundation. It'll look like nothing ever happened.'

'We could have caught him, Angie. I yelled at Cabral – the guy who was driving the car – on principle, but in reality he probably saved my life by slamming on the brakes. I could have been killed. I haven't let any of my men know this, but I was scared shitless when we were speeding towards that bridge.'

Angélique's hands trembled slightly as she tucked a few stray hairs behind her ears again.

'I understand.'

'You understand what?'

'The fear. The fear of an accident. That moment of panic before the impact.'

Marianne's eyes bored into her friend's. Angie rarely spoke about herself. She had confided a great deal when they first met: what she hated, her fears, her *want-to-kill*, her redemption. That had sealed their friendship forever, like poison that is poured from one bottle into another, so that Angie had become an empty vessel again; a very pretty exclusive little bottle, made of glass. A hairdresser's mirror. Sometimes transparent, at other times reflecting back the other person's image.

The ideal friend.

The two women were complementary. Marianne was pragmatic, calculating, strategic. Angie was romantic, idealistic, naive. There was just a hint of vulgarity in her demeanour, an indefinable failure of taste that men always spotted. It could probably be corrected, this fault, with a little psychological surgery. Easier to take than a nose job or liposuction.

'Have *you* been in an accident before?'

'Yes. A long time ago.'

Angie hesitated. The waiter, all smiles, brought them some ice cream profiteroles. Salted caramel sauce, with a miniature umbrella and a fan-shaped biscuit on the side. He leant even closer to Angie this time, but this time her face remained hidden.

'I've never talked to anyone about this, Marianne.'

'I'm not forcing you to . . .'

Angie drained her glass. Too quickly. A few ruby-coloured drops tricked down her chin.

'I was twenty-one. I was with a guy named Ludovic. A good-looking boy, the same age as me. Loud-mouthed. The type I went for back then. The type I still probably go for now, in fact. We'd been together for seven months when I got pregnant. I wasn't surprised by his reaction when I told him – I wasn't that dumb. Obviously, he didn't want me to keep it, the poor little thing. The loud-mouth's bravado suddenly went out of the window. He gave me the whole shebang: the hug, the puppy-dog eyes, the address book and the chequebook, an uncle who was a doctor, his parents who would pay for the abortion. I whispered into his ear: "I want to keep it." It was like an electric shock! I kept talking, turning up the voltage. "It's my child. I want to keep it. I'm not asking you for anything: you don't have to pay me a penny, you don't even have to acknowledge the child. I'll take care of it on my own. But I want to keep it."'

Marianne was holding her friend's hand now. In the distance, a crowd of people were emerging from the Volcan and dispersing through the Espace Oscar Niemeyer. The captain had never set foot in Le Havre's legendary theatre.

'Obviously I didn't understand men at all at the time. Or Ludo. He looked at me as if I was crazy. He went to get himself a whisky, came back, and calmly told me that it didn't work like that. That even if he didn't acknowledge this kid, he would still know it existed. He got another whisky. He said he'd be bound to think about it every day; the fact that a little brat that looked like him was living somewhere – another whisky – and that, even if he forgot about it, one day he might end up face to face with a teenager he'd never seen before who was his spitting image. And that no, he didn't want to grow old with the feeling that he'd left part of himself, a younger part, to grow up elsewhere.'

Marianne stroked Angie's hand, but didn't interrupt her. The vanilla ice cream melted, cracking the shell of salted caramel.

'Ludo lectured me for an hour. The bottle of whisky disappeared, but he could handle it – he was used to it. I replied to every point he made. It was the most banal argument since Adam and Eve. I said it was my body, my womb, and that no one but me had the right to decide to put a scalpel to it. He said it was his sperm, and that no one had the right to make clones of him without his agreement. I didn't give in. I didn't care anyway: he could say whatever he wanted, I would still go through with it. Whether he chose to help me bring it up or not, I was keeping that child. It was my right, and I knew it. In the end, Ludo seemed to understand that and calmed down. We even made love, then around midnight he said: "Shall I take you home?" I lived in an apartment in Graville back then.'

Her glossy lips twisted into a sad clown's face.

'There are about a dozen bends on the way to Graville. Coming out of the fourth one, Ludo's 205 GTI went straight on. He didn't move the steering wheel, didn't touch the brake. We went straight into the wall. We must have been going fifty kilometres per hour, sixty at the most. We were both wearing our seat belts. We escaped with only grazes.'

Marianne held tightly to her hand. Angie's voice had grown very weak.

'But the child died instantly. That's what the doctors told me. Ludovic had 1.2 grams of alcohol in his blood. He admitted all the undeniable things: he was drunk, he was disoriented, he'd just found out I was pregnant. But to imagine, your honour, that I would deliberately drive into a wall to cause Angie to have a miscarriage . . .'

The vanilla ice cream had turned into a beige liquid and the umbrella had been swept away by a thick, salty landslide. An empty tram went past without stopping, and the lights in the Volcan went out, leaving Place Oscar-Niemeyer in darkness. The last shadows of the night.

'I've thought about it so much since then. I've put myself in Ludovic's place. He was right, really. I couldn't have raised that kid on my own. Not behind his back. Not against his wishes. I paid dearly for my naivety. He was more cunning than me, that bastard. After a few examinations, the doctors at the Monod hospital confirmed that the damage to my fallopian tubes was irreversible and I would never be able to have a child. Ludovic still lives in Graville. I see him occasionally on the tram. He has three kids. He seems like a good father.'

The words froze in Marianne's throat.

'It's no big deal,' said Angie. 'It's my life. What can you do. There are people worse off than me.'

She got to her feet, put on her old leather jacket, wrapped a frayed scarf around her neck, over the fake pearl necklace she wore. Marianne paid for the meal. Angie's gaze was lost in the iron grille that covered the window of the clothes shop across the street.

She gave one last smile.

'If I find your Timo Soler for you, will you get me some of the robbers' haul? With a Hermès dress, a Gucci jacket and some Dior shoes, I'm sure I'd look beautiful.'

'You're the most beautiful person there is, Angie. The most beautiful of all. Even without all that.'

# 17

*Little hand on the 11, big hand on the 3*

The curtains twitched like a whirlwind of birds taking off a few seconds before the storm broke.

Then the window suddenly opened.

The glass shattered, as if an invisible monster had burst through it to get into the room. A thousand shards of glass rained down on the bed.

Malone only just managed to shield his face with both hands. Between his index and his middle finger, he saw Gouti holding out his paw before he too was carried away by the gale.

It was impossible for Malone to take his hands away from his face. Impossible to help his toy.

Gouti disappeared. Two other hands reached out, but he still couldn't reach them. Maman's hands. They were red.

Then she flew away too, spinning around faster and faster as she was sucked up by the void.

Malone screamed.

He wanted to move too. To join Gouti and Maman in the darkness. Beyond the wind.

Two arms held him back.

'It's OK, sweetie. It's over. Maman is here.'

Malone was drenched with sweat. He crouched on his bed and let Maman-da rock him, gently, for a long time, until he finally lay down again.

'It was just a nightmare, sweetie. Go back to sleep. Just a bad dream.'

Already, Malone's eyelids were growing heavy.

# WEDNESDAY

The day of the journey

# 18

*Little hand on the 8, big hand on the 4*

Pa-di's yelling woke Malone. Still in his pyjamas, he walked out of his room and stood at the top of the stairs.

The yelling was coming from downstairs. From the kitchen. This time, there was no need to leave Gouti in a corner so he could listen to their secrets and tell him afterwards; Pa-di was shouting so loud that Malone could hear everything.

'Seven-thirty in the morning! Can you believe it? Max sent me a text at half past bloody seven this morning!'

Sounds of water in the sink, cups, the fridge door opening and closing. Maman-da must be getting breakfast ready while Pa-di drank his coffee.

'You know who Max is, right? The lad who works for the parks department. His kid, Dylan, plays as a goalkeeper for the under-7s. He was chatting with Mrs Amarouche, the lollipop woman at the school. She overheard the shrink talking to the teacher. She's certain: that Romanian isn't going to leave us alone.'

Malone went down three steps. All he could see of the kitchen was the three top shelves, the ones where the sharp objects were kept. Pa-di and Maman-da, still deep in their discussion, were not even aware that he'd woken up. Which gave him an idea. He went down another three steps, barefoot, careful not to make a sound.

Pa-di's voice sounded even louder.

'According to Mrs Amarouche, the shrink wants to see Malone again tomorrow morning. He's going to turn up at the school. The headmistress is OK, but she's not standing up to him. He's just a shit-stirrer.'

Silence. He must have been taking a sip of his coffee.

'The answer's simple, Amanda. We won't send Malone to school tomorrow.'

Tinkling sounds. Glasses and plates being piled up. Maman-da emptying the dishwasher.

'That's not a solution, Dimitri. He'll have to go back to school at some point, whether it's the day after tomorrow or next week.'

Malone stood in the hallway. He quietly pulled up the little wooden chair that he sat on when he was playing, colouring or putting on his shoes. He placed it in front of the door.

'So what do you suggest? That he changes school?'

'I'm going to see Teixeira. He's the deputy mayor. He's grateful that I'm letting his son play centre-forward even though he hasn't scored since the start of the season. I'll ask him to speak to the mayor. We need to put some fucking pressure on this guy!'

The sound of a machine gun, and three rifle shots. Forks and knives being put away in a drawer, cupboard doors banging.

'What's the point of that, Dimitri? The mayor can't get mixed up in the school's affairs, any more than the cops can. A school is like a church. The teachers can do whatever they want. You just have to listen to them, and that's it.'

Malone had climbed on the chair, still soundlessly. He turned the handle until the door opened, then got down, pushed the chair away and pulled the door almost closed behind him, leaving just enough light so that he could see beneath the stairs.

'You might be right about the cops, Amanda, but parents have a right to get involved in school stuff. So I'm going to put pressure on him. And I'll do some digging too. Even though we signed that paper agreeing to let the kid see the shrink, maybe we can still stop it. Or choose another shrink.'

Pa-di was really yelling now. Next to his ogre-like voice, Maman-da sounded like a whispering fairy.

'It won't make any difference, Dimitri. I'll speak to him.'

'Speak to who?'

'Malone. I'll explain to him that he's hurting us by telling these stories. He's a big boy now. He'll understand. He . . .'

As he moved under the stairs, Malone could hardly hear Maman-da's voice. He'd already been in the big cupboard the day before, but he couldn't help looking again at the board with his name on it.

MALONE

Couldn't help observing the dead ants again, stuck there to make the shapes of the letters. It felt as if there were thousands of other ants, alive, crawling up his back. Quickly, Malone turned away. It was the other boxes that interested him now – the ones piled on top of each other, with little transparent boxes inside, the kind you put pearls or pencils or coloured stickers in.

He got on his knees and started rummaging through the first one, which was almost as big as him. He couldn't hear what Maman-da was saying any more, but Pa-di's voice continued to rumble through the cupboard door, like a bear that had just returned to its cave.

'All right, we'll do that then. You can try the softly-softly approach with the kid. And if that doesn't work, we'll try my style of softly-softly approach with the shrink, man to man.'

He laughed.

The smash of cymbals. A dustbin, being closed with a pedal. Maman-da's voice became audible again.

'He has everything, though. Toys. Books. Everything. Us. What more does he want?'

Malone had picked up a little plastic crate, the size of a shoebox. A shoebox for grown-ups. It was held shut by elastic bands. Through the transparent lid, he could see small black shapes.

Sweets? Liquorice? Toy figures?

The box felt light, but the elastic bands were so tight; he found it hard to get his fingers underneath them so he could take them off.

'What more does he want? Maybe something other than your softly-softly approach! All you have to do is take that damn cuddly toy off him. He spends too much time with that thing. How do you expect him to move on if his only friend is a rat he's been sucking since he was born.'

'Dimitri, it's normal for his age. All the kids have a cuddly toy . . .'

The sudden din drowned out the rest of her sentence. Amanda rushed out of the kitchen and shot a panicked look up the stairs.

'Malone?'

Nothing.

The door of the cupboard under the stairs was half-open.

The cries of a child, deep inside.

'Malone!'

The door flew open. Light rushed in.

Malone was on his knees, Gouti at his feet. A Tupperware box had fallen next to him. It was open. Amanda spotted Malone just before Dmitri's figure in the hallway blocked the light from the ceiling, plunging the cupboard into darkness again.

A few seconds of horror.

Her little boy had spilt the contents of the plastic box all over himself.

He was choking, reaching out in panic so that Maman-da would pull him out of there, out of that hell, out of that bottomless pit.

In the dark, he screamed even louder.

He was covered in insects.

Dead insects.

Hundreds of flies, beetles, ladybirds, stinkbugs, woodlice, bees. In his hair, on his pyjamas, on his bare feet, in Gouti's fur.

# 19

*Today, he said I love you, you know. But having a*
*child, bringing it up, me, you know . . .*
Want to kill
*I'll have the kid anyway. Behind his back. And I'll*
*call him Oedipus.*

*Convicted: 323*
*Acquitted: 95*

www.want-to-kill.com

Vasily Dragonman stood up and looked out through the window at the marina. From the twelfth floor of the Résidence de France, the motorboats, yachts and catamarans looked practically identical, like vehicles parked in a vast dealership. Almost all of them white. Almost all the same modest size. No luxury yachts to disturb the peace of the little boats; no high masts towering over the others. It was a marina for ordinary people who loved the sea.

Vasily moved even closer to the window, more than forty metres above the port. None of the rare passers-by on the Boulevard Clemenceau or on either of the port's sea walls could possibly see him.

Even standing there so immodestly.

After climbing out of his rumpled bed, Vasily had not bothered getting dressed. He now offered a three-quarter view of his naked buttocks, his hairy chest and his dangling penis to the pretty girl who remained under the sheets.

She got up and walked over to him, then pressed her bare breasts to his back, wrapping her arms around his waist and playing with the hair on his lower abdomen.

'I should go.'

'It's Wednesday,' the girl pouted. 'The schools are closed today, aren't they?'

'I've got a meeting with that female cop.'

'Your captain? That Augresse woman? I could be jealous.'

Vasily turned around and gave his lover a long kiss, then pulled himself free before his desire grew too intense. She stepped back and held her body against the pane, like a child's toy suckered to the glass.

Slightly upset. And then, a moment later, slightly amused by Vasily's clumsiness as he sat on the bed and struggled to pull his skin-tight jeans over his erection.

His grey woollen jumper was tight too, and his hair dishevelled. She thought he looked good.

'Where are you meeting her?'

Vasily hesitated before answering. He wrapped a cream scarf around his neck. A dark linen jacket that matched his eyes. No time to shave – unless he preferred not to in order to look even sexier.

'At the police station. I'm sure her deputies will be there too, probably half the brigade.'

'I hope so!'

He put his hand on the door handle.

'I feel as if it's beginning to get to you, this story about the kid. You shouldn't let it get in between . . .'

She didn't finish her sentence. Her skin, still stuck to the window-pane, now had goosebumps.

'In between what?'

At that moment, a shy ray of sunlight peeked between two clouds, projecting its spotlight into the apartment and turning her naked skin a beautiful shade of gold. She turned around and squashed her breasts against the burning glass.

'In between us,' she whispered.

He left.

# 20

Lieutenant Jean-Baptiste Lechevalier and Lieutenant Pierrick Pasdeloup had been waiting for nearly an hour in the VW Touran parked outside the Hoc pharmacy. They'd been there since eight that morning; Marianne Augresse had insisted that they be there well before the shops opened.

It was the only pharmacy in the Neiges quarter. If Timo Soler had someone helping him, it wasn't difficult to imagine a scenario in which his accomplice might go to the nearest pharmacy to buy whatever he needed to ease the pain. They had established with Larochelle the list of products likely to be used to treat the robber's wound, those recommended by any medical website: *Povidone-iodine, cetrimide, chlorhexidine gluconate, lidocaine, tetanus toxoid, metronidazole . . .*

The woman at the pharmacy was in on the plan. If any of her customers asked for one or more of these medicines, she would take off her white coat as soon as the person was out of the door and hang it on the coat rack behind her. This was their code. All the police would have to do then was discreetly follow the suspect.

Assuming that the suspect would be stupid enough to get his supplies in the neighbourhood.

JB and Papy had taken the first hour of the stake-out in order to make sure everything was in place. After that, two other agents would take over from them. The Rue du Hoc was still deserted, with the exception of a few customers at the pharmacy. It was as if the entire district had decided to take the day off, right in the middle of the week.

Papy was developing his own theory as they sat there. Twenty-six per cent of the Neiges quarter's population was unemployed,

123

according to the statistics provided by the local police. And the rate was double that among people aged eighteen to twenty-five. Why the hell would youngsters in search of work bother to get up any earlier than the employees at the Job Centre?

JB pressed his fingertip against the radio search button until he found a station.

101.5. Cherie FM.

Papy looked at him quizzically.

'Are you serious?'

Daniel Lévi was singing the ballad, '*L'envie d'aimer*'.[1]

'That was my wedding song,' said Lieutenant Lechevalier, with a smile. 'I still get shivers every time I hear it.'

'You baffle me, JB.'

He glanced outside. Still nothing happening. Not even a bin lorry. The cats and the seagulls seemed to be working part-time around the skips at the end of the street.

'Why?'

'Oh, no reason. Well, lots of reasons, actually. You've got the body of a Greek god, JB, and the handsome face of a gangster. You're a cop. Yet you live your life as if you work for the Post Office.'

Daniel Lévi was still wailing on the radio, along with his crew of backing singers.

'Sorry, Papy, I have no idea what you mean.'

'For fuck's sake, JB, do you really want me spell out what the whole force is saying behind your back?'

'No. Not really.'

Elton John was on the radio now, singing 'Your Song'. Lieutenant Lechevalier turned up the volume. Inside the pharmacy, a mother was holding hands with her two children while she waited to be served.

Papy decided to ignore his colleague's wishes.

'First of all, there's your wife, Marie-Jo. We all wonder what the hell you're doing with a girl like her. She gives you shit every time you have a stake-out at night, calls you ten times a day, forces you to

[1] The desire to love

124

be home by midnight even when we're celebrating the end of a case we've been working on for weeks. You take care of everything – the kids, the shopping on Saturday, DIY on Sunday, the parent–teacher meetings during the week – and on top of all that, she's not exactly Miss World, your Marie-Jo, is she? You have to admit that!'

JB did not get upset. He just looked a little surprised.

'Is that really what people are saying behind my back?'

'Well, yeah. You're the sexiest guy on the force. You won a vote the other day, next to the coffee machine. All the policewomen fantasise about you. So, obviously, we're intrigued by your Marie-Jo. Even the captain is sexier!'

Lieutenant Lechevalier smiled openly this time.

'Especially with her nose smashed in! You know, if Marie-Jo did ever dump me, I could definitely see myself with a woman like that.'

'Like what? A woman with balls, you mean?'

'Well, if you like . . .'

'And why would Marie-Jo ever dump you?'

'Dunno. Because I'm a cop. Because I work crazy hours and get paid fuck-all?'

Papy narrowed his eyes. A man in a hat, collar turned up, had just entered the pharmacy. He replied to JB without taking his eyes off this customer.

'Yep, it's official. You really do baffle me. All you have to do is be the first to find the Deauville robbers' hoard, preferably a few days before Valentine's Day. Then sneak a few trinkets into your pocket.'

An old Rolling Stones hit was playing now: 'Paint it Black'.

JB lowered the volume without replying, but Papy wouldn't let it go.

'Or better still, you could give them to a different girl. Someone prettier, nicer, sexier.'

JB remained silent for a moment, as if hesitating, then suddenly winked at his partner.

Strange, thought Papy.

He did not have time to wonder what that wink meant, though, because the woman in the pharmacy had taken off her white coat

125

just as the guy in the hat came out carrying a bag of medicine.

Lieutenant Pasdeloup aimed the camera at the man, zoomed in, then suddenly exclaimed: 'Jesus Christ, it's Zerda!'

JB nodded almost imperceptibly: he too had recognised the fourth Deauville robber, or at least the man who was strongly suspected of playing that role. He got out of the unmarked police car, forcing himself not to rush.

The man was calmly walking along the pavement. After twenty metres, he went into the grocery shop on the corner. Lieutenant Lechevalier followed in his footsteps while Papy crossed the street to the pharmacy.

There were about ten people in the cornershop, more than there were outside on the streets. Alexis Zerda – if it really was him – had stopped in front of the beer aisle. Lechevalier moved closer, pretending to look at the various brands of rum.

And then he bit his lip with rage.

*Fuck it!*

Alexis Zerda raised a six-pack of Corona up to his eyes.

*Holding it in both hands.*

The bag of medicine had vanished.

JB stared around in panic. Customers kept coming and going. Three were queuing at the till. Outside the shop, on the pavement, two women were serving themselves from boxes of fruit.

Lechevalier went even closer to Zerda, just to be sure that he wasn't hiding anything under his leather jacket, but in truth he had already understood. Zerda had handed the bag of medicine to an accomplice.

A man or a woman that he'd not spotted. They could follow Alexis Zerda for hours, even days, as they'd been doing on and off for months, but he wouldn't lead them to Soler.

While Lieutenant Pasdeloup checked with the woman in the pharmacy what the man had bought from her – sterile compresses, Betadine, Coalgan and sticky microporous tape: the ideal combination for tending to an open wound – Lechevalier was passing behind Zerda.

Back to back, face close to the rows of pastis on the shelf – Ricard, 51, Pernod – he turned his head just for an instant.

It was enough. Identity confirmed.

Not only did the man who was putting the Corona six-pack back down next to the Desperados look exactly like the portrait of the supposedly anonymous motorcyclist from Deauville, but JB spotted, beneath his hat, a large silver earring in his left ear lobe. And when the lieutenant brushed past him, he distinctly recognised a skull-and-crossbones tattoo at the base of his neck.

# 21

Marianne Augresse hesitated before answering, but as soon as she saw the name of her deputy on the screen, she feverishly pressed the green circle on her iPhone.

'JB. Any news?'

The captain felt a delicious rush of adrenalin in her veins while Lieutenant Lechevalier replied.

'We almost . . .' In a few words, JB described their stake-out at the pharmacy, the appearance of Alexis Zerda and the probable intervention of an accomplice whom they had not been able to identify. It took all the captain's self-control to stop herself from yelling that it was hardly worth putting two policemen in an unmarked car if they were going to be fooled that easily. After the previous day's fiasco, she knew it was better for her to stand by her men.

Directly opposite Marianne, three rubber-clad creatures made aquatic-aerial movements as their kite-surfing sails caught the wind and bounced over the waves. Half-bird, half-dolphin, she thought.

'OK, JB. Don't lose Zerda. There are about a hundred pharmacies in Le Havre, so I doubt it's coincidental that he went into the one in Neiges. It's the first link we've had since 6 January between Alexis Zerda and the Deauville robbery, so let's be positive.'

JB replied quicker this time, reassured that his captain had taken the news philosophically.

'I agree, Marianne. It's a sign that the wolves are cornered and will have to come out of the forest, sooner or later. I'm going to get Bourdaine to follow Zerda. I'll see you at the station?'

'I'll be there soon. Maybe just a little bit late.'

Instinctively the captain covered her phone with one hand so that the lieutenant wouldn't hear the seagulls in the air above her.

Then she hung up and turned to Vasily with a big smile.

'Sorry. An emergency . . . I'm all yours, though not for long.'

The immense Le Havre beach stretched out in front of them. A crescent of bourgeois buildings was encircled by the wide concrete sea wall, which was brightened up by the presence of potted palms, European flags floating in the wind, and freshly mowed strips of lawn. An infinity of pebbles. Ferries drifting across the Channel. Marianne wondered how Nice had ever managed to steal from Le Havre the reputation as the most beautiful urban seafront in France.

They walked, shoulder to shoulder, along a little pathway that consisted of a few planks placed over the pebbles, maintaining the illusion that they could approach the sea below them without spraining their ankles. The hundreds of white beach huts were ranged between the sea wall and the empty beach, like an extra line of defence against the sea.

As soon as they were past the beach huts, Marianne twisted her neck round to look up at the psychologist, who was twenty centimetres taller than her.

'I kept my promise, Mr Dragonman. I ordered one of my officers to conduct a discreet investigation into the Moulin family. His conclusions are clear. I'm sorry, but the parents are clean. Malone really is their child, and has been ever since he was born, even if it sounds a little strange to phrase it like that. There's no doubt.'

The beach was a desolate place in November – the huts locked up, the seafront restaurants closed – compared to the hive of activity in summer. Marianne, however, adored this slightly melancholic autumnal atmosphere. All the place needed was a shady tree-lined terrace where she could sit and have a coffee, watching the ocean liners pass by in the background, and Vasily's golden-brown eyes in the foreground.

'A normal family,' she continued. 'The couple have no secrets. Dimitri Moulin spent a few months in prison, but that was years ago. Since then, he's been a perfectly ordinary husband and father, involved in village life.'

Vasily frowned.

'If your definition of a model father is . . .'

Marianne did not rise to the bait.

'You can look at the problem from any angle you like, Mr Dragonman, but it's simply not possible that Malone *isn't* their son . . .'

'I understand,' said the psychologist. 'Thank you for trying.'

There were large black and white photographs pinned to some of the huts, reminiscent of the Roaring Twenties and the days of the *Titanic*: transatlantic liners with couples on the deck, dressed in their Sunday best. If it were a hundred years younger, Le Havre would have been a very romantic place.

While her gaze drifted over the posters, Marianne's mind filled with idiotic questions: Was Vasily still single? Or in love with another girl? Aroused by walking with a woman next to the sea?

Well, if he was, the bastard certainly wasn't showing it. He seemed to be brooding, refusing to give up on his belief, like a child who wouldn't admit that mermaids and unicorns don't exist. He turned to her.

'What is your earliest memory, Captain?'

'Sorry?'

The psychologist's face was illuminated by a wide smile.

'I love this test! Everyone has to think about it at some point. Go on, try to remember: what is your earliest memory? Not something you've been told, but a real memory, precise images.'

'Well, um . . .'

Marianne closed her eyes, so that only the sound of the waves could distract her, and opened them again a few seconds later.

'You've caught me off guard. I don't feel very sure . . . I think I'd say a holiday at my aunt's farm. I saw her milking a cow and I think I can remember picking up a little stool so I could copy her. I don't think I've ever told anyone about that.'

'How old were you?'

'I don't know . . . Four?' She hesitated. 'No, probably five, or maybe even six. It was in the spring.'

'So before that, for the first five or six years of your life, there's just a black hole? You have to rely on other people to know what happened to you, correct? In terms of images, there are old photographs in an album. And emotionally, there are the stories your mother told you one Sunday after dinner. For landmarks, you have the places where you've been told you used to go: a nursery school, a house – yours, your childminder's, the house where you spent your first holiday.'

He caught his breath, sucking in the sea wind, then went on:

'Malone Moulin isn't even four yet, Captain. Everything he's experienced – and will experience for several months to come – he will forget. The only thing he'll have left are those "ghost" memories I mentioned. As I've explained before, the memory of a child under four is like plasticine, which adults can shape in any way they want. So I believe you when you tell me that Malone really is the son of Amanda and Dimitri Moulin; but in that case, we have to look at the case in a different way. Those memories didn't enter his head by accident.'

'What do you mean?'

'Before the age of three, a child has no autonomous self-awareness. The "I" is associated with what we psychologists call the "communal psyche". His mother, his father and his childminder are, in a way, extensions of himself. So when Malone tells us about his previous mother and the memories that he associates with her, there is one thing we can be sure of: those early images do exist. And for them to exist, someone must have planted them in his mind, and then tended them. Someone who belongs to his communal psyche. Someone who has done all they can to make sure Malone remembers. As if he were their last witness. The guardian of a secret, if you like. Consequently . . .'

He paused. Ahead of them, on another hut, a sepia image of a man with a moustache wearing a bowler hat, pushing aside the veil on a hat in order to kiss a pretty, short-haired girl.

'And consequently,' the psychologist went on, 'if someone made so much effort to ensure Malone would remember these things then, naturally, it is in other people's interests that Malone should forget them.'

'Malone's parents?'

'For example. This might seem stupid, but everything that boy has told me gives me the impression that these things are clues that have been deliberately placed in his brain, like beacons, landmarks that will help him when the time comes.'

Vasily was getting carried away. He was waving his arms about and his lips were trembling slightly. The captain found this charming, intriguing, even convincing. Except that his argument had one major fault.

His hypothesis presumed that some Machiavellian person was filling Malone's head with memories by constantly repeating to him the details of a previous life.

And that was what struck her as wrong.

Because the being that was supposedly filling his head was Gouti, his cuddly toy. That is what Vasily had told her.

Ridiculous.

Marianne let the swell cradle her thoughts for a while, as if they could rise above the clouds and accept the dreamlike, the supernatural. She did not want to pour derision on Vasily's passion. Nothing in this romantic landscape invited that response. Against all logic, she decided to take the psychologist's fears seriously, or at least to pretend to.

'So that would be the explanation? That Malone is in some kind of danger. And these memories serve to protect him?'

'Maybe. How else do you explain his fear of rain? The way he always feels cold? As for all the other factors, they don't resemble a classic case of trauma. The images are too precise.'

A gust of wind blew Marianne's hair across her face. Hair like the tentacles of a dead octopus, red face, her coat buttoned up to her chin . . . so many sexy details to add to her smashed nose.

'Come on,' said Vasily. 'Let's go inside. I want to show you something.'

He pointed at an open, empty beach hut a few metres further on, identical to a dozen others that were being repainted by a local government employee.

Two metres by two metres. Inside, the persistent smell of damp contrasted with a surprising sensation of warmth. But clearly Vasily

Dragonman had not led the captain into this private nook in order to kiss her.

He knelt down and spread out a 1/25,000 map that he'd taken from his backpack. In order not to step on it, Marianne had to lean against the wooden wall. The paper was covered with colourful arrows, cross-hatched geometrical forms, circles in different colours.

'I've been trying to get a clearer picture of what's going on,' Vasily explained, looking up at her. 'So I've attempted to represent Malone's stories on paper. You see, I'm not so eccentric really. The hypothetical-deductive method. Isn't that how the police proceed too?'

Marianne observed the map in more detail, almost amused by it. It was true: she and her men often used identical material to organise investigations, based on witness accounts of varying reliability.

'According to Malone,' Vasily went on, 'his house – the previous one – was by the seaside. He could see the sea from his bedroom window. So I cross-hatched all of the inhabited coastal areas. There aren't that many, in fact, if you take into account all the cliffs, nature reserves, industrial zones, and so on. Next, Malone constantly talked about a pirate ship. Those are my circles. I've circled all the places where it's possible to see a boat, any kind of craft from a fishing vessel to a super-tanker. Everywhere that has a view over the fishing port, the marina, the commercial port. I even thought about the wooden boats in the playgrounds in Mare-Rouge, Saint-François and Bléville. Look, Captain, even if you cross-match the areas of habitable seaside with the views of a ship, the space that's covered is hopelessly vast. It includes a good part of the central zone of Le Havre that was rebuilt by Perret, for example.'

His finger pointed to circles and lines.

'What about the other things? The forest and so on? Malone also says he lived next to a forest full of ogres and monsters.'

The psychologist wasn't phased. He pointed to the green patches on the map.

'We're spoilt for choice. The forest of Montgeon, naturally, and the hanging gardens around the fort of Sainte-Adresse, the woods

133

at the entrance to the Jenner tunnel . . . But nothing overlaps. Or rather, all of it does. As soon as you go higher up in Le Havre, you can see the sea from a long way off.'

'And the rockets?'

Vasily seemed pleased that Marianne had remembered all these details. The wood-and-embers flicker of his eyes stirred something in the captain.

'No idea about the rockets. There's the airport at Havre-Octeville: that's only one kilometre from the sea, not far from the shopping centre in Mont-Gaillard, but Malone was positive: he said it was a rocket, not an aeroplane. To be completely honest with you, Captain, I also haven't found any trace of a castle with four round towers either. The closest are the Chateau d'Orcher, which has only one tower, and the Chateau des Gadelles in Sainte-Adresse, which has eight. I did make a list of anything that resembled a keep or manor house, including water towers: they're represented on the map by those little blue crosses.

Marianne looked down for a moment at the overlapping colours. Dragonman would have made a good cop. Much more imaginative than most of her colleagues. Vasily gave her a sorrowful smile.

'So, no single place fits all the criteria. It feels like trying to assemble several different jigsaw puzzles with the pieces all jumbled up in the same box. As if several layers of memory have all been mixed together. How can we know which ones fit together? Which ones to put aside? Which ones to eliminate?'

Captain Augresse had no idea. A bluish halo briefly lit up the darkness of the beach hut.

A message on her mobile.

*When will you get here?*

*JB*

Marianne took a step towards the door of the hut. As if the text from her deputy had suddenly woken her from a doze.

What the hell was she doing here? Hunched over a treasure map invented by a three-year-old child and a crackpot psychologist! While two criminals who'd shot policemen in cold blood were running free, two criminals they'd been hunting for nine months and who'd hidden stolen goods worth nearly two million euros somewhere in the region.

'I have to go, Mr Dragonman. We'll talk about this later. I've put a man on the case. He's young, but he's good. He'll keep digging, just in case.'

They exchanged a slightly strange handshake. The wind lashed at Marianne as soon as she went outside. She quickly walked to her car, parked opposite Victor's chip shop, the only place that was open on the seafront.

*
*   *

As he folded the map, Vasily Dragonman watched the captain walk away. Some teenagers got off a tram, wearing rollerblades, and set off in the direction of the skate park. Opposite him, a girl was running along the boardwalk, her ponytail beating against her shoulders, the earbuds of her MP3 screwed into her ears.

How far would the captain go in her support of him?

How long before she laughed in his face, like all the others had done?

And even if she didn't, how could he convince her to continue, to keep digging, deeper, faster, before all the clues sown in Malone's head dried up, like rotten seeds that would never flower? Before his life was stolen from him for good. His real life.

Malone had trusted him. This was the first time in the psychologist's career that he'd had to bear such responsibility.

He carefully put the map away inside his backpack. He was that child's last hope. A piece of driftwood, tossed about by the waves, to which Malone was clinging. If he let go, the boy would drown.

It was terrifying.

The jogger was pretty. She stared at him as she passed, although she didn't slow down, certain without even having to look back that the man's beautiful dark eyes would follow the sway of her buttocks in her skin-tight leggings all the way to the end of the beach.

The small pleasures of everyday seduction.

But she was wrong!

One second later, Vasily could no longer see her, lost as he was in his thoughts. Astounded by the suddenly obvious revelation that had exploded in his mind.

He had just realised how Malone communicated with his cuddly toy.

# 22

*Little hand on the 10, big hand on the 7*

With his red and orange hat, his mismatched scarf and gloves, and his boots tickled by the badly mown grass, Malone looked like a garden gnome.

Amanda took the bicycle with stabilisers from the garage and placed it on the driveway, just in front of the fence.

'We'll go to the duck pond.'

Only Malone's head moved. He may have been a garden gnome, but at least he was a luxury model, with an articulated neck and a built-in barometer. Boots firmly planted in the grass, Malone looked up with fear at the menacing sky.

*It's going to rain.*

Amanda lifted him off the ground and placed him on the saddle.

'Come on, lazy boy, start pedalling!'

Malone pedalled one metre forward before the wheels got stuck in the gravel. Amanda sighed and gave him a push.

'Go on, you big baby! I'm sure Kylian and Lola don't need their stabilisers any more.'

Her comment had little effect. She pushed Malone's back harder to help him gain some momentum, and at the same time she lifted up his hat, which had fallen over his eyes.

The boy's hair was still wet. He'd screamed in the shower earlier that morning. Malone always took baths. Every evening, he spent an eternity in the tub. He hated the sensation of water falling on him – it made him visibly terrified – but this time, Amanda had had no choice. She'd grabbed him, undressed him, and forced him into the bathroom. Malone's hair, face, arms and hands were covered in dead insects.

Dead, just dead. Not dirty.

When she'd found Malone in the cupboard, that was what she'd said to her son, and her husband, forcing herself to smile, as if it were all a big joke. Those insects on his skin and his clothes were no worse than confetti, or a cloud of flour blown into his face, or dandelion seeds.

Dimitri had barked in reply: 'Get the kid in the shower and then sweep this up!'

Obediently, Amanda had bent down, holding Malone in her arms and, using her free hand, had picked up the corpses of flies, beetles and bees, before dropping them, one by one, into the plastic box.

Dimitri had stood observing her for a moment, dismayed, then had exploded with rage. Malone had put his hands over his ears.

'And throw all that crap in the bin!'

This time, for once, Amanda had resisted.

'No, Dimitri. No! Please don't ask that of me.'

She had thought he was going to do it himself, tear the box from her hands, pick up a broom for the first time in his life, and clean up the mess. But no, he'd just started yelling again.

'You're mad! You're as mad as that kid!'

And he'd slammed the door as he left the house.

The housing estate sloped gently towards the pond. Malone hardly needed to pedal. He'd put Gouti in the basket attached to the handlebars and he let the bike roll along the smooth, black tarmac, as if it were a Formula 1 race track.

There was no danger here. There were never any cars in this street except those belonging to the inhabitants of the other houses on Place Maurice-Ravel. The architects who had designed Les Hauts de Manéglise were experts in the construction of labyrinths. They had explained to Dimitri and Amanda, when they bought their house, that their estates worked on the principle of what they called social control: no one could enter or leave without being seen; each resident looked out for the others' houses. Everyone had their own bit of street and their own parking space. The genius of this idea consisted in giving the impression that you were alone in your own home, of being able to grow flowers, trees and vegetables in your own little garden in complete freedom, while at the same time remaining surrounded by other, identical houses. To feel as if you were cut off from the world, the city and even the rest of the village, while remaining encircled by shopping centres, activity zones and motorway junctions.

They were good, those urban planners.

And in the middle of this strategically arranged model estate, the children could play in absolute safety.

There was even a pond, right in the middle, carefully maintained, like another proof of the visionary talent of the architects.

Amanda held Malone back by the collar to regulate his speed. He laughed – for the first time that day. She loved moments like this. They always made her think of the lyrics of a song by Renaud, which she listened to over and over again, to sear these memories into her head. Songs were good for that, she thought, even the dumbest ones – for making you remember stupid emotions.

Then she remembered the last words of the song, before the final piano notes, when Renaud sang about time as a murderer, taking away the laughter of children.

Stupid truths too.

There were no ducks near the pond. There hadn't been any for weeks now, since the first cold mornings in September. Amanda knew this, but she still pretended to be disappointed. Malone didn't seem to care: he grabbed Gouti and ran into the bulrushes to look for nests and eggs, just as he'd done last spring when the ducklings were born, before the neighbourhood cats devoured them.

Amanda let him play, watching tenderly.

This little patch of countryside, fifty metres from their house . . . For Malone, it was the edge of the world, an infinity to be explored, a shoreless ocean, which would shrink in his eyes as he grew older. This housing estate would also grow smaller over the years. The confines of his present universe would become merely a stunted planet, navigable in only a few steps.

A prison. Like the one in which King Minos locked up young Greeks for eternity. A deliberate trap made of dead ends and cul-de-sacs, walled in thuyas and privet hedges. In reality, the architects of the estate had constructed a labyrinth without an exit.

The ducks were the only ones who had made it out.

Even Amanda, when she was sixteen, had sworn to leave Manéglise and never return. And yet she had returned, just like the ducks did. Because that's how life was. Because even if you travelled all around the world, seeking sunshine and love, finding them or not, in the end it didn't matter. This was where the ducklings had to be born.

And be devoured.

A drop pierced the pond's oily surface.

Malone didn't notice, but Amanda did. She realised they would have to go home before it started pouring and Malone woke the whole neighbourhood with his screams.

'Where are the baby ducks, Maman-da?'

*This is where the ducklings have to be born*, thought Amanda again, without replying to Malone.

And be devoured.

*Unless she prevented it.*

Diced tomatoes. Hamburger. Homemade chips. An episode of *Jake and the Never Land Pirates* while she cooked lunch. Another while Malone ate his food.

And a third episode, just one more, Malone begged, but Amanda didn't give in.

'Time for your nap, cabin boy!'

Malone did not protest. He already knew all the episodes by heart – they were always being repeated on television – and besides, he liked being in his bedroom. Too much, probably, but how could Amanda reproach him for that?

Malone lay in his bed, only his head – and Gouti's – visible above the top of the duvet. Amanda sat down next to him.

'Listen, darling, I know Papa shouts very loud sometimes, but he does love you. A great deal. It's just that sometimes he gets angry.'

Malone didn't dare reply.

'Do you feel like Papa is often angry?' asked Amanda.

Malone turned his eyes to the calendar pinned to the wall next to his bed. The rocket had landed on Mercury.

*The day of the journey.*

Malone preferred the night to nap time, because it was dark then and the planets and stars really shone.

'You see, sweetie, when you tell stories – at school, for example – when you say that I'm not your mother . . . For me, it doesn't really matter, because I know it's not true. But it makes Papa very angry.'

Amanda gently stroked her son's hair. He stared at her now, eyes wide. The sunlight, filtering through the drawn orange curtains, filled the room with a copper glow.

Malone mumbled a few words: 'So you don't want me to say that any more?'

'I don't want you to say that any more, and I don't want you to think it either.'

Malone seemed to consider this deeply.

'But that's not possible, because you're not my Maman.'

Amanda's right hand continued stroking Malone's hair, while her left hand tensed on the duvet, crushing Woody, Buzz Lightyear and Bullseye in the hollow of her fist.

'Who told you that, Malone? Who put that idea in your head?'

'It's a secret. I can't tell you.'

Amanda leant closer and thought about raising her voice. But in the end, she decided to speak even more quietly.

'You know that those secrets make Maman sad.'

Without waiting for a response, she held him tight. A long, silent hug that Malone was the first to break away from.

'I don't want you to be sad, Maman-da. I . . . I love you . . . I love you forever!'

'So you mustn't say that I'm not your mother. Promise?'

'Even if I still think it in my head?'

'Even if you still think it in your head. Don't worry, sweetie, those ideas will go away, like the germs that make you sick, like the spots you got when you had chickenpox, remember?'

Malone sat up and twisted his body free of Amanda's embrace.

'I don't want them to go away, Maman-da! I have to remember them always. Always.'

This time, Amanda could not hold back her tears. She wiped her hand against Malone's pillow, then hugged him again, even tighter than before, and whispered into his ear:

'You mustn't say that, sweetie. You mustn't say that any more. People will end up believing you, and then they'll separate us. Do you understand? You don't want us to be separated, do you?'

'I want to stay with you, Maman-da!'

She pressed him to her chest. She was so afraid.

'Me too,' sobbed Amanda. 'Me too!'

The three seconds that followed were perhaps the sweetest of her life: the sensation of warmth, the taste of dried tears, the inviolable cocoon of this child's bedroom, safe from the world, timeless, the feeling that this happiness could never escape her . . . until Malone caught his breath and finished his sentence.

'I want to stay with you until Maman comes back to get me.'

# 23

*Today, the guy in front of me at the bank deposited a cheque for 127,000 euros.*
*Want to kill*
*I'll seduce his widow.*

*Convicted: 98*
*Acquitted: 459*

*www.want-to-kill.com*

Amid general indifference, a jingle announced that it was 5 p.m. Hardly anyone in the police station was listening to the radio, which played quietly in the background, except for one minute every hour when the news headlines were broadcast.

Already, the journalists had stopped mentioning Timo Soler's escape after the failed interception at the port. Since that morning, local radio journalists had been bombarding the police station with calls, in the hope of obtaining new information. One journalist had even camped out on the station's front steps for two hours.

Nothing new, Marianne had systematically responded. And this was not just surliness on her part, even towards the camper, who had zig-zagged away on his scooter after the captain had threatened to slash his tyres.

There simply was no news.

Lieutenant Lechevalier put on his jacket.

'Five o'clock. I'm going home.'

Marianne looked pained.

'Yeah, you'd better go. With the traffic the way it is, you won't even get home in time for *Going for Gold*.'

'Just after,' said JB, proudly exhibiting a handwritten list which he'd taken from the pocket of his jeans. I'm going to do the shopping at Mont-Gaillard.'

'Quite right,' joked Papy, looking up from his computer. 'If Soler reappears, we might be on non-stop stake-out for a week.'

The captain nodded.

'Listen to Papy, the voice of reason! You'd better stock up if you don't want your family to die of starvation.'

Papy added: 'And if mummy's available, you need to make the most of your window of opportunity. In '95, when Khaled Kelkal was on the run, we were on stake-out for eleven nights running.'

JB was already walking down the corridor, and didn't bother to respond.

'Let her know in advance, JB,' Papy insisted. 'Always in advance. With my ex-wife, I called it a warning shot.'

This time, Lieutenant Lechevalier turned and managed a smile.

'You've got my number if anything happens. But if you want my opinion . . .'

He didn't even bother finishing his sentence, and deep down Marianne had to admit that JB was probably right. What was the point in staying at the station all evening, twiddling your thumbs and reading the same reports over and over again. She'd had Alexis Zerda followed all day long, from the moment he emerged from the grocery shop on Rue du Hoc until he got home (on Rue Michelet), via a Ford dealership, the Admiral Nelson bar and the Physic Form gymnasium.

All for nothing.

Several times, Officer Bourdaine, tasked with tailing the suspect, had called Marianne to ask for instructions, weary as he was of constantly trying to remain hidden.

'Zerda isn't in hiding! He's living this laid-back life like he's a retired gangster. Either this guy is as pure as the driven snow or he's taking the piss.'

Pure as the driven snow, Marianne repeated in her head. That seemed to have a particular meaning in this context – he was living in the Neiges quarter, the Snows neighbourhood, after all – but ultimately the captain had no doubt.

'He's taking the piss!'

She did not believe in coincidences, the miraculous chance that might have led Alexis Zerda to that particular pharmacy the day after the failed attempt to catch Timo Soler; with him buying exactly the medicines needed to treat an open wound. Nor was there anything innocent about those medicines mysteriously vanishing a few minutes after he came out of the pharmacy.

He was the fourth robber. He was protecting Timo Soler. All they had to do was trap him!

'Don't stop following him!' the captain thundered into the telephone. 'He'll end up leading us to Soler. Either that, or he'll have to let him rot wherever he is.'

Then she added, in a gentler voice: 'But watch yourself, Bourdaine. Don't take any risks. Timo Soler might be some poor bastard who got in out of his depth, but Alexis Zerda is a dangerous madman. A cop killer. A killer, full stop.'


On the radio, a series of listeners called up to talk about the economic crisis. One of France's main logistics companies, employing 157 people, had just filed for bankruptcy. In a carefully organised contrast, each unemployed caller was given twenty or thirty seconds to rail against the system, before being succeeded by someone in work, furious at having to pay for the unemployed. To each, his own revolution.

While half-listening to this, Papy had spread out the entire haul from the Deauville robbery over his desk. He had printed a colour photograph of every stolen item and then cut each object out.

A Piaget tiara, a glasses case by Lucrin and a few dozen other luxury items. Treasure fit for a princess. When the case was over, he would send all the cut-outs to Emma, his granddaughter. For the moment, he amused himself by moving the objects around the

145

table, inventing an avant-garde fashion parade for an invisible man and woman.

'Actually, what surprises me is the opposite,' grumbled the lieutenant.

'The opposite of what?' Marianne asked.

'Everyone panicked after the Deauville armed robbery, you know? We were all so surprised, so worried. But what staggers me is that armed robberies are so rare. That passers-by are not tempted more often to help themselves from the shops. Don't you find it strange, Marianne? All those people walking by the shop windows without wanting to smash them? All those people content to look through them, without even daring to imagine that they have as much right to these objects – which they could never afford – as anyone else. Those people who never think to themselves: since money is something invented by the rich, why shouldn't the poor invent theft as a mode of transaction?'

The captain yawned in front of her screen, but Papy was on a roll.

'Frankly, don't you find it amazing that all those people who fill their trolleys continue obediently to pay for their items at the till just to make multi-billion-euro companies even richer, instead of all running out together and smashing through the revolving doors? Don't you think it's crazy that people can still drive around the streets in their Porsches without having stones thrown at them? That they can wear a Rolex on their wrist without having their arm cut off? That people with nothing left to lose agree just to withdraw from the game, without even gambling the little they have left, just for honour's sake, or to impress their girlfriend, or to save face in front of their kids . . . Jesus, even in poker, you don't get down to your last chips without going all in!'

The captain took advantage of a brief pause in Papy's tirade. Once he got started, Papy could monologue for hours.

'That's because we're good at our job, Papy! And we're even paid for it. We're supposed to scare people. Guardians of the peace – the civil peace and the public peace – that's been our title for a hundred and fifty years. Even if the world has gone to hell.'

'So, more Cerberus than St Peter? I get it, Marianne.'

With the back of his hand, Lieutenant Pasdeloup pushed aside a cut-out of a Longines watch, then continued:

'Alexis Zerda is a dangerous nutcase and we should lock him up – I agree. But according to the dossier, Timo Soler was a fairly good guy. Same goes for Cyril and Ilona Lukowik. To me, those youngsters from Potigny, with their underage parents, seem more likeable than the CEO of some faceless multinational.'

'I don't know, Papy. I don't know. I'm not sure we should even ask ourselves those questions. Do you remember the three tons of counterfeit Nikes we intercepted a month ago with the customs guys, which had come in a container from Cebu? Why throw all those in the skip, eh? The Philippines is in more need of development than the USA. Poor countries have nothing to lose, when you think about it. The world's just a big poker game? So why not go all in, little countries!' She rolled her eyes. 'It doesn't work like that, Papy, and you know it. There have to be rules, and good little soldiers like us to enforce them.'

Papy nodded, Sphinx-like, while his fingers twisted a strip of brown paper: a Hermés-Paris belt.

'You're right. One last thing, do you know who Hermes was?'

'A Greek god, wasn't he?'

'Exactly! One of the stars of the Pantheon with his headquarters on top of Mount Olympus. He was both the god of trade, and thieves. The Greeks understood everything, didn't they? More than three thousand years before the Central Bank confirmed the oracles of Delphi.'

The captain gave a brief snort of laughter, pushed back her chair and paced around the corridor for a while. The station was emptying. She typed a text to Angélique while pouring herself a coffee.

*Fancy a drink at Uno tonight?*

The reply arrived a few minutes later.

*Not tonight. Going to see my folks. Need cash.*

Marianne smiled as she crushed the plastic cup in her hand. She had no desire to go home alone, no desire to run alone on the treadmills of the Amazonia, no desire to eat alone, to go to bed alone, to get up alone the next morning. She suddenly thought about Vasily Dragonman. She had his mobile number, but she wasn't about to call him and invite him to dinner. What excuse could she invent?

'You staying late?' she asked Papy.

'Yeah. I won't leave this place before three in the morning.'

'You aren't paid overtime, you know.'

'I know. I'm just waiting until it's 8 p.m. in the United States so I can call my daughter in Cleveland on the office phone. If I do it at home, it'll cost me half my month's salary!'

Marianne didn't pursue the matter. She didn't even wonder if Papy was joking or not. She put on her coat and went out.

Alone.

# 24

*Little hand on the 5, big hand on the 11*

Malone slept for three hours. He slept a lot in the afternoons, much more easily than he slept at night.

Before his afternoon snack, Amanda gave him a new toy. A green and yellow aeroplane, with a propeller, sky-blue wheels and five little figures who all had bendable knees, a brown helmet and large black goggles.

Amanda gave Malone a new toy every Wednesday, making them appear as if by magic. And every Wednesday, this made Malone happy. During the days that followed, he wouldn't let the toy out of his sight. Nothing else counted for him but that toy – except for Gouti, of course.

A Happyland aeroplane this week; a fire engine last Wednesday; a dinosaur, a cowboy on his horse, a racehorse in the weeks before. And even when a new toy replaced the previous one in the order of his affections, Malone still remained keen to ensure that each object, each character, each plastic figure should find its rightful place in his imaginary universe – even if it had been stowed away in the bottom of a crate or lay scattered among a dozen other toys on the carpet. In accordance with an order that no one but Malone could understand, as if he were a budding God, blessed with an infinite memory that allowed him never to forget any of the creatures on the earth that he had created.

'Thank you,' said Malone, eyeing it admiringly.

He did not say 'Thank you, Maman-da'. Nor did he say 'Thank you, Maman', even though he realised that was what she wanted him to say.

He would have liked that, too. To call her *Maman*.

He wanted to do it every time she gave him a present, or kissed him, or told him 'I love you'. Which was pretty often, in truth.

*But he mustn't.*

As soon as Maman-da turned to prepare his snack, he ran to the dining room, put Gouti on the floor, rolled the aeroplane around under the table, and then – hidden between the chairs – he took the sheet of paper from his pocket.

It was folded up very small, so he could take it everywhere with him without anyone seeing it. Each time he felt that urge to say *Maman* instead of *Maman-da*, when he couldn't talk to Gouti because someone might hear them, in those moments, in order to avoid doing anything silly, he would unfold his drawing.

Or, rather, the drawing he had done with Maman. The secret drawing that he must never show to anyone, not even Vasily.

His little fingers unfolded the paper as he kept an eye on the open kitchen door. He looked quickly at the image: the star, the green tree, the tinsel, the candles, the presents, the three figures. He paused for a moment on the drawings of him and Maman. She had done them. He thought she was really beautiful with her long hair. He was too little back then; he didn't recognise himself in the drawing.

His heart beat very fast, as it did every time, but all the same he took the time to look at the letters at the top and the bottom of the drawing, those letters he knew by heart.

Ten at the top, above the star at the top of the tree:

**Noël Joyeux**

And thirteen at the bottom, next to the presents:

**N'oublie Jamais**

*A Merry Christmas.*

*Never Forget.*

His eyes moved from the top to the bottom, then very quickly he folded the paper up again. Maman-da was already coming back with his snack. She'd even put a straw in his strawberry cordial.

Malone was still playing on the dining room carpet when Dimitri came in.

Without even saying hello to the child, he headed directly for the refrigerator in the kitchen and opened a bottle of beer.

Amanda was peeling vegetables, indifferent.

Dimitri drank half the bottle in a single swallow before saying, 'We have to talk.'

Amanda went to close the kitchen door, but before she did, Malone got up on his knees, smiled at Pa-di, and used the tea towel on the table to wipe the crumbs from his chin and the red stain from around his mouth.

'Leave us for a minute, sweetie. Go and play in the living room with your aeroplane.'

Malone jumped joyfully to his feet. He didn't care. He was the cleverest! He'd left Gouti next to the television in the kitchen, leaning against the plastic box.

Dimitri paced in circles, his almost-empty bottle of Leffe in one hand.

'I've been thinking. All day long. Found it hard to concentrate on work, that's for sure. We don't have a choice any more. We have to call him.'

Amanda, who had not even looked at Dimitri to this point, her gaze focused instead on her carrot peelings, glanced up at him furiously.

'No way! We agreed, didn't we? There is no way we're getting involved with him again. Do you hear me?'

Dimitri pressed his foot on the pedal of the dustbin. The glass bottle clanked against the bottom and he cursed Amanda's obsession with emptying the bin when it was only half-full. He opened the fridge door, opened another beer, and licked the foam that quivered at the neck of the bottle.

'Fucking hell, Amanda, can't you see? It's the only solution!'

Amanda replied calmly, tersely, precisely, in rhythm to the vegetable peeler.

'The kid won't be telling any more stories. I talked to him. He promised.'

'But it's too late! The whole village is gossiping about it. Apparently the cops have been nosing around, asking questions.'

Amanda opened the bin and dropped the peelings inside.

'So?'

'So? They're going to be all over me. They'll bring up my record, the months I spent behind bars. They won't leave us alone.'

'And after that? What are they going to do? You think they're going to take the kid away from us because of some stories about ogres, rockets and pirates? Let them get worked up. They'll grow tired of it all in the end.'

'Not that shrink! He can't stand the idea that a kid like Malone could be brought up by people like us. He's the one who went to the cops. I'm calling. We have to put an end to this. He has to get us out of this shit.'

The second empty Leffe fell silently onto its vegetable bed. Amanda continued peeling more vegetables with the same mechanical movement, but inside she was choking on her fear.

*Put an end? Calling? Get us out of this shit . . .*

Just how naive *was* Dimitri?

While she was searching in vain for a way out, she noticed that her husband's hand was trembling as he reached for his phone.

He was hesitating!

Amanda seized the opportunity.

'So you're not capable of dealing with this on your own? Is that it? You can't talk to the Romanian man-to-man and make him leave us alone?'

She turned and stood in front of him.

'You didn't need help when I met you.'

In an instinctive gesture, she picked up the cuddly toy that was lying next to the TV and put it on Malone's chair. Dimitri had already put the phone back in his pocket, almost relieved, as if deep down he had been expecting this kind of reaction from his wife.

'If that's what you want. So I can deal with this in my own way, then?'

152

He stared at the plastic box next to the TV, the one in which Amanda had put all the insects that Malone had spilt, then added:

'If that's what you'd prefer . . . But I get the feeling that you're losing it a bit too.'

Amanda looked down at the insects, then at the cuddly toy, and then once again at the plastic box. Finally, she moved towards Dimitri. Clasped in her fist, the peeler looked like a pathetic fake knife, like the ones with a retractable blade used in the theatre.

'Well maybe I have reasons for being crazy, don't you think?'

# 25

The captain's footsteps faded, and the police station fell into silence. Lieutenant Pierrick Pasdeloup had turned off the radio. Papy enjoyed these moments of calm when he could sift through the evidence in an investigation, spread the exhibits out like a puzzle, take as long as he liked to put them in order, connect them, like a craftsman building a piece of furniture bit by bit, using the right tool for each part of the process.

He liked to let his mind slip away for a few moments, then sink back into the arcane details of the investigation.

And while he did so, he thought about his children, as he always did.

He had been only twenty when Cédric was born. Delphine had come next, two years later. His first two children were now over thirty and lived in the South. Both had become parents themselves; two children for Cédric, three for Delphine, a total of five grand-children, whom Papy hardly ever saw. The eldest, Florian, was already in secondary school. A few years more, and he in turn would leave his parents and probably live even farther away. The cycle of life.

Two photos of corpses on the desk. Cyril and Ilona Lukowik. Shot on 6 January 2016, on Rue de la Mer in Deauville.

Papy had gone through a divorce five years after Cédric's birth. He'd fought for months to get shared custody of his son and daughter; he'd even offered to change his job, but that bastard judge wasn't interested. In the following years, he had seen his children only every other weekend. Which meant that, with school on Saturday mornings, he'd probably seen them less than thirty-six days per year. Around one in ten . . .

When he met his second wife, Stéphanie, he was twenty-six and he already knew that they wouldn't last as a couple. She didn't realise it; she was in love. Stéphanie was too young, too beautiful, too fond of life. She was seven years younger than him and had never been with another man: it was inevitable that she would cheat on him eventually. They had two children together: Charlotte and Valentin.

When they divorced, four years later, after Stéphanie took a lover, Papy held all the aces. The break-up was obviously Stéphanie's fault. Even she felt guilty, and it was Papy who allowed her to share custody. For the kids' sake. He was a good sport.

Those were some of the most beautiful moments of his life.

Lieutenant Pasdeloup's finger caressed the photograph of a ruby tiara estimated to be worth fifteen thousand euros. When he thought about it, no one had paid much attention to the brief lives of this Bonnie and Clyde from Normandy. The investigation focused on the two fugitives, Timo Soler and his supposed accomplice, Alexis Zerda. On the haul too, which was the object of daydreams for readers and journalists alike. But Cyril and Ilona Lukowik, once their corpses had been removed from Deauville's seafront in two plastic body bags, had been more or less forgotten. Just a few routine visits from the Caen police to Potigny, the village that probably linked all of this together.

Papy had met Alexandra a few years later; she was thirty and she raised Charlotte and Valentin as if they were her own children, without ever asking for more, allowing him complete control over his kids. The perfect stepmother, who became a mother herself at thirty-three. A new child! The first for Alexandra, who hadn't particularly wanted children, and the fifth for Papy.

Anaïs was born in 1996. She was a little princess, adored by all. His princess, and his favourite. His reason for getting out of bed every morning. A dream of a girl, until she became a woman. Last June, she had passed her baccalaureate with flying colours. Now she was in Cleveland at a business school that cost ten thousand dollars per year. She had begged them to support her, and he'd spent the last eighteen years trying to make her happy, so how could he refuse? Even if, for him, it meant those eighteen years of happiness suddenly being swept away and scattered to the wind.

Papy had left Alexandra the day after Anaïs's exam results were announced.

At fifty-one, he still found Alexandra sexy, elegant, free, liberated even; now definitively freed from the millstone of motherhood. A full-time woman, at last.

They had made a wonderful family.

And Papy suddenly felt terribly old.


Lieutenant Pasdeloup somehow resisted his fatigue. His eyes, focused on the dossier, kept opening and closing. He only had to hold out a little while longer: in fifteen minutes, he would have Anaïs on the phone. That would be enough to wake him up.

He straightened up and concentrated on every detail of the investigation.

Timo Soler, Alexis Zerda, Cyril and Ilona Lukowik were all from Potigny, a little village in Basse-Normandie, that was renowned, for over eighty years, for having one of the biggest coalmines in western France. A village of miners' cottages, surrounded by woodland.

The Potigny mines had been shut down in 1989, leaving behind two generations and twenty nationalities of unemployed men, although the Poles – who had created a little Warsaw on the Caen plain – were definitely in the majority.

Four armed robbers. Four children from Potigny. Three boys and a girl. All of them unemployed, their parents unemployed too. One question gnawed at Lieutenant Pasdeloup: how and why had these four kids – who had all grown up together in the same working-class street in their village, Rue des Gryzóns – become, years later, an organised gang of criminals?

The Caen police had rummaged around in the village's collective memory, spending a few hours in the streets of Potigny, questioning people. It was all in the report.

The words danced in front of Lieutenant Pasdeloup's eyes.

What if the Caen police had missed something essential?

What if he could perceive what they had failed to perceive? If he could hear what they had failed to hear?

Papy felt convinced that the key to the whole investigation lay in that grim transformation. A group of four friends decide to attack some shops, armed with guns, in accordance with an almost suicidal plan. It was this that interested him, more than the possibility of finding the famous hoard or proving Alexis Zerda's guilt.

The lieutenant paused for a moment over the photographs of the four robbers. He moved the pictures of the two corpses together, so that they were lying next to each other. He was convinced that there was something here, even if no one seemed to have thought about this question. Ilona and Cyril Lukowik were the only ones whose guilt had been proven: shot down, Berettas in hand, without any possible doubt over their involvement, even if they'd never had the chance to explain themselves before a judge or talk to a lawyer. Yet that version of events bothered Papy.

Why had this couple agreed to take part in such a suicidal mission? Cyril had worked as a docker for years. True, he'd had only temporary jobs for the past ten months, but he'd left his past as a juvenile delinquent well behind him. He'd found love, marriage, a family. It was only the press that had depicted them as the region's answer to Bonnie and Clyde. He and the other cops knew that the couple led a steady, content life. How could Zerda have convinced them to commit to this murderous game? Them, and Timo Soler?

Was it just because of their friendship, forged in the Norman mining village?

Or a secret pact?

Some kind of debt? A contract? A threat?

Papy had an intuition that the key lay in Potigny, hidden deep in their shared past. After all, the village was less than a two-hour drive away. The simplest thing would be to go there and check everything in the report; to analyse everything that Ilona and Cyril had left behind them forever on the boardwalk at Deauville: their childhood, their youth, their friends, their family.

In particular, Lieutenant Pasdeloup felt he had to verify at least one detail, a detail that the cops from Caen, who had lost themselves in the mines of Potigny before him, had dealt with in less than thirty minutes. A detail that, he believed, changed everything.

# 26

'Couldn't you answer any quicker? I let the phone ring for at least three minutes . . . The cops are—'

'I'm dying, Alex.'

A brief silence.

'Don't talk crap. Isn't the medicine I got you helping?'

A hacking cough, in itself a kind of reply. Alexis Zerda imagined the gobs of blood that Timo was probably spitting over the screen of his phone. He held his own phone tight to his ear. Even if the car park outside the Docks Vauban shopping centre was deserted, there was probably a cop or two not far away, freezing his balls off, hidden behind a car somewhere. But wherever they were, they were too far away to hear what he was saying. In any case, the waves that were crashing against the sea wall of Quai des Antilles, less than ten metres away, were already practically drowning out Timo's voice.

Or his death rattle.

'I won't last much longer like this, Alex.'

*Just a bit longer. A few more hours. A day or two.*

'You'll make it, Timo! You're safe and sound. The cops won't find you. They're following *me* night and day. I can't go anywhere. So let's make this quick. Don't do anything stupid, OK? If you set foot outside, if you try to see a doctor – any doctor – or go to a hospital, they'll get you!'

'So what do you suggest?'

It was as if Timo had downloaded an *I'm-going-to-die* app from the Apple Store, thought Zerda. It was all there: the husky voice pierced by a whistling sound, the slow breathing, the tremble in his voice – and probably the rest of his body. Zerda could sense every little bit of life in Timo seeping away.

A wave broke against the wall and the spray splashed his trouser legs. He took a couple of steps back. No more than that, just in case the cops had a long-range microphone, or were accompanied by lip-readers. Although it hardly seemed likely that they'd have stuff like that in Le Havre.

'We're playing for time, Timo. The cops have connected me to this, because of that stupid fucking pharmacy. I went there for you, I can't do any more. We have to be careful. We can't lose everything, not now.'

While he spoke, Zerda tried to think of an excuse so he could hang up. He felt sure now that Timo wouldn't hand himself over to the cops. Not yet. Which gave him a bit more time. By the end of the pier, after the Quai de Marseille, a dimly lit yacht entered the port.

'Let me speak to him!'

It was a woman's voice in the background. Zerda froze in surprise.

'I said let me speak to him!'

This time, the voice drilled itself straight into Zerda's ear.

'Alexis. It's me. You do realise Timo is dying here? You do understand that, don't you?'

'What do you want me to do? Call an ambulance? Take care of that female cop who's running the investigation?'

'Why not? I'll let you choose. Anything that will create a diversion while we make a run for it.'

'Give me one more night. Don't do anything tonight. If we panic now, we're dead.'

'And what if Timo doesn't wake up tomorrow?'

Alexis Zerda was distracted by the electric blue lights of the yacht. Forty-five feet minimum. Steel hull and wooden deck. Must have cost a fortune – a few million at least. For a fraction of a second, he found himself wondering who lived behind those fluorescent portholes. What billionaire could possibly want to moor his boat in Le Havre, to bring his high-class whores to this dump?

Not him, anyway.

He forced himself to think again about Timo dying. His fiancée in tears.

'I love you, girl. You're way too good for him!'

*

     *    *

Timo fell back against the pillows, his back to the wall, as soon as the call ended. This was the least uncomfortable position he could find. He'd been in this position since the day before, half-sitting, half-lying, like some bedridden old man in a hospice who had nothing left to hope for in life but the comfort of a hospital bed.

'What a bastard!' hissed the girl.

Timo forced himself to smile. His wound had stopped bleeding a few hours ago. If he kept very still, it didn't even hurt any more.

'He didn't have to get those things from the pharmacy for me.'

She picked up a cream-coloured towel from a pile in the wardrobe, poured water on it, then lay down next to him. She put the damp cloth over the scarlet gauze that covered his wound.

Timo was trembling. His skin seemed to have turned even whiter, as if his natural colour were fading, turning the colour of the sheets, the pills he swallowed, the compresses that were accumulating in the bin. After only a few days shut up in this lightless apartment, he seemed to have lost the brown complexion he'd inherited from five generations of Galician peasants.

The brown complexion she loved so much.

She ran her fingers through his hair.

'Zerda's scared that you'll go outside, and the cops will catch you, and then you'll rat on him. That bastard would rather see you die.'

'I won't die if you look after me.'

Her hand touched the back of his neck. Damp. Feverish.

'Of course not. Of course not, Timo. You're not going to die.'

She leant over his shoulder and couldn't hold back her tears. They fell on his torso, trickling down to the damp towel. If only they were magic, she thought, and a single tear could heal his wounds, like they did in fairy tales. The next second, she told herself off for having such idiotic thoughts.

She had to keep going.

She lay for a long time in the same position. Timo fell asleep. Or he was dozing, at least. Finally, she managed to detach herself from him, taking great care not to touch his skin or disturb the mattress.

One foot on the floor. One step.

Timo's eyes flashed white in the darkness.

'You have to sleep,' she whispered.

The wound wasn't bleeding any more. The Betadine and the Coalgan were sitting next to the bed, along with a bottle of water.

She put one hand on his shoulder and gave him a long kiss on the mouth. Although his skin was damp with sweat, his lips were dry and hard.

'We're going to make it through this, Timo. We're going to make it through.'

He half-closed his eyes, then looked at her again.

'Both of us? You really think so?'

'All three of us,' she said.

He couldn't hide the spasm of pain. He grimaced, then continued.

'I couldn't care less about that bastard Alex.'

She didn't reply. She just had to remain quiet and wait. Wait for Timo to fall asleep. But, just for a moment, she felt disappointed that her fiancé had not understood.

# 27

*Little hand on the 8, big hand on the 9*

Under the duvet, Gouti had told him everything. Everything that Pa-di had said to Maman-da. But Malone had not understood any of it. And, like yesterday, he didn't feel like listening. He just wanted to hear his own story.

The story of Mercury.

This was maybe his favourite story.

He would almost have preferred to hear just that one, but it wasn't possible. Gouti told him a different one each night. Gouti always did what Maman had told him to do.

\*

\*    \*

*On his island, everyone called him the Baby Pirate. He didn't like that much, especially as he hadn't been a baby for a long time, but as he was the youngest in the family, with his cousins growing up at the same rate as he was, he always remained the baby.*

*Baby Pirate lived on a small island, a very small island, so small that when he walked around it by the sea, after only a few minutes he wasn't moving away from their small hut any more, but towards it.*

*Yet Baby Pirate didn't get bored. With his cousins, he would climb the palm trees to find coconuts. Except that Baby Pirate wasn't allowed to go up all the way to the highest branches.*

*'When you're bigger,' said his mother.*

*With his cousins, he also played hide-and-seek, even if it was difficult to find new hiding places on such a tiny island. They would bury themselves in holes in the sand, in rabbit burrows or in caves near the beach.*

*Except that Baby Pirate was never allowed to bury himself completely.*

*'When you're bigger,' said his Maman.*

*So, quite often, Baby Pirate would play with the only other person of his own age. Lily. Like him, she lived in a hut built on stilts above the sea, a hut that touched his. Indeed, ever since they were born, their beds had been leaning against the same bamboo wall that separated their houses. Lily was so pretty that Baby Pirate had only one desire: he wanted to marry her.*

*'When you're bigger,' said his Maman.*

*Once a year, but only once a year – at Christmas – Baby Pirate's small size came in handy.*

*That day, he would climb on his Papa's shoulders (he was the only pirate on the island who could still be carried on his Papa's shoulders) and his job was to put the big star on top of the tree decorated with baubles and tinsel.*

*'Only until you're bigger,' his Maman warned him.*

*One day, Baby Pirate had had enough of waiting to be bigger, of walking round and round his island. So he took the big boat that was moored at the beach and left. Alone.*

*He had hardly been gone ten seconds when he made an extraordinary discovery.*

*His round little island was not an island, but a planet!*

*His pirate ship was not a boat, but a rocket!*

*The sea all around his island was not sea, but the sky!*

*That's good, thought Baby Pirate. A rocket goes much faster than a sailing boat. A rocket goes at the speed of light, so he would travel light years.*

*On board the rocket was a little GPS showing the way to each planet, even the smallest planets in the most distant galaxy. Baby Pirate only had to follow the directions.*

*'After the third satellite, turn right towards the Milky Way. Keep left for three light years.'*

*'Make a U-turn immediately before the black hole.'*

*'Your itinerary includes meteor showers. Do you wish to continue? Yes or no.'*

The GPS also indicated the location of suns in each galaxy, and all he had to do was pass close to one of them – barely a few light-seconds – and the rocket would be filled with solar energy. The GPS was even equipped with a speed-limit system, except that was silly, because no one can go faster than the speed of light.

Baby Pirate travelled for twenty light-years. Surely that was enough, he thought, for him not to be a baby any more. Then he turned around and went back to his planet.

When he set foot on the planet once more, all his cousins, his Maman, his Papa and Lily ran over and hugged him.

His cousins had become big, bearded adults, his Maman and Papa almost looked like grandparents, and Lily had grown into the most beautiful of princesses. They were all twenty years older than when he had left them. He remembered his mother's words, so long ago.

'When you're bigger.'

That was now!

Or at least that was what Baby Pirate thought.

Because he hadn't noticed this yet, but he had forgotten one small detail, a stupid little detail, but one that changed everything: when you travel at the speed of light, you move as fast as time, and so you don't get any older.

Baby Pirate had spent twenty years in his rocket, but he wasn't a day older.

Everyone had aged except him.

And it was even worse than before, because none of his cousins wanted to climb the palm trees with him any more: they had become serious and strong, and were content to make the coconuts fall by shaking the trunk. He was the only one who could still crawl into rabbit burrows and caves, but no one else wanted to play hide-and-seek. When Christmas came, his father explained to him that he was too old and too tired to be able to carry Baby on his shoulders so he could put the star on top of the tree. As for Lily, such a pretty princess could never marry a baby pirate who was twenty years younger than herself . . .

Baby Pirate became the saddest pirate in the galaxy. And no matter how much he thought about the problem, he couldn't come up with a solution. He felt lonely too – the loneliest pirate in the galaxy. And yet, even if this might seem unbelievable, he would soon be even lonelier.

One morning, he woke up and everyone had gone. Everyone: his cousins, his parents, Lily. They had all got on the rocket and blasted off.

Everyone except him. They had abandoned him.

Baby Pirate began to cry. He didn't understand. He cried for three days and three nights in a cave, before climbing up the biggest palm tree on the island, since there was now no one left to tell him he couldn't.

And there, at the top of the tree, he saw the words written in the sand. They were very big. He even recognised his mother's handwriting. She had written: 'Wait for us.'

So, Baby Pirate waited. He was very brave, very patient, very well-behaved, and he stayed alone on his island for thousands of days, far from his parents, his friends and the princess he loved.

Because, finally, he had understood.

One morning, exactly twenty years later, the rocket came back and landed.

Lily came out first. She had not aged a day. But Baby Pirate, having lived alone on his island for all those years, had become a pirate as big and strong as his cousins who were next out of the rocket.

Lily and he were now exactly the same age and they were married the very next day.

'Now you are bigger,' admitted Maman.

And when Christmas came, Baby Pirate – although no one called him that any more – bent down, picked up his old Papa and put him on his shoulders so that his father could fix the big star to top of the tinsel-covered tree.

And as he did so, his Papa leant close and whispered these words into Baby Pirate's ear: 'It's hard to understand when we're little, but listen carefully. When you love someone – really love them – sometimes you have to let them go far away. Or wait for them for a long time. That is the real proof of love. Perhaps the only one.'

*    *

The story was over. Sticking his head above the duvet, Malone was soothed by the stars projected against the walls of his bedroom. As happened every night, as soon as Gouti had gone silent and fallen asleep, the mark returned. At first it was just a blurred shadow, the kind that his hand might make if he waved it in front of a lamp. Except that both his hands were hidden under the duvet.

It wasn't his hand.

Little by little, as his eyes got used to the darkness, the shape grew clearer, each finger appearing, exactly like the drawings he'd done with Clotilde when they put the palms of their hands on plates of paint - the pictures that were taped to the windows of the school.

Once all the fingers had appeared, it was time for the colour. Just one colour. Red.

Malone closed his eyes then, so he wouldn't have to see it. So it would disappear, like the stars on the walls, like the planets and the rocket that shone above him, like the bedroom, like everything.

And everything disappeared into the darkness, even Gouti.

Except the red hand.

Then everything else turned red too.

# 28

*Today, Laurent told me that he didn't love me any more.*
Want to kill
*The whole world, except him and me.*

*Convicted: 15*
*Acquitted: 953*

www.want-to-kill.com

Vasily Dragonman let the scalding water run over his naked skin. It had become a habit, an obligation, almost an obsession.

Taking a shower after making love.

The few times that he hadn't, because he'd fucked outside, had a quickie, or done it in a toilet cubicle, he'd felt as if the traces left by fingers, lips and genitals on his body were printed there indelibly. As if they would never be erased, that they would penetrate his flesh, melt into him, and he would lose a part of his identity, his privacy.

He cursed himself. Shrink. Lunatic. Him and his complexes. Not even capable of enjoying the feel of a pretty girl's skin on his own without turning it into a theory.

She opened the glass door of the shower.

She'd just pulled on a pair of orange harem pants covered with an African design. She was topless, her hair tied up. She looked like a village girl from one of the Kirikou stories, only lighter-skinned. That remembrance of his first adolescent yearnings only troubled him more.

'You got a message.'
She handed him his mobile phone. He turned off the water.
A text.
With his thumb, he wiped the condensation off the screen.

*Probably stupid of me, but I want to believe you.*
*Aware of urgency. I'll do my best.*
*Contact me, whenever.*
*Marianne*

'Your captain again?'
Vasily just made a sorry face, like a little boy caught in the act
but denying all responsibility.
Irresistible.
All the same, that was no reason to let this go.
'A text at midnight? She's hitting on you!'
She was aware that her jealous, angry pout was a lot less appeal-
ing than Vasily's innocent smile.
'I need her. I'm playing along.'
'For the sake of your kid. The little boy who talks to his toy?'
'Yes.'
He left the phone on the sink, then got back in the shower.
Turned the water on again. She followed him under the hot
waterfall, without even taking off her trousers. In only a few seconds
the cotton fabric formed a second skin clinging to her buttocks
and thighs, tattooing her alabaster skin with elephants, giraffes and
zebras.
She pressed her wet mouth against his neck.
'You're going to see him tomorrow morning at the school?'
'Yes. If they'll let me.'
'Can they stop you?'
'Yes, of course. Any of them could. His parents, the school, the
cops.'
'He needs you. It's all you've talked about for weeks now. The
way you're the only one he confides in. That you're being cautious,
taking it slowly. That if he clams up, then it's all over.'

She put some shower gel in her palm, rubbed her hands together, then placed them on her shoulders and ran them down over her body.

He took a step back. Her hands moved beneath the material of her Turkish pants, between her two skins. Her thigh pressed against the mixer tap and slowly, under the pressure of her coconut-vanilla caresses, moved it a few centimetres to the left.

The burning water turned lukewarm.

'Unless that's actually the best solution, Vasily. To let the kid forget whatever has traumatised him.'

Vasily's body was more like a rugby player's than a psychologist's. The slim muscles of a fly half. Her fingers followed the curves of his torso, venturing down over his abdominal muscles.

She whispered: 'If there is a ghost living in his head, wouldn't it be better to leave it locked up in its dungeon?'

Vasily replied quickly, before he got carried away.

'You forgot a stage.'

The water turned from lukewarm to ice-cold. They didn't move.

'What stage?'

'Before condemning the ghost to life imprisonment, before sending it to live in one of the cells in the boy's brain, my job is to find it, look it straight in the eyes, and tame it. To confront it, if necessary.'

After stopping the water with one agile foot, she stood on tiptoes and whispered in his ear:

'That's dangerous, no?'

They heard a succession of three electronic notes.

'Your little policewoman again?'

Vasily gave an annoyed smile before she could give him one of her pouts, and blindly grabbed hold of the telephone.

His expression suddenly changed.

'Problem?'

He lifted the phone up so they could both see the screen.

*Number unknown.*

A photograph and a message.

First the photo: a small marble tomb, its cross standing out

170

against a red sky. They couldn't make out any of the words or numbers engraved on the headstone.

The grave of a stranger? A child? A family?

Then they read the message below it.

*You or the kid. You still have a choice.*

She bit her lip, her desire suddenly extinguished.

'What are you going to do?'

'I don't know. Call the cops?'

'Your cop?'

He sat on the edge of the sink.

'I don't know. Jesus, what *is* all this?'

She stood in front of him. Beautiful. Her long hair fell over her naked breasts. Over her savannah legs. As beautiful as she had been the day he first met her, at Bruno's place. Slowly, she pulled down the elastic of her Turkish pants. There was nothing erotic about the gesture, though; it was more like a primitive ritual, an incantation.

She lowered the fabric a few centimetres, enough to reveal the top of her pubis. Modestly, without provocation, as you do when the doctor asks you to lower your underwear before doing an examination.

Her index finger circled her navel then moved down her smooth belly.

'Look at me, Vasily. Look at me and listen. You see this belly? It will never carry a child. You see this uterus? No life will ever come of it. Perhaps this doesn't seem the right moment to bring it up, and don't worry, I'll spare you the sordid details – you've had enough of those tonight, I suspect – but I just want to tell you that, contrary to what the bastard who sent you that message said, you don't have a choice.'

Vasily stared at her, incredulous, incapable of thinking clearly. Ten years working as a psychologist and ten years of theoretical study before that, and he still didn't have a clue what was going on.

'Protect that child, Vasily! Protect him. You're the only one who can save him. Understand?'

No, he didn't understand. He didn't understand anything any more. But at least she was right about one thing: he had no choice.

He took her in his arms and lied.

'I understand, Angie. I understand.'

# THURSDAY

The day of courage

# 29

*Little hand on the 11, big hand on the 6*

'Malone, listen to me. It's important. You have to tell me about your secret, if you want me to believe you. You have to explain to me how Gouti tells you all those stories.'

Malone did not reply. He kept his eyes firmly planted on the school desk that separated him from the psychologist, focusing on an invisible point, as if the response had once been written there and then erased. Gouti, between his knees, was silent too, even if his pink smile and laughing eyes did not seem affected by the psychologist's question.

'I have to know, Malone.'

Vasily hesitated. The bond of trust that he had built with this kid was as thin as a nylon string. If it broke, all of the kid's memories would go flying like pearls from a snapped necklace. And yet he had to stretch it. Carefully.

'If you want to see your mother again – the one from before, I mean – then you have to help me, Malone.'

The child did not raise his head. A prisoner of his silence. He just hugged his cuddly toy as if Gouti were the only person capable of helping him; as if the toy might suddenly open its mouth just to show this psychologist how limited his imagination really was.

But the grey and grubby cream rat remained silent.

Vasily pulled on the string again.

'Gouti has to talk to someone other than you, Malone, do you understand? He has to talk to a grown-up.'

Malone looked down at his toy. Vasily had the impression that the kid was asking Gouti's advice. Maybe they were communicating telepathically? Maybe all kids did that with their toys and only lost that magic power as they got older?

They had been sitting face to face in Clotilde's office for nearly an hour.

'Take your time, Malone. Take your time.'

He paused for a moment, and examined the headmistress's desk, which was cluttered with exercise books, large sheets of multi-coloured paper, pots of felt-tip pens and prizes for the school fete piled up in cardboard boxes.

In the corridor behind him, Clotilde walked past without even looking at him. Three-quarters of an hour before, she had made a pot of coffee without offering him any. She had even left the coffee machine percolating behind him, like an act of defiance.

Vasily looked up at the clock. In fifteen minutes' time, the mothers would begin arriving and it would be too late. Would he ever get another chance to question Malone?

The child still seemed to be begging his toy to help him. Too bad. Vasily had to speed things up, even if it went against every ethical code he knew.

'Malone, listen to me. A cuddly toy, like a teddy bear or Gouti, they can't talk! You know that.'

The child bit his lip and twisted on his chair. At least Vasily had managed to push one step further: he'd provoked a shock in Malone's brain, triggering a chain of events that would end with a reaction. He just had to wait.

He looked down at the table. Three sheets of paper were spread out before him. He'd printed them that morning, each with two columns.

To the left, questions, photographs, symbols.

To the right, the answers he had scrawled over the last few weeks.

Left column: a pirate ship, taken from an Asterix book.

Right column: Malone's reaction.

*No, it's not the same as my pirate ship. It was more black and without the thing in the middle.*

*The mast? So no mast, is that right? And how was it black?*

Vasily had groped around for several minutes before obtaining a precise answer.

*Black, completely black, like a warship.*

Left column: a castle – the Chateau de Pierrefonds – with its moat, its drawbridge, crenellations, towers and keeps.

*No, the towers were thicker, and not as tall. Without all that.*

*Without all what, Malone? Without the sloping roofs? Without the sculptures? Without the holes in the stone?*

Vasily had done seven drawings and each time Malone had shaken his head. Until the psychologist, having exhausted all possible architectural forms, lined up four simple circles.

O O O O

Malone's eyes lit up.

*Yes, like that!*

Vasily looked up.

Rain was hammering against the office window. Behind the glass, he could see the umbrellas gathering by the playground fence. Outside in the corridor, he could hear the children moving about, the little ones standing on tiptoes, grabbing their coats and scarves. In a few minutes, Malone would slip between his fingers.

And yet, he was almost there.

Malone was going to give in, Vasily could sense it. He decided to pull even harder on the invisible thread.

'Gouti talks in your head. Is that what you mean, Malone? He doesn't really talk to you. Gouti is a toy, he's not alive. He can't tell you stories every night. He just can't . . .'

'Yes he can!'

Malone did not say anything else. Arms folded. Mouth closed. Even if he was dying to prove the grown-up wrong.

Another few minutes, that was all Vasily needed. He pretended to lose interest in the child again and looked at his notes.

Left column: a rocket. Vasily had downloaded a photograph of Ariane 5.

*That's it!*

*You're sure? You've seen this rocket? You've seen it fly in the sky?*

*Yes. Yes, yes, yes, I'm sure. I remember. That's it!*

The psychologist stood up to turn off the coffee machine, the slow drip-drip-drip marking the passing seconds like a noisy old clock.

'Your Maman will be here soon, Malone. The one you call Maman-da. You'll go home with her. If you don't tell me how Gouti talks to you, then . . .'

For a brief instant, the macabre image of a tomb flashed in front of Vasily's eyes – the one that someone had sent him the previous night on his mobile. He had hesitated between deleting the text and forwarding it to Captain Augresse.

He hadn't made a decision yet. He'd deal with it later.

'Are you thirsty, Malone?'

He poured a glass of water and put it in front of the child.

Five to twelve.

He had no choice now. There was no time. If the string broke, so be it. The psychologist took a chair and sat next to the child. He leant down until their eyes were at the same level.

'They won't let me see you again, Malone. If you don't tell me your secret now – Gouti's secret – you will never see your Maman again.'

Malone stared at him.

This time, the decision was made. Without the child saying a word, Vasily knew that he had won.

Slowly, Malone held Gouti up. His hands rummaged in the creature's fur, as if caressing it, at the exact place where the fur changed colour, between the grey of the creature's little round belly and the grubby cream of the rest of his body.

Then he pulled. Gently.

Vasily couldn't believe his eyes.

Gouti's belly opened.

A simple strip of Velcro, hidden. Perfectly sewn, invisible,

178

impossible to spot, even if you held the toy in your hands. Not that any adult ever touched Gouti anyway.

Malone's little fingers rummaged inside the foam innards. First they took out a set of earbuds, child-sized, with the black wires in a tangle, which he patiently unrolled. After that, he unrolled another wire, also thin and black, presumably a power cord. More groping around inside the creature's belly, and then Malone extricated a tiny MP3 player.

A few millimetres thick, three centimetres long, with a small backlit screen that covered nearly its entire length.

Malone proudly exhibited the gadget to Vasily.

Instinctively, the psychologist reached over to the office door and pushed it shut with his foot.

'It's easy,' explained Malone. 'You just have to press these five buttons.'

The green triangle. To listen to Gouti.

The red circle. To silence Gouti.

The two lines. So that Gouti listens and tells you later.

And the two arrows, on two different buttons, pointing in opposite directions. So you could search around in Gouti's memory.

'So you can find the right story for each night. Is that right, Malone?'

'Yes.'


Vasily's hands trembled slightly. The explanation was so obvious. So simple, it was almost . . . childlike.

Seven files. One for each night. Seven stories, always listened to in the same order. Impossible to go wrong, even for a three-year-old child.

'Was it your mother who taught you how to use it? Your Maman from before. Did she make Gouti's heart and hide it inside him? Did she ask you to listen to Gouti's stories each night? Is it Maman's voice you hear? Is that right?'

Malone nodded in response to each question. He seemed to have grown up by two years in two minutes. Vasily did not have time to analyse the staggering consequences of what he had just learnt.

**179**

Why impose such a ritual on a three-year-old child?

How could Malone have hidden this secret from Amanda Moulin?

What were the stories about? What was their coded meaning? What effect did they have on this child's developing brain?

And, most of all . . .

Vasily stroked Malone's hair with one hand, in an attempt to calm his trembling.

What madness could have inspired such a strategy?


They heard the footsteps too late. The door opened. Malone reacted the quickest. Force of habit. Or instinct. In the same movement, he smiled reassuringly at Clotilde, hid the earbuds and MP3 between his knees, and dropped Gouti, belly down, on the table.

'Everything OK, Malone?'

A shy, natural-sounding yes.

Mankind, as a species, has a gift for lying.

The headmistress glared at the dormant coffee maker but didn't say anything. She turned to the child.

'Your mother is here. Can you go and get your coat?'

'He'll be there in just a minute,' replied Vasily in a conciliatory voice. 'We've almost finished.'

He made a show of sorting his notes on the table, while Clotilde shrugged and then left. The rain hammered even harder against the window. This time, Malone could not conceal a jerk of terror.

Vasily moved towards him and whispered.

'You have to give me Gouti's heart, Malone. I have to listen to what he says.'

Malone was scared. Because of the rain. Because of what Vasily was asking him to do.

'I know, you promised. You promised your mother. But I won't tell anyone.'

The child's knees slowly opened. His little hand reached out, holding the MP3 player and the two black wires that hung between his fingers like strings of liquorice.

The psychologist's hand closed around the boy's. They stayed like

180

that for several long seconds, sealing a pact that would link them from that moment on.

Vasily felt an immense responsibility fall on his shoulders, as if this child were handing him his very own heart, warm and still beating.

The bell suddenly rang.

That seemed to shake Malone from his terror. He nervously grabbed hold of Gouti and pressed him against his heart.

'I'll give him back his voice,' whispered Vasily. 'I'll give him back to you, I give you my word, in exchange for his. I . . .'

Vasily realised that he wasn't making much sense. He closed his hand around the MP3.

'Gouti is simply going to sleep for a while. He's going to rest. Don't worry, I'll give him back to you tomorrow, outside the school. I promise. I'll be there and I'll give you back his heart.'

Malone went to fetch his coat. Vasily watched him vanish down the corridor, jumping with fright every time he passed under one of the plastic skylights being pummelled by the downpour. Among the mysteries hidden deep inside this child's brain, there was also this fear of rain, like the permanent cold he felt whenever he went outside, forcing him to dress in more layers than the other children.

Would he find the answers to all these questions in the stories that Malone listened to? Vasily had a foreboding that, instead, these recordings would only deepen the mystery.

As he left the room, a classroom assistant walked over to open the school gates. The psychologist took out his mobile phone before putting the black earbuds and the MP3 in his pocket. Vasily's finger slid down the touchscreen, scrolling through the messages he'd received since the previous day.

***Angie. 9.18 a.m.***
A smiley holding a red, heart-shaped balloon.
*I love you. Take care of yourself.*

*Unknown. 12.51 a.m.*
A tomb, under a red sky.
*You or the kid. You still have a choice.*

He shivered. Feverishly his finger moved down to the previous message.

*Unknown. 11.57 p.m.*
*Probably stupid of me, but I want to believe you.*
*Aware of urgency. I'll do my best.*
*Contact me, whenever.*
*Marianne*

Without hesitating, he pressed on the CALL icon.

\*

\*   \*

Amanda Moulin stood outside the school gates, under a black umbrella, surrounded by mothers who were more interested in talking to each other than hearing their child tell them about his or her day.

Malone was just about to walk out into the playground when he froze, incapable of moving another step.

Before him, the rain was pouring down in a furious torrent.

He stood there for what seemed like an eternity, his eyes imploring Maman-da, who stood behind the gates with the other mothers.

A hand touched his back.

Vasily. He had come up silently behind him. The psychologist gently pushed Malone forward while observing the thin trickle of water running from the gutter in front of the classroom, fed by the last drops of the downpour.

'Go on, it's all right.'

Malone did not move. He stared at the grey sky, petrified.

This time, Amanda did react. Crossing the line that parents were not supposed to cross and entering the playground, she walked over to the classroom door. Without glancing at Vasily Dragonman, she lifted the umbrella above her son's head.

'Come on, sweetie, let's go home.'

Behind her, she sensed the mute protest of the other mothers who were obeying the school's rules.

The psychologist seemed annoyed too, standing there like a post behind Malone, eyes averted, hands stuffed in his jean pockets as if he'd just stolen a sweet. Amanda looked up at him.

'Leave my kid alone, sir. I'm perfectly capable of looking after him myself!'

Vasily's hand tensed inside his trouser pocket.

'I'm just trying to help Mal—'

'Leave him alone,' she repeated, louder this time. 'I'm begging you.'

The conversations on the other side of the gate went silent.

She whispered the rest.

'Leave him alone, Mr Dragonman. Or you'll make something bad happen.'

# 30

Captain Marianne Augresse waited. Irritated. Her eyes scanned the tram stop opposite, the cars moving down Boulevard George-V, even the Optimists and 420 dinghies sailing across the port.

How would he arrive?

And when?

She hated waiting like this, feeling vulnerable, dependant – especially here in front of the police station – when her usual daily life consisted of barking orders at people and making her own decisions about what she should do with her time.

Two officers, Duhamel and Constantini, walked past, rushing down the steps without even noticing her. She had no idea where they were going. That annoyed her even more, the absence of control over the movement of her men, particularly as she lacked the manpower to juggle all of the demands being made on the force.

She'd already had to give up on the idea of leaving an officer outside Alexis Zerda's house all night. The last one had gone off-duty at 11 p.m. and the next had not taken over until 6 a.m. the following morning. She couldn't have a cop tailing that man twenty-four hours a day, for weeks, when they had no concrete evidence against him. And that was without even mentioning Papy, who'd been pestering her all morning.

The Guzzi California screeched to a halt outside the station. The captain did not recognise Vasily Dragonman until he took off his helmet. His dishevelled dark hair made him look like a crow whose feathers had been ruffled by the storm.

'You're late, Mr Dragonman.'

Vasily did not even bother replying. He just got off his bike, walked up to the captain and extended his arm – so that she could see the object he was holding in his hand.

An MP3 player.

'The kid didn't invent anything,' Vasily muttered.

He briefly explained Malone's revelations: the MP3 sewn into the cuddly toy, the stories that the child listened to every night, earbuds in his ears, under the covers. An MP3 player that Vasily had promised to return to the child the following morning, outside the school.

Captain Augresse put one hand on the bonnet of the nearest car.

'Christ! That's unreal.'

'Not really, it's the truth.'

The captain's hand tensed.

'I know what you're going to say. You're going to go on about hidden memories and how the brain of a three-year-old is as easy to mould as a ball of clay. But what I'm talking about is the MP3 player and that cuddly toy. Did the kid really believe that his rat was talking to him?'

'I think so. Well, actually, it's more complicated than that. It involves psychological theories about child development that are still being debated.'

'Theories that I'm too stupid to understand?'

Vasily frowned in surprise.

'No. Why?'

'Too rational, then? Too much of a cop? Not enough of a mother? Not enough of a woman?'

The psychologist hesitated. He stared at Marianne. Clearly, he was more at ease with the neuroses of children than with those of grown women.

'I don't know, Captain.'

There was a silence.

'Well, go on then! Explain it to me!'

Vasily took a deep breath before starting to speak.

'Well, the question we have to ask, if we want to understand Malone's relationship with his toy, is when do children start pretending? Or, to be more precise, when do they become aware that they're pretending?'

Well, we're off to a good start, thought Marianne, frowning but not daring to ask the psychologist to repeat himself.

Vasily looked at her indulgently, then chose a different tack.

'OK, to give you a concrete example, let's say that from about the age of five, a girl who plays with a doll knows that she is playing with a doll, that what she's holding in her arms is a toy, even if she rocks it and cuddles it as if it were a real baby. She's become aware of the fundamental difference between the reality and her perception of that reality, and she can play on that difference through social codes. You follow me so far, Captain?'

Marianne nodded.

'I pretend to feed my doll with a bottle, but I'm aware that she is not really drinking and that she is not going to die if I don't feed her. I know that she is just a toy, even if that doll means more to me than anything in the world, even if my parents play along with me and talk about that doll as if she were a real person. That is what the game is for: imitating, codifying, transgressing. On the other hand, before, say, three years of age, children have no awareness of the difference between reality and their perception of that reality. For example, life and death do not really exist for them: a teddy bear is as alive as the bear they see at the zoo. Likewise, truth and falsehood are not notions that they can distinguish between: things exist or they don't, and that's all. For instance, it's impossible to have a true or a false mother. A child of under three will have a mother, and perhaps other female figures who look after him: a childminder, an auntie, a friend . . .'

He took a breath, and Marianne took advantage of the pause, like an attentive student.

'So, if I've understood correctly, for little Malone, his cuddly toy really *was* talking, even if he was the one pressing the buttons.'

Vasily shook his head. He seemed to be weighing each word of his reply in order not to upset her.

'It's not that simple, Captain. As I've said, this process of be-coming aware of their own perception, this cognitive detachment in children, generally takes place between the ages of two and five. But at what moment does it fundamentally flip from one to the other? Between two and five, we give kids the same toys to stimulate imagination, manipulation, and cognition. Most often toys that imitate real things: a car, houses, dressing up costumes (a doctor, a fireman, a princess, a pirate). Vast teams of marketing experts and education specialists work on this kind of thing, and kids are deluged with supposedly educational toys each Christmas. Children have never been as stimulated as they are now, but, most of the time, we still don't know anything about the kid's "black box" despite all those colourful objects we've invented for them. Is the child playing or not? Does he know that he's playing? Is he playing because we join in with his game? Or because he wants to join in with ours?

'So, to get back to Malone, this much seems clear to me. In his eyes, Gouti is neither an inanimate object nor a living being with its own feelings; those words don't really have any meaning for him; he is not capable of distinguishing between the two. Malone is obviously not aware that his attachment to Gouti is linked only to the projection of his own emotions on this cuddly toy. But a child of three *is* aware of what is forbidden and what isn't. The big difference between Gouti and an ordinary toy is not that he talks, listens and tells stories – most other toys can do that sort of thing in Malone's eyes: a television, a radio, a telephone – but that Malone's maman told him never to reveal this toy's secret, never to admit that his toy talks, listens and tells stories. And a child, even a very young child, knows how to do that: to obey. There is no awareness of what is good or bad – that comes later, even if you have to explain it to them as soon as possible – but he knows what he is allowed to do and what he isn't. It's later that this all gets a bit more complicated, when you have to align good and bad with what is permitted or forbidden. But thankfully for Malone, he has not yet reached that stage.'

A satisfied smile concluded this lecture.

While he was speaking, the captain had almost forgotten the comings and goings of her colleagues outside the station. This man fascinated her, unless it was simply the fascination she felt for all information about early childhood. Perhaps she would have been equally spellbound by an old, bald, myopic psychologist if he'd been expounding these same theories.

'OK,' said Marianne, forcing herself to focus on more pragmatic concerns. 'I'm with you on Gouti and I take back the word "unreal". So, how long do you think this, um, secret relationship with Malone has been going on?'

'Probably about ten months, which means that Malone has listened to each story more than thirty times, that they have become his reality, the only one he really knows.'

'Along with his normal daily life,' Marianne pointed out. 'Along with his school and his family.' She looked at the MP3 in the psychologist's palm. 'Have you had time to listen to it yet?'

'Yes. It's not very long. Seven stories, each one lasting a few minutes.'

'So?'

Two officers were entering the station. They saluted the captain while glancing, surprised, at the Guzzi parked on the pavement and at the man deep in conversation with their boss.

'Nothing is certain yet. There are some clues, lines of enquiry . . . that's all. The same obsessions keep recurring: the forest, the sea, the ship, the four towers of the castle. In a coded way, but also sometimes more precise. I've made some progress on the list of possible locations. It should only take me a few hours to visit the spots that could correspond to the place where Malone used to live, before.'

He leant down to the luggage carrier attached the motorbike. The captain thought he was about to unfold his annotated map in front of the police station.

'Unless,' she added a little brusquely, 'those memories are entirely fabricated. Unless little Malone has never lived by the sea or near a forest.'

'No! There's a meaning, a coherence to everything he says. I can sense it. It's my job to discover what that is. Your job, on the other hand . . .'

He left his sentence unfinished and opened the luggage carrier with the aid of a miniature key.

'I have another gift for you, Captain.'

He took out a little child's cup with a picture of Tinker Bell on it, rolled in a paper towel.

'Malone drank from the cup this morning.'

'So?'

'It's the only way of knowing if the Moulins really are his parents, isn't it? A DNA test. Should be simple enough for you, right?'

The captain sighed as she turned to look at the port. Kids wearing identical orange life jackets stood waiting to climb onto an Optimist. Their shouts mingled with the cries of seagulls.

Vasily waited, disappointed by Marianne's failure to react. The captain seemed to be suddenly immune to his charms when he was dangling proof under her nose.

'It's not that simple, Mr Dragonman. We would need an official complaint to conduct such an analysis, a letter rogatory ordered by a judge.'

The psychologist raised his voice then. If charm wasn't going to work . . .

'And you're going to hide behind Article 36b of the code of good conduct, are you? Don't you understand? What do you think *I've* just done? By giving you this evidence, I've betrayed the most basic rules of professional confidentiality. I've taken risks, Captain! Big risks.'

The image of the tomb flashed in his mind's eye. The captain did not seem overly impressed.

'Well, don't take any more, Mr Dragonman. Because, if you think about it, your main argument has just fallen apart.' She looked down at the MP3 player again. 'There isn't any urgency any more. We now know that Malone isn't going to forget his memories. They're stored on his hard drive. If they even *are* his memories.'

Now it was Vasily's turn to watch the children near the Optimists. Some of them were laughing, others crying. A few stood apart, petrified by the little sailing boats that they were about to board.

'Captain, this child has nightmares every night. He won't close his eyes because he prefers the dark night to the red screen he sees behind his eyelids. He thinks that raindrops are made of glass and are extremely sharp, that they will cut him to pieces if they touch him. And you're telling me there's no urgency?'

He had raised his voice again just as Benhami, Bourdaine and Letellier were entering the station, running up the steps, hands on the guns in their holsters.

Contradictory instincts were wrestling inside Marianne's head. She sensed that she shouldn't allow the situation to go on any longer. Not like this. And, above all, not here. In front of the station. With this man. Alone. Without even a cigarette in her hand as a pretext.

The cop stretched out her hand.

'Give me that cup. And we'll analyse the data on that MP3. If necessary, we'll ask the public prosecutor to open a preliminary investigation.'

She was silent for a moment.

'Don't worry, we'll be quick and efficient.'

Vasily Dragonman flashed a discreetly triumphant smile. As he put on his helmet, Marianne couldn't help eyeing his slim-fit jeans, his brown leather jacket and his matching eyes, which disappeared behind his visor.

Stubborn, cunning, impertinent, sure of himself and arrogant.

He was exactly her type.

Still holding the MP3, she forced herself to put her thoughts in order. Despite her promise to the psychologist, she had to consider her priorities.

Catching Timo Soler.

Replying to Papy, too. Lieutenant Pasdeloup had got it into his head to mount a further investigation into Ilona and Cyril Lukowik. Grey areas, he'd said mysteriously. He wanted to dig up a furrow that the cops from Deauville and Caen had already ploughed weeks ago, without any results. Papy was another of those men: stubborn, cunning, impertinent, sure of himself and arrogant.

But she needed him, here and now.

*

'Captain.'

Marianne looked up.

It was Dragonman. He hadn't left yet. Visor raised. Just his eyes showing, like lasers.

'I have one last question to ask you. Perhaps you could help me.'

'Yes?'

'It might seem strange to you. It's been nagging at me for weeks, and I haven't been able to come up with a satisfactory response. And yet I have the feeling that it's crucial. Maybe the key to it all, in fact.'

'Go on,' said the captain, with a sigh.

He took a photograph from his pocket.

'This is Gouti, Malone Moulin's famous cuddly toy. In your opinion, what type of animal is it supposed to be?'

And then he left the captain, standing dumbstruck outside the police station.

A moment later, he started his Guzzi California and entered the flow of traffic on Boulevard George-V. He disappeared quickly, without noticing the Ford Kuga pulling out of a parallel parking space a few seconds later and following him down the road.

## 31

Graciette Maréchal took forever to put her coins away.

Every morning, at the Vivéco minimarket, she bought her bread and a pastry – never the same one two days running – and her ninety-year-old hands trembled for an eternity as she placed each centime in her purse. This morning it was taking even longer than usual, thought Amanda, behind the till . . . Unless she was imagining it.

Nothing had changed in Manéglise over the last week. Nothing ever changed in this village, in fact. The same customers, same greetings, same newspapers, same scratchcards, same swear words, same rituals, same boredom. And yet, this morning, it was as if everything had been turned upside down.

Unless it was all in her head.

She felt as if the customers were coming to the shop just to spy on her, that the local papers were being bought just so they could find out sordid information about her, that conversations were started just to entrap her.

Was it just a feeling?

While Amanda was handing a baguette to Oscar Minotier, a labourer from Saint-Jouin-Bruneval who had been waiting behind Graciette for the last ten minutes, another customer entered and headed over to the newspaper stand. He was wearing a navy blue anorak with the collar turned up. She had never seen him before.

Amanda was suspicious of everything.

Everything happened so fast in a village of less than a thousand inhabitants. The houses, the gardens, their hedges, their lives . . . all of it was nothing more than straw, dry grass, dead branches. It took merely a spark, the flame from a match, to ignite it all. An employee at the mayor's office overhearing part of a conversation outside the school; a teacher speaking a bit too loud; a neighbour opening her door to a curious stranger. And the blaze spread, impossible to contain.

An internal, invisible fire. Rumour.

The mothers had smiled at her earlier, when she went to pick up Malone. As they did every day. As if there were nothing going on. But she wasn't fooled.

Amanda had spent time in every corner of Manéglise since she was a child; she had spent more time sitting on the bench of the bus shelter in the Place de la Mairie than she had in school. She knew the boredom that takes hold of you and doesn't let go in villages such as this, the routine, like gangrene in your dreams, those trivial things that become important because the slightest snag in normality is made to seem extraordinary. At best, a wedding, an inheritance, a journey. At worst, a dead husband, a cheating wife, a broken law.

A child who says that his mother – yes, his maman, you know her, she works behind the till at Vivéco – well, her kid, who's only three, keeps telling everyone that his mother isn't his mother.

Gangrene.

A godsend.

# 32

With the headphones over her ears, Marianne did not hear Papy come in.

Gouti had just found his promised land. Hazelnuts, acorns and pine cones buried under the sand had given birth to the most beautiful and dense of forests.

'Marianne? MARIANNE?'

The lieutenant was not giving up. Since nothing was happening in Le Havre, he insisted that she let him go.

The captain put the headphones round her neck.

'What the hell are you going to do in Potigny?'

'That's where Ilona and Cyril Lukowik are buried.'

'So?'

'It's also where they were born. Just like Timo Soler and Alexis Zerda. It's where they all grew up. Where Cyril Lukowik's parents still live now.'

'You're a pain, Papy! If the cops from Deauville or Caen find out that you've been sweeping up behind them . . .'

Pasdeloup was a pain in the arse, but he was also an excellent investigator. Imaginative rather than methodical. He begged her with his cop-on-the-verge-of-retirement-who-wants-one-last-stab-at-glory eyes; his old-footballer-sitting-on-the-bench-who-wants-to-go-on-at-the-last-minute-and-score-the-winning-goal eyes.

The captain passed him a photograph. Lieutenant Pasdeloup stared in surprise at this picture of a cuddly toy: a sort of grey and cream rat, with a pink, pointy nose, dark eyes, and worn fur.

'Here, this should keep you busy! Figure out what kind of animal it is. If you do, I'll even buy your ticket to Potigny.'

He didn't have time to negotiate or protest, because at that moment JB burst through the office door. With the drawn face and dangling arms of someone whose luck had just run out.

'We lost Zerda! Bourdaine's just called. He was following him outside the Espace Coty shopping centre. Zerda was going from shop to shop. Apparently, there were lots of people around. He lit a cigarette and, the next thing Bourdaine knew, Zerda was gone.'

'What a fuckwit!' screamed the captain, tearing the headphones from her neck.

JB attempted to calm his superior's wrath.

'Bourdaine says it was impossible to tell if Zerda shook him off deliberately or not.'

'Oh really? So he thinks Zerda didn't notice the cops following him around all the time? For goodness' sake! How long ago was this?'

'Maybe an hour ago.'

'And he's only calling now?'

'He thought he might be able to find him again.'

The captain held her head in her hands.

'Ha! He's outdone himself there! Did he think that Zerda had gone off to save him a spot on the terrace of the Lucky Store? Shit! Triple the patrols in the Neiges quarter! After all, maybe Bourdaine did us a favour. If Zerda is taking risks like that, he must be trying to get in touch with Soler. Maybe he doesn't have any choice, if his friend is suffering so badly. Alert all the doctors and pharmacies in the city!'

JB was gone the next instant. Papy stayed there a while longer, observing the strange photograph that he held in his hand: a grey and cream cuddly toy with sweet eyes that looked like an innocent creature being pursued by a police force gone mad. Then he put the photo in his pocket and followed his colleague out of the station.

\*

\* \*

In the minimarket, the guy in the navy-blue anorak was concentrating on his magazine.

**195**

*Wakou. For young nature lovers aged 4 to 7.*

Which didn't explain why he looked like a frightened teenager trying to sneak a look at the naked girls in an adult magazine. Amanda was almost amused.

The cop! Her friends had been thrilled to share their description of him. Side-parted blond hair, a long, giraffe-like neck, the slender fingers of a pianist . . . or a strangler.

A trainee cop at that. Barely out of school, by the looks of him. He'd been asking questions around Manéglise, with all the discretion of a roller-blind salesman on commission.

Amanda gave him a foul look. At worst, he would think she was just an employee doing her job. You read it – you pay for it! More likely, it would give him a scare, dissuade him from going too far, from getting too close to them.

To her. To Dimitri. But, most of all, to Malone.

Clearly, that snotty-nosed little policeman had done a good job. A good job of being a shit. Amanda's neighbours and friends had had no qualms about talking to him. Letting him into their homes. Letting him listen.

A woman standing in front of Amanda handed her the receipt for a package she had come to collect. The shop also served as a depot for mail-order items. Amanda knew that, to survive, countryside shops such as this had no choice but to sell themselves to the online commerce that would eventually end up swallowing them.

She passed the woman her parcel and asked her to sign for it. Ultimately, she didn't care about the fate of Vivéco: she wouldn't be there when the last shop in the village closed down. She glared at the young policeman again as he leafed through another magazine like a false pervert.

*Toboggan* now – for six to nine-year-olds.

*'It makes you want to be big'.*

3.53 p.m.

Carole had better not be late for her shift. Not today of all days. Amanda was determined to be on time, to be waiting outside the school gates before the others got there. To confront the pack. They could say, think, spread whatever rumours they wanted. But no one would touch Malone.

No one would take her son away from her.

*

*   *

'Captain, it's Lucas.'

Marianne Augresse parked her car outside the Hoc pharmacy.

'Is it urgent?'

'Well, I'm in Manéglise. In the bus shelter. You did ask me to report in twice a day.'

Instinctively the captain scanned the empty pavements of Rue du Hoc. She'd ordered two other police cars to survey the area around the pharmacy and five to patrol the streets of the Neiges quarter.

If Zerda so much as showed his face . . .

'Go ahead. Keep it brief. Anything new?'

'Oh yes. You were right to ask me to dig deeper on the Moulins, Captain. Behind the shiny veneer, I found unexpected . . .'

'I said keep it brief!'

'All right, well, let's just say that there are a few differences between the version given to us by the Moulin family and what I discovered from a bit of digging. Amanda Moulin, for example: it's true that she has worked at the village grocery shop for the last six years. Except that she stopped work for three years while she was on maternity leave and only started again last June.'

Marianne frantically searched in the pockets of her jacket for a notepad and a biro.

'So she kept her son at home, under wraps, all that time?'

She contorted her body on the driver's seat: the notepad was stuck inside the jacket's lining. Three hours at the gym every week and she still could barely lift up her arse when her jacket was trapped underneath it.

'Not exactly, Captain. There are loads of witnesses who've seen Malone over the years since he was born. As a baby, then as a toddler. His doctor, friends, other people in the village. The kid never

197

had a childminder though. And he was never in a crèche. Not that there is one in the village anyway.'

'So Malone never had any contact with other children until he went to school, is that right?'

'Exactly, Captain.'

'Stop calling me Captain, it just wastes time. You said "for example" before, when you told me about Amanda Moulin's maternity leave. Any other new information?'

'Yeah, well some of it seems pretty odd. You remember I told you how the neighbours had sometimes seen Malone riding around the estate on a bicycle, always wearing his helmet? There's a pond at the end of Place Ravel, with ducks that nest there in the spring. It's quite pretty, actually, er . . . Marianne. A nice place to bring up a family. Not too far from Le Havre, not too expensive and . . .'

The captain's fingers finally got hold of the biro lodged at the bottom of her pocket. If the intern had been sitting next to her, she'd happily have stabbed him with it.

'Get to the point!'

'OK, Marianne, sorry. Well, the Moulins seem to have burnt their bridges a few months ago. No more family visits or meals, which is understandable since all the members of their immediate family live several hundred kilometres from Normandy, except for Amanda's parents, who are buried in Manéglise cemetery.'

The captain sighed.

'The Moulins stopped inviting people to their home, and the few times they went to other people's houses, it was always without the kid. They also stopped visiting the doctor, Serge Lacorne. The neighbours also noticed something else that seemed a little bizarre. Last winter, they would sometimes see Malone outside – in the garden, on his bike, by the pond – with his hat covering his ears and his scarf up to his nose. But when the weather improved and the days got longer, the kid didn't seem to be around as often. Now it's true that, in estates like this, when the sun is beating down, it can be as empty as Chernobyl – everyone goes off to the beach – but still . . .'

After one last twist of her pelvis, the captain gave up trying to reach her notepad. Her thumb and index finger had just pinched hold of another object stuck at the bottom of her pocket.

'OK, Lucas, so what you're saying is that the Moulins – the mother especially – protected their child until he was two and a half with a social life that was . . . minimal. And since he turned three, it's been a complete blackout!'

'Except he's been in school since September, Marianne.'

She preferred it when he called her Captain.

'Except he's been in school . . .' repeated Marianne. Except for the nursery school, which was mandatory for every child in France in their fourth year. Not enrolling a child in the village school would have been the worst way of attracting unwanted attention.

Carefully she retrieved the object from her pocket.

'Actually, Marianne, there's something else I need to tell you and it's important.'

'Lucas, please, stop calling me Marianne. Even officers who've been at the station for thirty years don't call me that.'

'Er, well . . . I think she spotted me . . .'

'Who? Amanda Moulin?'

'Yes.'

'So? We're cops, not secret agents!'

'You think so, um, Mrs Augresse?'

She sighed again and placed the object in front of her.

'Amanda Moulin will hate you, that's for sure. She'll hate your guts for nosing around in her private life. But I seriously doubt she'd kill you for it.'

She hung up without waiting for a response and then, impatiently, looked down to get a better view of the picture of Tinker Bell and her friends flying in the sky there on Rue du Hoc.

For a long time, she gazed absently at the cup. The cup from which Malone Moulin had drunk that morning.

What if Vasily Dragonman was right?

And the simplest solution was to open an official investigation and carry out a DNA test?

# 33

*Little hand on the 8, big hand on the 10*

Malone was crying. Maman-da was sitting on the bed next to him, but he couldn't tell her why he was sad.

He couldn't tell her that Gouti had gone to sleep, maybe forever.

That his heart didn't beat any more, that his mouth didn't speak any more. That he was now just like any other cuddly toy.

He had to stop crying, though. He had to stop sniffling, pick up the handkerchief, and dry his tears. He had to because if he didn't, Maman-da would never leave. She'd stay there, hugging him, telling him that she loved him, that he was her darling, her sweetheart, her big boy. She'd stay there until he calmed down.

And he didn't want her to do that.

He wanted to be alone with Gouti.

Tonight, since his toy couldn't speak to him, it would be his turn to tell a story. His story. Through his wet eyes, he saw the little rocket sitting on the caramel planet. The biggest of them all.

It was the day of Jupiter. The day of strength. The day of courage.

Maman-da didn't leave. She stayed there, a warm presence next to him. He could feel her breathe, almost as if she had fallen asleep. But no: from time to time, she would caress him or say 'shhhh' almost without moving her lips. Sometimes she kissed his neck and told him that it was late, that he should fly off to the land of dreams.

Malone understood. He realised that, tonight, Maman-da would stay in his bedroom until he fell asleep.

So he, too, started talking without moving his lips. He started talking in his head. Maybe Gouti could hear him, when he spoke in his head.

He knew the story of Jupiter by heart.

It was the most important one: Maman had told him that many times. This was the one that – when the right moment came – he absolutely had to remember.

When the moment came to fly away. Not to the land of dreams, as Maman-da wanted.

When the moment came to fly away to the forest of ogres.

And when that moment came, Malone would have to be braver than he'd ever been in his life. There was only one way to escape the monsters, not to be taken into their lair. Afterwards, it would be too late: you can't jump out of a plane. To escape them, there was only one way, Maman had told him, one place where they would never be able to find him.

And Maman had made him promise to think about it every night in his head. To repeat the words, to recite them to Gouti, but never to repeat them to anyone else.

EVERY NIGHT.

To think about that hiding place, again and again, always.

The most secret hiding place of all. And yet the simplest in the world.

# 34

*Today, at the petrol station, I got up the nerve to tell my family that I didn't even have enough money to fill up the car. Given that we were about to go off on our holidays, it didn't go down well.*
Want to kill
*With my 20 euros, I was able to pump 11.78 litres all over the ground. Then I dropped my cigarette.*

*Convicted: 176*
*Acquitted: 324*

www.want-to-kill.com

The lighthouse on the Cap de la Hève illuminated the cliff precisely every twelve seconds.

Vasily had counted each second in his head. He had a powerful torch, strong enough to light up the viewing area and to roam over the chalky grassed area at the top of the cliff, but not strong enough to illuminate the foreshore below or the ink-black sea.

Twelve seconds.

Vasily aimed his torch at the Guzzi he'd parked between two white benches, on the edge of the empty car park. An icy wind took his breath away. Not violent enough to knock over the motorbike, which stood on its kickstand, but too strong to allow him to check his map one more time. Instead he just visualised the circles of colour in his head, the lines and arrows, all the slow and patient work he'd done cross-checking clues.

He'd bought a new map earlier that afternoon, copied out the results of his previous theories, then spent a good part of the day listening to Gouti's stories, over and over again, through headphones, holding felt-tip pens, often pausing the stories and rewinding them, going back over the differences, the evidence, in order to isolate the place that best matched the majority of Malone's memories. The smallest common denominator, Vasily thought, moving through the dark junipers.

This place. Here.

In this jungle of brambles that clawed at the sleeves of his leather jacket – an almost brand-new Bering. Probably ruined already.

*What the hell was he doing here?*

The image of the death threat flashed in his mind – the tomb on the cliff – as frequently and regularly as the blinding glare of the lighthouse.

He walked slowly and carefully. His torch only had a reach of about three metres and the grass was slippery. He had no desire to have to grab hold of the thorny branches to stop himself falling.

He tried to push away the reasonable voices whispering to him that he should turn back, get on his bike and speed back towards the lights of the city. It helped to think about Malone.

Malone, feeling lost on the step outside his classroom, terrified, shivering, incapable of walking through the slightest drizzle, of being touched by the last few drops of a rain shower.

Vasily had promised himself he would take a look, check it out. If his intuition proved correct, if all the elements were in place, he would not come back, not even in broad daylight. He would simply call Marianne Augresse, and the accumulated weight of the evidence would oblige her to come, to get involved.

The torch beam flickered over the bushes. Through the tangle of branches, he found it hard to tell where the plateau ended and the abyss began. For an instant, he imagined that if he fell here, stupidly, in this inaccessible part of the coastline, no one would find him for days. Not until his corpse had been carried away by the ocean currents and washed up somewhere along the estuary, on a beach, against one of the quays of the port, embalmed in salt and oil and mummified in plastic bags.

This time, it was the image of Angie that helped him to push back these morbid thoughts. The desire to send her a text. To reassure her. To reassure himself. As soon as he got home, she was supposed to join him at the apartment in the Résidence de France. He wouldn't be gone long, he'd told her. Just five kilometres each way on his bike.

The whooshing sound made by the departing message broke the silence. Vasily checked the time.

10.20 p.m.

The seagulls were asleep. The sea seemed to whisper.

Twelve seconds.

The great beam of light crossed the undergrowth, dazzled Vasily, then continued on its way north, briefly lighting up the beach at low tide.

Four towers. In a line.

Malone's castle!

Vasily's heart sped up. He'd been right.

The light continued circling. It was coming back to him already. The psychologist narrowed his eyes, concentrated, staring at the sea, which sparkled gold as in a brief, intermittent sunset.

The pirate ship.

Black.

Cut in two.

Vasily tried to control his excitement.

The next flash would light up the strange houses and then, behind them, the bare wall.

Shadows? Ogres?

Was it possible to live there?

Could Malone really have lived there?

Wasn't he following a trail of clues that had been deliberately left for him, using a child's brain, like some soft version of the Rosetta stone?

He stayed there for a while, attempting to measure exact distances, to calculate the number of kilometres separating this spot from the airport, from Mont-Gaillard, from Manéglise. He realised that locating this place would not make much difference without the support of the police. Without a letter rogatory to search, one by one, these huts from beyond the grave. Maybe the ghost of Malone's mother would still be there, and with it the secret of his birth?

He waited a good fifteen minutes before heading back to his motorbike. In the end, he found a clearer path that enabled him to avoid the brambles. His torch illuminated a circle of ashes littered with three cans of beer and a dozen fag ends. A few other traces of life, clandestine and ephemeral.

He was close to the car park, which was half-concealed behind the last line of junipers, when he heard a message arrive on his phone.

*Angie.*

Seven words, full of mistakes.

*Be carful. Im wating 4 u. Kiss*

Vasily felt an inner warmth enveloping him, like a sweet energy driving a silent engine, a wonder of technology that accelerated his heart, his footsteps, his desire to reach Boulevard Clemenceau as quickly as possible, to be wrapped in Angie's arms once more.

Falling in love with a hairdresser . . . And yet that was what was happening to him.

His eyes lingered for a moment on the photograph of Angie displayed on the screen of his mobile phone.

He smiled as he kept walking.

Sea fennel and sea kale crunched under his boots.

His smile froze.

His thumb pressed against the phone to make Angie vanish into darkness.

The Guzzi was lying on the ground.

Like a dead animal left there on the tarmac: that was the first image that popped into Vasily's mind. He rushed over. The wind gusted against his back, making his jacket swell, but it wasn't strong enough to have knocked over a three-hundred-kilogram motorbike.

Dim light from a street lamp, a hundred metres away, vaguely illuminated the scene. Vasily bent over the Guzzi, assessing the damage. Theories flooded through his brain.

Was it an accident? A threat? Some guy who had deliberately run his car into the bike? No, Vasily would have heard the noise. And there would be traces of the impact. A man, then? Who'd come alone, silently? But why?

Vasily looked again at the bike's chrome bodywork. There was no smell of petrol. No dents. The bike did not seem any more scratched by the tarmac than his jacket had been by the brambles.

He breathed slowly, giving his heart time to go back to its normal rhythm. He probably just hadn't set the kickstand properly, hadn't paid attention to the slope of the ground. Because of his fear, because he was rushing. Idiot! He wasn't made for this kind of adventure. He should pass the baton on to the police as soon as he could, he thought. Then join Angie.

Love her.

Give her a child.

That was the last image that came to his mind. The child had no face.

And then there was darkness.

The smell. The pain.

Vasily had no idea how long he'd been unconscious.

A few minutes? More than an hour?

The pain was searing, from his cervical vertebrae all the way down to his lower back, but it was nothing compared to the terrible weight that was crushing his legs. Three hundred kilograms. Grinding his knees and tibias in a vice of chrome and metal. Vasily had tried, in vain. It was impossible to move the Guzzi.

Caught in a trap. His helmet had rolled onto the car park, a few metres away.

Vasily put his hands flat against the handlebars and pushed

again. All he had to do was move the bike a few centimetres and he'd be able to slide out. And the pain would be less intense, at least, while he waited for someone to rescue him.

He took a deep breath.

The smell of petrol was inhaled deep into his lungs. Like an invisible acid cloud burning everything in its path. Throat. Windpipe. Thoracic cage.

He coughed. That was another reason he had to get out. He was lying in a pool of petrol. Most of the thirty litres from his tank, probably. He'd filled the bike up at the 24-hour petrol station in Mont-Gaillard before he came here.

He closed his eyes and slowly counted to twenty, taking the time to relax his muscles – biceps, triceps and deltoids – before tensing them again and pushing the Guzzi with all the strength he had left.

He would repeat this sequence until he was completely exhausted. Until dawn if necessary.

He couldn't just lie there, like a pinned butterfly.

He inhaled deeply, despite the stench of the petrol, then held his breath.

Opened his eyes.

Push . . .


At first Vasily thought it was a star, or the red lights of a plane against the black sky, or some strange luminescent insect.

It took him some time to understand, because he couldn't see anything other than that light.

His nostrils quivered first. Because of the smoke. And maybe because they scented danger.

It wasn't a star, or a bug, or a beacon on a plane or a rocket.

Just the glowing red end of a cigarette. In the mouth of an almost invisible man, standing a few metres away from him.

# 35

*Today, I am 39. No kids.*
`Want to kill ME`
*To bite into a poisoned apple, to lie in a glass coffin, and wait.*

*Convicted: 7*
*Acquitted: 539*

`www.want-to-kill.com`

*Be carful. Im wating 4 u. Kiss*

Angie reread the message she'd written on her phone, which was resting on her knees, then lay trapped between her thighs. The glass screen, sliding against the nylon tights under her skirt, made her shiver slightly.

In front of her, Marianne was still talking.

They were in Uno. Her calzone, which she'd barely touched, looked like a volcano that had stopped erupting and gone cold thousands of years before. The waiter kept coming over to their table. As if he might end up sitting next to them and spoon-feeding the captain.

It was late. Nearly midnight.

Angie wanted to leave, to go home, back to her lover's arms.

But she couldn't tell Marianne that.

She couldn't talk to Marianne about men tonight. Especially not hers.

It was almost as risky as talking about herself. She hadn't touched

208

a drop of alcohol tonight; she'd said too much the last time. She had almost finished the bottle of Rioja on her own.

Angie listened automatically, the words entering her ears without making much sense; as if Marianne were speaking a foreign language that she barely understood; just a few words, like buoys, strung to the line of the conversation.

*Vasily.*

That made sense. Angie immediately concentrated.

'You're going to think I'm an idiot, but I saw Vasily Dragonman again. We chatted outside the station, with all my men running past, and him on his bike. He lectures like a pro, but he looks like an angel . . . as if Dennis Hopper had read every book by Françoise Dolto!'[2]

Angie had no choice but to pour herself a glass of wine. Just one. She rolled her eyes: half-surprised, half-scandalised. She was used to simulating amazement at her customers' most banal revelations. Hairdressers are the world's best actors.

A life spent in front of a mirror.

'That shrink of yours? You're dreaming, Marianne. He's ten years younger than you. Anyway, a shrink and a cop falling in love as they investigate a case together . . . it's a bit like some crappy TV thriller, don't you think?'

Marianne stuck out her tongue. Her eyes lingered on the waiter's bum as he cleared a nearby table. Angie grimaced at her, drawing it out a bit too long.

She wondered how Marianne would react if she found out that her best friend was the lover of the man she was fantasising about . . . Would she laugh? Make a toast to handsome, young lovers? Or would it be a blow to her morale – yet another one – which the captain would simply accept in silence? Either that or she'd slap Angie in the face.

Angie had got herself into so much trouble by suggesting that Vasily call the captain. She needed to change the subject.

'Why don't you tell me about your colleague instead?'

---

[2] French psychoanalyst and paediatrician

'JB? What do you want to know?'

'Everything!'

She forced herself to laugh, throwing her head back. The waiter returned, his gaze sliding down Angie's neck and clinging to the bright pendant she wore around her neck, as if attempting to stop himself falling further into the shadows of her blouse.

Marianne stared up at the heavens.

'Well, darling, Lieutenant Lechevalier is still just as married as he ever was, still just as devoted to his kids, and still as sexy as ever in his tight jeans.'

'All good, then. You just have to wait until it's your time. Love is simply a question of patience, Marianne. You have to be there at the right moment, that's all.' She took a sip of her red wine before continuing: 'That's what my father always told me. He was bald at seventeen, was only one metre sixty tall, and his chest was so hairy he had to wear his shirts buttoned all the way up to his neck. And yet he hit the jackpot: the most beautiful girl in his class, an Andalusian all the other boys were in love with. He always said that he just stayed close, faithful, stubborn, attentive, like a fan who's so desperate to be in the front row that he's willing to sleep in front of the stadium for two days before his idol's show. For a whole year, while the others came and went, my father held a candle for her – or an umbrella, or a box of tissues, whatever was needed. But he was there. Twelve months of hell so he could be happy for the rest of his life. He said it was the same for my baccalaureate, a lot of hard work but with long-term benefits.'

'And the Andalusian is your mother?'

'Yeah.'

'Wow. So you're a child born of love, then?'

Angie held the glass to her lips again, holding it with both hands and hoping that it would cover up the tears that had sprung to her eyes.

Facing the mirror at the hairdresser's, she was usually better at this.

Happy for the rest of his life, she repeated in her head. Yes, deep down, her father had been. He'd worked shifts in Mondeville, at the

Normandy Metallurgy Company. Her mother had worked shifts too. At home. She organised her lovers' visits to coincide with her husband's schedule at the factory. One each night, one each day, one on Sundays. All of them very polite with little Angélique, the silent angel who played in her room while Maman worked in hers with the gentlemen.

'A child of love,' whispered Angie. 'That's it exactly.'

The tram setting off from the Hotel-de-Ville station made her think of the Caen–Paris train she had taken on the morning of her sixteenth birthday, after one last night spent in her house on Impasse Copernic, after one last kiss on her father's forehead, before the cancer caused by asbestos carried him away six months later.

A child of love.

The expression was almost comical.

Angie thought back to her adolescence. The dark years before she met the man of her life. A child born of love who'd wanted to kill the whole world.

'So, basically, you're advising me to wait?'

Marianne sat with her glass in the air, looking at her friend questioningly. Angie cleared her throat.

'Patience and obstinacy, my dear. It's your only hope!'

'You cow!' replied the captain. 'I've told you about my countdown hundreds of times: I've got eighteen months, twenty-four at most, before I need a man to plant his seed in my belly and watch it grow with me!'

They both burst into laughter. Angie's wasn't really even forced this time. She couldn't help liking this bossy old policewoman. Marianne was like her: a goat trapped amongst a pack of hounds, tied to its post, with just its horns and its hooves to help it survive. A witch's outfit worn over the dress of a princess. The proof being that the captain had barely even talked about her investigation tonight. She'd only mentioned it briefly over aperitifs, when the waiter brought them a kir and a grapefruit juice: Timo Soler untraceable, Alexis Zerda on the run, Malone Moulin's crazy stories.

The waiter was busy erasing the day's menu from the slate.

When he'd finished, he tidied it away at the back of the restaurant. Marianne appeared to get the message and finally stopped talking so she could attack her cold calzone.

She'd just picked up her fork when her telephone rang.

'Marianne, it's JB!'

Like an excited teenager, Captain Augresse pressed the loud-speaker button while waving her hand at Angie. She pointed at the photograph filling the screen.

JB wearing a tie, stripes on his shoulders, hat down to his eye-brows, posing proudly on the stage at the thirteenth Territorial Police Congress. Sexier than anything she'd seen since Richard Gere in *An Officer and a Gentleman*.

'Speak of the devil,' whispered Angie, giving Marianne the thumbs-up.

'Marianne, are you there?' asked JB.

The two women silently touched their glasses together.

'Marianne?'

'Yep, JB. Have you fallen out of the conjugal bed?'

'No, I'm on call. There's a bonfire, on Cap de la Hève.'

Captain Augresse managed to make her voice sound more serious.

'Teenagers fooling around?'

'No. Looks more like a traffic accident. Some guy crashed.'

'Shit. Do you have any details?'

'Not many. We only found out a while after it happened. The nearest inhabited building is two kilometres from the spot. By the time we got there . . . well, I'd hardly be exaggerating if I said that all we found was a pile of ashes.'

'Christ. Just one fatality, then? You're sure?'

'Yeah. But identification is going to be a pain. The only clue we have is the guy's bike. A Guzzi California.'

The earth collapsed beneath Marianne's feet. At the same moment, the glass of Rioja fell from the captain's hand, while Angie's smashed between her fingers.

The white cotton tablecloth was covered with purple stains that grew larger and larger, as the wine from Marianne's glass mixed with the drops of blood dripping from Angie's thumb and index finger. The stains spread until they joined together, creating the illusion of a monochromatic Rorschach test, the kind used by psychologists to give shape to the ghosts of the unconscious.

# FRIDAY

The day of love

# 36

*Little hand on the 8, big hand on the 6*

The school gates had just been opened. Ordinarily, Clotilde would stand to one side for a few minutes and say hello to each child by name, with a smile for the parents.

A pleasant welcome to keep the families in her pocket.

For at least three generations. If Clotilde remained in Manéglise for a few decades, she would probably have to look after the children of these children.

This morning, though, Clotilde remained a few metres back, near the small vegetable garden, in deep discussion with a man. Not a father, not even a substitute teacher, and certainly not an inspector sent by the authorities . . . the man didn't look the type.

Her ex-boyfriend, perhaps? Clotilde was cute, and the man, though older, was undoubtedly charming with his stubble, his classy leather jacket, his fitted jeans.

In truth – and this is what the mothers who secretly looked at the stranger thought – the man looked like a policeman. Or, at least, the kind of policeman you always saw on television, played by one of those famous actors with a handsome face, a strong jaw, and bulging pectorals.

The mothers decided to hang around a bit longer than usual.

Though not as long as Amanda Moulin, who had not yet gone through the open gate. While the other children let go of their parents' hands and ran to their classroom doors, Malone stood still. He was wearing a dark blue duffle coat, mittens, a mismatched woollen hat, and was clutching Gouti to his chest. He scanned the playground, the classroom windows, the mothers on their way out, the few cars parked outside the school. There was no motorbike.

'I want to see Vasily!'

Amanda pulled Malone's hand and whispered to him.

'You saw him yesterday, sweetie. He's in another school today.'

'I want to see Vasily!'

Malone spoke louder the second time. He could feel his heart beating hard against his hand – the one that was pressing Gouti to his chest. He felt flattened. Empty.

Vasily had promised. Vasily had said that he would be here. That he would return Gouti's heart.

He was going to come. Malone would hear the sound of his motorbike. He just had to stay here and wait.

'Come on, Malone!'

Maman-da was hurting him, pulling his arm like that. Once, he had pulled the arm of a cuddly toy – not Gouti, an old teddy bear – and the arm had come away in his hand, with some threads hanging from it.

'I want to see Vasily. *He promised.*'

Malone had shouted this time, so loud that Clotilde had turned around. The man who was talking to her did the same. Instinctively, Amanda took a step back, trapping Malone behind the sign displaying the menu for the week. The other parents, walking past them, did not look too surprised by the yell of a kid who was obviously refusing to enter the classroom.

Just as any other mother would have done, Amanda raised her voice.

'All the other children are already in school, Malone! Please, hurry up.'

A few mothers were hanging around still, the usual suspects: Valérie Courtoise and Nathalie Delaplanque, who nodded in agreement with Amanda's harsh tone. As if encouraged, Amanda pulled even harder on Malone's hand, tightening her grip on his blue mitten.

She'd drag him there, if she had to.

Malone knew the charade. So did Gouti. He let himself slide as if someone had stolen his heart. He did his rag-doll act.

Suddenly the boy seemed unable to hold himself upright and he collapsed onto the tarmac. Amanda had nothing more in her hands than a limp piece of rubber.

'Malone, get up!'

Géraldine Valette, Lola's mother, had joined her two friends. They were no longer even pretending to chat to each other or to check out the man near the vegetable garden; they were silent, watching Amanda and Malone.

What choice did they have, anyway?

If they'd seemed indifferent, it would have been a blatant lack of solidarity for their fellow mother, and if they'd got involved that would have been even more upsetting for poor Amanda. After all, every woman knows that, once she becomes a mother, she will one day have her fifteen minutes of public humiliation. An impolite remark, the child peeing their pants, a hysterical tantrum . . .

Amanda shouted what any other mother would have shouted:

'Malone, get up, you're making your mother ashamed!'

She didn't dare literally to drag her son across the playground, for fear of hurting him. He stayed where he was, lying on the tarmac. Now there were eight or nine mothers standing in sympathy outside the gates.

'Malone, this is the last time I'll tell you. Get up, or Maman will . . .'

Suddenly, the boy yanked hard. Amanda's hand was left grasping a blue mitten while Malone got to his feet and ran between the cars, screaming as if he wanted the whole village to hear:

'You're not my Maman!'

# 37

Marianne Augresse was shivering.

She had been standing for nearly two hours at the viewpoint on Cap de la Hève.

She was facing out to sea, where the wind blew in from across five thousand kilometres of flat water before rushing up the Seine estuary.

At her feet, ashes. Already cold.

And the things that hadn't been burnt completely. The captain made a mental list. One Guzzi California without tyres, without rubber on the handlebars, without a seat: just a shapeless carcass whose only distinguishing feature was the symbol, a silver eagle with its wings outspread.

One helmet, black and oval, probably deformed by the heat from the flames, like the hollow skull of an extraterrestrial monster with a disproportionally large brain.

A body, burnt to a cinder, with the exception of a pair of glasses, a set of keys, a melted torch and mobile phone, a watch, and the buckle of a belt. As if the journey to heaven meant you had to go through a security check and leave behind anything vaguely metallic.

Mariane Augresse had no doubt about the identity of the corpse. *Vasily Dragonman.*

Around her, a dozen cops were busy bagging evidence. The first DNA results would be available in a few hours, and with them clear proof, certainty, the definitive end of her dreams.

In the meantime, to rid herself of the emotion that threatened to overwhelm her, the captain focused on her work, imagining hypotheses, posing objective questions.

*Why would someone want to murder this school psychologist?*

Because this was not an accident; the crime scene left no doubt about that. The police had found no trace of any collision or skid marks. Besides, Constantini, an officer who owned a Yamaha VMAX – a model that was fairly similar to the Guzzi – had noted immediately that the fuel in the bike's tank would not have been sufficient to feed a fire of that size and ferocity, at least not without an explosion. Someone had deliberately poured extra fuel on the ground here.

There was still the possibility of suicide by self-immolation. That was what Judge Dumas had instantly suggested when Marianne called her a few minutes earlier. Throat tight, the captain had replied that she didn't think so, without adding anything else, without giving any details of the images that flashed past her eyes: the rebellious look on Vasily's face; his childlike excitement at the beach hut, kneeling over his treasure map; the calculated pauses in his skilled oration; his calm determination; his timid self-assurance . . .

The captain walked over to the barrier surrounding the viewpoint. She could see the lighthouse, the sea stretching out into infinity. Nothing else: trees blocked her view of the beach at the foot of the cliff. To see that, she'd have had to push through this jungle of junipers, get close to the edge . . .

'Phone call for you, Captain.'

Officer Bourdaine stood ten metres behind his superior. Lost in her thoughts, she did not appear to have heard him.

Why had Vasily Dragonman come to the Cap de la Hève? In the middle of the night. With a torch. Did this fatal expedition have any connection with Malone Moulin's revelations?

In her pocket, Marianne's fist closed around the MP3 that the school psychologist had given her the day before. He was supposed to come by the station that morning, early, so he could give it back to the kid. He'd promised him.

Was that why he was murdered? For these seven stories, one for each night of the week?

Of course, she too had taken the time to listen to them. But all she had heard were seven fairy tales, gently moralistic, quietly

221

amusing, slightly scary, the kind of stories that are told to millions of children every night all over the planet.

What was the secret they were hiding? A secret so terrible that it had to be concealed inside a cuddly toy? A secret that a child was forced to learn by heart, like a prayer? A secret that someone was willing to commit murder for in order to protect it?

'Captain! Phone call for you,' Bourdaine repeated.

# 38

*Little hand on the 8, big hand on the 8*

There were eight hundred and fifty metres between the Manéglise school and Place Maurice-Ravel, in the centre of the Hauts de Manéglise housing estate.

Eight hundred and fifty metres across which she had to carry Malone home single-handedly.

He remained still in her arms for the first two hundred metres, then he became more agitated, kicking and punching Amanda in the chest and back, until she stopped, put him down, and yelled at him. She yelled very loud, too loud, and he collapsed in tears. Then she had to hoist the child over her shoulder again, calm and trembling now.

Eight hundred and fifty metres, and a bystander would have thought the Tour de France was about to go through the village.

Amanda had the impression that every single inhabitant had decided – on the same day and at the exact same time – to swarm out onto the pavements: the drinkers from the Carreau Pique bar, smoking their cigarettes outside; the Vivéco's customers – child-minders, mothers, people off work and people without work – who'd all chosen to do their shopping that morning; the park-maintenance boys, who'd been repotting petunias on the Route d'Epouville roundabout since the crack of dawn; the old women on the bench on the Route du Calvaire, who looked as if they'd been there all night.

Amanda didn't care. Screw them. Screw them all, the inhabitants of this village of the living dead, this open-air hospice. She'd hated them all ever since she was sixteen. Just like she hated the mothers who'd surrounded her outside the school, looking so pleased, so thrilled, to see a mother who was worse off than them, relieved to see misfortune falling on someone else, allowing them to reassure themselves in the light of Malone's hysteria.

*Did you hear the way he talked to her?*

*'You're not my mother.'*

*I swear, if my child said that to me . . .*

Screw those chattering magpies and screw the vultures at the mayor's office and the parrots in the streets. She'd grabbed hold of Malone and turned back towards home because she'd realised that the man talking with the headmistress was a cop. And not just any cop.

The rumours had been circulating outside the school, even before Malone had his tantrum. Rumours are good that way, like the morning news: informing you, and everyone else, of the latest catastrophe about to strike you down.

The cop was there because a corpse had been found at Cap de la Hève. And everything suggested that the corpse was that of the school psychologist who came to Manéglise every Thursday to talk to certain kids.

Amanda turned onto Rue Debussy.

The estate's cul-de-sacs formed a labyrinth of deserted streets where she would, at last, be left in peace. Everyone worked, leaving their houses early, getting back late, and going off for the weekend. The people who lived here were not really inhabitants, in fact; they were more like permanent guests at a hotel where all they did was sleep, a hotel that they'd had to buy with thirty years of debt, a hotel where they had to clean everything themselves, look after the garden, make breakfast, change their own sheets and unblock their own toilets.

Malone was sobbing quietly now, and clinging to her neck. He didn't feel as heavy in this position. Amanda even liked the coolness of his tears running down the back of her neck, the feel of his cuddly toy's fur against her skin, the rhythm of Malone's heartbeat echoing hers.

She'd be home in less than five minutes.

Safe and sound.

Or apparently so. Inside her head, her thoughts were flying all over the place.

What should she do next?

Stay alone in the house? As if nothing was happening.

Dimitri would return at noon, as he did every day.

Should she talk to him? Make a decision together. The right decision. If there was one . . .

Dogs barked, invisible behind hedges. Little dogs pretending to be watchdogs, probably. As if every inhabitant of this maze had bought their own personal Minotaur. Each villager barricaded inside his own home, tuned to Radio Village. The people of Manéglise talked to their neighbours. News of Vasily Dragonman's death would have spread across the village at the speed of a postman or a baker's van. A journalist had already posted an article about it on *grand-havre.com*, along with a photograph of a circle of ashes on Cap de la Hève and punctuated by an army of question marks in only three sentences. They knew *Who*, they knew *Where*. But they still had to find out *Why* and *By whom*.

Malone breathed softly against her chest, his body as limp as his toy's. Asleep, maybe. Amanda turned onto Rue Chopin. Their house was at the end of the cul-de-sac, seventy metres away. She cut straight through the empty car park, without changing direction or slowing down, without turning her face to the window of Dévote Dumontel's house opposite. The high-pitched yapping of another dog, somewhere behind her, sounding like an alarm.

Vasily Dragonman. Burnt to death. Good news, obviously.

Alive, he was a danger to them.

But now he was dead, wasn't the threat even worse?

# 39

Officer Bourdaine, standing like a maritime pine, his body twisted as though he'd been struggling against the wind in this position for the past century, didn't dare shout. Despite the urgency.

'Captain! Phone call for you!'

Marianne Augresse still had her back to him. Only her neck moved, slowly. Facing the Cap de la Héve, the captain observed every detail of the panorama that opened around her with the precision of a lighthouse beam.

*Vasily Dragonman had not come here by chance.*

She was going to ask the forensics team to go over the area with a fine-tooth comb. They'd complain, but who cared? Obviously, the psychologist had been looking for something.

She tried to unfold Vasily's map in her memory, but was incapable of recalling the places he'd mentioned, the lines he'd drawn, the circles and the colours. On the other hand, she remembered every one of his final words:

'I've made some progress on the list of possible locations. It should only take me a few hours to visit the spots that could correspond to the place where Malone used to live, before.'

They had had to start the investigation over again, from scratch. Using Vasily's notes, Malone's testimony, Gouti's stories. Marianne had also sent JB to the school in Manéglise to talk with the headmistress. He'd scowled a bit – he'd been up all night in the freezing cold – but the captain hadn't given him any choice in the matter. It was a detour of barely ten kilometres.

'Captain?'

Finally Marianne turned around.

Bourdaine stammered. 'A . . . a phone call for you. It's urgent.'

226

It was Papy. He was yelling into the phone.

'Marianne? For Christ's sake, what are you doing? Larochelle's called!'

'Larochelle, the surgeon?'

'Yes! Timo Soler has just contacted him. He said he's losing consciousness, that his wound's reopened, that he can't move. He's arranged to meet him.'

'Fuck. Where?'

'Get this. At home! Well, in his hiding place, I mean. Rue de la Belle-Etoile, in the middle of the Neiges quarter.'

Marianne closed her eyes for a moment, offering her face to the sea as if its spray might cover her face with a thousand salty drops. But there was nothing. Nothing but a cold, dry wind, blowing away the ashes of a man she might one day have loved.

'Let's do it, Papy. Let's go. Round up five vehicles and ten officers.'

# 40

*Little hand on the 11, big hand on the 10*

On Malone's bed, they were all dead. A dozen ants, a black beetle with red dots, three ladybirds and another insect – bigger, this one, but he didn't know its name. He'd picked them up in the hallway, while Maman-da was hanging up his coat, and had hidden them in his pocket. Maman-da hadn't swept up properly yesterday. Now, the creatures were lying on his Buzz Lightyear duvet, neatly lined up, like monsters from outer space floating between the stars.

Dead.

Like Gouti.

His toy was leaning against the pillow, eyes open. He looked as if he was just resting.

But he would never speak again. Vasily had lied to him. Maman-da had lied to him. Everyone had lied to him. Adults couldn't be trusted. Except Maman.

He turned to look at the calendar. He counted the planets.

One, two, three, four, five . . .

The moon, Mars, Mercury, Jupiter, Venus . . .

Today.

The day of love.

Tonight, once again, since Gouti couldn't speak, it was Malone who would tell the story. Very quietly, hidden under the duvet. He didn't mind. He knew the story by heart. He knew them all by heart.

Malone realised he had stopped crying. He hadn't even noticed. Anyway, there was no point crying when the grown-ups weren't there to see you.

Maman-da was downstairs in the kitchen. He was alone in his room. He turned to Gouti and an idea came to him: after all, today, he could tell the story whenever he wanted! He could choose. There was no longer any need to wait for night-time.

On the calendar, the rocket was on the green planet, but that wasn't his favourite. He preferred the ones where there was more fighting, where you had to be brave, to battle ogres, monsters, protect Maman.

His eyes flicked down to the bed, to the tiny ants, the ladybirds that looked like hardened sweets, the beetle with two legs missing.

An army of the stars only fit for the rubbish bin.

He moved closer to Gouti, put his mouth next to the toy's little pink ear, and began to whisper. He wanted to tell him his favourite story, the one that scared him most of all. The one about the chief of the ogres, the ogre with the shiny earring and the tattoo of a skull-and-crossbones on his neck. It was easy to recognise the chief of the ogres, but it was much harder to escape from him.

'Listen, Gouti. In the forest, there was an ogre who . . .'

He stopped. His mouth wanted to keep talking, but this time it was his nose that prevented him. He was disturbed by a smell that made him think of something other than the story, and ogres, and Maman.

The smell was coming from the kitchen, and it replaced everything else in his head. Now it was all he could think about. How good it smelt. How hungry he was. How he wanted to go downstairs, give Maman-da a hug and steal a piece.

He stared at Gouti as if seeking forgiveness. The toy still didn't reply. Gouti was often a bit annoying in that way, but even more so now that he was dead and didn't have a heart.

What did it mean, if Gouti didn't say anything?

That he was allowed to go down and eat a slice of cake with Maman-da, or that he had to stay in his room and finish telling Maman's story?

# 41

*The mechanic lying under the car had promised me that my Twingo would be repaired by this evening. It wasn't. He seemed so genuinely sorry, the idiot. Want to kill*
*I pulled out the jack.*

*Convicted: 1,263*
*Acquitted: 329*

www.want-to-kill.com

Officer Cabral was driving like a madman. Marianne had put on her seat belt this time. Cabral had refused to start the engine until she did, staring at her still-slightly-twisted nose, the scabs barely concealed by a layer of foundation. He hadn't needed to say another word.

'All right, I'll put it on. But hurry up!'

The river of cars opened up for them all along Avenue Foch. Marianne liked that about Le Havre: the American-style grid layout of the city centre, its wide perpendicular streets, even if the comparison only really applied during their rare car chases, when they would play Starsky and Hutch between Rue Racine and Rue Richelieu, siren screaming.

The volume of the GPS was turned up as high as it would go.

She had to press the phone against her ear to understand the few words said amid this racket. The captain almost didn't pick up.

*Angie.*

'Marianne? I saw an article on *grand-havre.com*. The headline was 'Motorcyclist burnt on Cap de la Hève.'

Angie was silent for a moment. She sounded out of breath.

'The article said the victim was a school psychologist. My God, was it Vasily, Marianne?'

Without slowing down, the car cut across the grassy avenue reserved for trams. A few schoolchildren waiting at the stop stared wide-eyed, the quickest of them aiming mobile phones at the speeding police car.

Angie must have been fretting about her. This was not the moment for a friendly chat, but Marianne understood her friend's concern: after all, she'd spent half the night praising the charms of that man . . . while he was being burnt to a cinder less than five kilometres away.

The horror of it! Even if the adrenaline pumping through her veins momentarily anaesthetised her emotions.

But she needed to concentrate on her mission.

*Catch Timo Soler.*

'Do you have any more news?' Angie asked, after a period of silence. 'Are you sure that . . . that it's him?'

'Not yet. It's good of you to worry, Angie, but I can't speak right now.'

Cabral slammed on the brakes on Rue Brindeau. There was no way he could cross the tramline this time: an 'A' from Mont-Gaillard was passing a 'B' coming back from the beach. Ahead of them, at the end of Rue de Paris, a grey container ship, as high as a five-storey building, offered the illusion that one of the quarter's concrete apartment blocks had decided to leave the city.

Angie wasn't giving up.

Marianne put her palm over her right ear so she could hear her friend's words.

'As soon as you have any news, will you call me?'

Her voice was trembling. For an instant, Marianne had the strange impression that it was Angélique, not her, who had fallen in love with the psychologist.

Or his ghost.

Officer Cabral sped down Rue Siegfried, heading towards the port.

'In five hundred metres,' the female voice of the GPS announced, as loud as a gospel singer, 'cross the Pont V, then turn left. Your destination is in front of you.'

Marianne had to hang up. She had to guide Cabral once they got to the Neiges quarter. The last thing they needed was to make so much noise that Timo Soler knew they were coming.

They would be there as soon as they crossed the bridge.

She had to forget Angie. Forget the shrink. Concentrate on this arrest.

'I'll call you tonight, dearest. I have to hang up.'

# 42

*Little hand on the 12, big hand on the 2*

Amanda had just put the last plate on the table when she heard the front door open.

Just in time.

Table set. TV on. Bottle of Faugères on the table. She opened the oven door so that the smell of the Carambar cake would cover up the odour of the beef in the frying pan. Malone loved to smell his favourite cake slowly baking.

Malone was sensitive, gentle, intelligent, intuitive. Amanda had realised long ago that a keen sense of smell was a sign of sensitivity in a boy. The most important sense, along with touch, whereas most men were content with sight and taste.

While little Malone was incapable of eating an entire Carambar, he loved the taste of them, liked to suck them until they stuck to his fingers, chew on them a little bit, and best of all empty a whole packet into a saucepan with butter and sugar so they would melt. When he wasn't sulking, as he was today.

Before Dimitri came into the kitchen, Amanda turned the beef. It was already a bit too late for that: the meat was slightly over-cooked. Dimitri's culinary advice would constitute the majority of their table talk during their meal, along with a few enlightened remarks about the current state of the world, as seen from his house.

She was surprised by her husband's smiling face. He didn't go so far as to kiss her, but he did put a hand under her apron, which was tied at the waist.

'Did you hear? It's all everyone's talking about in the village. That fucking shrink went up in smoke!'

Amanda detached herself from his embrace and signalled for him to speak more quietly.

He poured himself a glass of wine while glancing over at the frying pan, as if the smell of Carambar was coming from there. Next to the frying pan, a saucepan of mixed vegetables was simmering. He didn't make any comment. You get used to quality, he'd told her one night after scolding her for a fallen soufflé.

His special way of paying her a compliment.

Dimitri lowered his voice and pulled out a chair.

'Our troubles are over. He won't be bothering us any more.'

Amanda shrugged and turned off the gas under the frying pan.

'The cops will investigate. He spent a lot of time with Malone.'

'Half a day per week. He must have been dealing with at least twenty other kids in the area. All of them nutcases.'

Amanda didn't rise to the bait. Putting on an oven glove, she took the cake out of the oven. She imagined the smell escaping, invisible, climbing the stairs and sliding under the door of Malone's bedroom. Like a delicate invitation that he alone would understand. Nothing else mattered.

As long as he never forgot that smell.

As long as he never forgot the taste of nice things. Only mothers could give that to little boys: sensitivity. If they followed in the footsteps of their fathers, idolised them, obsessed over football and cars and DIY, they were screwed: they'd end up being just as stupid. Generation after generation of idiots. Only mothers could try to put an end to this curse.

'You're right,' admitted Amanda. 'Anyway, we have no reason to feel guilty.'

Silence. Amanda dusted the cake with a layer of chocolate sprinkles. A pointless yet essential detail. The difference between men who would guard palaces in the future, and the refined men who would live inside them.

'Do we know what happened?' she asked. 'An accident at Cap de la Hève, that's what I heard. He crashed his bike. Is that right?'

Dimitri emptied his glass and smiled again.

'Yeah. That's what they'll say. He slid on a patch of black ice and, unlucky for him, his tank was full. He ended up underneath the bike, squashed. And then the whole thing caught fire. Maybe that dumb Romanian felt like having a fag while he was waiting for the ambulance to arrive.'

He laughed.

Amanda thought for a moment. Yesterday, Dimitri had been with her all evening, even if it had been late when he came up to their bedroom. It was gone 11 p.m. when she heard the end of *Private Confessions*, and then he had turned off the TV. How could he have been at Cap de la Hève at the same time?

In her head, she visualised the distance from their estate to the coast. The viewpoint was only about ten kilometres away, less than half an hour there and back, and Dimitri had been alone downstairs for more than an hour, lying on the couch, watching television.

In Amanda's head, a lawyer continued to plead her husband's case. It was impossible that he could have gone out: she'd have heard him start the car outside their house; she'd have heard him come back in . . . unless he'd been very quiet, if he'd deliberately turned up the volume on the television, for example, if he'd parked the car further away . . . The defence lawyer, having run out of arguments, clung to one last certainty.

*Dimitri was not a killer.*

'What do you mean exactly?' Amanda asked, her voice shaking. 'You mean it's not an acc—'

There was a knock at the door.

The police, already?

The school, again?

Dimitri got up to answer it, not appearing particularly worried. Amanda watched him disappear through the doorway, then felt a slight draught of cold air as the front door opened.

Dimitri did not sound surprised.

'Oh, it's you? Good timing. Come in!'

Her husband burst out laughing. While she hadn't been attracted to him when they first met, that laugh of his had comforted her. He wasn't that funny, but he saw humour all around him, in everyone, in every situation. His sense of humour was fairly obvious, and generally his life and his friends did not disappoint him.

Amanda went into the hallway and saw two men. She immediately noticed, also, that at the top of the stairs, Malone's bedroom door was ajar.

The Carambar effect.

In that moment, Amanda loved everything. That smell, her kitchen, her little man who, after a tantrum, would come and hug her skirt. A friend who had dropped by unexpectedly to talk to her husband, and her leaving them alone so she could add another plate to the table before serving the aperitif.

Happiness, just as she had always imagined it. As if everything could simply stop in that moment.

*

*   *

Malone stood at the top of the stairs.

He was hungry. He would have preferred to start with dessert. He heard voices in the hallway. He liked it when Pa-di invited friends round; they would stay in the living room while he, having nabbed some of the snacks from the bowls, would go to the kitchen to eat dinner in front of the TV, which was tuned to the cartoon channel. When Pa-di ate with them, he forced Maman-da to watch the news, and Malone couldn't understand any of it.

He approached the banister, holding Gouti in his arms. He didn't even need to tell him 'Shh'.

In the hallway, Maman-da had seen him and smiled up at him.

Suddenly, Malone bit his lip. Pa-di had taken the man's coat and scarf as he came in.

And it was then that Malone recognised him.

Not him, not his face. Something else.

The shiny earring. The skull-and-crossbones tattooed on his neck.

There was no doubt about it.

It was the ogre. The ogre of the forest.

# 43

*He's been snoring for the past ten hours.*
Want to kill
*He's not snoring any more. He's sleeping on his side. His feet are a bit cold. There are traces of drool and blood on the pillowcase.*

*Convicted: 336*
*Acquitted: 341*

www.want-to-kill.com

It was a bloodbath.

That wasn't an expression, it was literally what Marianne Augresse saw in the little bathroom with peeling wallpaper. The hip bath – of the kind popular in the 1960s – had rusty taps and mouldy joints, and in the bottom of the tub was a puddle of blood, nearly two centimetres deep, the plughole blocked with hair.

It wasn't difficult to figure out the cause: a wounded man had been lying there, he'd been put in the tub, washed and dried, which couldn't have been easy in such an old-fashioned bath, its sides nearly a metre high.

Timo Soler, without a doubt.

Now they could be practically certain that someone had helped him. Helped him wash. Helped him dress.

Helped get him out of there, before they arrived.

Marianne would soon have confirmation of this: a dozen men were searching the one-bedroom flat on the fifth floor of the building on Rue de la Belle-Etoile. Timo and his accomplice had left in a hurry. The apartment had been left as it was, as if they'd popped out to the shops and would return any moment now with a baguette and a newspaper: a pile of clothes at the foot of the bed, dirty dishes in the sink, bowls on the table, radio playing quietly, shoes scattered in the hallway.

*As if they'd be back soon.*

Yeah, right! thought the captain. Soler had once again slipped through their net. Again, their attempt to catch him had ended in complete failure, even if, this time, she didn't see how she could have done things any differently. Her men had approached Soler's apartment with caution. They'd closed in gradually on the block, then the building, then the stairway. And yet the wounded robber had managed to flee before the first police car had even reached the area.

Why? Timo Soler had called Larochelle less than an hour before. According to the surgeon, Soler's suffering had become unbearable, but he refused to go to hospital or even to leave his hiding place. Soler had given his address to the surgeon: he was ready to pay a lot of money – a LOT – for a discreet home visit from the doctor. So why clear off fifteen minutes later, before a single policeman had even set foot in the quarter?

Men wearing gloves sifted through the clothes on the bed. The dressing gown was completely red. Trousers, underpants, T-shirts, all covered with blood.

Had the doctor not sounded convincing on the phone? Had Timo Soler, after hanging up, suddenly become suspicious?

*It was strange.*

Marianne Augresse surveyed the flat with more concentration. Her eyes flickered from place to place: the tea towels hanging from a peg, the socks drying on the rack, the newspapers piled under the living room table. Something about this set-up bothered her, something that didn't quite add up, a collection of insignificant details that, when you put them together, gave you the impression that you could view Soler's flight – the way he was living, the way he had found to survive, hidden away and wounded all these months – in another light.

The solution was here, close by, the captain felt sure of it. But she couldn't put her finger on the one thing that would illuminate the whole mystery.

She cursed again as she bumped into Constantini, who was casually shining the Polilight under the sofa. Was she the only one who could sense that something was not right?

*That was strange too.*

She became even more convinced that the answer was here, staring her in the face, like some familiar but forgotten word, nagging at your brain, on the tip of your tongue. She was looking around the kitchen again, mechanically opening the fridge, the cupboards, when her phone rang.

Lieutenant Lechevalier.

She didn't let him speak.

'Get yourself here, JB, we need you.'

'Isn't Papy there?'

'No, the stubborn bastard left for Potigny about an hour ago. You know, the village where the Lukowiks, Alexis and Timo grew up? He thinks the stash is hidden there and, like an idiot, I gave him permission to go and search the place. I'm going to be bollocked for this by Judge Dumas, even if there was no way I could have known what would happen this morning. Anyway, it's too late for Papy to come back. And the forensics boys have to do their thing now. All they need to do is search the streets of Le Havre and follow the drops of Soler's blood.'

'Before the seagulls lick it up. Did you know they've become carnivores, from eating the corpses of illegal immigrants floating in the port?'

Marianne Augresse ignored this.

'Where are you?'

'Boulevard Clemenceau. We've just arrived at Dragonman's flat. He was living on the twelfth floor.'

*He was living . . .*

The use of the past tense made a bomb explode somewhere inside her skull. A brief, intense pain. More brain cells giving up the ghost, probably. Marianne was finding it increasingly hard to keep

239

everything separate in her mind, to concentrate simultaneously on both cases: the murder of Vasily, the escape of Timo Soler. And yet she had to keep switching between the two.

'What about the school, JB?'

'Manéglise, you mean, this morning? I don't know how to put this, but it gave me a strange feeling.'

Marianne spoke louder.

'What do you mean?'

'I don't know, it just made me uneasy. You know, turning up at a school at eight-thirty, just before class starts, and standing in the playground being stared at by all those little kids as if I was some kind of pervert, when I can't even take my own children to school because of this shitty job . . .'

The captain sighed.

'Spare me your whining, JB! Did you find out anything there?'

'Nothing definite. Vasily Dragonman was the only school psychologist working in the northern sector of Le Havre. He was responsible for three cantons, fifty-eight communes, twenty-seven schools, and more than a thousand kids. He gave them all a test, then followed about thirty more closely because the test results suggested they were troubled.'

Despite herself, Marianne thought about the Weber case, the psychologist murdered outside his office one morning in Honfleur in 2009. He'd been seeing more than fifty patients – several hundred if you went back four or five years – from schizophrenic teenagers to frenzied alcoholics. So many potential culprits who might have killed him in a fit of insanity, for a forgotten prescription, for a secret they regretted telling him, for a meeting he'd refused to attend. Each and every one of those fifty patients whose names were in Weber's diary had a very clear motive for killing the psychologist.

Did that hold true for Vasily too? Did he look after other problem children whose parents drank, hit them, touched them? Had he found out family secrets that were so sordid that every adult denounced by those children might want him dead?

About thirty kids, the captain repeated in her head. But Vasily had come to see her about only one of them.

She asked again.

'I'm not talking about the other schools, I'm talking about Manéglise. Tell me.'

'The headmistress struck me as being quite nice. She had a row with Dragonman yesterday, but she seemed genuinely upset by his death. She's the one who gave me his address. He obviously kept all his files at home. He had an old laptop, but he tended to print everything: interviews, reports, prescriptions for doctors, and that's without even mentioning the kids' drawings, whole exercise books filled during meetings. I'm outside the building now. It's going to take a while to go through all his stuff.'

'We've no choice, JB. Concentrate on the file for Malone Moulin, to start with.'

Suddenly Vasily Dragonman's hazel eyes appeared superimposed on the grey Le Havre sky, which she saw through the dirty window of the kitchen. Eyes sparkling mischievously, the eyes of a free mind still in touch with childhood. A little voice hissed at Marianne that he had died precisely because of that, because of the treasure map on which he'd sketched the ravings of a child.

The captain stayed like that for a moment, watching the clouds slowly being stretched into filaments by the wind, until the memory of Vasily faded and she found herself once more looking through the kitchen cupboards. Dozens of tins, packets of pasta, coloured sauces in glass jars.

And still that same impression, that certainty that this decor, these objects concealed something obvious that she couldn't pin down.

She wasn't focused enough.

She blamed herself for not having been able to disregard all those stories about secret maps, pirates and ghosts. She'd long ago learnt to forget such tales and legends, to leave them behind as she climbed the ladder of the police hierarchy, to renounce the role of the clever girl in the detective teams of her childhood, all those idols to whom she owed her vocation: George, the tomboy in the Famous Five; Velma, the brain of the gang in Scooby-Doo; Sabrina, the least feminine of Charlie's Angels.

241

Although she was still gorgeous, thought Marianne, much more than she was . . .

'Marianne?' JB asked, concerned.

The captain's gaze, still drifting around the kitchen, suddenly halted on a roll of kitchen paper, hanging from a dispenser.

Her heart sped up. In a fraction of a second, everything became clear. She understood what had been bothering her about Timo Soler's flat all this time.

She watched all the other officers as they searched every square centimetre of the apartment.

All of them were men.

Of course . . .

'Marianne?'

The captain forced herself to arrange the clues in her head. It all fitted, there was no doubt: behind the apparent disorder, the dilapidated apartment, and the smell of damp, everything was tidy. Neat. Ordered. Almost tasteful. No man on the verge of dying would have felt the need to do that. Nor would another man, an accomplice. Certainly not Alexis Zerda.

It was so obvious: how had they not thought of it before?

She stared at the socks drying on the rack.

This flat had been occupied by a couple.

A woman had lived here with Timo Soler. His girlfriend, his mistress, his wife? It made no difference. But it was thanks to this woman that he'd survived. It was because of her that they'd escaped once again.

To die somewhere else, the two of them together?

She almost screamed, forgetting the mobile phone in her hand.

'Search everything! I want proof that a girl was living here.'

*

* *

A good fifteen minutes had passed. Marianne had asked JB to go upstairs to Vasily Dragonman's flat, start sorting through his archives, and keep her abreast of any developments. She had then followed the location of patrols in the Neiges quarter on her iPad.

The GéoPol app looked like a video game, a sort of sophisticated Pac-Man where the police vehicles had to drive along as many roads as possible without ever colliding.

In which of those streets was Timo Soler hiding? At the back of a car, covered with a blanket, his girlfriend at the wheel? The existence of the girl was no longer a theory; those searching hadn't had much difficulty in locating proof of a female presence in the flat. Long hair, pale chestnut, found in the shower; lipstick stains on a glass; a pair of lace knickers fallen behind the bathroom cabinet.

Very sexy. Size 8.

The captain's glare had been enough to dissuade her men from making any salacious comments about this unknown woman, whom they guessed was slim, probably young and pretty.

Officer Constantini, with the aid of his Polilight, had found blood on the landing, then on the top three steps of the staircase, but not on those below. Marianne had sent three men, each equipped with a Black Light lamp, to search for other stains outside the building, in the car park, and on the road, to give them some clue as to which direction the fugitives might have taken when they fled.

Although Marianne didn't really believe this would work.

The lovebirds had flown the coop.

In Marianne's mind, the two cases jockeyed for attention. Between barked orders, her thoughts drifted ceaselessly to Malone Moulin, to Vasily Dragonman. When she turned back to the windows of the flat, the childlike face of the school psychologist continued to smile at her from the sky, slightly blurred, his beard, eyelashes and hair whitened by the clouds, as if the photograph of him had been artificially aged. Proof that Vasily's charm would have survived the passing of time, thought Marianne, troubled by the images that haunted her mind.

If she'd been alone, she would have collapsed in tears. No, a face like that shouldn't vanish before the years had patiently sculpted it. No, such sparkling eyes should not be extinguished in a single night.

She suddenly thought back to Angie's odd questions, on the phone, a while earlier.

*Are you sure that . . . that it's him?*

After all, there was still hope. There was no categorical proof that the corpse found burnt to a cinder beneath the motorbike was that of Vasily Dragonman. He probably wasn't the only person in Le Havre to own a Guzzi California.

'Phone call for you, Captain.'

Officer Bourdaine stood motionless in a corner of the room, like a decorative fig plant that might be real or fake. Marianne turned her back to the policeman, observing, in the distance, the immense skeletons of the cranes on the port.

'Captain Augresse.'

'It's Ortega. I'm at the morgue. It didn't take as long as expected, Marianne.'

'What didn't?'

'We got lucky. We found his medical file straight away. His dentist was Kyheng Soyaran, on Rue Sery. They knew each other well; they went to medical school together. He sent me X-rays of his teeth by email. It took less than five minutes. Comparing them took a bit longer, but . . .'

'Comparing them to what?'

'To the jaw of the man under the motorbike. What did you think I was talking about, Marianne? Surely you knew his teeth were still intact?'

Marianne Augresse swallowed.

'So? Just tell me, for Christ's sake!'

'There's no doubt. Same jaw, same teeth, one hundred per cent. There's no need to wait for the DNA results. The dead man at Cap de la Hève is definitely your school psychologist, Vasily Dragonman.'

# 44

*Little hand on the 12, big hand on the 6*

> *I looked in poems*
> *For ways to tell you I love you*
> *I found some wise words*
> *Much too long for a child of three, like me*

Curled up between the wall and the toilet bowl, Malone did not have much space.

Not that he cared. He had remembered Friday's story, the one for the green planet, Venus, about love. The one where he flew away with his mother at the end.

But before he could succeed, he had to escape the ogre, the one with the earring and the tattoo. Thankfully, Malone knew the magic place where baddies couldn't enter; Gouti had told him that secret many times. Every time they landed on the green planet.

He had to lock himself in the toilet!

Every time he went to do a pee-pee, he thought about it. He was too short to reach the bolt, but if he stood on the bin and stretched up on tiptoes, it was easy. That idea – of standing on the bin – hadn't been in Gouti's story; Malone had thought of it himself.

Lock yourself in the toilet.

Wait for Maman to come and get you.

Go away forever with her.

To give himself courage, Malone again unfolded the Christmas drawing that he kept in his pocket. As his small index finger touched every detail of the picture – the star, the tree with its badly coloured-in needles, the presents traced in felt-tip pen – Malone thought that he mustn't forget to put it in his hiding place later, in his album, so that no one would find it. Not Maman-da, not Pa-di, and especially not the ogre!

All the same, he took his time looking at the three figures holding hands under the tinsel.

Him. Papa.

His finger stopped on the third figure, caressing his Maman's long hair with his fingertip, before tracing every letter, at the top and bottom of the sheet.

**Noel Joyeux**
**N'oublie Jamais**

These were the only words that he knew how to read, except for his own name. Oh, and the word MAMAN, of course.

> *So I looked elsewhere*
> *And I found in my heart*
> *The words that you taught me*
> *When I was still little*
> *Maman, I love you as big as that!*
> *I say it with my arms.*

'Malone, come out of there!'

Amanda's voice was as gentle as she could make it.

'Please, Malone.'

The smell of burnt Carambar clung to the walls, to the floor, to the staircase. Persistent, almost sickening. Amanda had hoped for a moment that the scent would be enough to persuade Malone to come out of the toilet, but she had quickly understood that he wouldn't fall for such a crude trap.

Malone had recognised Alexis. He must be going through some sort of trauma, contradictory messages colliding in his head; perhaps seeing Alexis Zerda had triggered other memories for Malone, too, the way a broken watch will sometimes start working again if it's dropped on the floor.

Or maybe it was all in her head. Maybe that bastard, the way he looked like a vampire, had simply scared her kid.

Amanda sat on the worn carpet, outside the upstairs toilet. She was trembling, scratching the door like a little cat that wanted to come in, speaking softly, ceaselessly, like a mother watching over her sick child. Strong, caring, close.

Except that they were separated by a door.

She listened to the jagged breathing of her child and guessed that he was holding back sobs.

She was furious.

*Thousands of stars in the sky*
*Thousands of flowers in the garden*
*Thousands of bees in the flowers*
*Thousands of seashells on the beaches*
*And one, just one maman.*

'Forget it!' shouted Dimitri from the living room. 'He'll come out in the end.'

Her husband was a moron. She could hear the clinking of ice cubes in his whisky. Alexis wouldn't drink anything, not even a beer. He had a whistling sort of voice. To start with, it was possible to find this almost pleasant, almost sing-song, but eventually his lisping and shrill intonation became unbearable. The first time she'd met him, Amanda had even thought that if snakes could talk they would sound like Alexis. Not the Parseltongue of Harry Potter's basilisks, but the language a rattlesnake would invent after it had gone mad from slithering alone for too long through the desert.

'Forget it, Amanda.'

Alexis Zerda's orders brooked no discussion.

After slowly going downstairs, Amanda sat in the imitation leather club chair, between her husband and Alexis. Dimitri held the glass containing his malt whisky in both hands, as if to melt the ice cubes as quickly as possible.

'You've fucked up,' said Zerda.

He turned to Dimitri, but Amanda knew that his words were aimed at her. Alexis was too intelligent not to realise that Dimitri

247

had been out of his depth for a long time now.

'The cops will show up,' Alexis continued.

Dimitri looked as though he was about to respond, but Zerda ordered him to remain silent with a single hand gesture.

'The cops would have come here, anyway. They'd have come with the shrink, if he were still alive. And if that had happened, you know as well as I do what the result would have been. By getting rid of the shrink, we've won ourselves some time. Although not much.'

Amanda leant forward. Each time she moved, she felt the springs of the chair pressing into her flesh.

'Did you kill him?'

Without even bothering to reply, Zerda glanced towards the picture frame that was hanging on the wall. Inside felt-tipped hearts, short poems had been handwritten; simple Mother's Day rhymes that children learnt by heart, decorated with dried flowers and pinned butterflies.

'You'd better get rid of that too, before the cops show up.'

He swivelled to face Amanda, his green eyes staring directly into hers. His voice grew even more high-pitched.

'The boy should have forgotten everything a long time ago. For fuck's sake, with a kid that age memories usually vanish within a few months. That's what all the experts said. We did enough research. How can he still remember . . .'

'You?'

Amanda smiled.

'All of it,' Zerda went on. 'All of it. That little brat had better shut his mouth if the cops come calling. He's pissing me off with all his stories!'

'Don't talk about him like that,' Amanda said, raising her voice.

Alexis stood up and went to take a closer look at the butterflies and dried flowers. He paused to listen for any sounds of the door opening upstairs.

Nothing. Malone hadn't moved from his cell. Finally, Zerda replied.

'You take things too much to heart, Amanda. If the kid keeps his mouth shut, the cops won't have anything on us; they won't be able to make the connection. There's nothing concrete, you see? No proof. Just some brat's vague memories that should have been erased from his brain months ago. That was your job, Amanda. Wiping clean his past.'

During this conversation, Dimitri Moulin had poured himself another whisky. The other two were no longer paying any attention to him.

'And what if they take him away from us?' Amanda insisted. 'What if they take him without even making the connection with everything else?'

'They won't take away your son, Amanda. He's intelligent. He's in good health. He loves you. Why would they want to separate you?'

He shot a contemptuous glance at Dimitri, who, as if to save face, had only dared pour himself a small drop of Glen Moray. Amanda had long ago realised that, to Alexis, Dimitri was nothing more than a pawn to be sacrificed in this game of chess.

His old friend.

Dimitri had just been unlucky. He'd found himself in the same cell as Alexis in Bois-d'Arcy. Her husband had already been looking for a strong man to admire, to protect him too, the kind of man in whose shadow he could shine. He might have ended up with a bear, a shark, or a wolf. Instead, he drew the worst card possible. He ended up with a snake. A snake who would eliminate him as soon as he represented any danger, just as he'd eliminated Vasily Dragonman. As he would eliminate all of them. Her. Malone . . .

'Go get the kid,' said Alexis in a soft voice. 'If he doesn't open that fucking door, I'll smash it down myself.'

While Amanda went upstairs, Zerda called after her:

'I can't stay long. The cops could show up at any moment, and I don't want them to find me here. They were at the school in Manéglise this morning. As soon as they confirm the identity of the dead man on Cap de la Hève, they'll visit every family that nosy bastard shrink was involved with, and yours will be top of the list.'

Two steps higher.

'The kid just needs to cooperate. I don't care if he keeps banging on about pirates and rockets and all that shit; the cops'll get bored with that after a while. The important thing is that he plays his role. Just the bare minimum, Amanda, you understand? He can't remain silent, locked in the bathroom like a terrified oyster, or the cops will want to start opening his shell to find out what's inside.'

Another three steps.

'If you want to keep him with you . . .'

Amanda did not reply. The only sounds were the rustle of her dress against the banister and the soft shuffle of her slippers on the carpet.

> *Maman, Maman, my Maman dear*
> *Maman, Maman, take me in your arms*
> *Maman, Maman, a little kiss*
> *(Smack)*
> *Maman, Maman, a little secret*
> *(Whispered)*
> *I love you*

*<br>*   *

She came back downstairs five minutes later. Dimitri had drained his glass but had not poured himself another whisky. Alexis, standing, was examining the collection of butterflies in the frame, while keeping one eye on the view through the window.

Amanda clung to the wooden banister.

'He wants to talk to his mother.'

'What did you say?' asked Zerda, surprised.

'Malone says he wants to talk to his mother.'

'Impossible.'

'He says he won't come out until he's talked to his mother,' Amanda went on. 'He says if she can't come here, he wants to talk to her on the phone. But I agree with you, Alexis, letting him do that would be the worst thing we could do.'

They were silent for a few moments, and didn't notice Dimitri standing and quietly picking up the cordless phone. He took a look through the window at the empty car park, and then spoke.

'I've been living with this kid for a while now. It's hard to know what's going on in his head. He's as stubborn as a mule.' He left a calculated silence. 'But as blinkered as he is, there is one fool-proof way of making him obey.'

Alexis froze, suddenly interested.

'His mother.'

Amanda glared at her husband. Zerda looked away from the window for a moment.

'Go on, Dimitri.'

'Let the kid call her. Just for a minute or two. You can't fool him – he'll know it's her. And then, when he's hung up, we can do what we want with him. Lies are the best thing ever invented to keep kids in line. You see what I mean, don't you Alexis? We could say something like: "You'd better be good, boy, if you ever want to talk to your mother again." It's exactly the same as people saying "if you want Father Christmas to bring you presents" or "if you want the tooth fairy to come tonight".'

Amanda moved away from the staircase and stood in front of Dimitri. He was forty centimetres taller than her. Tears were streaming from her eyes.

'For God's sake, Dimitri. Surely we didn't do all of this for nothing? You can't . . .'

Alexis's warm hand touched her shoulder.

Warm and sticky.

'You know, what Dimitri's suggesting is actually quite smart. Your kid is already convinced that you're not his mother anyway. A quick phone call might buy us some time. A lot of time, in fact. And that's exactly what we need.'

'And then what?'

Without waiting for Zerda to respond, Dimitri handed him the phone, smiling faintly, as if telling Amanda she was out of the picture. That the men would take care of this.

Poor mad bitch.

'You promised me,' she stammered.

The ground gave way beneath her feet. Her hands and fingers

trembled, and a long shudder travelled up her spine. She could guess what would happen next. Alexis would liquidate them, one after the other. As soon as he'd found what he was searching for.

Zerda looked up at the stairs.

'Dimitri, go get the kid. Tell him we agree: he can call his mother. Tell him he can talk to her for one minute.'

# 45

Marianne Augresse had opened the two panels of the patio doors and was standing out on the balcony. A view of the port, the grey cargo ships, the empty sky. Empty forever.

The tulle curtains billowed in the wind, and inside the apartment a door banged shut. She didn't care. Just like she didn't care about the message Judge Dumas had left on her answering machine, expressing her surprise that Timo Soler had been allowed to escape again.

What could she do about it? Her men had sealed off the Neiges quarter less than fifteen minutes after the surgeon's call. If Soler had become suspicious of the surgeon, or had fled for some other reason, it wasn't her fault.

'Speak louder, Papy. I can barely hear you.'

She had gone out onto the balcony to get better reception, but it was clearly Lieutenant Pasdeloup who was having problems. Marianne leant her backside against the iron railing and, holding her phone to her ear with one hand, used her other hand to scroll down the messages on her iPad.

Managing two cases at the same time prevented her from taking a breather, from dwelling, feeling emotion. It was a bit like reading a thriller with two parallel stories, with the switches between the two threads speeding up as the book progressed, forcing you to move from one thought to the next without mixing them, without even having the time to ask questions. Probably the same thing that a woman might feel if she had a husband and a lover. Thinking of one, talking to the other, without tripping up.

Marianne had neither.

The last man to have smiled at her had gone up in smoke on

Cap de la Hève. One day later, all that remained of that smile was his jaw, kindly sent to her by Dr Ortega. She observed it on the tablet, hovering weightlessly thanks to the miracle of 3D-modelling software. The macabre proof that Vasily Dragonman's mouth would never kiss another girl.

'Marianne, I've just passed Caen. I'm in the Laize valley. Do you want me to turn around?'

Marianne opened another window on the iPad. On GéoPol, police patrols symbolized by red dots were moving around, searching for Timo Soler.

'Nah, doesn't matter, Papy. We're not getting anywhere here, anyway. Just try to find somewhere with better reception.'

'OK. I'll leave the valley and call you back.'

With her right index finger, Marianne clicked on another window. JB's messages were accumulating along with a shower of attachments, at least ten with every email. All of them children's drawings, taken from the dossier on Malone Moulin, which they'd found at Vasily Dragonman's flat.

Marianne opened them and zoomed in.

Strange lines, bright colours, complicated shapes.

Each drawing had been annotated in Vasily's round, meticulous handwriting.

```
Pirate ship, 17/9/2015
Rocket flying over the forest of ogres, 24/9/2015
Four towers of the castle, 8/10/2015
An ogre, 15/10/2015
```

Marianne's gaze lingered on the potato-shaped head of the supposed ogre; on the lines for the eyes, nose, and mouth (unless that was a scar); on the black dot to the side that might have been a beauty spot, a badly drawn eye, or an earring.

What could she do with all these scribblings?

In his first message, JB had said that the drawings reminded him of those of his five-year-old son, Léo. He'd then asked if he could have some time off in the afternoon, an hour towards the end of the school day, so he could surprise his wife and children.

Marianne had refused. Too much work today. She couldn't take the risk. JB had responded with a vicious text: a smiley with a raised middle finger (normally, he'd just send her the one with its tongue sticking out), along with a few words:

*If you had kids, you'd understand.*

Touché. Right to the heart. Bastard!

Yes, she had no children. That was possibly even why she'd been made a captain. But right now, she would almost certainly swap all the promotions in the world for a child who would wake her up in the mornings after she'd spent the night on stake-out, for a little brat who would throw himself in her arms as soon as she got through the door and make her forget all the sordid cases she had to deal with. But in the meantime, JB and the other males under her command – no matter how indignant they were, or what perfect fathers – were all on duty until tomorrow.

Papy's round head appeared on the screen of her phone.

'OK, I'm on top of the church bell tower in Bretteville, and I've got a good signal.'

'Just stop! While you're busy being a tourist, we've got a corpse on our hands, a man on the run who's probably bleeding to death, Alexis Zerda who seems to have completely vanished since this morning, and Timo's mysterious girlfriend. And the only thing we know about her is that she wears lacy knickers . . .'

'Is that all? Listen, I'm going to make you happy. I've found the answer to your existential question.'

Marianne frowned at two officers who were moving the chest of drawers in the living room, a silent request for them to make less noise.

'Which one?'

'The key question. The one that will open every door.'

'Just spit it out.'

'Don't you remember? Yesterday, in your office. The photo of the cuddly toy, "Gouti". You asked me what kind of animal it was.'

The captain sighed and, instinctively, moved along the balcony while pulling the doors together.

'So? What is it?'

Papy's happy-sounding voice contrasted with the anxious scrabble inside the apartment.

'I had a hard time – I spent most of the night doing research on the internet – but, in the end, it was pretty obvious. Your toy is an agouti.'

'A what?'

'An agouti! The clue was in the name – you just had to know that such an animal existed. An agouti is a sort of guinea pig, originally from Amazonia. It's a rodent, a bit bigger than a rat. Like a rabbit, in a way, but without the fluffy tail and the long ears.'

Marianne clicked on another drawing.

*Gouti*, it said next to it, in Vasily's handwriting.

Malone's drawing could only be deciphered as an association of ideas. Two circles, perhaps representing the animal's body, were placed on a carpet of red and yellow dots. Blue lines flew up to the top of the page.

'Great, another dead end. So Malone Moulin was talking to his guinea pig. Fantastic. Where do we go with that?'

'Before you hang up, there is one other small detail I should tell you, if you've got time. It's surprising.'

'Go ahead, Papy. I don't have anything better to do than take zoology lessons.'

'The agouti is amnesiac.'

'Sorry?'

'It spends its life hiding seeds and fruit, generally taking the shell off them before burying them. In that way, it builds up a food reserve for periods of scarcity, or for when it ends its hibernation. Except that, when it wakes up, it usually forgets where it's buried its treasure.'

Marianne coughed. The sea breeze sneaked into the gap between her coat and her neck, freezing her whole body.

'Brilliant, Papy! So the agouti is the dumbest rodent on the planet!'

'The most useful, in fact,' replied Lieutenant Pasdeloup. 'Unwittingly, it scatters and plants the seeds that a forest needs to regenerate, year after year. The agouti is the gardener of the equatorial world. So basically, it hoards treasure, hides it, then forgets it. And while it is dying of hunger, the forest grows back!'

'Shit . . .'

The captain stared blankly at the carpet of coloured dots on the child's drawing on her iPad. Seeds? Fruit? Pieces of gold?

She tried to recall a few fragments of Gouti's stories, which she had already listened to several times on the MP3 player. They would have to listen to them all again, deconstruct and decode them. Maybe they could find a connection between Malone's tales and the death of Vasily Dragonman.

But first, she had to catch Timo Soler and his girlfriend.

Her phone beeped a few seconds later. An email. From the Regional Judicial Identity Service: a standard secure message, identified by a file number that meant nothing to her. Without thinking, she clicked on the attachment.

The next second, her hand grabbed hold of the railing, as if she'd suddenly got vertigo. Stupefied, she read the three lines describing the DNA analysis.

# 46

*Little hand on the 12, big hand on the 8*

Malone was sitting on the sofa, next to Gouti.

Alexis Zerda had retreated a few steps, so he didn't frighten the child even more, while Dimitri handed the child the phone and explained for the third time that he was going to talk to his Maman. Just for a little bit, a few phrases, just hello, how are you, I'm fine, and then they would hang up and he would have to be a good boy, a very good boy, and stay with his other Maman, the one who looked after him now. Maman-da. Otherwise, he would never be able to talk to his Maman from before again.

Amanda turned her back on them. Silent. Nose pressed to the windowpane. A round car park was the only view. A thin mist was falling over the estate, as if it were all just a bad dream on a bad set. She didn't even have the strength to conjure up anywhere else. Her planet was confined to this circle of tarmac. In the reflection in the window, she saw the shape of Alexis Zerda.

Before Dimitri came downstairs with Malone, Zerda had casually opened his jacket to get a handkerchief. And to show them the revolver hanging from his belt.

Not that Dimitri had noticed, the fool.

The trap was closing on them. They had sealed a pact with the devil, had let him into their home, into their lives. For a moment, she almost wished to see a police car surging through the mist.

But if that happened, the cops would take Malone from her.

Dimitri dialled the number.

Amanda's eyes looked up at the frame above the sideboard: the hearts, poems and butterflies. It was all Dimitri's fault, everything that had happened to them. This succession of misfortunes, each one worse than the last, every time he tried to repair the irreparable.

If they both had to die, her only wish was that Zerda should kill her husband first, so she would have the pleasure of watching his face crumple against the cold tiles and, in the instant after, see those stupid eyes of his go blank forever. As if they still hadn't understood what was happening.

As if none of it had been his fault.

*
*   *

The telephone rang a third time. It was on the table in the hallway, next to the coat rack and a picture of the Étretat cliffs. The apartment's landline. None of the police had dared pick it up yet.

They were all waiting for their captain's orders. She was still out on the balcony, staring at her mobile.

Suddenly she came back into the flat, walking quickly, and picked up the phone, without even taking the precaution of putting on gloves.

She said nothing, only listened.

'Hello? Hello, Maman?'

A boy's voice. Very young.

Silence. One second, perhaps? An eternity.

Marianne thought about responding, afraid he might hang up.

'Hello, Maman? Can you hear me? It's Malone!'

Marianne froze, as if electrocuted. Officer Bourdaine, who was standing two metres away from her, instinctively called out:

'Is there a problem, Captain?'

Then, abruptly aware of his mistake, he clapped his hand over his mouth.

The boy had already hung up.

Marianne just had time to hear a muffled echo, maybe the sound of a gunshot.

Or a falling object? A body?

259

There was no time to think. Marianne screamed so loud that even the men in the car park twelve floors below could probably hear.

'Timo Soler's girlfriend had a child! And I know who that child is!'

# II
# Amanda

# 47

Malone trotted along the corridor in the small airport. He almost had to jog to keep up with Maman, taking three steps to her one.

Gate 1
Gate 2
Gate 3

He held Maman's hand tightly while he tried to count in his head the planes behind the glass. Ahead of them, people dressed as if they were going to war were marching; all of them men, with close-shaven hair. One of them had an earring and another had tattoos, on his arms and neck. Maman lowered her head as she walked past them, as if she was a bit scared too. Scared that she would be recognised.

As soon as they were far enough away, Maman started saying the same thing, over and over, almost whispering as she leant close to him:

'*Hurry up, hurry up, hurry up . . .*'

But he was the one who'd waited for Maman earlier, when they'd gone through the door where they had to take off their watches, belts and glasses, because it had made a noise and Maman had been asked to go through it a second time, after taking off her necklace.

Gate 4
Gate 5

He'd tried to get away then, just after he'd got past the door. He hadn't gone far – just to the end of the corridor – but when he saw the big poster, at the same moment when Maman called him, he realised that it was a stupid idea.

He had to stay close to Maman, be a good boy, a big boy, a brave boy.

He had to do everything exactly as she said.

Gate 6
Gate 7

Even if he was sad about Gouti. He missed his cuddly toy. It was more difficult to be brave without Gouti. Maman's hand still held his fingers tightly.

'*Hurry up, hurry up, hurry up . . .*'

One, two, three. Thumb, index finger, middle finger of his other hand. There were three planes on the other side of the glass: one white and blue, one white and orange, and the other one completely white. Malone didn't know which one went to the forest of ogres.

Gate 8

It was the white and orange one. Maman pointed it out to him. People were queuing up outside it.

Maman still didn't let go of his hand – it wasn't to make him go faster now, but so that he would stay in the line without moving.

So Malone didn't move. He just concentrated on gathering his courage. He had to do everything he'd been told, as Gouti had taught him, as his Maman before had asked him to.

His Maman before, not the one who was holding his hand.

People were starting to get on the aeroplane. The moment had come.

Malone repeated in his head the words he didn't really understand, even after saying them hundreds of times, in secret, in his bed, before going to sleep, and remembering them every day when he woke up.

*It's a prayer, it's your prayer. You must never forget it.*
*It's very simple. You can do it.*
*Just before you get on the aeroplane, you have to say a sentence, a sentence you've already said a thousand times, but you have to say it at exactly that moment.*
*Even if it's not true. They have to believe you.*

He tugged on Maman's sleeve.

*Even if it's not true. They have to believe you.*

'Yes, sweetie, what is it?'

# Four hours earlier

# 48

*Little hand on the 12, big hand on the 10*

Malone was sitting in the back of the car. There was no booster seat, like there was in Maman-da's car, and because of that he couldn't see outside, only a bit of roof with some foam and the grey dish that looked like a flying saucer that had flown too low and hit a chimney. The seat belt covered his face, from his left eye to the right side of his chin, like a big pirate's eye patch.

He clutched Gouti to his chest. Sometimes, in Maman-da's car, he would put a seat belt on Gouti too – the middle one – even if it annoyed Maman-da because it wasted time. But today, he was holding Gouti instead, the two of them sharing the same seat belt. Because he was a bit scared.

Maman-da seemed a bit scared too. She sat up front and kept turning around to him and winking at him, saying: 'You're going to have to be brave, my pirate. You're going to have to be very brave.'

Zerda had not raised his voice. He had put them in the Ford Kuga in the car park, just like any father in a hurry to get back to work.

Jacket buttoned up to his neck, he had bent down to Amanda.

'You take care of the kid. Make sure he doesn't do anything that will get us noticed. I'll be there in a minute.'

He had stood up, taken a step forward, then bent down to the Ford Kuga again.

'Wait for me in the car! Don't try anything, if you care about the kid.'

This time he had headed straight for the house, crossing the gravel driveway in three strides, without turning around.

As soon as the door of the house closed behind him, Amanda had scrambled into the driver's seat. She had to bite her lip to stop herself screaming. She bit it so hard, she drew blood. She had to keep quiet so as not to make Malone any more frightened than he already was.

No key in the ignition!

For a brief moment, she thought about undoing Malone's seat belt, taking him by the hand, and running away, losing themselves in this labyrinth of thuyas, opening the first gate she found and releasing the dogs; or simply running to Dévote's house, across the road, and barricading themselves in.

But only for a brief moment . . .

She stared into Malone's eyes.

Her life didn't matter. The only thing that mattered was her child's life.

*

* *

Dimitri looked up and wiped the corner of his lips. His right hand froze, the glass of whisky paused midway between the table and his mouth. The glass, three-quarters full, shook perilously; he felt like a ridiculous little kid who, as soon as his parents' backs were turned, had stolen a whole handful of sweets.

Alexis Zerda was silent, as if hesitating.

Dimitri stammered: 'What were the cops doing at Timo's place? Fuck, do you think they've caught him? Or found his corpse?'

Zerda undid three buttons of his jacket.

'That was a stupid idea of yours, Dimitri, making the phone call. Another stupid idea.'

Dimitri sniggered and took a long, defiant swig of Glen Moray.

'You agreed with me, didn't you? Maybe you know more about child psychology than I do? Did the Romanian give you a few lessons before he went up in smoke?'

He drained his glass while Zerda undid the last few buttons of his jacket.

270

'You're in the shit, Alex. Not me. I've no connection with Timo Soler or any of your problems. I just did you a favour. Full stop.'

Zerda walked across the living room and stood in front of the only window, the one that looked out over the estate. Amanda and Malone were still waiting inside the Ford. There was no one else in the car park or the gardens that surrounded it. He had to act quickly now.

'You're an idiot, Dimitri. Even at Bois-d'Arcy, you were the stupidest guy in the entire prison. I actually felt sorry for you. That's probably how you managed to find a woman. And a kid.'

He put his hand on the windowpane.

'You don't deserve them, Dimitri.'

Zerda abruptly pulled the curtains shut. The room fell into darkness, as if the sun had fallen on its face.

Dimitri slammed the whisky glass down on the living room table.

'What are you doing?'

'You realise you're responsible for the death of a child?'

'The kid's not dead.'

'For Amanda, he is.'

Dimitri licked his whisky-soaked fingers, then stared through the dim light, trying to follow Zerda's slow movements. One hand in his pocket, the other near his belt.

He rubbed his index finger over his gums and giggled. The forty per cent alcohol anaesthetised the urge to cry out. Alexis was right. He was an idiot. Even now, when Zerda was about to point a gun at him, he was incapable of reacting as he should have done. He had no idea what Alexis wanted to hear, what he was searching for. His terror transformed into another giggle.

'I may have lost one kid, but I found her another one. Better than the first one! You've seen Amanda, you know it's true. She prefers this one.'

Alexis Zerda took out his pistol as casually as if he were reaching for a handkerchief. In the darkness, all Dimitri could see was an arm with a long, narrow shape at its end. He thought he could recognise the weapon: the Zastava, that Serbian pistol that Alexis had bought from a half-mad soldier who'd come back from Kosovo nearly fifteen years ago.

Zerda whispered as he took a step forward.

'You see, Dimitri, I'd regret having to get rid of Amanda. Very much so. But you? Not at all . . .'

Dimitri had stopped giggling now. Laughing in the face of death, Dimitri realised, was not going to help him out of this situation. Nor would turning his back on it.

He stood up, staggering slightly.

'Stop messing around, Alex. What good would it do you to kill me? I don't know anything about the loot, or about the kid. I don't know anything about anything.'

'The cops will be here in a minute or two. You'll hold them up for a while. Like the shrink has. I'm like Hansel and Gretel, dropping bodies behind me instead of breadcrumbs. Big bodies blocking the path, that take time to move, which gives me time to vanish.'

Dimitri continued to stare at the barrel of the Zastava. He could see it clearly now. It was lit by a single shaft of light coming through a gap in the curtains, like a theatre spotlight. According to the lunatic soldier who'd sold it to Alexis, that gun had killed dozens of Bosnians; men, women and children.

He stammered: 'I'd delay them a lot longer if I were alive, Alex. You go off with the kid, and I'll keep them busy. I can talk for hours if I have to. I'm good at that. You'll have time to go wherever you want.'

'I know. And you're right. You are good at bullshitting. So let's just say that I'm doing this for the pleasure of it.'

*Bang.*

The ten-millimetre bullet went straight between Dimitri's eyes. He collapsed on the carpet, knocking over the table, the glass and the bottle of Glen Moray.

Alexis looked at him for less than two seconds, just enough time to check he wasn't going to get back up, then headed over to the window.

Opened the curtain.

And shuddered.

Amanda was standing there, looking at him.

Zerda's first reflex was to look past her. He exhaled with relief. The kid was still in the car, seat belt on. His eyes were drawn back to Amanda's face.

The two of them stayed like that, staring at each other, separated only by the dirty window.

Alexis could read fear on Amanda's face. No pain, no sadness, no compassion for the body stretched out on the carpet in a pool of alcohol.

Just fear.

Stranger yet, he thought he could see what looked like the ghost of a smile on Amanda's lips. As if she were relieved. Maybe even attracted to him. Yes, that was what Zerda thought when he went over the moment in his mind afterwards as he was driving the Ford Kuga: that this determined little woman, who was still almost pretty if she put her mind to it, if you took the time to look deep into her eyes, asked her to put on some make-up and wear nice clothes; that this woman, while she might have been terribly scared of the man standing opposite her, with a gun in his hand, couldn't help admiring him too.

When Amanda's lips moved behind the window, almost imperceptibly, leaving a small circle of condensation on the glass, he thought he could lip-read what she was saying. Two words.

*Thank you.*

# 49

The police car emerged onto Avenue du Bois-au-Coq.

'Manéglise, 17 kilometres, 18 minutes,' indicated the GPS fastened under the rear-view mirror. Officer Cabral was hoping to get there in half the time. He accelerated again, siren wailing, overtaking the tram on his left. In the distance, the corrugated-iron village stood out against the aluminium-coloured sky.

Marianne yelled into the phone:

'Don't bother going through the files now, JB! Just grab a basket – or a cardboard box, or a bin liner or whatever – and throw all of Dragonman's dossiers into it. I want to know everything he might have heard, written or guessed about Malone Moulin. The kid's drawings, the shrink's notes, bring me everything! If you hurry up, you can meet us in Manéglise in less than fifteen minutes. You can do a presentation!'

'Wouldn't it be better if I . . .' Lieutenant Lechevalier stammered.

'We've been barking up the wrong tree this whole time, JB. Just before Malone called his mother at Timo Soler's apartment, I received the DNA test results on that cup the kid drank from. The analysts compared the boy's saliva with Dimitri Moulin's genetic fingerprint, and they're certain: Dimitri Moulin is not Malone's biological father! They pulled the wool over our eyes, JB. We've been playing ping-pong between two cases when in reality this was always one case. So get a move on.'

Officer Cabral entered the roundabout almost without slowing down. The traffic was denser now. Other vehicles swerved out of the way as the police car snaked in and out, like a rude child pushing its way through a long queue.

Marianne now called the station. Lucas Marouette, the intern, was on duty. He would have a fresh eye on this whole business. He'd know where to look; he'd already proved that.

'Lucas? I want you to read through the Deauville robbery file, concentrating on Timo Soler. I want his whole life story, from childhood on. Papy's in Potigny, the village where Soler grew up. He might find new information there, but in the meantime, give me everything you can find on the man's private life, especially any clues that he might have had a child, a child he was bringing up with his girlfriend. Better still, identify her.'

Cabral slammed on the brakes behind a Peugeot 207; the learner driver seemed to have been panicked by the siren. Marianne grabbed hold of the door, without letting go of her phone, briefly thinking about her poor, battered nose.

'I want that girl's name!' she yelled at Marouette, without giving him time to reply.

The police car overtook the 207, which was blocking the only entrance to the shopping centre ahead of them. They went past a car park that seemed to go on forever, like a field of tarmac where some mad farmer had sowed some cars. Multicoloured, lined up in perfect rows, ready to be harvested.

Marianne's gaze fell on the red and green bird looking down from the immense façade of the Auchan hypermarket. At noon on a Friday, the Mont-Gaillard shopping centre was already as busy as it was during a weekend sale.

Officer Cabral went across another roundabout, as the cars moved to the side to let them pass.

'I should use the siren next time I want to go shopping here,' he joked.

Marianne wasn't listening. She had turned off her mobile and her eyes remained glued to the shop signs that were flashing past. According to Vasily, it was here – in this shopping centre – that young Malone claimed to have seen his mother for the last time. His real mother, the one before Amanda Moulin.

A mother who was hiding out in an apartment in the Neiges quarter with Timo Soler? Who'd handed over her child, ten months before, to a stranger?

But why?

Why hand over her child, and at the same time concoct the craziest of stratagems – an MP3 player sewn into the belly of a cuddly toy – so that the boy would remember her? How was it even possible since that kid, Malone, had lived with the Moulins since birth, had grown up with them during the first three years of his life?

Could he have two families? Alternating custody, shared between two mothers? Each trying to erase the memory of the other in order to keep the boy for herself?

'Manéglise, 12 kilometres, 9 minutes,' the panicked GPS corrected itself.

Cabral had gained seven minutes on the duration of the trip announced by the stubborn female voice. As if it were a personal competition between them.

'Go faster, Cabral,' Marianne hissed.

No female solidarity.

Ahead of them, a water tower, entirely painted with marine motifs, looked like a lighthouse lost in the middle of some fields. Was it there to direct tractors lost in the countryside?

It's all one case, thought Marianne again. Timo Soler, Alexis Zerda, Vasily Dragonman, Malone Moulin. All of it connected, right from the beginning.

Two families.

One child.

It didn't make sense.

# 50

*Little hand on the 1, big hand on the 2*

The Ford Kuga crawled forward. The narrow road ran between two embankments covered with vegetation; there was barely room for the SUV to pass between the branches of hornbeams and chestnuts. The Kuga's large wheels rolled smoothly over the road's ruts and the tufts of grass growing through the tarmac.

Zerda turned to Malone.

'Open your eyes, boy. My car is a time machine. You know, like in *Back to the Future*? Are you ready for your trip?'

The child looked at him, not understanding. Ahead of them, the horizon seemed to grow wider between the thick silhouettes of oaks that were almost intertwined.

Amanda, sitting in the passenger seat, wrung her hands.

*A time machine.*

She thought about telling Zerda to be quiet. But, really, what would that change?

Alexis had no idea how to communicate with a young kid. She did, but what could she do apart from pray that Malone had erased everything from his brain and that the snake behind the wheel believed it? Pray that Zerda was convinced that Malone no longer represented a danger to him.

She imagined the brain of a child as being something like a computer. Even when you put things in the bin, when you thought you'd got rid of them – emails, files, photographs – they were still there, somewhere, hidden. All you had to do was ask someone who knew about computers and they could find them, months or even years later . . . The only effective method was to throw the computer

277

out of a window, from the fifteenth floor, drive over it, or toss it in the fire.

She just hoped that Zerda wasn't thinking that way. He was driving in silence now, wearing sunglasses even though what little sunlight there was came filtered through the trees.

Amanda turned to Malone. He was calm, staring through the window, as if used to long silent drives. The timid sun was playing hide-and-seek with his light brown hair. Next to him, on the back seat, Amanda had thrown the bag in which she kept all the important documents: family record book, passports, medical files. Zerda had told her to bring everything, without giving any indication of where they were going.

As she swivelled to look at Malone, Amanda's legs came closer to Alexis's. He stroked her left knee, just before putting the car into second gear.

Amanda sat back in her seat again.

He wasn't even coming on to her, she thought. There was nothing sexy about her any more; she had long ago stopped believing in all that stuff: attraction, seduction, and so on.

Amanda's idea of attractiveness was limited to smiling at her customers in the minimarket and looking clean and well-rested, not even elegant or made-up. For the rest, she had given up on the game of romantic love. There were too many cheats. She thought of love as a swindle aimed at suckers, like those lottery tickets she sold to her customers. They never won, or if they did it was always a tiny amount, just enough to keep them wanting to play, never the jackpot that would set them up for life.

She might not be the cleverest person in the world, but at least she understood that. Disappointment. Dimitri had taught her well on that particular front. No, Alexis's hand on her knee was not an attempt at seduction, it was simply a reflex, born from an assumption of male dominance.

Zerda fiddled with the car radio. He turned up the volume at the back of the car while reducing it at the front.

RTL2. Freddie Mercury was singing the first words of 'Bohemian

278

Rhapsody' against the notes from a piano.

Amanda realised that Alexis wanted to talk to her without Malone hearing. All the same, she had to listen hard to catch each word that whistling voice of his uttered. No way was she going to move even a centimetre closer to him.

'Don't worry, Amanda. I know what you're thinking, but I won't hurt him. If I was going to do anything to him, I'd have done it a long time ago, which would have made everything a lot simpler. I'm a dangerous man – a piece of shit, a bastard, call me what you want – but I wouldn't harm a kid.'

He'd lifted up his sunglasses so he could look at her with his snake's eyes.

It was impossible to trust him.

His hand slid off the gear stick and back up Amanda's thigh.

Caressing her jeans. Crappy jeans, bought for ten euros at the local market.

Just a reflex, showing he's the dominant male, she repeated in her head. A habit. Almost a form of politeness.

Without a word, she gently pushed his hand away.

A thin smile spread across his face, although he turned his eyes back to the road.

'I'm not like Dimitri,' he added. 'I don't hurt kids.'

With his right hand, he rummaged inside the glove compartment, then handed Amanda a photograph that had been trapped beneath a road map.

'I took this with me before I left. Dimitri gave it to me. Do you recognise it?'

*Malone.*

'You have to speak to the kid, Amanda. It's better if you explain it to him rather than the cops. I'll be long gone by then.'

For an instant, Amanda stared at the landscape that opened up behind a new house surrounded by low hedges, then the path forked and they were driving between thick embankments again.

'Think about it, Amanda. So he understands what's happening to him. I don't think they'll let you keep Malone after this.'

He turned up the volume on the radio with his fingertip. Freddie's piano faded and Brian May's guitar took over.

Amanda's brain was a computer too. It had resisted a ten-metre fall, a truck driving over it and the flames of Hell.

Her memory was still intact. A simple photo placed in her hand was enough to bring back images of the past, stored in her brain like a DVD kept at the back of a drawer.

*Malone.*

It was ten months ago – 23 December, to be precise.

Brief scenes flashed past. The birth of Malone. Malone crawling outside his bedroom on the upstairs carpet. Malone standing in the park. His first steps. His first words. His first teeth. Malone crying. Malone laughing. His mother sweating, in a permanent state of alert. Malone, such a daredevil, climbing, exploring, walking tightropes. His mother's infinite precautions: the bars screwed to his cot, the straps fastened to his high chair, the bolted barriers at the top and bottom of the stairs, always closed behind her.

*Malone.*

In her nervous hands, the photograph warped, distorting the child's face.

She remembered how she'd screamed when she found Malone's body at the bottom of the stairs, the laundry basket falling from her hands. Dimitri, glass in hand, who was supposed to be watching over the child. Ten metres away from him, and he saw nothing, said nothing, did nothing.

Accident and emergency. Hope. Waiting.

The diagnosis.

A few hours in a coma. Brain trauma. Malone would live.

Probably.

But we don't know any more than that. We have to wait.

Coming out of the Joliot-Curie private clinic, eleven days later, away from the eyes of neighbours, cousins, friends, suspicion and shame. As far as those people were concerned, they had gone on holiday to Brittany to visit Mont-Saint-Michel, the ramparts of

Saint-Malo and the aquarium. They'd have time to explain, later.

The return to Manéglise, with Malone.

The after-effects.

Malone the daredevil who now never left his chair; Malone the tightrope-walker, now incapable of dressing himself, feeding himself, going to the toilet; Malone the explorer, who now moved nothing but his eyes, and who seemed only to see what was minuscule – smaller than himself, at least – insects, flies, ants, butterflies. Those things that moved around him when he was put down somewhere.

The rest – the bigger things, the real, important, living things – he no longer noticed: not flowers, not trees, not cars.

Nor even his mother.

Amanda touched her fingertip to the sad face of the boy in the photograph. Malone had just come out of the hairdresser's; he had a right-hand parting with the fringe covering his forehead and he was wearing his check shirt from Du Pareil Au Méme, the one that was too tight for him. Strangely, she didn't think he was handsome any more. His eyes were inexpressive, too close together, and his nose was too big – he got that from Dimitri. She turned slightly towards Zerda, shielding the photograph with her left hand, so Malone – who was still staring out the window – wouldn't see it.

Freddie was still singing. This song went on forever.

Amanda had never talked about the accident with anyone, except for Professor Lacroix, head of the department that treated Malone at the Joliot-Curie clinic. She'd decided to wait until Malone was better before she told those around her; laughing about the huge scare they'd had, the terrible ordeal they'd been through. According to Professor Lacroix, there was a fifteen per cent chance that Malone would recover completely. And if fate went the other way – towards the thirty-three per cent chance that everything would quickly get worse – she would close the shutters, barricade herself in her house and never speak to anyone again.

It was a question of love, Professor Lacroix had told her. Love and money, Amanda quickly understood. On the internet, she found an American laboratory that operated on cerebral lesions, replacing the damaged neurones through the stimulation of new axons, or at least that was her understanding. They were the only team in the world to practise that kind of neurosurgery. It cost hundreds of thousands of dollars for even a simple operation, but Professor Lacroix seemed sceptical when Amanda handed him the printout.

It's a question of love, Mrs Moulin, not money.

No need to draw her a picture. She got it. She knew all about disappointment.

The days passed. Malone's condition stabilised. Or appeared to.

Except that other kids of his age developed, started talking more, counting, drawing. He didn't.

Or at least he did, but only with flies, butterflies and ants. She helped him as best she could, taking an interest, playing with those damned insects the way other mothers would collect pearls or beads for their children.

He was examined every three days. To establish a longitudinal diagnosis, as the doctors explained.

Amanda looked at the photo again. Read the words on it.

*Malone, 29 September 2014.*

The picture had been taken in front of the Needle Rock in Étretat, three months before the accident. That day, Malone had spent the afternoon running after the seagulls on the sea wall.

The last letter from the Joliot-Curie clinic arrived on 17 January 2015, along with two bills. Amanda had learnt how to read between the lines of the medical reports. She wasn't so stupid, when she put her mind to it. She'd gently let the sheet of paper fall from her hands.

Malone was doomed. He had only a few weeks to live. They'd found a crack inside his brain, a tiny crack, but it was growing little by little, at increasing speed, endangering his vital functions; a fissure between the brainstem and the spinal cord, precisely in the part of the brain known as the pons Varolii, which controls motor functions and the senses.

And it was cracking.

Inexorably.

Malone's life expectancy was no longer than that of a dragonfly, a butterfly, or an ant.

A mayfly.

It was as if he'd always known.

Amanda opened the window and slowly tore the photograph into strips, before tearing them again until the picture was confetti, which she scattered in the wind. Alexis Zerda, hands on the wheel, still wore the same frozen smile. Like some facial tic. Unless that was his way of trying to look reassuring.

Amanda closed the window.

Freddie came to the end of his song, his voice very quiet, in contrast to his usual vocal pyrotechnics.

Piano and voice, back to the beginning.

Dimitri hadn't said anything that morning. He'd just read the clinic's letter, then put his glass on the table and put on his coat.

She could still hear the door banging shut, the car starting up.

He hadn't dared talk to her about it. He'd been thinking about the idea, at the back of his head, for a few days now.

Maybe he was hoping for forgiveness. As if Amanda might one day look at him without that contempt, that absolute disgust.

He left without a word.

To find a second child.

The way you might replace a dead dog with another one.

# 51

*Today, Christmas Eve, that bearded fuckwit turned up without an iPhone 6, without an iPad, without a Nintendo 3DS, but with a language exchange trip to Frankfurt and a subscription to Acadomia.*
Want to kill
*My little sister never even had a chance to believe in Father Christmas. He's up the chimney, burning with his sack.*

*Convicted: 853*
*Acquitted: 18*

www.want-to-kill.com

'Maybe he didn't want to try his Carambar cake?'

Marianne Augresse rolled her eyes at Officer Bourdaine. She was standing in the entrance hall, next to the cherry-wood coat rack, looking from room to room. The kitchen and the living room. In fact, Bourdaine's inappropriate comment didn't seem that stupid, on the face of it.

In the kitchen, you would have sworn that Amanda Moulin was about to appear at any moment – tea towel in one hand, sponge in the other – and shout cheerfully to her family: 'It's ready! Come and eat!'

The table was set. Tomato and mozzarella salad in the fridge. Fresh bread. Cake in the oven, slightly burnt. That was the only false note.

In the living room, everything had gone mad. Dimitri Moulin was lying on the rug with Japanese patterns that vaguely resembled water lilies. They were now floating, not on a lake, but in a pool of half-dried blood.

A bullet between the eyes.

No weapon visible.

And no witnesses; Amanda and Malone Moulin had disappeared.

The Moulins' car was still in the garage; they'd checked. Everything suggested that Amanda Moulin had shot her husband, then fled with her son. Or her supposed son, anyway. On foot?

Marianne Augresse took a step forward, to the door of the little cupboard under the stairs. She was still struck by the contrast between the two rooms, one scene homely, the other the scene of a crime, as if the two places were separated by an insurmountable barrier; two universes that could not be connected. At least not like this. Not so brutally.

There was something else.

Marianne forced herself not to get drawn into hypotheses that, for the moment, led nowhere. After all, she just had to let the forensics team do their job; it wouldn't take them long to find out if someone else had been in the room, even if there was only one glass of whisky on the living room table; even if – according to his boss – Dimitri Moulin had left work at about eleven thirty, and had, therefore, been killed less than thirty minutes after arriving home for lunch.

Constantini and Duhamel were patrolling the neighbourhood in search of witnesses. Two other vehicles were driving around Manéglise and the surrounding area. If Amanda Moulin really had panicked and had walked off somewhere with her son, she couldn't have got very far.

Except Marianne didn't believe for a second that was what had happened.

She approached the window and saw Lieutenant Lechevalier's car come screeching to a halt outside the house. She waited while JB bent over the back seat and picked up a large plastic box, gathering a few sheets of paper that had scattered over the floor. Presumably the collection of documents found at Vasily Dragonman's flat.

JB had got here quickly. He was a good, efficient worker. Even if he was furious that he hadn't been able to see his wife and kids since the day before – furious with his captain in particular. JB would be useful, the most useful of all of them when it came to sifting through every month of a three-year-old child's brief life.

The captain turned around and stared at Dimitri Moulin's corpse. She wanted to think about something else.

A bullet between the eyes.

The shot was clean, precise. The work of a professional, not of a woman holding a revolver for the first time in her life, upset after an argument, or trying to defend herself, or take revenge; a woman who might have panicked and pressed the trigger in a moment of desperation. Marianne didn't believe it was premeditated either. Even the most conscientious, the most submissive wife wouldn't place a plate, a glass, a fork and a knife in front of the chair belonging to the man she was planning to kill as soon as he got home.

The captain's mobile buzzed. A text.

*Angie.*

Her friend was still worrying about the body found at Cap de la Hève. Marianne didn't have time to call her back, to confirm that yes, it really was Vasily Dragonman who'd been murdered. The two of them would commemorate him by getting drunk one of these nights, but right now, her pretty hairdresser couldn't say anything that would help her find her way through the labyrinthine passages of the psychologist's brain. There was no rush; she would call her back later.

Marianne Augresse put one foot on the first step of the staircase, then said to Officer Benhami:

'Tell JB to join me in the kid's bedroom. If the box is too heavy, you can help him bring it upstairs. We'll stay up there while you play with your cotton buds and test tubes.'

\*

\* \*

JB had spread Malone's drawings over the bed, about fifteen A4 sheets that Vasily Dragonman had kept in his file.

The bedroom couldn't have been more than fifteen square metres and had a slightly sloping ceiling on the wall opposite the stairs. Marianne was obliged to bend down to turn on the little CD player on the bookshelf, before hooking it up to the MP3.

The recording broke the silence in the child's room. A soft, calm voice, which could have been masculine or feminine. If you were only half-listening, you might even have thought it was the voice of a young child, the kind of voice you heard on cartoons, the kind of voice a cuddly toy might have, if it could talk; in Malone's mind, at least.

Because after listening more carefully, Marianne felt quite certain that it was a woman's voice, although the higher-pitched sounds were sometimes a little exaggerated and there was a metallic ring to certain intonations. Marianne was fairly sure that the voice had been altered, probably put through some basic sound-processing software. That, too, should be easy enough to check.

*Gouti was just three years old, which was already pretty big in his family, because his mother was only eight and his grandfather, who was very old, was fifteen.*

What was the point of distorting Gouti's voice?

*They lived in the biggest tree on the beach, which had roots shaped like an immense spider. Their place was on the third floor, first branch on the left, between a tern that was almost always away on trips and a lame owl who had now retired, but who used to work on the pirate ships.*

The answer seemed obvious. The voice had been modified so that it wouldn't be recognised. So that, should Gouti and his heart end up in the hands of a stranger, or if Malone talked too much or wasn't careful enough to hide his stories under his duvet, no one would be able to track them back to the storyteller.

His real mother? Timo Soler's girlfriend?

This answer was only partially satisfying. How could anyone be identified if their voice was the only clue? Because the police already knew this person? That was the most logical explanation, even if it did not seem fully convincing. If the girl had a criminal record, if she'd known Soler because they belonged to the same criminal circles, it wouldn't have been difficult to identify her, whether her voice was camouflaged or not.

Marianne was hardly even listening to the story, which she'd played so many times the day before, but JB seemed entirely concentrated on the tale delivered by this robot voice, like something from a Japanese cartoon. As there was no space left on the bed, he'd unfolded the map on the little desk. He knew the rules. Marianne had already told him what kind of game they were playing: a treasure hunt! Picking up the game where Vasily Dragonman had left off. Same map, same clues, although they had one big advantage over the psychologist: they were going to look first at the areas around Cap de la Hève, because that was where Dragonman had been murdered. Because he was getting too close?

The captain looked around Malone's room for a few seconds. There were a lot of toys, almost too many for a family as poor as the Moulins, though Marianne knew it would be stupid to see that as abnormal. Malone was an only child, and everything in this room spoke of the parents' love – or the mother's, at least – for this child.

The captain took a closer look at the fluorescent calendar hanging above the bedside table, with the rocket on one of the seven planets – today's, Friday. So that was how Malone kept track of the days, when some kids his age were incapable of distinguishing evening from morning.

Everything had been calculated. Planned in infinite detail. Malone had been manipulated for nearly a year by his adoptive parents; or by that woman, unknown to the Moulins, so that he would retain some trace of his life before, despite the efforts of his new family.

Marianne sat down on the little bed, pushing the drawings out of the way and leaning back against a Buzz Lightyear pillow, the twin of another bearing the likeness of Woody. Below, she could hear the heavy footsteps of the forensics team. She had no desire to go downstairs. Marianne felt good, at peace, in this pastel-coloured room that seemed like a sanctuary. JB brushed past her to pick up some large, multi-coloured magnets, them used them to fix a few other drawings to the yellow radiator.

She had been sharing the intimacy of this little room with him for several minutes now, and she had noticed how at ease her deputy seemed. In this unfamiliar environment, he had almost instinctive points of reference. You could tell it was natural for him to lift up the sheets of a bed and find the toy hidden there that was causing the bump; to tidy up a toy the way other men would pick up a scrap of paper; to find a book just by glancing along the spines of the hundred or so arranged on the bookshelf; to walk around the carpet without crushing any of the Playmobil figures or small cars scattered around, his movements assured and reassuring. Elegant.

A Chippendale in a Toys R Us magazine.

It was totally seductive. He was the cream of the crop. Those bodybuilders at her gym could sweat all their lives without even coming up to JB's ankles.

She imagined his giant shadow as he walked past the nightlight on his daughter's bedside table to give her a goodnight kiss. And she felt, like a fantasy, what those parents must feel when they go to hide a coin from the tooth fairy under their child's pillow, to tell a story in a whispered voice, to share a three-way hug – or ten-way if you included the cuddly toys; that daily complicity that gives couples who hate each other a reason to stay together, who go on putting up with each other for those seconds of eternity that no orgasm can replace.

For an instant, Marianne thought of the bedroom in her apartment, the one next to hers, unoccupied but crammed full of never-opened cardboard boxes, her dusty guitar, her collection of faded Peruvian dolls, and a drying rack hung with underwear that did not excite anyone. For an instant, she imagined it with a rainbow mobile hanging from the ceiling, pink cat wallpaper, giraffe curtains, a carpet covered in clowns . . .

Christ, Marianne! Get a grip!

On the wall facing her was a square painted slate-grey on which you could draw, erase your drawing, then start again. The box of chalks was lying next to it.

To get her mind off the emptiness tugging at her belly, Marianne picked up a piece of white chalk. Then she wrote:

Who is Timo Soler's girlfriend?

Is she Malone's mother?

Why did she disguise her voice?

Why did she hand over her child to Amanda and Dimitri Moulin?

Why did she give a cuddly toy the memories her son was going to lose?

What was he supposed to remember? Was there a precise aim? For a precise moment?

Does the answer exist, encoded in Gouti's stories?

The chalk broke as she was writing the ninth question mark. She picked up another piece.

Who is Gouti? Why is Malone's cuddly toy an agouti, an amnesiac rodent?

She then changed her chalk to a pink one, and wrote in a mixture of joined-up writing and capital letters:

WHO killed VASILY DRAGONMAN?

WHO killed DIMITRI MOULIN?

WHO will be the next victim?

WHO is the killer? Who are the killers?

WHERE is AMANDA MOULIN?

WHERE is MALONE MOULIN?

WHERE is TIMO SOLER?

WHERE is ALEXIS ZERDA?

WHERE is the loot from the Deauville robbery?

Nervously, she used what remained of the chalk to trace a circle around all of these words, then wrote, diagonally:

WHAT CONNECTS ALL THESE QUESTIONS?

JB looked at her.

'Is that all? Just twenty questions?'

Marianne calmly put away the chalk, then checked her watch.

'One last one, for good measure. Why hasn't Papy called me back?'

# 52

Federico Soler. 1948–2009.

In the Potigny cemetery, the dead were not very old. That, at least, was what Lieutenant Pasdeloup was thinking as he wandered slowly among the gravestones, doing macabre mental calculations.

Sixty-one. Fifty-eight. Sixty-three.

Seventy-seven, almost a record.

The closure of the biggest mine in western France, in 1989, had not had much effect on the life expectancy of the miners who had become unemployed. For them, it was already too late. Or too early. Those who could, got away; the rest were trapped here. Behind the cemetery, Papy spotted the bell tower of the Polish chapel, Notre-Dame-de-Czestochowa, but the flags on the graves in front of him and the languages on the epitaphs betrayed the presence of a score of other nationalities who had washed up here and would now never leave.

Italians, Russians, Belgians, Spaniards, Chinese.

A few minutes later, the lieutenant stopped in front of another grave, larger, a coffin for two.

Tomasz and Karolina Adamiack, the parents of Ilona Adamiack, who had changed her name to Lukowik when she married Cyril. The two of them had died in the same year, 2007 – at fifty-eight and sixty-two respectively. Papy now had all the elements of the dossier in his head, the precise life story of the four members of what he thought of as the Gryzoń Gang. Four kids, all born here, a few houses apart. The parents of Cyril Lukowik were the only people who still lived in the village, still at the same address: 23 Rue des Gryzoń. Alexis Zerda's parents had moved south, to Gruissan, on the Languedoc coast, about ten years before.

Papy lingered a while longer in the small, empty cemetery. Before entering it, he had quickly made a tour of the village. In the centre, everything had been almost completely reconstructed. Traces of the village's past were reserved for insiders. Small iron trolleys used as flowerpots at each entrance to the village; a Rue de la Mine; a Stade des Gueules Rouges (Red Faces Stadium) with its Mining Petanque court; a water tower in the shape of a derrick.

As if that time were lost.

As if the children who had grown up here were lost.

No more mine, no more parents, no more work.

It wasn't an excuse, just an explanation.

Here, in Potigny, dire poverty. Over there, in Deauville, barely fifty kilometres to the north, the sea.

Two villages of the same size, in the same region, but which did not even seem to belong to the same world.

It wasn't an excuse; but it was a temptation . . .

Papy approached the cemetery gates, on his way back to his car. Yes, it was easy to understand why the Gryzoń Gang had wanted to go shopping in Deauville, using a Beretta 92 and two Maverick 88s instead of a chequebook or a credit card. It wasn't even a question of necessity. More like identity.

Being born in a Norman mining village? What a joke! Growing up in one of those little cottages in the Pays d'Auge, without any cows or apple trees . . . who could believe it? Not even a local singer like Pierre Bachelet to give themselves a semblance of pride. Nothing but some crappy mining tunnels, worked for a few decades and then abandoned. A sacrificial generation, from all over the world, who came only to end up dead and forgotten here, in this tiny cemetery. Apart from the Poles, perhaps.

It was the opposite of his own life, thought Papy, pushing open the gates. His own family – children, grandchildren and ex-wives – had dispersed all over France, all over the world. For a few seconds, he thought about his daughter, Anaïs. It would be 7 a.m. in Cleveland now. She was probably still asleep.

His phone buzzed as soon as he got back to the street. Marianne. A message left fifteen minutes ago. Papy had turned off his phone in the cemetery. Not out of fear of disturbing anyone – he was the only living person there – but out of respect, out of superstition rather than religion. While it hadn't been proven that the radiation from smartphones was toxic for the living, maybe they disturbed communication between ghosts in the hereafter.

'Papy? Are you in Potigny?'

The captain's voice sounded loud and excited in his ear.

'Yeah.'

'Fantastic! It was maybe a good idea, in fact, you going there. I want you to collect everything you can find on Timo Soler. We're looking for a girl, you know that, right? And maybe even a child that he might have had with her. Timo Soler must still have family, friends, neighbours in the village?'

Lieutenant Pasdeloup pictured Federico Soler's grave and the information collected about his son. Timo had been raised solely by his father, until his father's death in 2009, at the age of sixty-one. Lung cancer. His mother, Ofelia, had gone back to Galicia when Timo was just six.

'Timo Soler left Potigny eight years ago. Since then, silicosis has wiped out the generation that knew Timo as a teenager. Seriously, it's worse than a cholera epidemic.'

Marianne's response was a slap in the face.

'Well figure something out, Papy. You're the one who wanted to visit Potigny. It's your responsibility. Find an old teacher, his friends at the football club, a priest, a baker who knew him as a kid, anyone.'

*Anyone . . .*

The streets of Potigny were deserted. The shops were new. The village seemed to have exorcised the ghosts of the mine long ago.

'I had no way of knowing, Marianne.'

'Knowing what?'

'Knowing what would happen this morning. There'd been nothing new on the Deauville robbery for ten months!'

Marianne sighed. Papy reached the long, straight shopping street that ran through the village.

'So what were you hoping to achieve from this little pilgrimage of yours?'

'I have a feeling, an intuition. It's too early to say, but it's a sort of matrix that would connect all the pieces of the puzzle, something that would explain everything. The Rue des Gryzóns, their adolescence here, the empty spaces on their CVs, and all the entries on their criminal records. Also the things Malone Moulin said, that story about the rocket, the fact that this kid has an agouti . . .'

'You're really beginning to annoy me, Papy! Do you realise how much fun we're having here? We're listening to the stories told by a cuddly toy and trying to draw fairy tales on a treasure map. To be honest, you'd be more use to me here. You know this area better than any of my men. Thanks to you, JB's going to be stuck in a child's bedroom, looking at drawings, and he can't even pick up his own kids from school or kiss his wife.'

Just then, Lieutenant Pasdeloup spotted the school, at the end of the street. Opposite it, a pretty girl was emerging from a hairdressing salon. Short skirt, high heels, and blonde hair – although the last detail was perhaps only about ten minutes old.

Papy couldn't help laughing as he thought of the captain's last words.

'What's so funny, Papy?'

'Sorry, Marianne. It's just an image that clashed with what you were saying. JB is the perfect father – that's true. But if you think he leaves the station at four o'clock to pick up his kids . . .'

'What?'

Marianne stood up suddenly, almost banging her head against the sloping ceiling.

'He doesn't really go to see his children,' Papy explained. 'He goes to see the mothers, if you know what I mean. Handbags, not satchels.'

'Huh?'

Papy sighed. 'Yeah. He likes to study all right, private lessons with pretty teachers . . . I was quite shocked too when I found out yesterday. It was JB's wink that tipped me off, but apparently the whole station knew about it already!'

Marianne leant back against the wall with the painted slate on it, her jacket erasing the chalk words that she had written there. All that remained were a few question marks left hanging in the air, a few barely legible words.

*Mother, child, memories, killers . . .*

The captain stared at Lieutenant Lechevalier, who was semi-prone on the bed, covered in a child's sketches. Fully focused on the investigation.

A pro.

Except he wasn't working on Vasily Dragonman's notes or Malone's drawings. JB was looking through the file on the Deauville robbery: the shoot-out on Rue de la Mer.

More interested in gangsters than scribbles and fairy tales, thought Marianne. A liar. Another bastard.

JB turned away from her, and she took the time to examine him, and the details of this child's room.

The cream of the crop? The ultimate fantasy?

In the end, JB's infidelities did not change her vision of family. In fact, they strengthened them. Yes, sharing a few magical seconds with a child is, for a couple, a moment of complicity as intimate as an orgasm. Or, to be more precise, a moment that gradually takes the place of an orgasm for the couple.

And then the mamans can find it with another man.

And the perfect papas cheat on the mamans.

Well, JB did, anyway.

And yet they always demanded shared custody if they were caught.

Marianne said calmly into the phone:

'OK, Papy, call me when you have any news.'

She turned off the phone and turned towards JB.

'Close that file,' she said, her voice harsh. 'We've already been through it a thousand times. You know about children's drawings, about nursery school psychology and early childhood, don't you? You've got kids, right? So get to work! Vasily Dragonman found out something, and surely we're not more stupid than he was!'

JB looked surprised by his boss's sudden anger. He was about to reply when there was a yell from downstairs.

'Captain Augresse. It's Bourdaine. We've found a witness. Dévote Dumontel – she lives in the house across the street.'

Marianne walked out onto the landing. Bourdaine was out of breath from running across the car park. He was waving a piece of paper, his arm curved like a tree branch in December under the weight of its last leaf.

'I showed her the photo, Captain. She's certain she saw Amanda and Malone Moulin get into a car, a black SUV she'd never seen before. She didn't recognise the make, but we can find out. He joined them a few seconds later. The mother and the kid looked terrified, she said. She also offered me a coffee, but I . . .'

'Who, for fuck's sake? Who joined them?'

Bourdaine waved the photograph as if, from three metres above him, Marianne would be able to recognise the portrait.

'Zerda!' he shouted. 'Alexis Zerda!'

Captain Augresse grabbed the banister.

Her mind jumped back to Dimitri Moulin's bullet wound, straight between the eyes. The corpse would already be on its way to the morgue, inside a body bag. Next, she went through the interminable list of crimes planned by Alexis Zerda, the murders he was suspected of: two dead at the BNP bank in La Ferté-Bernard, two others in the attack on the Carrefour van in Hérouville.

And now, since yesterday, two more corpses to add to his list.

Vasily Dragonman. Dimitri Moulin.

And two more to come, probably, in a few hours.

A woman and a three-year-old child.

Why would Zerda stop now?

Marianne ignored Bourdaine, who was, as usual, rooted to the spot while he awaited his orders. She had to take stock, at the speed of a computer that spat out an answer the second you pressed *Return*. They had no idea which direction Zerda had gone, but if he was taking Malone and Amanda Moulin with him, then there had to be some connection with the child's memories. A crazy idea suddenly occurred to her: the only person who might know their destination was Gouti, and Malone probably had the cuddly toy with him in the back of that SUV.

Their only informant.

And – this idea seemed even crazier than the first one – they were able to communicate with him.

Marianne turned to JB, who was still sitting on the child's bed. Still looking through the photographs of the robbery.

On top of Malone's drawings, he had spread the photographs of the two corpses outside the Deauville spa, plus those of the blown-out windows on Rue de la Mer, the cars riddled with bullet holes. Obviously, the two-faced bastard would rather play cops and robbers than actually do any work. This annoyed Marianne, who had, after all, given him perfectly clear instructions a minute ago. But before she could open her mouth to vent all her fury and disappointment at him – the fury of a powerless cop doubled by the disappointment of an innocent woman – he raised his hand and spoke in a confident voice.

A cheat, but a self-assured one.

'I've found something in the file, Marianne. The connection between the robbery and the kid! This explains his trauma, his fear of rain, his double identity and the rest.'

# 53

*Little hand on the 1, big hand on the 5*

It's not rain, Maman-da said.

Rain falls from the sky to the earth, and that's why it hurts – because it falls from so high up, from the clouds above our heads, clouds that we think are small but which are really bigger than anything we know. The tiniest of clouds is bigger than the entire earth. The drops fall all the way through the universe, past the stars and the planets, before smashing down on us.

But not these drops that are wetting your face, Maman-da assured him, even if Malone found it hard to believe her. These drops, she went on, are brought by the wind. They don't smash down on us, they fly away. They come from clouds too, but little clouds made by the waves, white foam that crashes against the pebbles, bounces up and is carried by the wind to the beach, and sometimes even up the cliff.

To convince him, she then used other words that he didn't know. Froth. Swell. Spray.

Still, he didn't trust her. He protected his face with the hood of his coat. When he looked straight ahead, the sky and the sea were the same thing. They were the same colour – grey – and all mixed together. As if the person who was colouring them had messed up. There wasn't even a line to separate them.

It scared him, not to be able to tell the difference between the rain that cut you and the rain that only made you wet. So, Malone lowered his head, under his hood, and looked down.

The castle towers. The pirate ship. The houses, he couldn't see those yet, but he knew they were there. They had to go a bit further down a small staircase, after the big one. His house was the third one.

He didn't know why, but he was sure of it. Everything was just the way it was in Gouti's stories, but now he remembered the images too.

*
*   *

'Give him your hand,' said Zerda's voice.

Alexis scanned the horizon. There was no one in sight. It was a godsend, this icy wind. No walkers to disturb them, here or on the beach below. Even hang-gliders, which were pretty common in this area, would not risk going out on a day like this. As an extra precaution, the SUV was parked behind a copse of chestnut trees: it was impossible to spot, even if you drove slowly along the Saint-Andrieux road.

From this improvised car park, however, you had a view over the entire coastline to the Cap de la Hève. An autumnal Norman landscape, painted in black and white. Zerda imagined for a moment that Vasily Dragonman's ashes were adding to the greyness. The cops had already left the crime scene, the viewpoint where his motorbike had burnt; Alexis hadn't noticed any movement there when he passed by a few minutes earlier. He'd just slowed down, for the pleasure of closing his eyes for a second and reliving the moment when he'd flicked the cigarette end into the puddle of petrol. One corpse after another. A trail of them behind him. At this very moment, the entire Le Havre police force was probably trampling all over Amanda's living room carpet in Manéglise.

How long would it take for the cops to find them? It had taken the Romanian shrink weeks. And even with their greater resources, Zerda doubted the police would be any more intelligent. That was no reason to hang about, though, nor to change his tried-and-tested method . . . the Hansel-and-Gretel strategy.

He put his hand on Amanda's back, then leant down to her ear, opening his other hand and bringing it to the side of her head to protect her other ear from the wind.

'Time to go, Amanda. We'll go down to the hideout, get what we came for, and then we're out of here.'

His hand slid a few centimetres down, to the hollow in her lower back. A curve that he imagined more than his fingers actually felt, beneath all the layers of clothing.

Amanda did not react.

Still impervious to my charms? wondered Zerda. That will come. It's bound to after a life spent with that brute Dimitri. A life spent feeling him inside her, on her, behind her, while the rest of her skin never felt the slightest caress or kiss.

Slowly, his hand descended to the top of her buttocks, as if to urge her forward, to urge her to take Malone by the arm and lead him down the steps carved into the cliff.

*

\*    \*

They had already descended thirty or forty steps. Amanda went first, holding her son by the hand. Malone said nothing, his head lowered, apparently preoccupied by the drops of sea spray. His little legs did not even seem to tire as they went down the steps.

Amanda could sense Alexis close behind her. She knew that if she slowed down, or stopped to catch her breath, he would stand one or two steps above her and put a hand on her shoulder, gently touch one of her breasts, move his body a few centimetres from her mouth, using urgency as an excuse. Don't hang about. Hurry up. We've got to grab the loot, the cops are after us, we have to protect Malone.

All this as an excuse to fondle her.

She wasn't an idiot. He was playing with her, but she did feel aroused. Despite everything. Despite herself. She wasn't so naive as to imagine that she was desirable, that she had any particular charm, that there was any chance of softening Zerda up with a wink and a sway of her hips. She simply calculated that Zerda might want to take advantage of her. Before going on the run for several weeks or months, he might want to make the most of the situation. To rape her, if necessary.

Malone slipped on a step that was higher than the others. She grabbed him at the last second, her grip firm.

Maybe that was a stroke of luck, in the end. Not for her, but for her son. Maybe she could place herself between the boy and the killer? She could be his shield. She liked that image. The extra weight she'd put on might come in useful in that role.

She felt Malone's little hand gripping hers more tightly with every step. Malone was the only male who found her beautiful. The only male for whom she was soft, tender, sensitive. Unique. The only one capable of loving her, without judging her. The only man, when it came down to it, for whom her life was worth living.

She looked down: the stairs seemed to go on forever. At the very bottom, the black carcass of the boat seemed to come apart with each wave, sinking deeper into the dark water each second that followed. And yet the wreck had been there for an eternity.

Still smiling at her son, Amanda pulled on his arm and went a bit faster, trying to put at least three steps between her and the snake at her back.

*

\*    \*

Malone felt reassured. He always felt reassured when he was holding hands with Maman-da. She was as strong as a mountain. She always held him – without him being able to resist, hold back, run or fall – when they crossed a road or walked down a street, or to prevent him tumbling down a staircase, like she'd done just now. Maman-da's hand was like a big elastic band, holding him close.

Malone thought that it must be the same for him and Gouti. He must be a big elastic band for Gouti. Even bigger, in fact: he could do things with Gouti that Maman-da couldn't do with him, like holding him by the hand with his feet not touching the ground, carrying him around all day, throwing him in the air and catching him. He could even sew his arm back on. Yes, Maman-da was much nicer to him than he was to Gouti.

He was never scared, with Maman-da.

He wasn't scared of the ogre behind them either.

He knew how to escape him. He remembered it all now. Almost all, anyway: only the forest and the rocket were missing. The rest was all here. Soon he would be back in the house where he had lived before, with Maman. The third house, the one with the broken shutters. Maybe Maman was waiting there for him. Maybe all three of them were going to live there together: him, Maman and Maman-da.

He was still cold, but he wasn't scared any more.

Except of the drops – the ones from the sea – even hidden like this under his hood.

# 54

JB stood up and stared at the captain, his blue eyes on hers. Those charming eyes, those clever eyes. The eyes of the man who had found the solution before anyone else.

How many girls had he seduced with those eyes?

'Look,' said JB, holding a photograph from the Deauville file under Marianne's nose.

Marianne observed the picture, which she had already examined dozens of times. The Rue de la Mer, outside the spa. The Lukowiks dead in the middle of the street. Cars riddled with bullet holes, parked across from the casino. She didn't see where her lieutenant was going with this.

'You remember, Marianne, that we wondered how Cyril and Ilona thought they would escape, what their plan was for getting out of Deauville? The most likely theory, given that they couldn't run with those bags, was that a car was waiting for them.'

'I know, JB, I know all that. We checked all the registration plates on the cars parked nearby. We didn't find anything.'

'Look at that Opel Zafira. In the foreground, a few metres from the bodies.'

Marianne tried to concentrate, but JB was impatient: he placed his index finger on the glossy paper.

'There, Marianne.'

'Shit,' the captain hissed.

In the back of the grey sedan, they could make out the shape of a child's car seat. The window at the back of the Opel had been shattered by police bullets into thousands of tiny shards that were covering the vehicle's back seat . . . and the booster seat.

'A shower of glass,' said JB. 'Remind you of anything?'

'Malone Moulin's phobia about rain.'

'Timo Soler's supposed son.'

JB and the captain stood side by side in the little, toy-cluttered bedroom. She felt JB's leather jacket brush against her arm, glanced at his stubble, smelt the scent of his ever-present after-shave – Diesel, *Fuel for Life*, or something like that. The concerned father and the submissive husband were now gone; the mask had fallen.

He was just a predator, like the others. A wild beast.

A bastard.

But a good cop.

'So what's your theory?'

The lieutenant gazed at the captain again, his blue eyes like two bullets at point-blank range.

'Just follow the thread, Marianne, you'll come to the same conclusion. We always thought that a driver was waiting for the Lukowiks outside the casino, and that the driver must have got rid of the stolen goods afterwards. But we couldn't prove it; there were probably a hundred cars parked nearby at the time of the robbery, and lots of them disappeared in the scramble that followed the shoot-out. So let's modify our theory a little bit . . . What if the driver was a woman? Timo's girlfriend. And sitting in the back of the car was their son, a boy less than three years old.'

The lieutenant examined the picture again: the bodies, the crowd around them.

'That would actually have been a pretty shrewd idea. Deauville was likely to be blocked off by police barricades after the robbery, but who would suspect a family with a little kid in the back seat?'

'Except that they were shot before they reached the Opel.'

'Yes. If I'm right, then Timo Soler's girlfriend and child were among the dozens of people who were on Rue de la Mer just after the shoot-out, and who vanished soon after.'

'Hundreds, you mean. All those people walking on the beach, along the streets, coming out of the Grand Hotel, the casino, the beach huts, the spa. Once the hail of bullets was over, the whole of

Deauville showed up to cover the event. That could be an advantage too, JB: if the registration number of the Opel Zafira doesn't give us anything, we have hundreds of amateur photographs in the file, a whole CD of them. We'd just have to go through them all, hoping to find little Malone Moulin on one of them.'

'Holding his Maman's hand.'

Marianne touched the photograph again with her fingertip, cautiously, as if the shards of glass might cut her.

'Those lunatics,' she whispered. 'Involving a child of two and a half in an armed robbery . . .'

'He was away from the action, though,' JB pointed out. 'With his mother. The gang thought they could escape without spilling a drop of blood.'

The captain glared at him. His explanations sounded like excuses to her, and his excuses were a sign of irresponsibility. She was being unfair, almost ridiculous, but she didn't care.

'Fucking hell, JB . . . You've got children! That kid saw it all! People shot dead right in front of him, perhaps only a metre away. Possibly people he knew.'

Marianne felt a furious desire to keep spitting her hatred in JB's face. Using a child as bait during an armed robbery, cheating on his wife at the risk of destroying his family, the lives of his innocent children . . . The same crime! Same punishment!

Except that the lieutenant did not seem to notice the anger that was bubbling up inside Marianne. He just put his hand on her shoulder, his eyes flaring with excitement, like a bloodhound catching the scent.

'People he knew . . . You're right, Marianne. That's it! That's the key!'

In the next moment, they were both sitting on Malone's bed.

'Let's go back to the beginning,' said JB. 'A group of friends from Potigny are organising a robbery. Cyril and Ilona Lukowik, Timo Soler, with Alexis Zerda presumably being the fourth musketeer. And then there's also Timo Soler's girlfriend, whose name we don't know.'

'This probably took several weeks of preparation,' Marianne took up the thread. 'Months maybe. Except that, on D-Day, the perfect plan falls apart. Ilona and Cyril are killed before they reach the car and Timo Soler is identified . . .'

'And the police figure out the identity of the fourth robber to be Alexis Zerda, although they don't have any proof. Not a single witness. None of Timo Soler's friends will talk, no one seems to know anything. No one could have imagined at that time that there were two other witnesses: Timo's girlfriend and their son.'

JB moved a little closer to Marianne so he could sift through Vasily Dragonman's file. The captain immediately shifted away from him, crushing Buzz Lightyear's spacesuit beneath her. Buzz protested with a noise that did not sound even remotely interplanetary.

Surprised, Marianne slid her hand under the duvet and took out a small, soft photo album, the cover decorated with monkeys, parrots and tropical trees, which made a noise a bit like a xylophone when you pressed it.

She opened it.

In the first photograph, a baby sleeping in a wicker basket, protected by a kind of delicate white sheet, like mosquito netting or a slightly kitsch piece of lace.

Was that Malone?

She couldn't recognise him . . . Even though, in the cradle, placed next to the baby's little pink mouth, was a brand new, perfectly clean Gouti.

'Two other witnesses,' JB went on, paying no attention to Marianne's discovery. 'If we'd known after the robbery that Timo Soler had a girlfriend and a kid, we'd have questioned them. The girl could have lied to us, of course . . .'

'But,' the captain interrupted, 'we'd have got the truth out of the kid! About his parents. And his parents' friends.'

'About the Lukowiks, and especially about the shadowy person who must have been to the Solers' flat plenty of times, to have a drink, study the map of Deauville, then ride his bike down Rue Eugène-Colas, stopwatch in hand. Alexis Zerda.'

307

'Alexis Zerda,' repeated Marianne. 'Malone knew him – of course he did. He might have sat playing with his toys when he was in the room, or spotted him when he woke up at night to do a pee-pee or sat in his mother's lap. Even subconsciously, he would have remembered his face. If we got to that kid, we'd have proof that Zerda was involved. It's even possible that the Solers, the Lukowiks and Zerda were living together in the same hideout, away from prying eyes and ears.'

'The hideout we're looking for now. The one buried in Malone's memories, surrounded by pirates, castles and rockets. The place that Vasily Dragonman must have found.'

Marianne turned to the next page of the photo album. The plastic pockets were grimy from having been touched by damp, sticky fingers.

The baby was a few months old. He was sitting in the grass. The weather must have been nice, because the baby was wearing only a nappy and a little red bandana on his head that made him look like a pirate.

A boy. Almost bald. Eyes narrowed in the sunlight, so it was impossible to tell what colour they were.

Malone? Maybe . . . She still couldn't be sure.

In his chubby little hand, he was holding Gouti by his hind paw; the toy already looking a little rough around the edges, but still relatively new.

'So that's the theory,' said Captain Augresse in a quiet voice. 'They make the child disappear. Give him to a local foster family, while the affair dies down. And, more importantly, buying themselves time for the child to forget everything he's seen. Alexis Zerda's face in particular.'

Before continuing, she thought about what Vasily had told her regarding the memory of a child, the theories he'd explained in her office less than five days earlier.

'It doesn't take long, JB, for a kid under three to forget his past and become a mute witness for the rest of his life. Only a few weeks to forget a face. A few months, a year at most, to forget everything he's experienced before . . .'

JB moved closer to Marianne again to look at the photo album she had found in Malone's bed.

'Clever. More than that, in fact: it's all very logical. But that still leaves a lot of unanswered questions. How could they pull the whole thing off? How would they find this foster family? And change the boy's identity, at the age of two and a half? And, above all, why take such a risk? All Soler's girlfriend had to do was hide somewhere with her child, because we didn't even know of their existence. We're getting warmer, Marianne, but there's still a piece of the puzzle missing.'

She turned to the next page of the album.

This time, the baby was more than a year old. He was standing up, and disguised as an Indian. Behind the tree where he was leaning, they could see the pond at the centre of the housing estate in Manéglise and the cream-painted houses a bit further off. This time, it was Malone, without any doubt, because the photograph was taken closer up, the face better framed and the light clearer.

No trace of Gouti or any other cuddly toy.

She turned more pages. Malone on a merry-go-round, in front of an aquarium, next to a birthday cake, with Amanda and Dimitri. Three candles.

And then the last page: Malone standing next to a Christmas tree. Curiously, the captain thought this last picture seemed thicker than the others. She slid her finger into the plastic pocket, under the photograph, and removed a sheet of clumsily folded paper.

It was a drawing. Done by an adult, but coloured in – scribbled on – by a very young child.

Malone?

The picture represented a classical Christmas scene: a family together in front of the presents and the sparkling tree; one of those drawings that a parent might do with an over-excited child the night before Christmas as a way of persuading them to be patient, and which they say they will give to Father Christmas when he drops by. The three family members – Papa, Maman, child – were crudely drawn; there was no way it could be used to produce descriptions

. . . although the mother did have long hair, much longer than Amanda Moulin's.

Marianne noted one last detail: the drawing was accompanied by four words. The first two were written next to the star at the top of the tree: *Noel Joyeux.*

The last two were written next to the presents: *N'oublie Jamais.*

She examined the sheet of paper for a moment. It was worn, presumably from being held by Malone for hours on end. The four words were written in a feminine hand, probably his mother's. They would have to compare this handwriting with Amanda Moulin's. What did all of this – the four words, the three figures, the Christmas Eve celebration – represent for this child?

The questions collided in the captain's head.

A new mystery? Another clue? How could they be sure? Every object in this ordinary child's bedroom could have been put there for a reason. To fulfil a planned function, fabricating another reality, the one they wanted Malone to accept. Were these simple toys, or traps cunningly laid? That calendar depicting the solar system? Those stars on the ceiling? This *Toy Story* duvet? That Happyland aeroplane? That crate full of cuddly wild animals? Those Playmobil pirates? This photo album . . .

As she continued to leaf through it, Marianne thought about her deputy's theory. Who was this child in the photos following the first three years of his life, as if it were a fairy tale?

Was it the same child?

Or two different kids, their identities merged through skilfully retouched photographs?

Or, more plausibly, the same baby, but one who had been given two versions of his life. The first version until he was three years old, until the armed robbery, the tragedy, the terrible trauma. And then the second, in order to forget the first, to protect the adults he'd been around since his birth. Sacrificing him in order to protect him.

What mother would accept that? Accept losing her child, even for a few months, if those few months were enough to erase every memory and turn her into a stranger in the child's eyes?

More shocking still, what mother would agree to exchange her child for another? Because they had the proof, after Lucas Marou-ette's excellent investigative work: Amanda and Dimitri Moulin really did have a child, Malone, born on 29 April 2012, at the local clinic.

If Timo Soler's child had taken that other Malone's place, then what had happened to the first child?

Had he, too, flown away?

# 55

*Little hand on the 1, big hand on the 11*

After descending more than half of the stairway, they had almost reached the level of the top of the four large cylinders. The boat was floating in front of them. To their right, the first abandoned houses were beginning to appear.

Amanda had never come here. She had sometimes heard about this strange place, but she'd never made the connection with the stories Malone told.

Now, she understood.

Malone was still holding her hand. Docile. Obedient. Lost in his thoughts. His memories, perhaps.

Zerda was just behind them, moving at the same pace. She could sense that he would have liked to go faster, but he didn't say anything. The boy kept going without whining about it, and that was surely the best that Zerda could hope for.

He didn't say anything either when she stopped for a few seconds to take off her trench coat and sling it over her arm. She was soaked beneath the acrylic, the cold drops of sweat trickling down her back. The fear. It was a difficult descent. The icy wind lashed her face, but all the same she undid two buttons on her blouse.

Her throat bare. Sheer madness. She'd catch her death. Or maybe she'd just delay it. The excuse of the physical effort from the descent was ridiculous, but what other weapon did she have? What choice did she have but to send Zerda a few crude messages?

That she was a woman.

That, if he wanted . . .

This was the only thing she could sacrifice to give Malone a chance of escaping with his life. She had not been able to protect her first child. She had to save the second.

She kept going, one step after another at a steady tempo. There were another hundred or so before they reached the beach. The stairway to hell.

The one that Malone fell down.

The other Malone. The dead one.

On 17 January 2015, the day when she received the letter from the Joliot-Curie clinic announcing that her son had only a few weeks to live, that the lesion was opening up his brain like a crack splitting a stone . . . that day, Dimitri had not said anything when he left.

He had come back that evening.

With another child. To replace the first – the doomed one sleeping in his bedroom upstairs.

The promise of another child, to be more precise; if she agreed.

At first she had thought he was insane. She didn't understand any of his story about the lost friend he hadn't seen in years. Alexis, a friend willing to do them a favour, a mutual favour, an exchange, a swap, a good deal, those were the words he had used, the kind of words you use when you are negotiating with your neighbours at a car boot sale.

Except that they were talking about a child. Their child.

It was temporary, that was what Dimitri had said at first; just for a few weeks, a few months at most, enough time for her to grieve, for the pain to fade. A sort of anti-depressant; a kid in the house, laughing, needing a mother, needing games and hugs. Then, quickly, he realised that this was not the right strategy. Even if he was incredibly stupid.

The image of her husband's corpse passed briefly through Amanda's mind. Temporary. Dimitri had been right, in fact. Temporary – which was prophetic, for him at least. A few months: that was exactly how long he'd had to live.

But that evening, still alive and kicking, Dimitri had changed tack. He'd pronounced the necessary words, the only ones that would have changed her mind, made her accept this infernal plan.

*Maybe we can even keep him.*

Amanda had only asked questions later. She wanted to know the story of this child, a gift from God to replace the other one, she wanted to understand why they had to protect him, why his mother and father wanted to distance themselves from him, to start with. And maybe never see him again, if Dimitri's promise was not merely another lie.

*Maybe we can even keep him.*

Amanda had still hesitated. What an idiot she'd been, when she thought about it now. But to think that, if she'd refused Dimitri and Alexis's proposal, she'd never have felt the warm hand of a little boy in hers again, the warm heart of a sweet little thing against hers, the damp lips of an imp against her flabby cheek.

Thankfully, in the end, she'd said yes. She'd realised that this child they were offering her was a chance – a second chance.

Malone was doomed. He hadn't spoken to anyone but his damn insects in weeks. Maybe he communicated telepathically, with invisible antennae, but he never spoke or expressed his feelings out loud. No joy, no pain. It was the doctors who diagnosed the ache that was gnawing at him, the pain that all the pills he swallowed could not diminish, any more than they could re-solder the fissure that was cleaving his brain. Fevers, migraines, delirium. That cursed, collapsing pons Varolii. He never showed them that he was suffering.

Maybe it had been better for Malone to fly away, to escape his suffering, and for his mother to be given the chance to raise another baby, to protect another child. That seemed so clear to her now, so obvious.

The sea licked at the pebbles. Amanda wondered if the tide was coming in or going out. In the absence of any wet marks on the stilts, any seaweed sticking to the wood, she concluded that it was coming in. They had to move fast.

*

*   *

314

At last, they had reached the final steps. All that remained was a concrete parapet for them to get over, and then they were on the beach. Amanda tried to help her son, but he evaded her, agile, and hauled himself up, only offering her his hand after he'd crossed it, his head covered by the hood of his coat.

A little monkey.

Of course, she'd thought, in tears as she'd looked at Malone sleeping in his chair, drooling, pissing himself, weary like a dying animal. Of course, this one, the new baby, she wouldn't love him as much, he wouldn't be hers. It would just be a way of earning forgiveness from her real child, of proving to him that she could be a good mother, generous, attentive, protective, so that he could be proud of her, there where he was, where he wasn't suffering any more.

She squeezed her son's hand before jumping down onto the pebbles. A little jump of a metre or so. She squeezed hard. Too hard.

He didn't complain. He never complained.

She couldn't have known, back then, just how much she would love this other child, who had to take the same name as her first son.

He was intelligent, imaginative, reserved. He was the kind of man she loved. The kind of man she could have loved, would have liked to love. Kind, thoughtful, sensitive to poetry and flights of fancy, more interested in rockets than cars, loving magic wands more than swords, roses more than balls, dragons more than dogs.

She was prepared to do anything for him, even if he didn't love her, not like a mother, not yet, but with time that would come. And if there wasn't time, at least he could love the memory of her, if she died for him.

For an instant, without even turning to Zerda, she imagined that the salty sea spray dripping down her bare throat made her seem desirable.

Now they'd reached the beach, they were progressing even more slowly. Amanda was sure of it now: the tide was rising fast, the waves rolling over the dry pebbles, a few centimetres higher each time, and them dragging them back, wet, with a noise like a construction site.

Zerda had gone in front. He gestured at the third house, the one with broken shutters, not even glancing at Amanda, never mind noticing her soaked cleavage. In fact, he went to the opposite extreme, exaggerating his indifference, leaning towards Malone, as if his mother no longer existed.

'Hurry up, child. We're not safe here any more. Apparently you told a stranger about our secret hideaway.'

He winked at him, to show him that he wasn't angry about this.

Standing up, he did now look intently at Amanda: a vertical gaze, from her face down to her chest.

'There's no time to lose,' he insisted.

She trembled, thought about putting her jacket back on.

*No time to lose?*

Amanda no longer had the strength to fight. In a few metres, they would reach that abandoned house on this deserted beach. Doubts swirled through her mind; the shifting pebbles beneath her feet prevented her from thinking; the slightest noise broke her concentration; when it came down to it, she was no more intelligent than Dimitri. She would end up the same way, lying in a pool of blood, a bullet between her eyes.

She watched the tide rise higher.

The sea would carry her body far away, to the muddy estuary, where she'd join the other refuse fallen from container ships. Her hand was wet, and Malone's slipped around inside it like a fish fresh out of the water.

Her body, her life, this Calvary . . . she didn't care about any of it, as long as her son survived.

*

\*   \*

Zerda stopped outside the house and grinned at them. Amanda could see the butt of his Zastava again, now he'd opened his jacket. He seemed to be able to read the internal battle she was having with herself, as if he had somehow bugged her brain. She was panicking, hesitating, still hoping at least for a truce, a reprieve. Let him spare the boy. Let him fuck her before he killed her. Let him be content with the loot.

Perfect.

He had no doubts. There was no reason to change his plan. After all, why not continue with his Hansel-and-Gretel idea, leaving bodies behind like breadcrumbs. In the eyes of this kid, he was already an ogre anyway.

He'd wasted too much time over the last few months. Looking after Timo so he wouldn't go to the police. Leaving his treasure in place. Waiting for the kid to forget. For the cops' attention to waver.

He climbed the three steps up to the wood and corrugated iron house, which was in the same dilapidated state as the other ten huts on this crappy beach, then he took the key from his pocket, although it would have been just as easy to open the worm-eaten door with a simple kick. He had to struggle against the euphoria that was rising inside him. He mustn't let it drown him, or intoxicate him.

But it was difficult.

He knew that he would, in a few minutes, emerge from this house where he had spent all those weeks before the robbery, with Timo, Ilona, Cyril and the kid, that he would emerge from this pirates' den, as they'd called it, and he would be rich.

And alone.

# 56

*Saint-Lazare station. Line 14. Friday evening. I'm one of the hamsters rushing up the escalators.*
Want to kill
*I left a bomb down there. They don't understand – they think it was Al-Qaeda. But it was just me.*

*Convicted: 335*
*Acquitted: 1,560*

www.want-to-kill.com

She'd always hated car parks. It was almost a phobia.

Especially the gigantic car parks that you find in shopping centres, those steel plains that were prohibitive to pedestrians, whose exits seem to slip away as soon as you get close to them, but which you had to walk across.

Once, when she was young, she got lost in one.

At the Mondeville 2 shopping centre, in the suburbs of Caen. She'd come into the centre's car park through the north door, feeling sure herself, sulking because her parents had refused to buy her the latest Poke Ball. She, Papa and Maman had entered the centre through an identical door. The south door. Her parents had spent an hour searching for her in the S2 car park, the purple one, while she was crying in N3, the green one. Panicking. Abandoned.

The security guards had found her there.

*Want to kill.*

Car parks. A phobia.

Even as an adult, she lost her car in these places, almost every time.

Today, it was where she lost her love.

Timo's dark blood continued to leak out of him, slowly. Beneath him, the stain was spreading over the ivory-coloured seats of the Twingo, like a sugar cube dunked in a cup of coffee. Timo's face and arms and neck, on the other hand, were growing even paler.

She stroked his thigh, lovingly, reassuringly. Timo was sitting in the passenger seat, which was reclined back as far as it would go, strapped in place by the seat belt. The people wandering around the car park couldn't see anything; at most, those who turned their heads as they walked past the car and tried to look through the windows, like nosy neighbours, might think they were a couple who were in no hurry to move, deep in discussion.

Timo's quivering lips, seen from the other side of the glass, might have made people think he was speaking.

And he was trying to, although all she could understand were a few sounds, one syllable in three, one in ten. Timo's mouth sighed as it closed again.

'. . . *care* . . .'

She smiled at him and her hand moved up to his torso. She had always found Timo handsome. Girls used to stare at him, before, when he could still walk around without the danger of being recognised.

'. . . *care* . . .'

What was Timo trying to say? What was he talking about?

How much he cared about her?

How scared he was?

Something else, before he died . . .?

'You have to live, Timo. You hear me? You have to live . . .'

She forced herself to speak slowly too, pronouncing each syllable, as if encouraging Timo to do the same.

But there was no reply, only a quiver of his lips.

'You have to live, my love. For our son! I need to leave you for a few moments, you know that, but you must stay strong. After that,

I'll call the hospital, and I'll give them everything: the aisle number, the colour of the zone, our car's registration number, and they'll come and find you. They'll save you. They'll keep you in hospital for a few weeks, and you'll spend a few years in prison, but then you'll get out, you'll still be young, my love, and your son will still be a boy. We'll see each other again. You understand, don't you, my love? You *have* to live. For us. For the three of us.'

As she spoke to him, she kept an eye on the luminous figures on the dashboard.

14.13.

Timo pronounced another word, unfathomable, except for the first letter. L. The rest was lost in a gurgle of saliva and blood.

A word beginning with L.

Love?

Later?

Lost?

She put her lips to his. They were dry. Hard. Cracked. Above them swung the little pine tree hanging from the rear-view mirror, the odour of vanilla mingling with the smell of stale tobacco without managing to overpower it.

Before she could staunch the memory, that pine tree made her think, inevitably, of the drawing she'd hidden behind the photograph of her baby.

**Noel Joyeux.**

**N'oublie Jamais.**

The only thing that still connected him to her.

Everything was in place. Everything had been planned. Now she just had to trust to luck.

She made sure that Timo would not tip over, that his position was comfortable – or bearable, at least – lying on the passenger seat; then she pulled the sun screens down to be certain that no one in the car park would be able to spot him.

Timo could hold out. Timo was going to hold out. He'd held out all those months since the robbery, all those days, since that bastard of a surgeon had tricked them. He could hold out a few hours longer, just a few hours.

Want-to-live.

She got out of the car and smiled one last time at Timo. Her lover's eyes were already closed. His mouth was still trembling, but no sound came from it.

She staggered slightly and had to put one hand on the car to steady herself. Behind her sunglasses, the tears were falling, deforming the face of her wristwatch as if it were the clock in a painting by Dali.

14.23.

At the end of the car park, the electric sliding doors opened as people came and went. She was right on time.

# 57

Papy stood staring at the chasm below. Stunned.

Five hundred and sixty metres!

Around the hole, everything seemed to have been abandoned. Obviously, he was lost. His GPS had not taken into account the recent renovations in Potigny, the latest destruction of the industrial wasteland and the new streets that crossed through the vanished factories, ruined cottages and old brick buildings – the way you pass through a ghost without feeling anything other than an inexplicable shudder. The lieutenant had found himself outside the village and had stopped his car before making a U-turn in a rubble-strewn car park.

He was looking for Rue des Gryzons, a little mining street that would also be demolished one day, when all the miners were dead, and be replaced with apple trees and meadows. Wiping out this anomaly forever.

In the north of France, there are mines, pyramid-shaped slag heaps and red cottages with flower-lined streets; in Normandy, there are farms, half-timbered houses and wells in courtyards. Real landscapes end up resembling those produced by the collective imagination. In the north, people wanted to see Zola; in Normandy, Flaubert or Maupassant. A kind of cosmetic surgery that was performed by men to the places where they slept, rather than to the women they slept with. Another way of fighting against the march of time and erasing the ugliest parts of the past.

Papy liked to put the world to rights, alone, in his head, with no one to contradict him; not even the honeyed voice of the GPS that told him to go down streets that no longer existed and ordered him to 'make a U-turn immediately'.

In defence of his GPS, Lieutenant Pasdeloup had not really been paying attention to the directions. Although driving slowly, he had also been checking the messages that Marianne had sent him: drawings by that kid, Malone, and the same old clues.

A boat.

A forest, a rocket.

A castle with four towers.

The captain's messages, accompanying the drawings, were increasingly urgent in tone.

*Come on, Papy, you've lived in the area for more than fifty years – you must have some idea!*

True, but . . .

The policeman was no longer really concentrating on those drawings either. Each man had his own job. There were fifteen cops in Le Havre, staring at those sketches. An investigation is a team job, and he liked to sniff out leads the other cops hadn't followed. He liked to work solo, a bit like a private detective. A few months from retirement, he thought he was owed a certain degree of freedom. He called Lucas Marouette, the intern who was holding the fort at the station, and fired questions at him. He wanted to have as many cards as possible in his hand when he found that damn Rue de Gryzons, when he walked around the street where Timo, Ilona, Cyril and Alexis were born, had grown up, at exactly the point in time when the mines were closing. They were like kids who'd survived the bombardment of their village and had to invent games to play in the ruins, their laughter drowning out the lamentations of the old. Like the children of Oradour, the babies of Hiroshima: the unfounded hope of children running around a grave, without understanding, without any respect for what was sacred.

A grave that was five hundred and sixty metres deep. A grave he stood next to now, in which a hundred years of local history had been carelessly thrown away.

The lieutenant had got out of his car and read the little sign before leaning over the chasm. The Aisy shaft was the last industrial remnant of the village's mining past. Five metres wide, but almost bottomless. Ore had been extracted from it right up to the late 1980s, and a sort of concrete blockhouse had been built around the hole, surmounted by a tower, thirty metres high, square in shape, and covered with narrow windows, their panes all now broken.

Papy stood there for a moment. What the hell was that intern doing? He'd asked Lucas some precise questions that would only need a quick search on the internet, even if they might have seemed a little odd. Was the old lieutenant going soft in the head, the younger man must have wondered? First of all, Papy had wanted to know about the life cycle of an agouti, a strange South American rodent! Absolutely everything. Yes, it might seem a stupid request, young Marouette, but it wouldn't kill you to give me the answer. And, even easier, tell me the meanings of a few Polish words (any translation tool would do the job) . . . Gryzońs, and other names linked to the Polish colony in Potigny that he'd been able to spot.

The key lay in an association of ideas, a coded memory; Papy felt sure of it.

Lastly, and more difficult to find – but Marouette needed a bit of a challenge – he wanted as much detail as possible on the lives of Timo Soler, Alexis Zerda, Ilona Adamiack and Cyril Lukowik, from their childhood to the present day. Not their criminal records – he knew those details already – but everything else, the kind of stuff that normally didn't interest the police or lawyers.

And so he waited.

A message arrived one minute later. But it was Marianne, not Marouette.

Papy cursed.

The boss was growing impatient.

She'd sent him a drawing by Malone Moulin, which to his eyes looked just like all the others. A scrawl, which only held his interest for a second or so because it was just like the ones his grandchildren did, and which were stuck to the front of his fridge with magnets.

Four vertical black lines and three vaguely horizontal blue lines.

The famous castle by the seaside, according to Malone.

*A castle, FFS!* Marianne had written. *Papy, find me a fucking castle in the estuary with a view of the Channel.*

There isn't one, Marianne!

The child is making it up.

Papy waited a while longer, savouring those moments of reflection by the bottomless grave, then headed back to the car. He was on his way to Rue des Gryzoń, with or without ammunition.

The message from Lucas Marouette reached him while he was arguing with Anna, the bossy voice of the GPS. Although normally the lieutenant liked bossy women who stood up to him.

There were three attachments.

The first contained about thirty pages on the life of an agouti. Lieutenant Pasdeloup quickly scrolled through it. Later . . .

The second was only one page long, a table with two columns: Polish words in the first, French translations in the second.

Only one line interested him in that particular moment.

*Gryzoń.*

The lieutenant felt his heartbeat accelerate. With a movement of his thumb on the touchscreen, he reduced Anna to silence.

So he'd been right all along!

He clicked, a little feverishly, on the last file. Two pages: a few scraps of information about the Solers and Lukowiks. The intern was quite resourceful: he'd unearthed some old CVs from the job centre. He'd remembered that all these criminals had been claiming benefits in the months leading up to the robbery. No one had looked into their prior work experience, any training courses or temporary jobs they had done. Even less so for the Lukowiks, whose unemployed status had ended that morning in January 2015, on Rue de la Mer. All anyone remembered was that they'd worked at the port for a while, him as a docker and her as an accountant.

Papy looked up at the sky. Now he had everything he needed. Might he be wrong? Should he speak to Marianne about it? It wouldn't help her, right now, in finding Timo Soler, Malone Moulin, Amanda Moulin or Alexis Zerda. But at least he now knew how this madness had come about.

Another message. Marianne again. She was obsessed with those bloody drawings . . .

*Papy? Did you get my last message?*

Sighing, the policeman looked again at Malone Moulin's latest masterpiece.

Four black lines . . .

The kid had told the shrink about the cylindrical towers, but there were no castles still standing anywhere near Le Havre. And certainly not by the sea. The whole area had been bombarded during the war.

Marianne was getting on his nerves. He wished she'd just let him get on with his side of the investigation! If everyone did their job, followed their own threads, they could talk about it once the ball of wool had been disentangled.

The policeman's eyes followed the movement of the clouds for a moment, until they stopped on the tower above the Aisy mine shaft.

And then the penny dropped. There was a shifting of gears inside his brain. Suddenly, it seemed as if the immense concrete block rising up towards the sky began to waver, to tremble, before it collapsed into the gaping hole beneath it.

Hand shaking, he grabbed his mobile phone. After all, he loved to satisfy the desires of bossy women. He scrolled down his list of contacts and pressed *Boss*.

'I've found it, Marianne. I've found your bloody castle by the sea!'

# 58

*Little hand on the 2, big hand on the 7*

Malone was sitting on the steps of the house on stilts, facing the sea. Gouti was perched on his knees in case the tide suddenly came in or an especially big wave crashed close by. Gouti didn't have a hood. He didn't have anything on his head to protect him from the drops. The ogre had told him not to go inside the house, to stay outside, and wait.

He didn't mind. Even if it was cold, he preferred to stay out here. In his memories, the boat was prettier: it had large white sails and a black flag at the top. This one was ugly, half-sunk in the water. It almost looked like a rock.

Like the castle. It didn't look very solid either, and the towers didn't protect you much and you probably couldn't see very far from the top of them, if you could even get up there, because there were no windows and no stairs. Just four towers. Not even any walls between the towers for knights to look down from. All it would take was one big wave and it could all disappear, like the boat, like the ogre's house, like Gouti.

No, not Gouti. Because he was holding him tight, between his knees. Even if he was dead.

Malone wanted the sea to hurry up and go out. He remembered that too. Sometimes, the sea went out a long way, further out than the round stones, leaving sand behind it. Malone had built castles with Maman, in front of the house, big sand castles that stood for a long time before the sea returned.

It had been right here, he was sure of it, even if everything was now hidden under the water. Maybe when the sea went away again, his Maman would come back to play with him.

His Maman from here, not Maman-da.

The horrible scream made him jump. It was the ogre. Instantly, Malone pressed his hood against both ears, and a moment later put two fingers in Gouti's ears, so he wouldn't have to hear it either.

*
*   *

With a sudden movement, Alexis Zerda knocked over the plywood cupboard. It exploded over the damp carpet, the walls, doors and drawers. He used his feet to turn over the debris; the wood, glass and crockery, the broken ornaments, the yellowed sheets of paper. Nothing.

Nothing but a useless mess.

Still angry, he tore the bookcase from the wall and pushed it over. The few books, records, vases and tins were all crushed by the weight of the overturned piece of furniture.

Still nothing, except for the pile of shit they'd left behind when they'd abandoned their lair.

No trace of the loot.

Zerda frantically searched through the remaining furniture, under the beds, tore out the plasterboard from the thin walls that separated the five rooms – bedrooms, kitchen, living room – driven by nothing but pure fury, because he'd realised the truth ever since he'd lifted up the trapdoor under the fridge: someone had beaten him to it!

The loot had been hidden in the crawlspace under the house – accessible only by moving the refrigerator – in three suitcases, each the exact maximum size for hand luggage that could be taken on a low-cost airline. Two million euros' worth!

The bed in the first bedroom smashed violently against the wall. The blade of the dagger that he held in his hand carved a large incision in the mattress, unleashing a flurry of foam.

Only four of them had known about the hiding place. Timo, the Lukowiks, and him. Even the kid didn't know. Nor did Dimitri or Amanda, obviously. He had hidden the loot as planned after the

328

robbery, so he could wait for everything to settle down and have time to get in touch with his fences – some Chinese guys, living on the other side of the world, without any possible connection to the police's informers over here.

So who had betrayed him?

Zerda disembowelled a second mattress, which was already mouldy from the damp, then let it fall to the floor like a slaughtered corpse, barely even bothering to search through its guts.

There was no reason why the piece of shit who'd retrieved the hoard from under the trapdoor would have hidden it somewhere else inside this house. And he remembered perfectly well where he had left the three suitcases when he'd come here the night after the robbery.

Who?

Who could have come here after that?

Not Timo. Not in the state he was in. Zerda had left him half-dead in his apartment in the Neiges quarter. And definitely not the Lukowiks, as Cyril and Ilona were already in the morgue in Le Havre by then, being examined by the forensics experts.

That left only one possibility. Someone had talked.

Timo? To his girlfriend? To the kid?

Zerda froze for a second and glanced over at Amanda, who was sitting on a chair in the living room, looking pensive, as if staring at an invisible television.

He'd take care of her later.

He took three steps towards the front door, paused to take a few deep breaths, and then went out and sat down next to the kid.

*You never know.*

*
*   *

Amanda stared at the wall. At a crack in the wall, to be precise, which reminded her of the mortal fissure in a child's brain. The house would end up collapsing too – it always started like that, with a tiny fissure, that then became a gaping hole, creating an emptiness, a chasm, without you even realising it, a void into which

**329**

everything would fall, everything you cared about.

She stood up quietly. Zerda no longer seemed to be paying any attention to her, but she knew him: he was as alert as a wild animal, like a tiger, even when he appeared relaxed. Ready to pounce, at any moment, on anyone.

That crack intrigued her.

She approached it and pressed her nose to the wall. Close up, it looked more like a thread that led from the ceiling to the floor, ran along the skirting board, then rose up again to a little Formica table with a single drawer. As if a colony of ants had found a hoard of sugar and was meticulously transporting its plunder.

Amanda touched her finger to the wall. Stranger yet, the crack in the wall was not natural. It had been traced, in black felt-tip, in tiny dots, a striking imitation of a discreet line of insects.

As if someone had wanted her to notice it – and only her. As if it had been drawn by someone who knew the secret of her son, who knew that the only living beings who'd accompanied him to heaven were insects, marching in procession beneath his skull.

She turned back to look at Zerda. He was talking to Malone, outside the front door.

What could he be telling the child?

It didn't matter. At least she had a few seconds to herself. Clearly, whoever had traced this line had wanted her to open that drawer.

She opened it, taking care to place her body in front of it so Zerda wouldn't see. Old road maps, badly folded. She pushed them out of the way, searched beneath them.

She didn't understand.

Her trembling fingers grasped hold of two rectangular cards.

She was holding two aeroplane tickets . . .

Two seat numbers, 23 A and B.

Two names: Amanda and Malone Moulin.

A place of departure – Le Havre-Octeville – and a destination. Caracas, via Galway, Ireland.

Flight leaving Le Havre at 16.42. In less than two hours.

What did it mean?

Were these tickets what Zerda had been searching for? Was this how he, too, had hoped to get away? But that was impossible: the entire French police force would be searching for him. There was no way he would get through a security check at an airport.

So who, then?

Her thoughts were interrupted by a violent coughing fit. Zerda looked round at her, suspicious. Opening the buttons on her blouse had been a stupid idea: all it had achieved was to expose her chest, and her lungs, to that icy wind, enclosing her heart in a coffin of frost.

She was going to die in a few minutes, anyway, her nose full of snot. Ridiculous, pitiful, just like her whole life. She should be concentrating on just one thing right now: distracting Zerda, and screaming at Malone to run away, to run as fast as his little legs would carry him away from this hovel, before the tide imprisoned them here for good.

\*

\* \*

'You've lost your treasure?'

Malone wasn't afraid of ogres, so he could help him. Especially as this one seemed completely lost, nothing like the big ogre in the story of the Naive knight, with his dagger that could cut even the moon into pieces.

'Do you have an idea, Malone? Do you know where it's hidden?'

He sounded like a baddie, pretending to be a goodie.

'You're like Gouti, then . . .'

'What do you mean, like Gouti?'

'Yes, like Gouti. Don't you know the story? Gouti, his treasure, he hides it before he goes to sleep, so he can be sure to find it when he wakes up.'

'Go on, Malone. What does he do to find his treasure?'

'Well, nothing. That's the point of the story. He never finds it. Each time Gouti buries treasure, he loses it and doesn't remember where he's hidden it.'

A flood of insults smashed together inside Zerda's head. It was as if someone had put all these ideas in the kid's head just to fuck with him.

And yet he made his voice go softer. High-pitched, but children liked that. He knew how to control himself when he had to.

'But if Gouti never finds his treasure, then . . . who does? Who stole it from him?'

'No one.'

Malone looked out at sea, pressing Gouti between his knees, then went on.

'No one and everyone. That's the point of the story. Gouti's treasure is a seed, a seed buried in the ground that grows and makes a big tree so that everyone can enjoy it, and eat from it, and sleep inside it too.'

Zerda leant closer to the child. He could feel the barrel of the Zastava rubbing against his thigh.

*

*   *

Her curiosity too strong, Amanda continued to search through the drawer, while making sure she was blocking it from Alexis's view. She lifted up one last map. Yvetot. Code 1910 O. But she moved it too quickly, and the object hidden beneath it also moved. There was a noise, only a faint one, probably drowned out by the sound of the waves, but even so it made Amanda shudder.

This time, as if playing the Operation game, she took infinite care as she put the road map down on top of the table, revealing what lay beneath.

She narrowed her eyes to be certain that she wasn't dreaming.

There was no other explanation possible. Someone had put it there deliberately. For her.

# 59

*Today, Stéphanie gave birth to our third child.*
*Except there were two in her womb.*
Want to kill
*I asked her which one she wanted to keep.*

Convicted:  1,153
Acquitted:  129

www.want-to-kill.com

*Gouti was just three years old, which was already pretty big in his family, because his mother was only eight and his grandfather, who was very old, was fifteen.*

Five cops were busy working around Captain Augresse and Lieutenant Lechevalier.

Dimitri Moulin's corpse had been removed, along with the blood-soaked rug, and now the cops could come and go around the crime scene without taking any precautions; there was even a map spread out on the Moulins' living room table.

This is urgent, the captain had shouted: we have to prevent two more murders, one of them of a three-year-old boy. And since Papy had called, outlining his conviction, they finally had a proper lead.

*Malone didn't draw the towers of a castle, but of a factory . . .*

Lieutenant Pasdeloup had had this sudden revelation while observing the tower of a mine that looked strangely like a keep. They weren't looking for four towers but four chimneys, or four tanks, or four cisterns.

Facing the sea. Should be child's play . . .

The five policemen around the table each had a laptop in front of them and were staring at the screens like a team of geeks playing some online game with more geeks on the other side of the planet.

Google Earth, Google Street View, Mappy, the local Urban Planning office's information system . . . they were checking any site that contained georeferenced data, photographs or maps. Two other cops, Benhami and Bourdaine, had been ordered to call the port authorities and the Chamber of Commerce and Industry.

Captain Augresse supervised the operation. Papy was the best cop in her team, and his intuition had proved itself once again. What a shame that the stubborn bastard insisted on working alone . . . She would happily have swapped him for JB. Not that she didn't enjoy the sight of the lieutenant's tight little arse bent over the table, and not that he wasn't an effective cop either – he'd proved he was when he'd spotted the child's booster seat in the Opel Zafira parked outside the Deauville casino. But Papy's presence would have reassured Marianne, even if she couldn't say why exactly. It was stupid, but she no longer felt able to fully trust JB.

*Once upon a time there was a big wooden castle that had been built with the trees from the large forest that grew all around. In this big castle, which could be seen from far away because of its four high towers, lived the knights. In those days, the knights each bore the name of the day when they were born . . .*

After the initial euphoria following Lieutenant Pasdeloup's suggestion – 'Look for a factory!' – the enthusiasm in the room had waned.

Nothing seemed to match.

Most of the team were focusing on the port's industrial zone, but that was a long way from Cap de la Hève. Along the sea front, there were no refineries or power stations or steelworks or chemical factories. Production sites were mostly situated upstream, near Port-Jérome, the biggest refinery in France. The police had also searched on the other side of the Seine, towards Honfleur, but all they could find there was a marina, a few fishing boats, a lighthouse, and no towers of any kind . . . There was nothing to the north either, towards the Antifer oil terminal, nothing resembling Malone Moulin's descriptions.

Marianne cursed as she glared at her watch.

14.40.

They were getting bogged down . . . At least JB would have a good excuse for arriving home late that night. He'd be able to kiss his children and wife without worrying about her smelling another woman's perfume on him. The captain could even write him an excuse note without feeling any qualms.

They were getting nowhere on the other aspects of the investigation too. The lead on the Opel Zafira's number plate had ended up in a dead end. The car had been moved after the robbery – either a few hours later or the next morning – without anyone noticing. According to the registration number, it belonged to a pharmacist from Neuilly, who almost never came to Deauville and kept three cars in his garage. He only reported the theft three months later, on 9 April. And, at the time, no one made the connection between this stolen car and the list of twenty-seven other vehicles parked along Rue de la Mer on the day of the robbery. What a mess! The Opel had probably been burnt somewhere in the estuary since then, or pushed off a quay into the port.

From this, only two conclusions could be drawn, neither of them particularly new: the first, that the robbers had prepared their crime in meticulous detail, and second, that it was in this car – since it had been stolen – that Ilona and Cyril Lukowik had planned to flee, and also in this car that the loot had disappeared.

One last hope remained: picking out Malone Moulin on one of the photographs taken by bystanders before, during or after the shoot-out. Lucas Marouette was on that job. Nothing to report for now, though, and unless he got lucky, it was likely to take him a long time to get through all the photographs. The IT wizard was going to have to zoom in on several hundred pictures, searching out just one face amid a crowd of tourists.

*On his island, everyone called him the Baby Pirate. He didn't like that much, especially as he hadn't been a baby for a long time, but as he was the youngest in the family, with his cousins growing up at the same rate as he was, he always remained the baby.*

In the Moulins' living room, the distorted voice of Gouti continued to tell his stories, from Monday to Sunday, on a loop. He'd been doing it for nearly an hour now. Marianne had insisted that they didn't stop the MP3 player until they had discovered the coded meaning of all those places, even if the nasal voice playing in the background gave a weird, almost surreal aspect to the scene.

Cops playing on their consoles while listening to fairy tales.

*You see, Gouti, the real treasure is not what we spend our life searching for; the real treasure was buried close by all the time.*

The captain moved away from the table to answer her mobile, which was vibrating in her pocket.

*Angie.*

Perfect timing!

Marianne pressed her phone against her ear and walked out onto the terrace of the Moulins' small back garden.

'Marianne, are you there?'

'Angie? What's up? Is there a problem?'

'No . . . it's just that you were supposed to call me back, to tell me what was going on. So, your shrink, was it him, that pile of ashes?'

The captain rolled her eyes, then looked around the garden, which was enclosed by three privet hedges. A pile of firewood under a lean-to, which the man of the house would never bring in; a lost ball under a plastic chair that his son would never see again; a rusted barbecue that would never be lit . . .

'Yes, it was him,' said Marianne.

There was a long silence. Interminable. It was the captain who broke it.

'And the list has grown longer since then. I really don't have time right now.'

'I . . . I understand . . .'

Marianne's fingers toyed with a piece of paper in her pocket. She took it out and read it.

*Noel Joyeux. N'oublie Jamais.*

The drawing found in Malone's photograph album.

'Are you . . . could I see you tonight?' Angélique asked shyly.

'No, probably not.'

Marianne felt bad about her curt reply, but she couldn't be on the line to Angie for more than a minute. All the same, Marianne did decide to ask one last question.

'Are you OK? Are you at work? You sound strange.'

'I'm OK. I'm fine. You're very important to me, Marianne, you know. I need you.'

She'd said this in a soft voice, almost a whisper, as if speaking to a child, or a lover. The captain felt moved. She felt a great deal of affection for Angie. Inexplicably, given that they'd only really known each other for a few months. Almost certainly because she and the dreamy hairdresser shared the same mixture of absolute despair and uncontrollable passion for a fairy-tale ending; and that only a fierce sense of humour allowed them to bear the huge gap between those feelings.

Want-to-kill.

Want-to-live.

Want-to-blow-up-everything.

Want-everything, want-nothing.

But not now, not tonight. They'd have time to put the world to rights while downing a bottle of Rioja when this case was closed. To put their own little world to rights, at least.

'Thank you, my lovely,' whispered Marianne. 'I'll get back to you soon, I promise. But you have to hang up now.'

'No problemo. Ciao.'

*

Marianne went back into the hive, where ten of her worker bees were gathering nectar. JB was getting annoyed, shrugging, and clicking from one screen to another, as if his belief in Papy's hunch was decreasing by the minute. Replacing towers with chimneys, knights with factory workers. Time was passing, and the poor darling was stuck here with them.

Angie's voice continued to echo in Marianne's head.

*I need you.*

More than a declaration of love, it had sounded like a cry for help.

Marianne chided herself, feeling simultaneously like a strict teacher and an unruly child. It was ridiculous – she wasn't going to start stirring up all those parasitical ideas in her head. Besides, it wasn't difficult to find something else to concentrate on; all she had to do was move a bit closer to the speaker next to the mahogany sideboard, from which Gouti's voice emerged.

*He took out his big knife. The blade gleamed in the night, as if the moon in the sky above them were merely a piece of cheese that this immense weapon could slice into pieces.*

Officer Bourdaine was standing to attention in front of her, back straight as a lamp post.

'For me?'

He nodded, keeping his body completely still.

'Captain Augresse. I'm listening.'

'The name's Hubert Van de Maele. I'm an engineer at the seaport. Well, a retired engineer. The director called me. Apparently you're looking for a specific site, in connection with an investigation? He didn't have time to deal with it himself, so he asked me. I don't mind, keeps me busy. Helps the fight against Alzheimer's, Alexander, Parkinson's and Huntington's, all those diseases that might come to get you once you're thrown on the scrap heap. The director knows that I never say no. So what exactly are you looking for?'

Wearily, Marianne explained. A site that might resemble a castle, close to the sea and to a boat that might resemble a pirate

ship . . . but they hadn't found anything, even looking fifty kilometres further up the estuary, or following the coastline from east
to . . .

Van de Maele cut her short:

'Did you think about the old NATO base?'

'Sorry?'

'The abandoned NATO base. In Octeville-sur-Mer, just after
Cap de la Hève, near the airport.'

Marianne's heart started pounding.

'Go on.'

'In the early sixties, in the middle of the Cold War, the French
state, which was still a member of NATO, decided to build a small
base five kilometres north of Le Havre, in case the main port was
bombarded. Sixty-centimetre-thick concrete walls, four fuel tanks,
each capable of holding ten thousand cubic metres, anchorage for
oil tankers and battleships, all of it hidden at the foot of the cliff,
with a stairway of four hundred and fifty steps leading up to the
top. The army occupied the site for twenty years, but it was kept
secret. As in *The Tartar Steppe*, they waited for the enemy for years
on end, but no Cossack or red submarine ever came near, as you can
imagine. The base was never really used at all. In the early eighties,
it was put out of service. They poured cement into the oil tanks,
the doors of the blockhouse were soldered shut, and the place was
abandoned. All that remains is a rutted path and the stairway. Ten
or so houses were built there, making use of the access to the sea
and the old equipment. All completely illegal, of course, like a squat
with a sea view. But then everyone, except for a few environmental
charities, forgot the whole story.'

'The four tanks, what do they look like?'

'They're lined up, facing the sea, above the concrete blockhouse.
They're pretty big. If you're down there, they're all you can see. It
isn't hard to imagine the place being the set of a science-fiction film,
or the villain's lair in a James Bond film.'

'So, you told me the base was never used. There aren't any boats
there then?'

'No. All the quays were destroyed when the base was shut down.

339

And five spikes planted in the seabed are supposed to prevent anyone mooring there.'

Another red herring?

'Although,' Van de Maele added, 'just to give the place an even more sinister feel, between the rusted fuel cisterns and the corrugated iron huts on the beach, no one ever had the courage, the time or the money to get rid of the wreck.'

'The wreck?'

'Yes. It's part of the decor too. A ship that washed up there, a good thirty years ago. First-generation tanker, cut in two. At high tide, it looks like it's still afloat, like a ghost ship, but at low tide, when the sea pulls back, you can see that it's mired in the sand. It's black. Standing almost proudly in the mud, but trapped there forever. Because of a war that never took place. Just like *The Tartar Steppe*.'

Marianne wasn't listening any more. She had already handed the phone back to Bourdaine, without even thanking the retired engineer. She paused for a moment by the child's drawings spread out on the table, then called over Lieutenant Lechevalier, thinking that they had to act fast – as fast as possible.

'The place does exist, JB! The kid didn't make anything up, he just distorted reality a bit. It all fits. This has to be the place where Malone spent the first years of his life.' She took a deep breath, attempting to slow her racing heart. 'And where he might be spending his final hours.' Slow down. Breathe. 'He could be there right now, with a killer . . .'

# 60

*Little hand on the 2, big hand on the 9*

Alexis Zerda watched the stilts vibrate, tremble, become as soft as rubber. The rising tide had almost completely covered them and the bolder waves were now reaching the terrace of the house. They had to get out of there.

The kid didn't know anything, that was obvious. He just repeated what had been imprinted on his brain: that story about the Amazonian rat that buries its treasure and never finds it, searching for it until it grows crazy.

The kid was just a parrot who'd learnt a fable by heart. The person who had engraved this tale in his head was obviously the same person who'd stolen the loot. Mad bitch! To taunt him like that, and then leave the kid into the bargain . . .

Zerda slid his right hand under Malone's hood and caressed the boy's hair, while his left hand moved slowly along his belt, reaching for the Zastava. He had to get rid of Amanda first. He'd take care of the kid later. He found it hard to understand why, but for society a kid was worth a fortune, an incredible amount, more than three suitcases containing two million euros' worth of goods. So for a mother, how much more was a child worth?

'Amanda, let's go.'

Zerda gave the order calmly.

He turned his eyes to the house's interior, went in, and closed the door behind him. Amanda was standing motionless at the back of the living room, amid the smashed-up furniture. He thought she looked almost sweet like that; almost desirable with her blouse open, her body trembling, the life she was starting to regret, now that it was over. Almost beautiful, even with the imploring look in her eyes.

*Do what you want with me, but leave the child.*

That look of total abandonment . . . Would he ever encounter such complete submission in his life again? Such absolute resignation? Such self-sacrifice? No, he probably never would. Not in any woman. Even if he tortured her.

The love of a child made women sublime.

But vulnerable and predictable too. He took a step forward, taking care to check that Malone was still standing where he had left him, playing with his rat and dreaming about pirates. He moved the Zastava behind his back.

Zerda would be with other girls, even if he had to pay to seduce them. Pay through the nose.

The love of money also made women sublime. Other women. Elsewhere.

Blindly, his thumb released the safety on the pistol.

'I won't hurt him, Amanda. I won't touch the kid, you have my word.'

His way of ending this with dignity. Cleanly. His index finger touched the trigger. He would whip it out and fire at the same time, so Amanda wouldn't have time to realise what was happening. She wasn't being executed by a firing squad for desertion; she was just another breadcrumb on his path.

Get rid of her, then get the hell out of there.

'I know, Alexis,' said Amanda. 'I know you won't touch the kid.'

She was smiling. It was better this way. Zerda was relieved that she was taking it well. He just had time – a fraction of a second – to think how ridiculous that idea was.

Taking what well? Her death? Her execution?

He heard Amanda's last words as if in a fog.

'Because you won't have the time.'

Suddenly his attention was fixed on the arm that Amanda held out, pointed at him. In her hand, a revolver.

She fired. Four bullets.

Two hit Zerda's chest, the third went through his shoulder blade, and a fourth went a good metre to his right, into the plasterboard wall.

Zerda collapsed.

Dead on the spot.

Amanda performed the gestures that followed automatically, making a list in her head just like she did every day for the usual myriad tasks of a housewife and mother. She put the revolver – which she'd found in the drawer – into her right-hand pocket. She would throw it in the sea once she got outside. Into her left-hand pocket, she put the two aeroplane tickets. Then she would tidy up, a little.

Create a diversion – as much as she could – the way Zerda would have done. Alter appearances so that the police would be stuck in the place for as long as possible.

Then get the hell out of there.

*

\*   \*

'I'm tired, Maman-da.'

Malone had climbed less than a quarter of the way up the stairway. Amanda tugged harder at his hand. One step more, one of the three hundred that remained. The wind pummelled at their backs.

'I want to stop, Maman-da. I want to rest. I want to go back to my house, the one near the sea. I want to wait for Maman.'

Amanda did not reply. She pulled his arm. One more step.

298.

'It's too long. It's too high!'

297.

'Stop! You're hurting my arm!'

296.

'You're nasty, Maman-da. You're nasty. I don't love you.'

296.

'I don't love you. I only love my mother. I want Maman!! I WANT MY MAMAN.'

296.

Abruptly, Amanda let go of Malone's hand. Then, before he

could react, she tore the cuddly toy from his left hand. The child's eyes registered panic in the face of Amanda's cold fury. Not another word escaped his mouth.

Amanda didn't hesitate for a second – she threw Gouti as far as she could. He landed a few metres below, bouncing like a rag doll on the bare limbs of a hazel tree, above a ditch filled with brambles and nettles, finally coming to rest – arms crossed, head hanging – suspended from a thorny branch.

Gouti!

Malone stared at his toy open-mouthed, eyes full of tears, incredulous.

Amanda's firm hand grabbed his five little fingers, like five irritating little insects. Then she pronounced four words, only four, each one separated by a long silence, and the wind whipping the cliff face seemed to make the words echo for a long time, carrying them right up to the top.

'I am your mother!'

# III
# Angélique

# FRIDAY

The day of love

# 61

Angélique was in pain. Her position was almost unbearable. Her thighs, buttocks and back were resting on cardboard boxes, but she was desperately trying not to crush them, keeping still because the slightest movement might make them collapse under her like a house of cards.

She had to stay balanced, like a tightrope walker sitting on a glass stool balanced on a rope suspended over a void. Whenever one of the boxes showed the faintest sign of weakness, she would press her hands against a wall, to take the strain off it by redistributing her weight. Her muscles were almost paralysed from having to maintain this pose.

A blindfolded tightrope walker at that. Yes, she was crouched there in total darkness too, just to spice things up.

Angie was prepared for more pain, an eternity of pain if need be. How could she complain about the blood that she lacked in her curled-up legs and her flattened fingers when blood had been leaking out of Timo's body for the past three days? How could she curse the foul odour that rose to her nostrils – this mixture of ammonia, lavender and shit – when the smell of death had embalmed the body of her beloved, that stink which she could only combat by pressing her body against his?

She had to hold firm, for these endless minutes, just as she had been doing for nearly an hour. Just as Timo was holding firm, in the Twingo, out in the car park.

The screen of her watch gave off a dim light, just enough for her to be able to read the time without anyone spotting her.

15.23.

She would call for an ambulance as soon as she was safe.

Millimetre by millimetre, she accentuated the pressure of her hands on the walls, and that tiny movement was enough to help her maintain her balance. Or at least, so she imagined. So she had read. She'd read everything that might be useful to her. Written down everything, planned everything, to give herself the best possible chance of succeeding, even if that chance was only one in a hundred, or one in a thousand.

Angélique heard footsteps break the silence. Doors opening, banging shut. Very few words, no laughter, no music, only footsteps, noises and sighs. She held her breath, even if no one could possibly have suspected that she was there. So close by.

Silent images appeared to her in the darkness. The Deauville robbery, Ilona and Cyril shot dead before her eyes, their corpses lying on the ground near the spa, the bullet that smashed the back window of the Opel Zafira, the rain of glass, the crowd of vultures around them, and her casually brushing the shards from her son's hair as if she were sweeping away bits of confetti after a carnival.

Time accelerated and she saw Alexis Zerda's face, his panic, his fury at Ilona and Cyril, even though they were dead; his anger with Timo – even though he'd been wounded – when his helmet had fallen off and bounced on the pavement outside the racecourse.

Zerda had left their hiding place and walked down to the beach. It was evening, and there had been no one else at the foot of the cliffs for kilometres in either direction. Zerda had said the cops were bound to connect the robbery to him, if they managed to identify the other three robbers; all they'd have to do was think about the street where they'd grown up together: Rue des Gryzons.

'They don't have any proof, Alex,' Timo had found the strength to murmur. 'And even if they put me in prison, I won't say anything.'

Timo's comment wasn't calculated, a ploy so that Zerda wouldn't leave him to die like an injured dog, or put him out of his misery. He was sincere. Yes, Angélique thought, her simpleton lover had felt sincerely sorry for that bastard Zerda; he was sincerely ready to apologise for having allowed his helmet to fall off, for having taken a bullet to his lung, for not having been able to measure up to the perfect plan conceived by the gang's brains – a man who did not even dare meet Timo's tear-filled gaze.

No, those snakelike eyes, Angie had immediately understood, were avoiding Timo's so they could linger on the face of her son.

Malone. She had to call him Malone now.

Zerda had stared at the two-and-a-half-year-old boy for a long time, with the same look in his eyes as he had when he stared at cops, informers, anyone who got between him and his freedom.

*Malone knew Alexis's face.*

If the cops traced the clues back to this child, all they would have to do was show him a photograph – any of the photographs taken in Potigny, at the football club or in the local Bar de la Mine – and Malone would nod his head and say yes. A toddler probably couldn't be summoned to testify in court, but his testimony would nevertheless constitute proof in the eyes of an investigating judge, enough to get Zerda arrested, locked up, enough to set in motion the entire machinery of the police and the judicial system.

In fact, it would be better than proof, if Malone nodded to say yes, he knew Zerda: it would become a certainty to the investigators. From then on, they would know that the four of them had spent months preparing the robbery together, watched by this child, that they had spent hours talking through every detail. Timo wouldn't say anything, even if he was taken, and neither would she, if the cops managed to identify her. Only the child represented a danger.

Angélique's brain had had to work as fast as a windsurfer skimming over the dark sea behind the fuel tanks. She had to convince Zerda that Malone was not a dangerous witness, or at least that he was less dangerous alive than dead; the arguments had come to her naturally, just after she sent her son out to play on the beach.

'A three-year-old kid forgets things, Alex. He forgets quickly. In a few weeks – a few months at most – your face will have been wiped from his memory. We just have to wait, play for time, leave the loot where it is for a while.'

Alexis Zerda had observed Malone for a long time, watching him in his red boots as he picked up bits of lichen from the beach and put them in a circle between tiny piles of pebbles.

Perhaps, deep down, Zerda had realised that he had no choice; that, if he decided to eliminate the child, he would have to kill his mother too, before she strangled him with her bare hands – and he didn't want to kill her.

Zerda had always had a soft spot for her.

The idiot.

Her plan had been born in that moment, as she looked out at the three different horizons that opened up before her: the rusted door frame of this house on stilts in the foreground; Malone's red boots on the vast beach in the middle ground, and the immensity of the sea in the background.

It was a crazy plan, a house of cards that might collapse at any moment.

A meticulously prepared plan, developed over months, its final details added at the last minute; last night, in fact, when she'd realised that Alexis Zerda was beginning to scorch the earth around him, getting rid of any inconvenient witnesses.

In the darkness, the irritating sound of high heels clacking on the ground dragged her from her thoughts. Rapid, jerky footsteps. An employee, late for her shift? A working girl in a hurry? An elegant woman rushing to meet her lover?

So close to her. Invisible.

Angélique forced herself to remain focused on her memories. Yes, that plan was unreal, mad, unrealistic, but she had no choice. She had to build that house of cards, wall by wall. Each one was fragile, but together they could hold each other up. She just had to separate them, compartmentalise them, and be the only one who knew the plan in its entirety. That wasn't difficult, when it came down to it. She knew all about the arts of seduction and persuasion.

Seducing a single man was easy: she had everything she needed to do that.

Seducing a single woman was perhaps even simpler. Single

women are suspicious of men, not of the perfect new best friend.

Vasily Dragonman. Marianne Augresse.

The rest was in the hands of her son. Malone. She had to call him Malone, to cram that name into his head. Had he followed her instructions to the letter? Had he listened to all those stories that she'd recorded, disguising her voice, and hiding all this from Alexis of course. How could that killer have imagined that her vengeance would take the form of fairy tales and a cuddly rat that knew the only way to get rid of ogres?

The sharp heels were already receding, giving way for the first time to laughter. Children's laughter. And, louder than that, a few seconds later, the yelling of a mother.

Crude, vulgar. Without any humour or tenderness, without any justification; the yelling of a prison guard, as if her children's joy was an insult to her existence, as if her children's lives belonged to her, like they were objects to be tidied away. To be polished until they shone. To be broken, out of negligence or anger.

*Want-to-kill.*

The kids were already moving in the other direction, followed by the mother's clicking footsteps.

Her plan, when Angélique thought about it, reminded her of her oldest memories. Strange memories that dated back to when she was fourteen, and to a collection of short stories that her French teacher had made her read, a science-fiction book with a series of stories about the colonisation of Mars by humans. Crazy stuff. The Martians, before they were all killed by the humans, possessed strange powers, such as their appearance changing, depending on who was looking at them. One of the last surviving Martians was hidden in a remote farmhouse, where the human colonists had viewed him as their son, a boy who'd died years before. He'd stayed there, loved and sheltered, until his adoptive parents took him to the city. Bad idea. In the street, one woman saw the Martian as her husband, who'd died a few days earlier, another man as the wife who'd left him, another person as a friend who'd remained buried in the earth . . . Even though the Martian tried to flee, someone always recognised him, took him by the hand, or the waist, or the neck, begged him to stay, not to disappear again. And that was how he died – torn apart and trampled on by a crowd of grieving humans who loved him without being able to share him.

Now, she understood that story. It was what must not happen to her son.

Malone, for Amanda.

Malone for her too, from now on.

Her son, even if he bore another child's name.

A cardboard box crumpled beneath her weight, and Angélique had to hold on to the two walls, praying that the entire edifice would not collapse. She breathed out: the pyramid held firm, even if she had the impression that her improvised throne was continuing to subside, imperceptibly, millimetre by millimetre. That she might crash to earth at any moment.

Not now, she prayed, not when she was so close to her goal. Her cardboard house only had to stay up a few minutes longer.

After that, they would have an eternity to build another, in the brightest clearing in the biggest forest in the world.

Far away.

A house of stone, solid, indestructible.

For her family.

Herself, Timo and their child.

# 62

*Today, for my hen party, my three friends decided to parade me along the Champs-Élysées dressed as a Mexican whore, wearing fishnet stockings, fake breasts and a sombrero.*
Want to kill
*I didn't say a word when the tourist bus arrived just as they were stepping back to take a photo of me. Moments later, they were disguised as enchiladas.*

*Convicted: 19*
*Acquitted: 1,632*

www.want-to-kill.com

Lieutenant Lechevalier did not hesitate before taking off his shoes and rolling his canvas trousers up to his knees. He paddled through the thirty centimetres of water that lapped at the stilts, apparently untroubled by the cold bite of the rising sea. After reaching beneath the rickety wooden house, he stood up, soaked, exhibiting a coat covered in blood.

'That's all I found.'

Marianne, in the dry on the doorstep, observed the trench coat: obviously a woman's, but quite large. JB insisted on sliding his latex gloves over the saturated cloth.

'Given the amount of blood soaked up by the material, I think it's safe to say that Zerda didn't just give Amanda Moulin a scratch.

Going by the stains, I would say several bullets, to the chest, stomach and lungs. She has to be dead.'

The captain grimaced. JB was rarely wrong about the ballistic aspects of an investigation.

'Hardly a surprise,' she sighed. 'No sign of the body?'

'No,' JB confirmed. 'Nor of the kid, for that matter.'

'With a bit of luck, Zerda will stick to the same strategy: one corpse for each location. The kid is still with him.'

'You think Malone will be next on the list?'

Marianne stared at her deputy.

'Unless we stop him. Take this house apart, bolt by bolt if you have to, and find Amanda Moulin's corpse. Zerda can't have carried it back up the steps, and it wouldn't have been carried away by the tide yet. This was the place where the Rue des Gryzons gang spent months planning their robbery. So I also want you to find me a nice collection of souvenirs of their seaside holiday.'

JB went into the house, barefoot, his wet sky-blue shirt sticking to his skin. Marianne, phone to her ear, mobilised the operational logistics division of the DCPJ, the judicial police's central management.

'Can you hear me? Yes, it's Captain Augresse! I want the highest alert possible put out for Alexis Zerda and Timo Soler. Photos, posters, emails, faxes . . . flood the entire region!'

For a moment, she glanced up at the sky.

'And make sure that their photos are all over the walls of the Havre-Octeville airport. Make sure everyone working there gets to see them. We're only five kilometres away and I don't believe in coincidences.'

*

*   *

The sea had risen an extra twenty centimetres or so. Police officers were going to and fro, from the stairway to the house, carefully carrying the equipment necessary to analyse the crime scene. They hadn't dared take the time to remove their shoes and trousers, so they were walking fully-dressed through the knee-high water, staggering on the smooth pebbles scattered by the swell.

Inside the house, Marianne stepped carefully along the vinyl flooring, which was coming unstuck in places and was slippery from the puddles of water left by the policemen's soaked boots. Alone in the bedroom, JB seemed indifferent to the general bustle around him. He was sitting at an improvised desk that consisted of a plank and two trestles, eyes riveted to the screen of a laptop.

The salty water was still trickling down his back, and his shirt clung to his more prominent muscles: trapezius, lats, and lower back. Marianne thought he looked sexy, indifferent to being wet, like those footballers who play for ninety minutes in the pouring rain, hair slicked back, thighs gleaming, so focused on the match that they don't even notice the torrent. That was the only interesting aspect of watching a football match, as far as she was concerned.

So handsome, those idiots, those bastards.

JB, sensing her presence behind him, turned to face the captain.

'It's Zerda's laptop. He's erased everything, but I'm going to try a bit of digging. You never know.'

Marianne did not object. Logically, they should have passed the computer on to the Central IT and Tracing Department, but time was short. JB was a whizz with computers. And a child's life hung in the balance . . .

If he was still alive.

The captain feared that a DNA analysis would reveal that the blood found on the trench coat or the carpet was mixed with another person's – that of a three-year-old boy – and that they would find not only the mother's corpse, any minute now, in a cupboard or under a floorboard, but two corpses. One of them smaller.

She shivered.

'You OK, Marianne?'

The captain thought about telling her deputy where to stick it. He was the one who was soaked yet she was the one who was shivering.

Handsome, stupid and proud as a peacock.

*

'Captain? It's for you!'

Bourdaine stood outside, both feet in the sea, reminding Marianne of a weeping willow: thin legs close together like a trunk, and wet arms holding a phone a few centimetres above the water's surface. Marianne grabbed it.

'Boss? It's Lucas! You're going to be proud of me – I found young Malone in the photo!'

'Photo? What photo?'

Lucas started again, more slowly, like an old hand explaining things to a confused newbie.

'One of the six hundred and twenty-seven that were gathered after the shoot-out in Deauville. Kindly taken for us by the dozens of tourists who immortalised the scene for our police archives.'

'OK, keep it short. You're sure it's Malone?'

'Absolutely, boss! I've sent you a J-PEG. Officer Bourdaine has opened it already: all you have to do is slide your finger from left to right.'

'Thank you,' said Marianne sarcastically. 'I do know how to use a touch screen!' Her thumb slid across the plastic while the intern went on:

'And that's not all, boss. Guess who's holding Malone's hand in the photo?'

Annoyed by the way Lucas kept calling her 'boss' every three words, the captain was about to reprimand him when the image appeared, at the very moment Marouette answered his own question:

'His mother.'

In the small photograph, a crowd of several dozen people were gathered in a line outside the casino. Nervously, Marianne put her thumb and index finger on the screen to enlarge the picture and then scrolled past a row of faces, the vast majority of whom belonged to couples in their sixties or older.

'Under the one-way sign, boss,' said Lucas. 'Next to a big bald guy, who's about a head taller than everyone else.'

A one-way sign.

A big bald guy.

Go down.

When she saw Malone's face, Marianne immediately thought of Munch's *Scream*, that distorted face expressing sudden, unbearable madness and horror.

The captain's eyes dwelt on Malone's features, as if fascinated by the terror in his eyes, contrasting with the almost indifferent reactions of the other bystanders. Then, at last, her gaze moved along slightly until it was resting on the woman who was holding his hand.

His Maman. Timo Soler's partner.

For an instant, she thought the house on stilts was tipping over into the water, being carried away by the sea.

No, she was the one who was keeling over.

She grabbed the doorway with her left hand while her right hand suddenly lost all its strength and dropped the mobile phone into the sea.

Bourdaine, stupefied, continued standing there, not moving a muscle to rescue the phone.

\*

\*   \*

*Angie . . .*

Angélique was Malone's mother.

Everything flickered quickly, very quickly, through Marianne's head . . .

Their meeting, ten months ago, after they first encountered each other on the *want-to-kill.com* website. An anonymous complaint about that site had been personally addressed to the captain. It was just another website, one of millions across the globe, only this one was hosted somewhere in Le Havre. The captain had no difficulty locating it, with help from the IT Department. She summoned the girl who was hosting the site, Angélique Fontaine, who confirmed that she'd created it years before, when she was a teenager, a trashy version of the better-known *life-is-shit.com*. For years, *want-to-kill. com* had gone on without her. A few people still posted messages

359

sometimes, but it got no more than a few hundred views per month. Angélique didn't mind if the site was closed down; her adolescent ravings were a thing of the past now. The captain had sent a standard report to the state prosecutor and let him decide what action was to be taken.

There had been an instant connection between her and Angélique. She was pretty, cheerful and kind, without having completely lost her teenage insolence. It was Angélique who had got back in touch with her the following day, on the pretext of providing her with additional evidence for the *want-to-kill.com* file: old copies of emails and invoices from the site's host. They went out for a drink one night, as Angélique worked in a hairdressing salon during the day. Then they met up again one week later, for dinner at Uno. Of course, it had all been calculated, a set-up. Including the anonymous letter that had started it all.

Marianne looked down at the mobile phone floating on the surface of the water. The waves lifted it up, leaving grey foam on the screen, but it didn't sink, presumably because of the silicon shell.

She had not been suspicious of Angie. Why should she have been? She had hardly told Angie anything about the investigations she was running. Just Malone Moulin's name and details of her conversation with Vasily Dragonman. She had not even mentioned Timo Soler before she'd tried to catch him in the Neiges quarter, when Angélique had called her in the police car. She must simply have heard the GPS blare out: 'Cross the Pont V . . .' Which would have made it easy for her to realise that it wasn't Dr Larochelle on his way to treat her beloved, but the police . . . Angélique had been skilful enough not to question Marianne directly about any of her investigations, being content to monitor her, to know where she was and when she was there. To keep control of her, in some way.

Lucas Marouette's voice continued to bellow through the telephone-raft, as if the young policeman were enclosed in a miniature coffin floating in the sea. His words were inaudible, or Marianne didn't hear them.

She was trying to remember, going over the long hours they had spent in conversation, anything about the case that she might have revealed to Angélique.

Almost nothing. They'd talked about men, clothes, books, films . . . and children. Children most of all.

Other people's children.

Nothing too serious. Just a monumental case of professional misconduct.

From her pocket, her fingers extricated the drawing she'd found behind the photograph in Malone's album. Five words. The star, the tree, the presents, the family.

**Noel Joyeux**
**N'oublie Jamais**

Feminine handwriting. A mother with long hair. How could she have been so stupid?

Nobody said 'Noel Joyeux'. The normal expression was 'Joyeux Noel'.

And as for 'N'oublie Jamais' . . .

N.J.

When you said the letters out loud, it sounded just like . . . Angie.

Malone already knew how to recognise most of the letters of the alphabet. That drawing was a clever way of making him remember his mother's name, subliminally at least. A secret code to add to the tales of Gouti which she had recorded for her son. Captain Augresse understood now why the voice had been altered.

She'd been duped.

Marianne suppressed the desire to throw herself off the threshold of the house. It was a pathetic urge: there wasn't enough water to drown her, and too much for her to break her neck. Bourdaine was still standing there, arms dangling, waiting for an order. He might have stayed like that until high tide.

The captain finally concentrated on Marouette's voice coming from the silicon rectangle. With a movement of her head, she ordered Bourdaine to pick up the phone.

It dribbled water onto her shoulder as Lucas continued shouting.

So it still worked, apparently.

'Boss? Where were you? I've got all the information you need on Malone Moulin's mother. Her name is Angélique Fontaine. And guess what, boss – she's from Potigny too! She grew up on Impasse Copernic, three streets away from Rue des Gryzoñs. I checked on Mappy. She was in the same class as Soler until she was fifteen. After that – on her sixteenth birthday, in fact – she left the village. I suppose she met Timo again afterwards and . . .'

Captain Augresse hung up, without even waiting for Marouette to finish his account. In the same second, she pressed another speed-dial.

'Operational Logistics? It's Augresse again. We've got more news, so can you get on this straight away! I want you to add a third photo to the ones of Zerda and Soler. It's a woman. Angélique Fontaine. Contact the station – they have the photo. I want it printed immediately and distributed everywhere in the area. Stations, toll booths . . . I want mobile brigades posted at every roundabout.'

Marianne pressed the phone closer to her ear. She waited until she was sure they'd understood her, then yelled down the phone:

'Yes, of course you should also put her picture in the airport at Le Havre! That's the number-one priority!'

The captain had not heard JB coming up behind her.

'You're right, Marianne.'

She answered without seeming to have heard him.

'Still haven't found Amanda Moulin's corpse?'

JB shook his head and repeated:

'You're right, Marianne.'

'About what?'

'About the priorities. The airport.'

Marianne's eyes grew wide as her deputy lifted the laptop up to her face.

'Look, I retrieved this from the computer's memory.'

The captain could see only a cluster of tiny symbols, impossible to read, on the dimly lit screen.

'Go on, Champollion[3], decipher it for me . . .'

---

[3] French scholar famous for deciphering Egyptian hieroglyphs

'You won't believe this, Marianne. It's the history of a search on one of the airline comparison sites. All the enquiries have the same place of departure and the same destination: Le Havre to Galway, and then Galway to Caracas. There's a flight leaving today. At 16.42.'

He checked his watch.

'That's in half an hour!'

He looked up at the sky, then down at the cold water, as if he were about to dive in. He checked the depth of the water, then put the computer under his arm and said, in a confident voice:

'The airport's less than a couple of kilometres away. We should be able to make it.'

# 63

*Little hand on the 4, big hand on the 3*

Amanda grabbed Malone by the waist and lifted him up so that the woman behind the counter could see him. It was a measly physical effort compared to what she'd just been through: carrying Malone up the last three hundred steps of the stairway at the cliff, before driving to the airport in Zerda's Ford Kuga. All the same, she hammed up her fatigue to the girl who was checking their papers and tickets. A complicit smile. The girl was not very pretty, stuffed into her blue uniform, but this was compensated for with a harmony of details – small, round, apple-green glasses; a little emerald cat on one ring; nails painted in the colours of the rainbow – that gave her more charm than the slender women behind the other counters with their perfect curves, powdered faces, lipstick and eyeshadow, like cloned Barbies, straight out of the box.

A shy girl, thought Amanda. A daydreamer. *Jeanne*, her name badge said. She liked children, that was obvious. Children and cats.

The woman signalled that Amanda could put Malone down. As soon as his feet touched the floor, he hid behind her legs.

Jeanne did not look like a jobsworth, but all the same she meticulously checked every document, presumably because of something to do with all these soldiers roaming the lobby, those photographs of Alexis Zerda and Timo Soler on the walls. Amanda felt the sweat trickling down her back, even as she repeated to herself that there was no reason to be afraid, that all her papers – and Malone's too – were in order, and that no cops would be calling the airport or putting her name on a blacklist because, even if they had found the old NATO base by now, they would assume she was dead.

'Have you ever been on a plane before, dear? Have you ever travelled this far away?'

Malone hid behind her again, and Amanda adored that reaction, like a frightened cat reaction. The woman went on.

'You're not afraid, are you? Because you know, where you're going, there's . . .'

A silence calculated to make Malone react. The drops of sweat running down Amanda's back had reached her jeans. It seemed impossible that this woman could not smell the bitter stench.

'There's a jungle . . . Isn't that right?'

Malone remained silent.

The stamp banging down twice against the passports sounded inside Amanda's head like two sledgehammer blows destroying the walls of a prison. 'But there's no reason to be scared, sweetie. You'll be with your mother!'

Soldiers walked past behind them. Jeanne glanced at them suspiciously before continuing to address Malone.

'Ask your mum. She'll tell you all about the jungle.'

Amanda thought she was going to faint.

And Malone wasn't even looking at her.

When that stupid, over-chatty woman pronounced the word 'mother', he had turned his head in the other direction, towards the wall, towards the posters that were pinned there, of Zerda and Soler.

*And Angélique Fontaine.*

The police had made faster progress than she'd expected. They'd already identified that woman, so presumably they knew that she was Malone's real mother. They knew everything now . . .

Amanda forced herself not to panic. Thankfully, Jeanne wasn't looking at her and was still focused on Malone.

The police knew everything . . . Except that she, Amanda, was alive, and that no one was going to steal her child from her! Angélique Fontaine had abandoned her child, she was an accessory to murder, she would end up in prison for years; Malone needed a mother who was free, a mother who loved him; he had already almost forgotten his previous life. In a few days, Angélique would be nothing more than a blurred face on a photograph. In a few weeks, she would simply never have existed for him.

The woman behind the counter was still looking at them, her face folded into a frown.

She couldn't fail now, when she was so close to her goal.

Amanda turned towards the posters on the wall and looked beyond them, at the aeroplanes behind the large windows, the tarmac runway, the sea, and casually ruffled Malone's hair.

A mother and her son, before the big departure, already dreaming that they were in the sky.

The moment lasted an eternity, punctuated by the heavy footsteps of  young soldiers in combat gear. Finally, Jeanne slid the passports through the opening in the glass window.

'Everything seems to be in order, madame. Have a good trip.'

'Thank you.'

These were the first words Amanda had pronounced.

At the end of the runway, a sky-blue KLM A318 Airbus was taking off.

*

*    *

Lieutenant Lechevalier looked up at the Airbus that was crossing the sky. He followed its progress for a moment over the oil-black ocean, before running down the steps.

Marianne was standing about fifty steps below, out of breath.

'I've got a witness!' he shouted. 'And not just any witness . . .'

He stood in front of the captain and handed her the cuddly toy.

'Where did you find that?'

'In the brambles, a few steps higher up. Alexis Zerda must have thrown it there before he disappeared.'

The captain did not reply. For an instant, he'd hoped for a compliment, a smile, something along the lines of 'Well done, JB'. The lieutenant was no fool: this toy was a crucial discovery. The kid was never separated from it; this ball of fur was his security blanket, the thing that calmed and consoled him. If Zerda had got rid of the toy, it meant he intended to get rid of the child. Maybe he already had, in a place more discreet than a thorny ditch next to a stairway.

Marianne grabbed the furry toy and hugged it in her arms with a tenderness that Lieutenant Lechevalier thought excessive, as if his superior officer had also started believing that this toy really could talk and was cuddling it to squeeze out its secrets.

'Let's go, JB!' said Marianne. 'Get a move on!'

Once again, the captain had barked her order without even glancing at him. In three strides, the lieutenant was already five steps ahead of her. He was baffled by the change in Marianne's attitude towards him. She seemed constantly annoyed with him, aggressive, in a way that couldn't simply be due to the pressures of this case, to their repeated failures, to the urgent need to catch Zerda and Soler. It seemed much more personal than that.

Special treatment. Directed at him.

As if their almost instinctive complicity had been smashed into smithereens and he was now nothing more, in his superior's eyes, than just another male cop competently carrying out his orders, one of dozens of other male cops competently carrying out her orders. It gnawed away at him, not being able to understand the reasons for this sudden change. He'd done a great job, after all: he'd spotted the kid's car seat in the Opel Zafira parked outside the Deauville casino; he'd unearthed the search history for those Le Havre-Galway-Caracas tickets on Zerda's laptop; he'd found Gouti in the brambles . . .

Seeing admiration in Marianne's eyes was, bizarrely, one of those things he was most fond of in his life. There was nothing sexual about it. For a change. There was nothing ambiguous like that in his relationship with his boss; they were just a good team, a bit like a couple of dancers or ice-skaters.

Another Airbus streaked across the sky. The airport in Le Havre was less than two kilometres away as the crow flies. The plane to Galway would take off in fifteen minutes; they would get there in time, even if – with all the warnings and surveillance – it was unlikely that Zerda, Soler or Angélique Fontaine could get through security.

One minute later, JB had reached the top step. He turned back to Marianne: she was thirty steps below, staring out to sea, holding Gouti the way a little girl might hold her handbag on the train. Trembling.

For a fraction of a second, he had the illusion that the cuddly toy had waited until it was alone with the captain to make a crucial revelation, and that Marianne was still in shock from it. It was a stupid idea, obviously, but that was just how the captain looked. As if, simply by observing Gouti, she'd realised that they'd been on the wrong track from the very beginning.

He crossed the car park. By the time he'd reached the car, started the engine and driven to the top of the stairway, Marianne would be there. He'd open the passenger door for her so she didn't even have to slow down.

Efficient. Quick-thinking. Syncopated. Like a pair of ice skaters.

As he flashed the car's headlights, one thought bothered him; he'd always wondered how they did it, those couples – whether dancing on wooden boards or thick ice – rubbing against each other for years without eventually falling in love.

# 64

Perhaps Anna was continuing to bark orders alone in the car. Papy didn't know. He'd turned off the engine, parked the Mégane and abandoned the GPS in order to move on to Plan B.

The old-school method: a good map of the village.

While it was easy to find his way around the modern part of Potigny – a main street with a row of shops, surrounded by new houses – the old miners' quarter hid modestly away from the few visitors who came by there. It consisted of about ten rows of dwellings, each two hundred metres long, divided into ten shabby little houses, all of them identical.

Lieutenant Pasdeloup had marked out Rue des Gryzoñs on the map, along with the addresses of each person involved in this case. Lucas Marouette had even found for him, in an old book on the history of Potigny, photographs of the area taken at the time when the mine was still working.

Federico and Ofelia Soler, 12 Rue des Gryzoñs
Tomasz and Karolina Adamiack, 21 Rue des Gryzoñs
Josèf and Marta Lukowik, 23 Rue des Gryzoñs
Darko and Jelena Zerda, 33 Rue des Gryzoñs

Before leaving the car, after Marianne's panicked message, he had added another cross. The one marking the address of Angélique Fontaine's parents, on Impasse Copernic, three streets away from Rue des Gryzoñs. That was the house he found first, a little cottage that was not touched by any of the others due to the miracle of a small garden. It was quite stylish. Or must have been, once. Now the shutters were closed, the flowers wilted, the gate rusted. A ghost house. Hard to believe that children's laughter or the shouts of teenagers had once rung out within those walls.

Potigny was not a village where you could grow up, only grow old.

He turned right onto Rue des Gryzoṅs. What struck him first was the uniformity and linearity of the architecture. Monotonous and monochrome, with nuances in the red brick that only a rare ray of sunlight could pick out.

Rust red, wine red, blood red.

The kids had left this place too. All that remained was a sign advising motorists to SLOW for CHILDREN AT PLAY and a sleeping policeman. The sign was probably only ever true once or twice a year, when the grandchildren visited for Christmas or a birthday.

Papy walked slowly. The street was straight, empty, windy. It felt a bit like the Wild West, with him the stranger in town, his progress tracked by hundreds of eyes behind the curtains. He almost expected Billy the Kid to appear at the other end of the street.

But there was no one.

He arrived at number 12, the Solers' house. According to Marouette's files, the house had been sold a few months after the death of Timo's father. A bargain price. Federico Soler had preferred to spend the few months of retirement that he'd slaved away his entire life for on home improvements rather than chemotherapy. Papy played spot the difference with the photograph of the house taken around the time when Timo was a teenager: the sandpit had been replaced by a flowerbed, the football pitch by a boules court, and the basketball hoop by a barbecue. A curtain twitched open, revealing a pink dressing gown. Papy kept walking.

Number 21: Tomasz and Karolina Adamiack. There was a sign on the fence.

*For Sale.*

The house's dilapidated state – it had clearly been abandoned years before – stood in stark contrast to the meticulous care paid to the gravestone of Ilona's parents.

Number 23, two houses further down: Josèf and Marta Lukowik. Lieutenant Pasdeloup decided that he would leave the Zerdas' former house, number 33, until last; the Zerdas had left the village more than ten years ago, whereas – if Lucas Marouette's files were correct – Cyril's parents still lived here. The shutters were the same pale green colour as they had been in the photograph from back then; same vegetable garden, same slide, same swing hanging from the high branch of the cherry tree. As if their child had never left home.

Papy walked up to the gate.

A letterbox. The logo of the Pays d'Auge. A doorbell, a few centimetres higher up.

His index finger trembled slightly as he pushed the button, as if the sound might not just wake up the house's occupants, but the entire neighbourhood, the whole village, even those who were sleeping in the cemetery.

Had he guessed correctly?

Was it the right thing to do, following this path, alone, without Marianne or any other colleagues?

The doorbell rang.

He waited for quite a while before the oak door opened.

He was expecting Marta Lukowik to appear, but in fact it was Josèf.

Short grey hair, matching jumper, the look of a Polish customs official on the Oder-Neisse line. All that was missing was the hunting rifle in his hands. Instead, his two dark, close-set eyes were trained on Papy like a double-barrel shotgun, ready to blow away intruders.

'Yeah?'

Despite the best efforts of Josèf Lukowik to intimidate Lieutenant Pasdeloup, to get rid of him as fast as possible, without even waiting to find out what he wanted, Papy didn't even meet his gaze.

371

Instead, he was looking beyond him.

Behind him.

Through the tiny crack between the open door and the corpulent mass of the retired miner. It had taken him only a fraction of a second to realise that he had not come here in vain. That he had guessed the truth, from the very beginning.

# 65

*Little hand on the 4, big hand on the 4*

'Maman-da?'

She turned to Malone, her eyes blazing. He immediately corrected himself:

'Maman?'

'Yes, sweetie?'

'Why are people taking off their shoes?'

Malone did not really understand the answer. He couldn't see the connection between belts, women's jewellery, glasses, shoes and the computers.

Maman-da – after all, he was allowed to call her that in his head – kept repeating the same two words to him:

'Hurry up.'

Her hand was on his back, and her arm propelled him forward. Two police officers – a man and a lady – checked their papers again. While Maman-da was handing them over, Malone took a step sideways. She grabbed him at the last moment.

'What's the matter, sweetie?'

Malone noticed that her voice was softer and kinder, probably because of the police. It was a bit like how they had to behave properly when his teacher was around. This was his chance.

'I want Gouti!'

Malone saw his toy again, Gouti's head caught in the spiky bushes. Maman-da had had no right to take him away!

NO RIGHT to leave him there.

NO RIGHT to go on without him.

Amanda stared stupidly at the police while she hugged the child tight in her arms.

'Where we're going, sweetie, there are lots of Goutis, just the same as him. I could buy you another one, a nicer one.'

Malone wasn't listening. His eyes were looking through the gap between Maman-da's locked arms. The airport lobby was big, but he could run fast. Faster than Maman-da, that was for sure. He just had to save himself. It wouldn't be hard.

He whispered, in a tiny voice.

'OK, Maman.'

Maman-da released him.

Immediately, Malone leapt away, before Maman-da could react. All he had to do now was run straight ahead, then turn after he reached the big posters on the wall.

'Malone, stop!' yelled Maman-da behind him.

He stopped.

Not because she'd yelled; it had nothing to do with that. Maman-da had probably made everyone in the airport turn to look by screaming so loud, but he had barely even heard her.

He was looking at the poster.

*It was Maman.*

There she was, with her big smile, her long hair, and she was looking at him too, as if to tell him off.

How stupid he was! To think he'd almost disobeyed her.

Only now did he remember her advice, the advice he was supposed to never forget, the advice she'd made him promise to repeat to himself every night in his head – which he'd done, with Gouti.

He had to wait, that was all.

Maman-da's hand took a firm hold of him.

'That's enough, Malone!'

He had to wait for the right moment.

And, before that, he had to act as if Maman-da was his Maman. They passed yet more police and Maman-da took off her glasses, her watch, took her phone from her pocket. Malone only had to remove the medallion from around his neck. They went through a door without a wall. Maman-da made it ring; he didn't. She had to take off a necklace and try again.

He waited patiently for her on the other side.

The police were laughing among themselves. There were others, a bit further away, with rifles, dressed as though they were actually going to war.

While they walked along the corridor, past the big windows and the aeroplanes they could see through them, Malone thought back to his mother's last words.

'Gate 8,' said Maman-da. 'Two circles, one on top of the other. Can you help me look for it, sweetie?'

Malone was looking the other way, at the walls, the shops, the doors.

He was going to have to be brave. He wished Gouti were with him. There was only one way to escape ogres! Only one way not to get on the plane that would take him to their forest.

Maman had repeated it to him, when she was saying goodbye to him, as he was holding Gouti to his chest.

*It's a prayer, it's your prayer. You must never forget it.*
*It's very simple. You can do it.*
*Just before you get on the aeroplane, you have to say one sentence, a sentence you've already said a thousand times, but you have to say it at exactly that moment.*
*Even if it's not true. They have to believe you.*

Two circles, one on top of the other.

Gate 8.

Maman-da smiled. A sort of big pipe, like an enormous vacuum cleaner, was connected to a white and orange plane. As if the people were just balls of dust. Or crumbs.

Malone pulled at Maman-da's sleeve.

*They have to believe you. Even if it's not true.*

*

'Maman.'

Maman-da smiled at him. All he had to do to make her smile was call her Maman.

'Yes, sweetie, what is it?'

'I need to go pee-pee.'

# 66

*Today, at nearly midnight, he said sorry love, I never go to bed with someone on the first date. Me neither. Not after the last 317 dates.*
Want to kill
*I left him my high heels as a souvenir - one in each bollock!*

*Convicted: 97*
*Acquitted: 451*

www.want-to-kill.com

The police car squealed to a halt outside the glass doors of the airport. The two car doors opened simultaneously, in perfect synchrony. Marianne and JB jumped out. The captain got ready to sprint, still holding Gouti in her left hand.

16.33.

The plane to Caracas, via Galway, was due to take off in nine minutes.

That countdown obsessed her, even if she knew that Alexis Zerda couldn't possibly escape on this plane, from this airport. Not with the kid, not with Timo, not with Angie.

Not on his own either. They had informed every airport employee, every police officer, every flight attendant. No way could he slip through the net in an airport this small. That search for flight tickets was probably just another diversion, or one of Zerda's many plans – Plan B, Plan Z, whatever, not the one he would actually follow. He was anything but stupid. He wasn't about to leap into the wolf's mouth.

16.34.

If in doubt, just keep going!

The sliding glass door opened in front of her. Marianne was about to go through it, when she felt something pulling her backwards. She was stopped in her tracks.

JB was holding her by the wrist.

The lieutenant's ear had been glued to his phone ever since they parked, but all he did now was shake his head.

'Wait, Marianne.'

The feel of her deputy's hand on her skin did not provoke any particular sensation. Three minutes earlier, when JB had put on a dry shirt in the car, she had shamelessly checked out his muscled torso and his perfectly sculpted six-pack. And yet the only image that came to her mind was of JB's children waiting outside the school for their papa while he was busy screwing some pretty girl.

It was a stupid sort of rejection. JB was still a good cop, a nice piece of eye candy to be enjoyed on the sly, in the rear-view mirror. But as far as her fantasies were concerned, it was over. For now, at least. Marianne would try again after the menopause, if handsome young JB hadn't put on ten kilograms by the time he reached his forties.

Handsome young JB who was not letting go of her hand.

'What the hell is it?'

'It's Constantini. They've found a corpse in the hideout at the NATO base. There was a ditch behind the house, filled to the brim with gravel, gobs of oil, seaweed and water because of the high tide. Constantini had to go in up to his shoulders to get the body out.'

'OK, JB. We were expecting that.'

Marianne turned to the door of the airport and tried to advance, but still Lieutenant Lechevalier held her back. The glass doors slid open again, then slid shut a second later, as if disappointed that no one was entering.

'What, JB?'

'There's just one problem. With the corpse.'

The lieutenant paused, squeezing Marianne's wrist as if he were taking her pulse.

One hundred and fifty beats per minute.

'Spit it out, JB!'

'The corpse. It's not Amanda Moulin!'

The lieutenant's hand tightened around her wrist.

One hundred and seventy-five beats per minute.

'It's Zerda. Two bullets in his chest.'

'Shit!'

At last JB let go of the captain's wrist. She leapt free, heading straight towards the airport lobby, still throwing questions over her shoulder at her deputy.

'Anything else, JB?'

He was only a few centimetres behind.

'Yeah, and it's even more of a surprise than the corpse's identity . . . It's Marouette, the intern. He's good. Fast. He's been doing some research into Angélique Fontaine.'

Marianne bit her lip. The backlit glass door reflected her image, deformed. JB was about to tell her that they'd found a photo of Angie or, better yet, a witness: the waiter at Uno. Angélique Fontaine had been meeting up every week with a woman who strangely resembled Marianne. Honestly, I'm not kidding, she's your spitting image!

'Marouette checked out her whole life story,' JB went on. 'From her childhood in Potigny up to today. She works in a hairdressing salon in Le Havre, and she lives in Graville . . .'

A hot flush enveloped Marianne. Of course, she would explain things. Of course she would admit how stupid she'd been. All she was asking for was a few minutes, so she could save the kid.

'So?' Marianne stammered.

Two soldiers, armed to the teeth, were marching towards them.

'There's no trace of any kid! Nothing in her background since the age of twenty that makes it possible she even had one!'

Marianne thought back to their conversation at Uno: Angie's car accident, when she was pregnant, deliberately caused by the child's father; how upset she was never to be able to have children. All those secrets that made sense only in this final scene.

'How could she have hidden a child?' Lieutenant Lechevalier asked. 'And for three years? There's always so much paperwork, for God's sake: maternity wards, crèches, childminders, grandparents, doctors, neighbours. You can't hide a baby in your apartment while you go to work, or keep it under your coat when you go shopping. Marouette and the others could not find any trace of a child in Angélique Fontaine's life. None at all!'

The two soldiers were standing less than two metres away.

A disillusioned voice sniggered inside the captain's head. Well, yes, JB, we all have our little secrets. You and your floozies. Me and my best friend.

Marianne held up her police card to the soldiers and kept running forward, enjoying her pathetic show of authority over the boys with shaved heads. A sort of gallant last stand. For a second, her gaze lingered on the posters pinned to the wall opposite.

The faces of Alexis Zerda, Timo Soler and Angie stared back at her.

And all for nothing. It was Amanda Moulin they had to search for in this airport; she was the one who was going to try to board the aeroplane with the kid she'd adopted, who bore her name. And the customs officials had no reason to stop her. Very clever, Amanda . . .

The captain checked her watch as JB, too, came to a stop in front of the posters. He was probably thinking this case was drifting out of control. Poor man.

Less than five minutes to take-off.

She continued running through the lobby, still holding Gouti in her hands. JB might be a good cop, but he was wrong on that point. He'd been left behind by events, with no grasp of the situation.

But she understood, thanks to this cuddly toy.

Amanda must not be allowed to fly away with Malone. Absolutely not! Not because she was guilty of Alexis Zerda's murder; she probably had a good case for having killed him in self-defence. No, there was another reason.

Angie hadn't lied to her. Angie had simply put a message in a bottle and thrown it into the sea, an SOS that echoed her own. In a way, she had even told her friend the truth. That was where the urgency lay – only there – and as for the rest, she would sort through her feelings later, in front of the police's internal affairs committee.

Still without slowing down, in an almost intuitive ballet with her deputy, Marianne pointed towards the security officers while she headed towards the check-in desks. No need to explain. They were pros, perfectly coordinated.

Marianne found herself facing another soldier, barely twenty years old, who was looking incredulously at the cuddly rat she held in one hand and the captain's badge in the other. She was about to put him in his place when the phone in her pocket buzzed.

She surprised herself by praying. Which wasn't like her at all.

Dear God, please let it be Papy!

Let him help her to make the right decision, this time; let him confirm what Gouti had revealed to her a few minutes earlier, as she was climbing up the stairway of the abandoned NATO base.

Three simple words sewn into his fur, which no one but her had noticed. Banal. Unexceptional. The same words sewn into thousands of identical cuddly toys sold all over the world . . . and yet they shone an unearthly light on the truth.

Angélique was not Malone's mother . . .

# 67

*Little hand on the 4, big hand on the 7*

There was hardly anyone in front of them now. The vacuum cleaner must have hoovered up most of the dustballs. Whoosh . . . straight into the plane.

Malone pulled a face. The hand that was holding his hurt him slightly, especially the ring that pressed against his skin. He forced himself not to cry.

He looked up.

One, two, three.

Three last dustballs ahead of them. The queue was advancing quickly. The lady in a suit was much faster than the others, faster than the one behind the glass earlier when they had handed over their papers, faster too than the one who had asked them to take off their belts and watches. This one barely even looked at people as they went past, never mind the passports with their photographs that they held out. All the lady did was take the little piece of card, the one you needed to get on the plane, tear part of it off, and then hand back what was left.

One, two, three, Malone counted again.

This was the third time they'd had to show their papers. It was normal that this lady was paying less attention the third time round.

The mouth of the vacuum cleaner had swallowed up the last dustballs; it was their turn now.

Malone hesitated; he was a bit afraid of this lady. She had long red fingernails, fire-coloured hair, dark skin, black eyes, and a mouth that opened wide when she spoke and never closed completely, as if she had too many teeth.

Malone understood.

She was a dragon.

She guarded the entrance to the cave, the one that led to the forest of ogres. She allowed the other dustballs in – she didn't care about them – but would she let *them* in?

The dragon took their passports, hardly even glancing at them, then tore the piece of card and opened her mouth without looking up.

'Have a good trip, madame.'

It was quite dark inside the vacuum cleaner. A bit colder too. At the end, Malone saw another hole: the doorway to the plane.

*The forest of ogres . . .*

This time, Malone couldn't hold back his tears.

The hand in his was soft. The voice in the tunnel was gentle.

'You've been very brave, my love.'

Malone didn't care about being brave. He didn't care about ogres. He didn't care about the dragon. He didn't care if the plane took off with or without them.

He just wanted Gouti.

He wanted his cuddly toy.

'You're going to have to be a bit brave again, my love. Gouti would be proud. You've done exactly what he wanted you to do.'

She took Malone in her arms.

'OK, my love?'

Malone sniffed, then they continued walking. Just before he came out of the vacuum cleaner and into the plane, there was a little gap: you could see the tarmac of the runway beneath. And just after that, there were another two ladies in suits who asked for the torn-up piece of card. Not their passports this time, just the card. The numbers of their seats were written on it – Maman-da had explained that to him. These two ladies had mouths with too many teeth too, but they kindly showed them where they should sit on the plane.

The hand gripped his more tightly.

'Ready, my love? I promise: Papa will join us soon.'

She kissed him. Malone sniffed. Without Gouti to stroke, he didn't know what to do with his hands. His eyes continued to cry, but he managed to smile in the end.

'OK, Maman.'

# 68

*Today, he came back to buy bread. He's handsome.*
*He's an engineer, or something like that. He wears*
*a suit and tie and he makes his children laugh by*
*carrying them on his back. He didn't look at me once*
*as I handed him the baguette. Not once did he glance*
*at my low-cut blouse. Not once did he look at me like*
*I was anything more than a stupid shop assistant.*
Want to kill
*I invented a story and emailed it to his wife. She*
*smashed his skull in with an iron – I read it in the*
*local paper.*

*Convicted:  2,136*
*Acquitted:  129*

www.want-to-kill.com


The figures coming up behind Marianne looked like ghosts. Immense, translucent . . . the closer they came, the bigger they grew, until they were now as big as the airport's white and red control tower, dwarfing the two Boeing 737s on the runway. For a brief instant, they became darker, almost menacing, then vanished in the next second. A cloud in the sky, probably, which had been enough to erase the reflection of the two policemen rushing towards the captain.

Marianne didn't look behind her though; her gaze remained fixed on the runway.

Gates 5 to 9. Amsterdam. Galway. Lyon. Barcelona.

JB stood beside his boss, out of breath.

'Marianne? Listen to this. We've found Soler! An anonymous phone call from a woman. He was lying on the passenger seat of a Twingo parked in the airport car park.'

Marianne, abruptly dragged from her torpor, turned away from the planes and faced her deputy.

'Timo Soler . . . At last! How is he?'

'Not good. A punctured lung, an open wound on his shoulder blade, internal bleeding. But he was still alive when Bourdaine and Benhami opened the car door. They even spotted a few signs of consciousness – fluttering eyelids, trembling lips, that kind of thing. But don't expect him to start confessing!'

The captain stared at her deputy.

'What's your prognosis, JB?'

'Hard to say. The ambulance is on its way. A one-in-ten chance, maybe? One in a hundred? Soler has survived until now, after all. It's a miracle he's not dead already.'

To their right, the man in charge of airport security was getting agitated. Clearly, he didn't give a damn about Timo Soler's chances of survival. He was a small man in a suit and tie, with thin-framed glasses that slid down his steep nose and drops of sweat that trickled down his bald head into what remained of his hair between his neck and his ears. He was flanked by a flight attendant with red hair and painted fingernails, a good head taller than him, and two young shaven-headed soldiers wearing combat fatigues, machine guns strapped over their shoulders. The four of them looked like Mafiosi. A shady businessman, his moll, and two bodyguards. He had the cold, cutting voice of someone without natural authority.

'What are we going to do, Captain?'

Marianne did not respond. She stared at the Boeing 737 behind the window again, her mind running through what had just happened.

Timo Soler had been abandoned half-dead in the airport car park, but the emergency services had been called in time for him to have at least some chance of surviving, however slim. That was logical, after all, since every episode of this story had been written in advance. Marianne was ultimately just a puppet in a toy theatre, a character whose role had been plotted out, chapter by chapter.

She thought about the second-to-last event, less than five minutes ago.

A scream had echoed through the airport while she was questioning one of the women behind the check-in desks. It had come from the direction of the women's toilets that were just beyond all the security checks. JB and Constantini had run straight over there and Marianne had followed, a few metres behind. She'd understood as soon as she saw the door smashed down by Constantini's shoulder and, behind it, the body laid out on the floor.

One more illusion.

Amanda Moulin had been taken by surprise and knocked out in the women's toilets. Her attacker had then dragged the unconscious body into the nearest cubicle, crudely gagged and tied it up. A rushed job.

'He was hiding here,' JB said, pointing at the door of the maintenance cupboard opposite. 'He was hiding in that tiny box room, waiting for Amanda Moulin.'

Marianne observed the tiny cupboard, with its crushed cardboard boxes, its mops and bottles of detergent.

'Crazy, isn't it?' JB went on. 'How long was he waiting there?'

'She . . .'

'She?'

The captain examined the narrow rectangle, about thirty centimetres wide, one last time. Amanda Moulin, sitting on the toilet, the gag now around her neck, was looking shell-shocked.

'She! Only a woman could hide in there. A thin, flexible woman.'

*Angie.*

The image of Amanda's face slowly faded from her mind, along with that of the cupboard full of toilet paper and bleach. They were replaced by the Boeing 737.

Security Man was still watching Marianne. Nervously, his gaze hopped from the flight attendant's breasts, at eye level for him, to the henchmen's machine guns, then back to the captain's face. Security Man seemed unused to seeing a woman with a gun on her belt. A woman he was obliged to wait for while she made a decision.

Marianne was thinking. Quickly. It was all clear now. Angie had taken Amanda Moulin's seat on the plane! She must have gone into the airport a few hours earlier, before her poster was distributed to the customs officers. She must have booked a seat on another flight – it didn't matter which one – and then she'd waited, hidden in the toilets. All she had to do was wait for Amanda Moulin – whom no one suspected at the time, whose poster was not plastered all over the walls of the airport – to arrive with Malone, get through the baggage check-in, past the customs officials, past passport control and the security checks. The last check – the one before boarding – was purely a formality, as the queue of one hundred and twenty passengers had to be herded onto the plane in a matter of minutes, the flight attendants merely glancing at the passports, and focusing on the seat numbers on the boarding passes. After all, the passengers' passports had already been checked twice.

A mother and a child. Two passports. A vague resemblance. All Angie had to do was conceal her face a little, and she'd have no worries about being stopped at this stage.

The perfect plan. Angie had shown incredible daring.

Security Man, at his wit's end, seemed to be desperately seeking help, any kind of support, but the two soldiers looked as if they'd been turned to stone, the attendant to a wax doll.

He was on his own. He sighed.

'So, what should we do?'

Marianne responded by pointing outside.

'Is the plane to Galway still on the runway?'

The man rolled his eyes and clapped his hands, then pointed at the Boeing on the tarmac.

'Yes! And there are three others waiting in line behind it. The girl and the kid are on board, we checked. We're just waiting for your orders, Captain. Judge Dumas has made it clear that the aeroplane mustn't be allowed to leave without your agreement. I have fifteen men ready to go as soon as you . . .'

Marianne did not reply. Security Man lowered his eyes and grimaced. This was driving him mad. This indecisive police captain, wandering around with a disgusting cuddly toy in her arms, and no one even batted an eyelid. You'd think he was the only one who'd noticed. This whole episode was crazy.

As if to torture the man even more, Marianne's fingers began to squeeze the toy, running over the seam in Gouti's fur. The captain re-read the four words on the toy's label. Gouti's secret!

She couldn't stop a small smile creeping across her face.

Four words, before their very eyes, ever since the beginning, and no one had paid them any attention.

*Made in French Guiana.*


Yes, Angie had written everything in advance, this whole story, down to the last chapter! But it was up to her, Marianne, to choose the ending.

Angie's confidences at the table in Uno had been designed just for this. To prepare this moment. To make her hesitate . . . All those evenings, all those hours when Angie had pretended to be her friend.

Manipulation?

A cry for help?

Security Man stood on tiptoes and shouted like a yappy little dog:

'My God, what are we waiting for, Captain?!'

Marianne's calm reply sent him into a complete meltdown.

'A phone call.'

# 69

*Today, Léonce asked me to turn off his life support.*
Want to kill
*I couldn't.*

*Convicted: 7*
*Acquitted: 990*

www.want-to-kill.com

The child swung slowly, yet without any awareness of the danger.

The two ropes that held the cracked wooden board were frayed and attached to the swing's frame by rusted snaplinks. The rain and the years had also left their mark on the other equipment: a worm-eaten bar, asymmetric rings, a rope net full of holes.

The child wasn't moving: the swing was just swaying on its own, its movements not slowed or accelerated by the slightest gesture, not even a blink. The child's gaze was fixed, as if, for him, everything else was moving: the grass, the trees, the house, the entire earth.

From the conservatory, Marta Lukowik observed this child, covered from head to foot, from mittens to hat, for a long moment, then put her coffee cup down on the table. A whole series of plants and shrubs were growing in the glass-walled room, carefully arranged in earthenware pots lined up next to the windows: orange trees, lemon trees and gooseberry bushes providing a sophisticated mix of colours.

Josèf, sitting opposite Lieutenant Pasdeloup, pointed to the little garden enclosed inside three high brick walls. Papy thought he was going to talk about the child.

'You wouldn't guess it, but that's south-facing. We had the conservatory built in 1990, just after the mines closed, with the compensation we received. Madness . . .'

He coughed and pulled a cup of coffee towards him.

'We're still paying for it, twenty-five years later, but maybe I wouldn't be alive today if I wasn't spending my days under glass, surrounded by all these plants.'

His cough transformed into a phlegmy laugh. Marta dropped a sugar cube into her husband's coffee, without him even asking her.

'And with the three walls around the garden,' Josèf added, 'the neighbours don't bother us.'

He flinched as his lips came into contact with the hot coffee.

Papy tasted his. It was bitter. It hadn't been easy, persuading Josèf Lukowik to let him in, and showing this retired miner his police ID had not helped matters. It had only been when he mentioned the names of Timo Soler, Angélique Fontaine and Alexis Zerda that Josèf had opened the door a centimetre wider.

The reaction was especially marked when he mentioned Alexis Zerda's name. Papy had responded instinctively.

'Alexis Zerda is dead. He was shot, less than an hour ago. We found his body on the old NATO base.'

The door had opened then, and Josèf had said simply:

'We'll go through to the conservatory. Marta, make us some coffee.'

That was all. As if Josèf had no wish for the lieutenant to hang around in the hallway with its old-fashioned wallpaper, as if he didn't want his gaze to linger on the *Solidarność* posters, on the photograph of Wawel Cathedral or the portrait of Bronisław Bula above the shoe rack.

Visitors were taken to the conservatory.

Where the neighbours wouldn't bother them.


Papy gulped down his coffee, forcing himself not to grimace, then stared brazenly at the child on the swing.

'So what happened?'

Marta Lukowik put her hand on her husband's. A wrinkled hand, covered with brown spots, as worn as the snaplinks of the swing, tired out from years of carrying children, before they grew up and left those hands behind. Lieutenant Pasdeloup realised that Marta's hand, placed on her husband's, meant that it was too late, that he should tell the whole story. A wordless connection. It was up to her husband to find the actual sentences, but it was the wife who was confessing.

Josèf coughed again.

'Alexis called us after the robbery in Deauville. I call him Alexis, you know. For us, Zerda was Darko, his father. I spent twenty years at the bottom of that hole with him.'

Marta's hand pressed more heavily on her husband's.

'He was the first one to call us, before the police, before the journalists, before the neighbours. Cyril had been killed by the cops in Deauville, on Rue de la Mer. Along with Ilona, who had also been shot. I remember, it was nearly noon; Marta was listening to Radio Nostalgie as she brought a camellia out into the conservatory. She turned the tuner to France Info. That was all they were talking about. Alexis was right. The pot fell from her hands. You can still see the mark, there.'

He pointed at a dent in the tiled floor.

'Marta and I didn't like the cops much, even before that . . .'

Papy didn't rise to the bait. In the garden, the child was still swinging, gently, regular as a pendulum.

'Alexis Zerda wanted to meet you?'

'Yes. We saw him barely an hour later, near the pond in Canivet. The place where all the kids used to go fishing, in the old days. He was alone. Both of us went to see him. Marta was driving. I was trembling too much. It's in moments like that that the bloody arthritis in my right hand comes back.'

Papy understood then that Marta's hand placed on Josèf's was a way of calming it, immobilising it, like a caress reassuring a frightened bird.

'Alexis was standing in front of the pond, near what remains of the hut in the bulrushes that he built when he was ten, for trapping frogs and moorhens. Two sheets of corrugated iron and three rotten planks. Alexis was shaking too. It was the first time I had ever seen him like that. Even when he was summoned by the teachers at the secondary school for extorting money from young Leguennec, he never lost his contempt for authority, that look of defiance, the same attitude his father had when he looked at the foremen in the mine. But that day . . . no. For the first time, he seemed – how can I put this? – vulnerable. And we all knew why.'

'Because he'd almost been killed? Because Cyril and Ilona were . . .'

'No,' Josèf cut in, punctuating his reaction with another coughing fit. 'Alexis couldn't have cared less about our son or our daughter-in-law, or even Timo, who had been wounded. In fact, that probably suited him: fewer people to divide the loot between, fewer witnesses. I never had any illusions about young Alexis, you know. When I saw him for the first time, it was here, in this garden, at Cyril's fifth birthday party. This might seem strange, but you can guess, almost every time, what a very young kid will become. And little Alexis . . . well, let's just say he wasn't the kind of kid who wanted to share his cake.'

Papy did not remark on this and turned the conversation back to the subject in hand.

'So what made him feel vulnerable then?'

'The last witness who was still alive.'

Lieutenant Pasdeloup played a card.

'Angélique Fontaine?'

Josèf smiled, and so did his wife.

'No. Angie would never have told the cops anything, and he knew it. No, what scared Alexis was the kid. That was why he took the risk of coming to see us. Because of the kid.'

'How old was he?'

'Nearly three. The kid had been with them all through the planning of the robbery. In his mother's arms, playing next to them, eating with them. Obviously, the cops would question the boy. Even at that age, he was smart, clever, chatty. The kid would have talked. At the very least, he'd have recognised Alexis's face in the photographs the cops would have showed him. At worst, he'd have repeated bits of conversation, dates, names of places, streets, shops. Kids are sponges when they're that young.'

'The testimony of a three-year-old child? You think the judge would have paid attention to that?'

Josèf looked across the conservatory. Imperceptibly, the swing had begun to slow, perhaps because it was tired of having to do all the swinging by itself.

'We did some research,' the retired miner went on. 'Since those paedophilia cases in the nineties, judges have listened to what kids say . . . And quite right, too.'

'What exactly was Alexis Zerda's plan?'

Josèf's abrupt response made Marta jump.

'To swap the kid.'

He was suddenly gripped by a coughing fit, stronger than the previous ones, so Marta took up the story, in her gentle voice.

'It was the only solution, really. The police were bound to discover the existence of that child. So they were bound to come and question him, and the kid would have told them everything. Even if we'd asked him to lie to the police – if it's even possible to ask a three-year-old kid to do something like that – the cops would have realized that he was hiding something and they'd have got it out of him eventually. The solution that Alexis Zerda came up with was very simple, if you think about it: he just had to make sure the cops questioned the wrong child. He had to replace him with another child, if possible a less chatty one . . . Better still, a kid incapable of communicating, traumatised, lost in his own little world. It was the only solution,' Marta repeated.

Her hand remained firmly on top of her husband's, but she couldn't stop her voice trembling. Josèf added:

'Alexis would have killed the kid if we hadn't agreed. He'd have killed the kid to stop him talking.'

The child in the garden had got off the swing. Either that, or he'd fallen off. He was lying in the grass, on his side. The tall grass covered his ears, his shoulders, his thighs. Almost without his head moving, his cheek caressed the nearest tufts, as if it were an animal's mane.

Marta stood up and asked the lieutenant if he wanted another coffee. He accepted, even though he felt sure he wouldn't be able to finish it. When Marta returned with the pot, Papy spoke again.

'Right. He had to swap the kid so the cops wouldn't question him. I get that, but still, it must have been quite some magic trick, mustn't it?'

Josèf took up the story again:

'Alexis had an idea. He'd found a donor. A mate of his who he'd shared a cell with in Bois-d'Arcy. Dimitri Moulin. His kid, Malone, had fallen down some stairs and was almost a vegetable. It was the perfect solution. It just took a few thousand euros to convince the father . . .'

He looked at Marta, then continued.

'It was a bit more difficult to convince the mother. She refused to be separated from her child, even for a few months. So, with the father's help, they tampered with the results of the hospital's latest analysis. They made the mother believe that her child was doomed, that he had only a few months left to live. We had to play along, that was the deal. We spent hours on the phone with Amanda; to start with, she would call us ten times a day, then gradually less often, and in the end she hardly called at all. We continued to send her messages, letters, photographs, to reassure her. Well, I say reassure her . . . Basically, just to tell her that Malone was still alive. There was nothing else to say. No progress to mention. Malone eats, Malone swings, Malone looks at butterflies, Malone looks at ants. Malone doesn't speak, Malone doesn't play, Malone doesn't laugh. Yes, we kept giving her updates, but by then we'd understood . . .'

He couldn't continue his sentence. Tears ran down his wrinkled face. At the bottom of the garden, the child stared at a point in the grass that he alone could see, presumably some tiny insect.

Papy came to Josèf's aid.

'You'd understood that, in Amanda's heart, the other child had taken the place of hers. Is that what you mean?'

'That's right,' confirmed Marta. 'Of course, we now have access to his medical files.' She glanced at the little boy's body stretched out in the grass. 'In reality, the kid could stay like that for years. He's not even in pain any more.'

Her voice was infinitely gentle.

'Alexis's plan might seem complicated, but really it was very simple. He just had to swap the children for a while, enough time for the child to forget his life before, or at least forget any faces, names and places that might be compromising. It was inevitable. After that, Alexis couldn't have cared less what happened to the two kids.'

The Lukowiks had agreed to the swap; they had agreed to cover for Zerda, in order to fool the police. Lieutenant Pasdeloup thought about the file lying open on the passenger seat of his police car. Josèf had got into trouble with the law a few times when he was young. Drunk and disorderly, fighting in the street, insulting a police officer . . . nothing too bad, and it was nearly fifty years ago, but it was enough to make him understand why Josèf and Marta were not the type of people to spontaneously go to the police.

There were still grey areas in the file, though. Angélique Fontaine had not had a child: there wasn't a trace of any child in the research. Lucas Marouette had been categorical about that.

'Tell me about Angélique Fontaine,' Papy said.

A broad smile spread over Marta's face.

'Little Angie was always the most intelligent one in the gang. Crafty, talented, gracious. A bit dreamy, too. When she was a little girl, in Potigny, you'd never see her without a doll or a book in her hand. And pretty as a picture . . . Pretty and romantic: you can probably guess the rest, detective. Angie's problem was boys. Boys, and authority in general. In the list of all her lovers, Timo Soler was the best. Not that there was much competition . . . He was still a bad boy, and they kept their relationship secret. That's why most people never realised Angie was sharing Timo's bed. For Angie, it all exploded in adolescence. Her mother was cheating on her poor father – everyone knew about it, including him – but I don't think that was even the problem. It was just that her parents weren't at her level any more; little Angie was an extraterrestrial for them; their house, in Impasse Copernic, had become a lifeless planet, and Angie was dreaming of another galaxy. But everything went wrong after she moved away. Her father's cancer, which killed him within six months; her famous blog, *want-to-kill.com*, and then the accident, of course.'

'Accident?'

Papy had jumped. Marouette's file did not mention any accident. Was this the missing piece of the puzzle?

'Angie was in a car crash in January 2005, near Graville, with her boyfriend at the time. Another one of her bastards. She collected them, seriously! He got away without a scratch, but Angie was a few months' pregnant. She lost her child and the doctor told her she could never have children again. And God knows she loved kids, Angie. I can still see her, the poor thing, as a little girl with her dolls, pushing them around Potigny in her little pink pram.'

Seeing the lieutenant's surprised expression, Josèf added:

'Not many of us knew about it, but we had the same doctor as the Fontaines, Dr Sarkissian – he still lives in Potigny, actually. We play boules with him every Friday afternoon. He's one of ours, as they say. Well, for a doctor to stay here, he'd have to be one of ours.'

Papy swallowed. Everything was becoming clear. Nearly. He put his hand on top of Josèf and Marta's, then asked his question before they could remove them.

'When was the last time you saw your son and your daughter-in-law?'

He felt the two hands wanting to escape, but he pressed down firmly.

Who would reply? He'd have bet on Josèf, but in fact it was Marta.

'It all depends on what you mean by "saw", detective. Cyril and Ilona dropped by briefly once or twice before the robbery, just for a coffee or a meal, not long enough to go for a walk or play a game of belote, but we were happy with that. It was better than before.'

'Tell me,' said the lieutenant.

'Cyril had had a hard time, when he was a teenager. The mines had just closed. He started dealing and selling stolen goods – dope, car radios, cars, alarm systems pinched from holiday homes. He was no angel, and neither was Ilona, but they paid for it. More than two years in prison, all told. After they got out, they married and went straight. I mean it, detective! They rented an apartment in Le Havre, in the Neiges quarter. He became a docker. He worked hard, he liked his job. Then after four years on the Quai d'Europe, they left.'

'To go to French Guiana, right?'

'Yes. In the large seaport at Remire-Montjoly, Maersk opened an extra line. The pay was better than in Le Havre, much better, but Cyril had to sign an overseas contract that would last several years.'

'But they didn't hesitate?'

'No. They left in June 2009. Six years ago now. I don't think I saw Cyril for more than seven whole days after that, before he was . . .'

New tears fell. She turned her face away and stared at the rusted swing at the bottom of the garden, as if it were a symbol of the life they had lost from this house. The ant-child was just another ghost.

Josèf took over.

'After five years, when Cyril came back to Le Havre, there was no more work for him on the docks. More than half the workforce had been laid off. Muscle power wasn't necessary any more: one guy could unload a ship with fifteen thousand containers using just a joystick. I'm sure you can guess the rest, detective: no job, no money . . . Cyril started seeing Alexis again.'

Marta dabbed at her tears with an embroidered handkerchief.

'They had responsibilities now,' Josèf said. 'We never thought, when they left for French Guiana . . .'

'You never thought what?' Papy insisted, although he already knew the answer.

Outside, near the child, in the badly mown grass, a butterfly took off. The boy didn't even react.

It was Marta who replied.

'We never thought Cyril and Ilona would bring us back a grandson!'

# 70

Papy left a long pause, to give himself time to recall the key points from the files, the ones that had intrigued him the night before when he'd stayed up late at the station before calling Anaïs in Cleveland.

*Intuition!*

Through the conservatory window, he looked out again at the child lying in the long grass.

'We never thought Cyril and Ilona would bring us back a grandson!'

According to the report, the police in Caen had gone to see Josèf and Marta Lukowik on 20 January 2015 to question the child belonging to Cyril and Ilona Lukowik. Everything seemed to be in order. The grandparents had taken over as guardians of the little orphan. They'd shown the boy photographs of all the possible suspects, including Alexis Zerda. They'd questioned him for a good hour. Nothing!

The kid, according to the report, seemed barely conscious, borderline retarded. The police had recorded this in the report without sounding particularly surprised: the child had just lost both his parents in the most violent way. They recommended psychological monitoring, and they'd had a conversation with the grandparents, but as far as the investigation was concerned, it was a dead end. It was logical, really: the questioning was purely routine, a simple case of not overlooking any possible lead. The report of the interview took up only ten lines in a dossier comprising several hundred pages of testimonies and expert opinions. No one, apart from Papy, had paid it the slightest attention.

Now, he saw every detail clearly.

'How old was your grandson, when you saw him for the first time?'

Marta's voice shook with emotion, as it had when she spoke about Angie.

'Just under two. He was born in French Guiana, it was the only place he'd ever known. He was used to the equatorial climate. That was the first thing I noticed: the kid was cold all the time in Normandy. I was always telling Cyril that he needed to wrap his son up in warmer clothes, but he didn't seem to care. The boy was very cheerful, and advanced for his age. He already spoke a lot, all the time, especially about the big Amazonian forest, about monkeys and snakes, about the Ariane rocket that took off from Kourou, even if he was beginning to forget things, and get them mixed up.'

With her eyes, she pointed to the plants around the conservatory.

'He used to have fun pushing the pots close together to make a little jungle. He would pile up glasses to build a rocket and imitate the noise with his mouth. He'd pretend to be a monkey, shrieking on the swing.'

'And I imagine he never let go of his cuddly toy?'

New tears welled in Marta's eyes.

'His Gouti? Oh no, he'd never let go of Gouti! His parents had bought the toy for him over there. They could have chosen a better-known animal – a jaguar, an armadillo, a sloth, a puma, a parrot – they were spoilt for choice really. But it was a nod to the street they'd grown up on. Gryzoń means "rodent" in Polish.'

Agouti, Gryzoń, rodent . . .

Papy had only solved the puzzle when he arrived in Potigny: that five-year stay in French Guiana mentioned in Cyril and Ilona's file, the cuddly toy named Gouti, and a few other clues, like that photo album that Marianne had told him about over the phone, decorated with monkeys, parrots and tropical trees, the photograph of a wicker cradle protected by mosquito netting, all the memories in the child's brain that mixed up the NATO base, the jungle, the rockets.

Marta stood up and raised her voice.

'A golden child,' she said. 'His head in the clouds. We saw him once or twice a month after that. At least that one could have been happy. He was born near the sky, not underground, like all the kids from this village. That one at least could escape. He had a chance, before . . .'

'Before what, Marta?'

The old woman leant against the cold conservatory. Her words turned to grey mist on the glass.

'Before he saw his parents being shot dead right in front of him! Do you have children, detective? Can you imagine a more monstrous plan than using a two-and-a-half-year-old child to help you get through police blockades after an armed robbery? To use your own kid? I'm talking about my son, detective! My son and my daughter-in-law! How could the child have survived that? Alexis told us how it happened, he didn't shy away from the details: how Cyril, already wounded, just had the time to put his hand on the door of the Opel Zafira and meet his son's eyes, before running away and getting another three bullets in his back. How could a child be expected to recover from a trauma like that? The poor kid is screwed, detective, just like all the others!'

She turned around and, still standing, held her husband's hand again.

'Screwed like Josèf, who spent his whole life digging a tunnel just to end up getting silicosis. Screwed like Cyril, struck down for wanting to touch all that glittered. A third generation screwed.'

She looked around the garden, at the three brick walls. The child lying in the grass seemed to have fallen asleep.

'He won't escape, lieutenant. Never.'

'Unless he forgets,' said Papy.

For the first time, Marta appeared to lose her composure.

'And how do you expect him to forget? That child has no parents any more! We're too old. As soon as his time with the Moulins is over, he'll just be shunted from foster home to foster home, with the mark of death engraved on his brain. A mark that can never be erased.'

*A mark that can never be erased.*

Papy thought again of the conversation he'd had with Marianne, about Vasily Dragonman's theories. Was it possible to suppress the memories of a child before his memory stabilised? Even of a trauma. Especially a trauma. To bury the memory rather than obliging the person to live with it for the rest of their life? How reckless, how desperate, how determined would you have to be to make that bet?

He didn't say a word, though.

Marta turned back to the garden and looked at the child sleeping on the lawn, with a smile on his face, a thin trail of dribble dangling from his lips, his hair mingled with tufts of grass that moved gently in the wind.

'This little angel will probably be happier.'

Josèf seemed lost in his thoughts. Papy stood up and pulled out his phone. He had to call Marianne urgently, now that he had the whole story. He took two steps away from the old couple. The changed angle of light showed him his reflection in the conservatory window. Whether because of his proximity to the Lukowiks or for some other reason, Papy suddenly felt old.

Three generations, all screwed, Marta had said. Despite himself, he thought of his own children – Cédric, Delphine, Charlotte, Valentin, Anaïs, all of whom had flown the nest – and of his six grandchildren, whom he hardly ever saw. Yes, he felt old. Was he screwed too?

He stood there a long time, observing his reflection. Marta thought he was looking through the window, at the child.

The old woman's voice turned nasty.

'Are you going to take that one away from us too?'

# 71

*Today, I am crossing the Pont des Arts.*
*Alone.*
Want to kill
*Like the straw that broke the camel's back, I would*
*like to be the one who fastens the last padlock*
*to this bridge, the padlock that finally makes it*
*collapse into the Seine.*

*Convicted: 19*
*Acquitted: 187*

www.want-to-kill.com

The fifteen soldiers deployed around the aeroplane appeared to be following a choreography directed by the head of security, with a simple hand movement, from behind the large airport window.

Marianne didn't even glance at him as she hung up the phone. Papy's words continued to echo through her head, mingling with those of Vasily Dragonman, a few days before.

Was it possible to erase a child's memory? To bury a trauma? To stop that trauma growing bigger, taking root, eating away at a life?

Why not?

The brain of a three-year-old child was like plasticine to be moulded. Why shouldn't this child forget that his parents were dead, murdered in front of him, since that memory was unbearable and a fairy godmother was ready to wipe it away with a wave of her magic wand?

Yes, that child believed that Angie was his Maman. Angie had manipulated him, in order to save him. Gouti had been her instrument, her accomplice. Angie had simply used the oldest trick in the book, opposing one truth with another, Amanda against Angie, an alternative that was already so complicated for his little brain. Two loving mothers, that was already too many, the best way of making him forget that the third was no longer there to bring him up, making him forget that she had died in front of him, forget the trace of the bloody hand print that his father had left on the car door. Making him forget that rain of sharp glass, and – soon afterwards – forget this ordinary rain too.

Under the frowning eyes of Security Man, Marianne gripped the cuddly toy in her hands.

Angie had wanted a child, more than anything. Angie would be a good mother. Malone would grow up happy, with her.

Angie had not killed anyone.

Angie had become her friend for this reason: so that Marianne would understand that she wanted to save the child. Because Angie was his only chance.

Angie had only accepted Zerda's plan – swapping the two kids – so that she could get rid of him more easily, when the time came. Alexis Zerda had been incapable of imagining how far a mother would go in order to protect her child. So two mothers, both wanting the same kid . . . You stood no chance, Alexis! The first one, Amanda, put two bullets in his chest with a gun that the second, Angie, had given to her.

The head of security seemed to have decided to put an end to this stand-off. He wiped his forehead, made a brusque hand gesture to tell the flight attendant with the painted nails to leave, and placed himself in front of Marianne.

'So, Captain? Are we going in or not? It's a woman and a kid. They're not armed. So what the hell are you waiting for? You were the one who gave the order not to let this plane take off!'

JB, still immobile behind them, accompanied by Bourdaine and Constantini, looked like he was keeping score.

Marianne did not respond. She suddenly felt dizzy. The aeroplane standing on the runway. The men in uniform encircling it. This bald dwarf barking at her. The stoical rigidity of the two soldiers. The flight attendant's rictus smile. As if everything around her had frozen, except for the yapping of Security Dog.

'Don't you understand? If you block one take-off, you block them all! I've got four flights waiting behind this one! For God's sake, there are over a dozen armed men on the runway. We can storm the plane in seconds.'

'Calm down,' said the captain, almost reflexively. 'We're talking about a child and his mother.'

The dog kept barking.

'Then why go to such extremes? Why keep this plane on the ground and delay all air traffic for twenty minutes?'

He was trying to defy the captain, pitting his authority against hers, his sense of legitimacy against hers, his physical power against hers if necessary. The intimidation dance of the dominant male.

Marianne didn't even deign to look at him. Instead, she turned to the flight attendant with the red smile and the fiery hair.

Putting a friendly hand on her shoulder, Marianne reached out with her other hand, to let the woman know that the captain was entrusting her with the most delicate part of this entire operation.

The attendant's hand closed. It was soft, even if she still didn't understand what was expected of her.

In a raised voice, so that everyone could hear, Marianne explained the situation to her.

'The kid forgot his cuddly toy. He can't leave without it.'

# 72

*Little hand on the 5, big hand on the 3*

The Cap de la Hève was now nothing more than a small dot on the horizon, disappearing in the next moment beneath the wing of the Boeing 737. Straight ahead, through the window, Angie could now see nothing but the ocean, with a few cotton-wool clouds floating above it. They went through the clouds without splitting them, like dreams passing through a feather pillow.

Malone had fallen asleep in her lap. Gouti was clutched tight against his chest. The cuddly toy rose and fell, as if it were breathing in time with the boy.

As if it, too, was exhausted. Sleeping the sleep of the just, like a hero in the epilogue of his greatest adventure.

Angie adored this sensation, this feeling of being trapped, unable to move an arm, a leg, feeling the numbness rise through her until it controlled her breathing. Nothing could wake her treasure.

A flight attendant walked past, smiled, and thoughtfully asked if everything was all right. Angie adored the tender expression on the face of that woman when she looked at her big sleeping baby.

She had spent so long dreaming of this moment.

Giving this child a second chance. Or was he the one who was doing that for her? It didn't matter. Like Gouti, she would match her breathing to Malone's from now on.

Gently, she lay back against the blue velvet seat and closed her eyes.

*

It had all been so easy, in the end.

Alexis Zerda was dangerous, but predictable. She'd had no trouble convincing him to spare the child, to simply swap him for a few months, long enough for the child to forget everything. That fool! The child would forget the worst, of course, but he would remember the rest, what he had to remember, when he had to remember it, thanks to Gouti.

How could she abandon that child, whom Ilona and Cyril had barely even looked after? For the months preceding the robbery, she had been his nanny, his big sister, his Maman even; she was the one who put him to bed, who got him up in the mornings, who washed him, who told him stories while the others went over their plan for the zillionth time, each street in Deauville, each centimetre of the map, each second of the hold-up that was not supposed to last more than three minutes but would give them enough money to last for the rest of their lives.

Gouti had not lied, not really. Angie was Malone's Maman, his real mother, long before his parents went to heaven.

Amanda Moulin had been predictable too, in a different kind of way. Of course, she fell in love with the new Malone. Of course, she was ready to do anything to keep him, to stay with him, to escape with him to the other side of the world, if she found two tickets to paradise; to get rid of anyone who stood in her way, if she found a weapon to help her. It hardly mattered if the cops had discovered the computer search for the plane tickets; that was just another way of covering her tracks. She'd bought them using Zerda's laptop, the one he'd hidden with the loot at the NATO base, but she'd taken care to delete all the files mentioning the names of Amanda and Malone.

The only unknown factor was Marianne Augresse. It was essential that she understood. Not too early, because that could have jammed the gears, and not too late, because she needed time to think over Angie's confidences. Sending her an anonymous letter had been enough to trigger their meeting, and after that Angie had given it her all, put her heart and soul into it. Never before had she gone to such lengths with a female friend.

Sincerity wrapped inside a lie. That was her strategy, her gamble. A desperate bluff, the price of her freedom.

One last time, she thought about the psychoanalytical assertions that she was sweeping away. She was fully aware of the fact.

Despite the long conversations she'd had with Vasily Dragonman about resilience, she had never been convinced by the idea that it was better to wake the ghosts, confront them, rather than simply letting them slide into oblivion.

She could never accept that it was better to make a child carry the burden of the truth for the rest of their life, in the name of their right to know, rather than allow them the lie that might give them the chance to tear out the page full of crossings-out and start again, on a blank page.

Of course, she didn't know anything about traumatic memory, the unconscious, and the chimeras that would haunt Malone throughout his life. But she couldn't believe that love – her love – wouldn't outweigh all of that on the scales of happiness.

The Boeing continued to rise, and the estuary shrank below them. In a few seconds, they would move above the clouds, to the other side of the world. In the growing darkness, the last traces of life in the city were the garlands of light that decorated it. She imagined that most of the cars down there would already have their head-lights on.

Before leaving this land and flying to another continent, Angie couldn't help thinking of Timo. That had been the only limitation to her plan. He couldn't escape with them. He was on the police blacklists. No way could he have taken the plane, or even got through security.

She put her hand to Malone's forehead, then whispered in his ear, to imprint the words in his dreams.

'Papa will join us later.'

She hoped that was true. She hoped it so much. Timo would be a wonderful father.

Taking care not to wake Malone, she leant towards the window to have one last look at the place she was leaving. The final image she saw, before the clouds swallowed up all traces of life on earth, was of the urban spiderweb, yellow and shining, with the exception of a single blue light weaving through the others at a faster speed.

# 73

*Today, I got the results for my first year of medical*
*school. I came 1,128th. They only keep the first 117.*
*Want to kill*
*Because wanting to heal got me nowhere! Now I just*
*have to choose my speciality. Executioner? Hitman?*
*Thriller writer?*

*Convicted: 27*
*Acquitted: 321*

www.want-to-kill.com

The flashing blue light and the screaming siren announced the
danger. As the ambulance hurtled out of Avenue du Bois-au-Coq,
the high walls of the Mare Rouge tower blocks were stained blue for
a very brief moment. It was enough to bring a few of the building's
inhabitants out onto their balconies, although they barely had time
to see the ambulance speed past, to hear the siren echo off the brick
walls.

The ambulance sped past the Mont-Gaillard shopping centre.
For three hundred metres, neon signs competed with the blinding
blue light, then they disappeared, along with the vast car park and
the vehicles trapped inside it.

The ambulance went down Avenue du Val-aux-Corneilles.

The Monod hospital was now only two kilometres away: *1 min
32 seconds*, to be precise, as the SMUR's signalling system always
was.

Just ahead, a motorbike braked suddenly. A van pulled off to the side.

Yvon continued at the same speed. He was an experienced driver. He wasn't trying to break any records, just get there on time.

It would have been madness to try to go any faster.

The ambulance dived into the city. Yvon went the wrong way around the next roundabout and continued along the bus lane.

*55 seconds.*

He just had to drive up Avenue de Frileuse, and they'd be there.

Yvon felt the gloved hand on his shoulder.

He was used to it. This happened once or twice out of every ten trips. Tanguy, the other paramedic, his colleague for more than three years, didn't even need to say a word.

They were driving along the bus lane. Yvon braked and shifted down a gear to park behind a bus. He stopped the siren and the blue light, then turned back to Tanguy. In the back of the ambulance, there was also Eric, the emergency doctor, and a girl he didn't know – very young, in a white coat, presumably a newbie.

It was Eric who spoke. This was his privilege, if you could really call it a privilege.

The last word, the last gesture.

Beside them, shadows rushed off the number 12 bus and disappeared one by one into the black mouths of the buildings along the pavement.

'It's over,' said Eric, covering up Timo Soler's boyish, handsome face.

# Six months later

# 74

On the terrace of the Brigandin Hotel, almost everyone was a man.
A single man.

Doctors, computer experts, logistical experts, technicians, all of
them working at the Guiana space centre in Kourou to help the
Ariane rocket blast off for the two hundred and seventeenth time. It
was almost routine now and blast-off was set for two o'clock. These
men in shirts and ties – or Lacoste polo shirts or khaki Bermuda
shorts, to help them bear the afternoon humidity – did not seem especially stressed by the situation. In fact, a little further off, behind
the wall of bamboo, the sound of laughter could be heard coming
from the hotel swimming pool.

Beyond the fence, a few hundred metres away, in the heat haze,
Ariane towered against the horizon, plunging the palm trees and
warehouses into shadow. It was tall and elegant, like a spotlessly
white cathedral, built in its own clearing even before a city encircled
it. A capricious cathedral that would blast off, defying God, and
sow metal angels in the sky.

Maximilien, mojito in hand, spotted her as soon as he set foot
on the terrace.

The only woman!

The dolls with brooms or the mixed-race waitresses with plunging necklines, behind or in front of the bar, did not really count in
his conception of equality.

The woman was lost in her thoughts, sitting in front of a mint
cordial. Young, pretty, with dark sunglasses covering her eyes, and
long braided hair falling down over her flowery dress, arms and legs
tanned but not too tanned. She must have been living in French
Guiana for several months, but less than a year. Maximilien, as an

enlightened connoisseur, had learnt to date the cooking time of female flesh simply by the colour of their skin.

He walked over.

'May I sit down?'

The terrace was packed. It was a reasonable excuse. The girl smiled. A good sign.

'Yes, of course.'

She lifted up her sunglasses for an instant. She found him attractive – that complicit look wasn't wrong. Another good sign.

He wasn't much older than her, five years at most. He had a long-term suntan, but its intensity was reduced by his alternating schedule: three weeks in French Guiana, three weeks in Paris. He'd explain to her, without much need for exaggeration, that the fact this rocket was able to blast off was partly due to him, that he was the leader of a team of thirty engineers and technicians, that each blast-off gave him a massive surge of adrenaline, and that even after fifteen of them, he'd never lost that feeling; he'd also tell her that he made a very good living, that he often came here, that he got a bit bored, after the launches, that he liked meeting people, that he'd dreamt of being an astronaut when he was a little boy, and he'd almost made it.

He offered the young woman his hand.

'Maximilien. But I prefer Max.'

'Angélique. But I prefer Angie.'

They each forced a laugh, the two perfectly synchronized. Yet another good sign. Max introduced himself, gave a rundown of his CV with tried-and-tested inventiveness, and made sure he listened to Angie, even if she remained much more discreet than he was. Almost worried. She explained to him simply that she was only here for a few days, to take care of business, and that she mostly lived in Venezuela. Observing the Western Union biro placed next to her, he was briefly reminded of the drug dealers who sought to evade the French police by swinging into France occasionally before returning to anonymity in the equatorial forest.

She looked as if she was travelling incognito, with her black sunglasses. That added to the girl's mystery.

She did not withdraw her hand when Max's fingers first began to caress it, then capture it. No ambiguity.

She wore a wedding ring. Max showed his hand, also without ambiguity. The privilege of expatriates, of the equator, of the humidity.

'You're beautiful, Angie.'

'And you're a charmer, Max.'

Their fingers intertwined, rubbing together for a first tango. Angie's eyes shone.

'And undoubtedly a wonderful lover. If I told you how long it has been since I last made love, you wouldn't believe me.'

Max seemed momentarily disconcerted by the girl's boldness.

'But all those qualities are not enough, Max. I'm looking for something else.'

'A challenge?'

The engineer was smiling again. This girl liked to play. He adored that. He didn't have time to ask about the nature of the challenge, however, because the answer materialised right in front of his eyes.

Lively and cheerful.

'Maman, can we stay a bit longer? The rocket's about to blast off!'

The four-year-old boy had appeared suddenly from between the tables and leapt up onto his mother's lap, making the mojito and mint cordial tremble even before the Vulcan engines had started spitting flames.

'Of course, my love. That's why we came.'

The kid ran off again, laughing mischievously, picking up a foul-looking cuddly toy that appeared to be a rat on his way. He kept running, weaving between tables and waitresses until he reached the guardrail that offered a perfect view of the gigantic white rocket.

Max downed half his cocktail, then asked the girl:

'Four?'

'Nearly five. The additional quality I'm search for is for him. I need a lover, he needs a father.'

'Two indivisible qualities?'

'Yes.'

417

'And this is non-negotiable?'

'I'm afraid so.'

Max laughed openly. He turned on his iPhone with one finger then put it on the table to show Angie the photograph on its screen.

'Sorry, Angie. I already have three of those! Allow me to introduce Céleste, Côme and Arsène, respectively three, six and eleven, as well as their mother, Anne-Véronique. I adore them all.'

He stood up, grabbing his mojito.

'Hasta la vista, señorita.'

He took one last look at the child, who'd climbed on top of a plastic chair to get a better view.

'Take care of yourself, Angie. Offer him the stars – he deserves them.'

He blew her a kiss.

'There's no lack of potential fathers here.'

Angie watched him walk away into the lobby of the Brigandin Hotel, then her gaze returned to the tables around her, where men – on their own, in pairs, in groups – were laughing, playing, looking bored. Dreaming.

# 75

Amanda Moulin was sentenced to four months in prison. The murder of Alexis Zerda was considered self-defence, without Amanda having to claim it, and without her lawyer having to argue it.

But Amanda Moulin also had to answer for other crimes: identity theft, failure to report an accident, attempted kidnapping.

She was incarcerated in the correctional centre in Rennes. For the first two weeks, she received a letter every morning, after her walk, postmarked Potigny. The address on the back was 23, Rue des Gryzońs, home to Josèf and Marta Lukowik.

She didn't open them. Not a single one.

She knew what they contained. Photos of Malone, always the same. The account of his days, always the same. Malone was not going to die; that was the first thing her lawyer had told her. Dimitri had, with Alexis Zerda, tampered with the results of the Joliot-Curie clinic.

True, in Malone's brain, there was a tiny crack through the pons Varolii, between the brain stem and the spinal cord, reducing his motor skills and sensitivity to almost zero, but no vital functions were affected.

She didn't care now. It was all the same to her. If anything, she'd have preferred Malone to be dead. Preferred it all to be over. For someone to leave her a nail, a sheet, a stool in her cell so she could hang herself.

Then, three weeks after her incarceration, she was told she had a visitor. A woman, younger than her. She was a social worker. She explained that the children's judge had made his decision. He was taking away the guardianship of Malone from the Lukowik

419

grandparents, as they weren't blood relations of the child, and there-fore had no rights, and no authorisation for him to be their ward. The child would be sent to a medical institution for the rest of her prison sentence.

'And then?'

The young social worker lowered her eyes, but said nothing. She just gave her some papers to sign, for the judge, for the Regional Health authority, for the institution. Amanda signed everything without even reading it.

The judge's order provided for a supervised visit every week.

Amanda, firmly held by two guards who gave her no choice in the matter, found herself face to face with Malone the following Wednesday, at ten thirty in the morning, accompanied by a female carer, in a small, windowless room.

For the ten minutes of the visit, Malone just stared at the fly that buzzed on the wall behind Amanda. The educator, who was also younger than Amanda, stammered a few questions to start with: Aren't you going to hug him? Or kiss him? Aren't you even going to speak to him? Then she, too, learnt to be silent.

Every Wednesday.

Amanda obediently attended each visit. There were no more buzzing flies.

Each time, Malone was accompanied by a different female carer. Strangely, this was what finally made Amanda react. This image of Malone coming and going with a different woman each week, like some troublesome object being constantly handed on. A burden.

Something inside her awoke, slowly. Then grew, Wednesday after Wednesday.

She began to hope again. In a few weeks, she would be released. Malone would be handed back to her. She would look after him. She would accept him the way he was.

One week before her release, the children's judge ordered further examinations, for Amanda as well as for Malone. Amanda answered the questions of the prison psychologist for half a day, and Malone spent two days in the paediatric neurosurgery department led by Professor Lacroix, the same doctor who had operated on him after his fall.

On the morning of her release, Amanda met Professor Lacroix. He made her wait for nearly an hour, even though there were no patients in the waiting room, not even a child playing in the Lego corner, just three secretaries giggling in the next corridor.

At last, the doctor received her. He had spent a long time talking to the judge.

Malone belonged in a specialised institution, he said.

Malone needed regular surveillance, care, treatment. Amanda could see him as often as she wished.

'Give me back my child,' Amanda said simply. 'Please, doctor . . .'

The neurosurgeon did not reply. He was playing with a silver pen, not even bothering to take the documents that Amanda had brought him out of their plastic folder: the authorisation for Malone to live at home. Only he could sign it.

'Please, doctor.'

There was no hostility in Amanda's voice.

Lacroix's response was to push the medical file towards her. Amanda read it mechanically. She already knew the results by heart. There was nothing new here. Stable condition. No development in his cognition or reaction levels.

'It's for the good of the child, Mrs Moulin,' the neurosurgeon told her. 'This is no reflection on you. Malone will be better off in a specialised institution, and that way he'll be able to . . .'

Amanda had already stopped listening. Her gaze wandered down to one of the pages of the medical file, even if she had read that quote from Harper University Hospital in Philadelphia dozens of times before. The only laboratory in the world to mend cerebral lesions by implanting new axons in the damaged neurones. A team of thirty qualified neurosurgeons to serve their patients, the publicity brochure claimed. Unique technical facilities, a vast tree-filled park to aid peaceful convalescence, a list of famous Americans successfully operated upon spread over three columns, even if none of the names were well-known in France.

Cost of the operation: $680,000.

'You understand, Mrs Moulin,' concluded Lacroix, 'I'm sorry for you, but I can't take the risk of leaving Malone with you. Not in his state. Not after everything that's happened.'

Amanda hated the neurosurgeon's smile as he put the silver pen in a drawer. That pen alone would probably cover about one-thousandth of the cost.

Nothing had changed on Place Maurice-Ravel. The neighbours had reserved seats by their windows for her return. The house was cold, dusty, empty. The bamboo rug had been returned but it still had red stains on it. The Mother's Day poems still hung in their frame, decorated with hearts and butterflies.

Amanda didn't even have the strength to cry.

She didn't leave the house for the next three days, didn't eat, hardly slept. It was the postman who broke through her inertia, knocking at the door since Amanda wasn't going down to the letterbox, where her post was accumulating.

A letter from French Guiana. The postman proudly showed Amanda the postmark.

Amanda opened it at the kitchen table, sitting in front of a cup of coffee, the only thing she could still swallow.

The first page was almost blank, except for two words:

*For Malone.*

And a signature.

*Angie.*

The second contained more lines, about ten of them, which Amanda read diagonally.

These lines apologised for not having written earlier, and mentioned a parcel sent to Venezuela, a jeweller in Anvers, a Dutch intermediary, a complicated distribution of the loot to clients in Singapore, Taipei, Johannesburg, Dubai.

Then nothing else, except for the last two lines.

Two letters, a series of numbers, and a name.

CH10 00230 00109822346
Lloyds & Lombard, Zurich United Bank

# 76

Marianne had decided not to set any limits.

Not to the number of guests, nor the number of bottles she would drink. Only one number was set in stone: the number of candles on her birthday cake.

Forty.

For one night, Marianne forgot the internal affairs investigation – the blame hanging around her neck, her possible suspension – and she mingled with her guests, glass in hand. She was wearing a skin-tight T-shirt with the words *No Kids* on it, and kept repeating:

'To freedom!'

JB turned up at about 11 p.m., on the arm of a girl ten years younger than him, who was dressed in a pair of denim hotpants with a fuchsia top that barely tickled her belly button. He was carrying a bottle of champagne behind his back, to celebrate his divorce and the judge's refusal to grant him shared custody. He stayed barely three hours, then planted a friendly kiss on Marianne's forehead and whispered into her ear that he was off to a club to meet some friends from Loreen.

The others began to disperse a little later, around three in the morning. By 5 a.m., amid glasses scattered here and there, card-board plates abandoned on the furniture, bottles that had not been recorked, crushed petits fours and slices of cake with only a bite or two taken out of them, the only guest remaining was Papy.

Marianne collapsed on the sofa, next to Mogwai, holding a bottle of Desperados.

'Shall I give you a hand tidying up, my love?'

'Don't worry, Papy. I'll deal with all this later. I've my whole life to tidy up.'

Papy opened another bottle of beer.

'Look who you're talking to.'

Lieutenant Pasdeloup had celebrated his retirement the week before. He'd taken it at exactly fifty-two years old, after twenty-seven years of service, as all active functionaries in the French police were entitled to do.

Marianne was drunk. She let go of the bottle she was holding and it fell onto the carpet, the beer spilling under the sofa.

'It's so stupid, calling you Papy. You're barely ten years older than me, and you're in better shape than most men my age. You're single. You're not answerable to anyone any more. Why don't you come over here.'

She curled up to make room for him, pushing Mogwai off the sofa with her foot. Papy just smiled.

'What exactly are you proposing, Marianne?'

The captain smiled back at him.

'Sex. To celebrate my new life. Yours too. Just sex. Nothing more, I swear. I'm sure you don't want any more kids. You've got plenty of those already.'

Lieutenant Pasdeloup was trembling slightly. He grabbed a chair and sat facing Marianne.

'Would you really offer me that, Marianne?'

'What? Sex? Yes, I told you . . . Just once, to see how it goes . . . There's no hierarchy between us any more.'

'Another kid, I mean. Would you offer me that?'

Marianne's head felt terribly heavy, but she nodded anyway. It was supposed to mean yes, or why not, or let's see.

Papy leant forward and took her hand.

'Really, Marianne? You'd offer me the possibility that in six months' time, I could put my hands on your round belly and feel a living part of me growing inside it? You'd offer me the chance to spend my nights watching over a crying kid who needs me instead of surfing the internet? The chance to have a tree and shining stars at Christmas instead of spending it alone? And with the white-bearded old man coming every year? The chance for the swing in my garden to start squeaking again? The chance for me to get the bike out again and a reason to go for walks along the port and start swimming again? An excuse to go on all the rides at the funfair and binge-watch cartoons? Really, Marianne? A little kid giving me a kiss every morning even when I'm in my sixties, jumping into my lap and saying, "Papa, you're bristly!" but kissing me anyway? Not ending up a miserable old sod who refuses to even call his grown-up children every week because they've got nothing to say to him, but instead having a kid demanding a story and hanging around my neck until my back breaks just so I won't leave his bedroom? Really, Marianne, you'd offer me that? You'd offer me the chance to start over, to turn back the hands of time, to rewind my life, to become twenty years younger overnight . . . You'd really offer me that, Marianne?'

Marianne took hold of Papy's hand and pulled him towards her.

The ex-Lieutenant Pasdeloup let her do it.

'You won't be disappointed. I'll be the perfect father.'

Marianne moved her lips towards his, and just before she kissed him she whispered:

'You'd better be. Because I'm going to be a real pain of a mother.'

A *Sunday Times* Crime Book of the Month

'A tantalising story that wraps the reader in myriad enigmas'
*Daily Mail*

'Outrageously entertaining'
*The Times*

'Agatha Christie updated and then cranked up to 11: a blast'
*Shots Magazine*

**Fécamp, 13 July 2014**

From: Lieutenant Bertrand Donnadieu, National Gendarmerie, Territorial Brigade of the District of Étretat, Seine-Maritime

To: M. Gérard Calmette, Director of the Disaster Victim Identification Unit (DVIU), Criminal Research Institute of the National Gendarmerie, Rosny-sous-Bois

*Dear Monsieur Calmette,*

*At 2.45 a.m. on 12 July 2014, a section of cliff of about 45,000 cubic metres collapsed above Valleuse d'Etigues, 3 km west of Yport. Rockfalls of this type are not uncommon on our coast. The emergency services arrived on the scene an hour later and established beyond a doubt that there no casualties resulting from this incident.*

*However, and this is the reason for this letter, while no walkers were caught in the landslide, the first responders made a strange discovery. Lying among the debris scattered over the beach were three human skeletons.*

*Police officers dispatched to the site found no personal effects or items of clothing in the vicinity that would enable them to identify the victims. It's possible that they might have been cavers who became trapped; the network of karst caves beneath the famous white cliffs are a popular attraction. However no cavers have been reported missing in recent months, or indeed years. We have analysed the bones with the limited* equipment at our disposal and they do not appear to be very old.

I should add that the bones were scattered over forty metres of beach as a result of the landslide. The Departmental Brigade of Forensic Investigation, under the auspices of Colonel Bredin, pieced together the skeletons. Their initial analysis confirms our own: not all of the bones seem to have reached the same level of decomposition. Bizarre as it may seem, this suggests the three individuals had died in that cavity in the cliff at different times, probably several years apart. The cause of their death remains unknown: during our examination of the remains we found no trauma that would have proved fatal.

With no evidence to go on, ante or post mortem, we are unable to pursue the usual lines of inquiry that would allow us to determine who these three individuals were. When they died. What killed them.

The local community, recently unnerved by a macabre event that has no apparent connection to the discovery of these three unidentified corpses, is understandably rife with speculation.

Which is why, Director, while I am aware of the number of urgent matters requiring your attention, and the suffering of those awaiting formal identification of deceased relatives, I would ask you to make this case a priority so that we may proceed with our investigation.

Yours sincerely,

Lieutenant Bertrand Donnadieu,

Territorial Brigade of the District of Étretat

# Five months earlier

## 19 February 2014

'Watch out, Jamal, the grass will be slippery on the cliff.'

André Jozwiak, landlord of the Hotel-Restaurant Sirène, issued the caution before he could stop himself. He'd put on a raincoat and was standing outside his front door. The mercury in the thermometer that hung above the menu was struggling to rise above the blue line indicating zero. There was hardly any wind, and the weathervane – a cast-iron sailing ship fixed to one of the beams on the façade –seemed to have frozen during the night.

The drowsy sun dragged itself wearily above the sea, illuminating a light coating of frost on the cars parked outside the casino. On the beach in front of the hotel the pebbles huddled together like shivering eggs abandoned by a bird of prey. Beyond the final towering sea stack lay the coast of Picardy, a hundred kilometres due east.

Jamal passed the front of the casino and, taking brisk, short strides, set off up Rue Jean-Hélie. André watched him go, blowing on his hands to warm them up. It was almost time to serve breakfast to the few customers who spent their winter holidays overlooking the Channel. At first the landlord had thought the young disabled Arab was odd, running along the footpath every morning, with one muscular leg and one that ended in a carbon foot wedged into a trainer. Now, he felt genuine affection for the boy. When he was still in his twenties, Jamal's age, André used to cycle over a hundred kilometres every Sunday morning, Yport–Yvetot–Yport, three hours with no one pestering him. If this kid from Paris with his weird foot wanted to work up a sweat at first light – well, he understood.

Jamal's shadow reappeared briefly at the corner of the steps that rose towards the cliffs, before disappearing behind the casino wheelie bins. The landlord took a step forward and lit a Winston. He wasn't the only one braving the cold: in the distance, two silhouettes stood out against the wet sand. An old lady holding an extending lead with a ridiculous little dog – the kind that looks as if it runs on batteries, operated by remote control, and so conceited that it goaded the seagulls with hysterical yaps. Two hundred metres further on, a tall man, hands in the pockets of a worn brown leather jacket, stood by the sea, glowering at the waves as if he wanted to take revenge on the horizon.

André spat out the butt of his cigarette and went back into the hotel. He didn't like to be seen unshaven, badly dressed, his hair a mess, looking like the sort of caveman Mrs Cro-Magnon would have walked out on many moons ago.

His steps keeping to a metronomic rhythm, Jamal Salaoui was climbing one of the highest cliffs in Europe. One hundred and twenty metres. Once he'd left the last of the houses behind, the road dwindled to a footpath. The panorama opened up to Étretat, ten kilometres away. Jamal saw the two silhouettes at the end of the beach, the old woman with the little dog and the man staring out to sea. Three gulls, perhaps frightened by the dog's piercing cries, rose from the cliff and blocked his path before soaring ten metres above him.

The first thing Jamal saw, just past the sign pointing to the Rivage campsite, was the red scarf. It was fixed to the fence like a danger sign. That was Jamal's first thought:

*Danger.*

A warning of a rockfall, a flood, a dead animal.

The idea passed as swiftly as it had come. It was just a scarf caught on barbed wire, lost by a walker and carried away by the wind coming off the sea.

Reluctant to break the rhythm of his run, to pause for a closer look at the dangling fabric, he almost carried straight on. Everything would have turned out quite differently if he had.

But Jamal slowed his pace, then stopped.

The scarf looked new. It gleamed bright red. Jamal touched it, studied the label.

Cashmere. Burberry . . . This scrap of fabric was worth a small fortune! Jamal delicately detached the scarf from the fence and decided that he would take it back to the Sirène with him. André Jozwiak knew everyone in Yport, he would know if someone had lost it. And if it wasn't claimed, Jamal would keep it. He stroked the fabric as he continued his run. Once he was back home in La Courneuve, he doubted he would risk wearing it over his tracksuit. In his neighbourhood, someone would rip your head off for a €500 cashmere scarf! But he would no doubt find a pretty girl who'd be happy to wear it.

As he drew near the blockhouse, to his right a small flock of sheep turned their heads in his direction. They were waiting for the grass to thaw with a lobotomised look which reminded him of the idiots that he worked with, standing by the microwave at lunchtime.

Just past the blockhouse, Jamal saw the girl.

He immediately gauged the distance between her and the edge of the cliff. Less than a metre! She was standing on the precipice, looking down at a sheer drop of over a hundred metres. His brain reeled, calculating the risks: the incline to the void, the frost on the grass. The girl was more at risk here than she would have been standing on the ledge of the highest window of a thirty-storey building.

'Mademoiselle, are you all right?'

Jamal's words were snatched away by the wind. No response.

He was still a hundred and fifty metres from the girl.

Despite the intense cold, she was wearing only a loose red dress torn into two strips, one floating over her navel and then to her thighs, the other yawning from the top of her neck to the base of her chest, revealing the fuchsia cup of a bra.

She was shivering.

Beautiful. Yet for Jamal there was nothing erotic about this image. Surprising, moving, unsettling, but nothing sexual. When he thought about it later, trying to fathom it out, the nearest equivalent that came to mind was a vandalised work of art. A sacrilege, an inexcusable contempt for beauty.

'Are you all right, mademoiselle?' he said again.

She turned towards him. He stepped forward.

The grass came halfway up his legs, and it occurred to him that the girl mightn't have noticed the prosthesis fixed to his left leg. He was now facing her. Ten metres between them. The girl had moved closer to the precipice, standing with her back to the drop.

He could see that she'd been crying; her mascara had run, then dried. Jamal struggled to marshal his thoughts.

Danger.

Emergency.

Above all, emotion. He felt overwhelmed by emotion. He had never seen such a beautiful woman. Her features would be imprinted on his memory for ever: the perfect oval of her face, framed by twin cascades of jet-black hair, her coal-black eyes and snow-white skin, her eyebrows and mouth forming thin, sharp lines, as if traced by a finger dipped in blood and soot. He wondered whether he was in shock, whether this was impacting on his assessment of the situation, the distress of this stranger, the need to grab her hand without waiting for an answer.

'Mademoiselle . . .'

He held out his hand.

'Don't come any closer,' the girl said.

It was more a plea than an order. The embers in her coal-black irises seemed to have been extinguished.

'OK,' Jamal stammered. 'OK. Stay right where you are, let's take this nice and slow.'

Jamal's eye slipped over her skimpy dress. She must have come out of the casino a hundred metres below. Of an evening, the hall of the Sea View turned into a discotheque.

A night's clubbing that had gone wrong? Tall, slim and sexy, she would have drawn plenty of admirers. Clubs were full of creeps who came to check out the babes.

Jamal spoke as calmly as he could:

'I'm going to step forward slowly, I want you to take my hand.'

The young woman lowered her gaze for the first time and paused at the sight of the carbon prosthesis. This drew an involuntary look of surprise, but she regained control almost immediately.

'If you take so much as a step, I'll jump.'

'OK, OK, I won't move . . .'

Jamal froze, not even daring to breathe. Only his eyes moved, from the girl who had emerged from nowhere, to the orange dawn on the edge of the horizon.

A bunch of drunks following her every move on the dance floor, Jamal thought. And among them, at least one sick bastard, maybe several, perverted enough to follow the girl when she left. Hunt her down. Rape her.

'Has . . . has someone hurt you?'

She burst into tears.

'You could never understand. Keep running. Go! Get out of here, now!'

*An idea . . .*

Jamal put his hands around his neck. Slowly. But not slowly enough. The girl recoiled, took a step backwards, closer to the drop.

Jamal froze. He wanted to catch her in his hand as if she were a frightened sparrow that had fallen from the nest, unable to fly.

'I'm not going to move. I'm just going to throw you my scarf. I'll hold one end. You grab the other, simple as that. It's up to you whether to let go or not.'

The girl hesitated, surprised once again. Jamal took the opportunity to throw one end of the red cashmere scarf. Two metres separated him from the suicidal young woman.

The fabric fell at his feet.

She leaned forward delicately and, with absurd modesty pulled at the remains of her dress to cover her bare breast, then stood, clutching the end of Jamal's scarf.

'Easy does it,' Jamal said. 'I'm going to pull on the scarf, wrap it around my hands. Let yourself be dragged towards me, two metres, just two metres further from the edge.'

The girl gripped the fabric more tightly.

Jamal knew then that he had won, that he had done the right thing, throwing this scarf the way a sailor throws a lifebelt to someone who's drowning, drawing them gently to the surface, centimetre by centimetre, taking infinite care not to break the thread.

'Easy does it,' he said again. 'Come towards me.'

For a brief moment he realised that he had just met the most beautiful girl he had ever seen. And that he had saved her life.

That was enough to make him lose concentration for one tiny second.

Suddenly the girl pulled on the scarf. It was the last thing Jamal had expected. One sharp, swift movement.

The scarf slid from his hands.

What followed took less than a second.

The girl's gaze fixed on him, indelibly, as if she were looking at him from the window of a passing train. There was a finality to that gaze.

'Noooo!' Jamal shouted.

The last thing he saw was the red cashmere scarf floating between the girl's fingers. A moment later she toppled into the void.

So did Jamal's life, but he didn't know it yet.

# AFTER THE CRASH

## Michel Bussi

**On the night of 22 December, a plane crashes on the Franco-Swiss border.**

All the passengers are killed instantly, apart from one miraculous survivor – a three-month-old baby girl. But who is she? Two families step forward to claim her, but is she Lyse-Rose or Emilie?

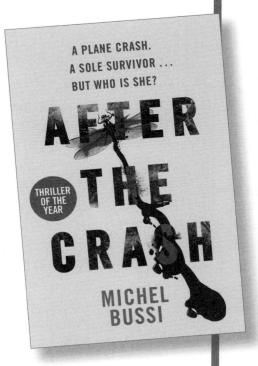

Two decades later, on the eve of her eighteenth birthday, the detective who investigated the case makes a discovery that could change everything . . .

**'One of the most remarkable books I've read in a long time . . . I doubt I'll read a more brilliant crime novel this year'** *Sunday Times*

# BLACK WATER LILIES

## Michel Bussi

Jérôme Morval, a man whose passion for art was matched only by his passion for women, has been found dead in the stream that runs through the gardens of Giverny. In his pocket is a post-card of Monet's *Water Lilies* with the words: Eleven years old. Happy Birthday.

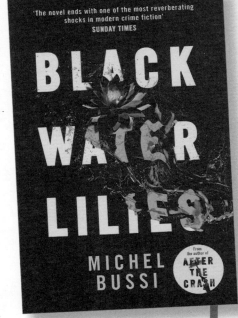

Entangled in the mystery are three women: a young painting prodigy, a seductive schoolteacher and an old widow who watches over the village from a mill by the stream. All three of them share a secret. But what do they know about the discovery of Morval's corpse? And what is the connection to the mysterious, rumoured painting *Black Water Lilies*?

**'Ends with one of the most reverberating shocks in modern crime fiction'** *Sunday Times*

# DON'T LET GO

## Michel Bussi

In an idyllic resort on the island of La Réunion, Liane Bellion and her husband Martial are enjoying the perfect moment: blue seas, palm trees, a warm breeze.

Then Liane disappears. Despite his protestations of innocence, the police view Martial as their prime suspect. Helicopters scan the island, racial tensions surface, and bodies are found.

**Is Martial really his wife's killer? And if he isn't, why does he appear to be so guilty?**

# TIME IS A KILLER

## Michel Bussi

**Summer, 1989. Corsica.** Fifteen-year-old Clotilde is the sole survivor when her family's car plunges off a narrow road into a ravine.

Twenty-seven years later she returns to the island with her husband and teenage daughter in an attempt to come to terms with her past. But then she receives a letter – from her mother, as if she were alive.

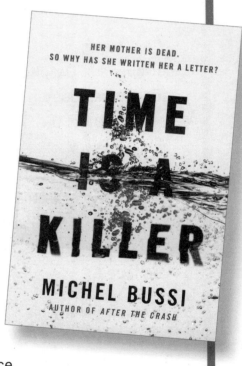

It seems impossible. Clotilde watched her parents and her brother die that day in the ravine. She has lived with their ghosts ever since. But then who sent this letter – and why?

**'Peels back layer upon layer of subterfuge to reveal a dizzying twist leading to a pitch-perfect ending'**
*Daily Express*